Perfect Pitch

A novel by

Ron Bitto

This is a work of fiction, names, characters, places and incidents either are the product of the author's imagination or are used fictitiously. Any resemblance to actual events, locales or persons living or dead is entirely coincidental.

ISBN-13: 978-0615722573
ISBN-10: 061572251

Dedicated to the memory
of my grandmother Albertine
and my father, who inspired
this story.

Other novels by Ron Bitto

Blind Sidetrack

Weddings and Funerals

Something Cool from Red Hot

Edited by Ron Bitto

Travels with Mary,
the Journals
of Mary Murphy Bitto

Available at www.ronbitto.com or
www.amazon.com

Chapter One

In the Top Hat Club's basement lounge, Albertine played a Gershwin ballad and was caught up in the music that she brought to life in the low, dark room. Yes, the old piano was out of tune, and two of its keys were dead, but "Someone to Watch Over Me" touched her deeply and made her wish that her husband loved her more, loved her enough so she wouldn't have to be afraid of his temper, or suspicious of the way he looked at other women. If Hendrik loved her more, their life would be more exciting, and she might not have to spend so much time at the club.

Albertine had come to the Top Hat in a scarlet chemise and a pink cloche hat. Her black hair was bobbed and crimped, and her lipstick was as red as her dress. Her fingernails had to be short because of the piano, but she kept them polished red, too, in beautiful contrast to the white and black keys. Her piano teacher, Madame Corbet, (the organist at the Notre Dame church) would not have approved of her nails or her music, either, because Madame had taught her Chopin, Schubert and Debussy along with the sentimental songs of the day. Perfect pitch had made Albertine a star piano student, but it was the chance to play at the Top Hat Club that made her believe her life could be different and special.

When she finished the Gershwin number, she looked up to see that a small crowd had gathered to start their evening in the old speakeasy before moving upstairs at nine to hear the featured band. A young man, alone at the table closest to the piano, stood up and called out to her, "Play 'Paper Moon' for me, Albertine." He came toward her extending a dollar bill that he stuffed into the beer glass on the piano.

"Sure, Monty," she said and began the wistful song as he stood over the piano and gazed at her longingly.

Only twenty-one Monty Matheson was a professional boxer who liked to dance with Albertine. He had thick, copper-colored hair, dreamy eyes and a badly broken nose. While all the other men in the lounge were smoking, Monty chewed gum. Albertine had heard that he hadn't lost in fourteen matches and that if he won a few more bouts he'd probably go to New York to fight the middle weight champion.

Monty stood close enough to see Albertine's green eyes and her full lips that pouted as she concentrated on the music. She was only five-foot-two, but her trim legs seemed long when she danced and held herself high and proud. And for such a small woman, she had a very nice bosom. Monty was sure she dusted her breasts with perfumed powder. How different Albertine was from the rough life he led in the gymnasium and boxing ring. He wished he could do more than just dance with her.

For her part, Albertine hoped Monty would get discouraged and move along before she finished her set. Sure, he was a good enough dancer, but he didn't laugh at her jokes, and he never had much to say. And he followed her around like an abandoned puppy, which put her off entirely. If she was going to forget about Hendrik for a while, it would to be with a real man and not with a sad boy like Monty Matheson.

Then as she was finishing "Paper Moon," Monty nodded thanks to her and left in a hurry, and two other men came to the piano and slid money into her tip glass. But this was not good news. Albertine knew they were small-time crooks who earned their living by doing the dirty work for big-time gangsters.

Tino Capoletti looked sharp-faced and brutal with his cold black eyes, broad chest, and shiny suit. Tino's friend, Nick Trantini, was short, wiry and mean. A hungry rat, Albertine thought, who got his thrills by hurting people.

"Was that fighter bothering you?" Tino asked her as she stood up from the piano and straightened her dress.

"What fighter?" she pretended not to know.

"Bubble gum boy," he sneered. "If he was bothering you, we can fix him."

"Yeah, we'd like to fix him," Nick chuckled.

"No, I hardly noticed him. Leave him alone. He wasn't bothering me," she shrugged, trying hard to seem indifferent. If they were jealous of Monty, they could make sure he never fought again.

"We thought you might take a ride over to Cicero with us tonight," Tino suggested. "Have a few drinks. Watch us gamble."

"Cicero's not the same since Mr. Capone went to jail," Albertine teased him. "And the music's better here."

"This place don't hold a candle to the Napoli!" Nick scoffed. "There's no action here. Not even a dice game."

"Our pal Nick has a tin ear," Tino reminded her. "He likes to go to Navy Pier to listen to the calliope on the merry-go-round."

"And I've got perfect pitch!" she laughed. "Maybe some other time. What do you boys want me to play for you tonight?"

"How about 'Ain't We Got Fun'? That might make you change your mind," Tino said and squinted as he gave her a wise grin.

"I'll play it," she said and shrugged again nervously, "but my mind's made up."

As she began the tune with a flourish of quick rag time chords, she remembered the time she had ridden out to Cicero with Tino. He got so drunk he ripped her dress and passed out before he could drive her home. The other hoodlums thought she was his girlfriend and invited her upstairs for a private drink. But she had a different idea. She reached into Tino's jacket and pulled out a pistol and a switchblade before she found his billfold. Then she took out enough money for a taxi and left before he came to. She'd been afraid that Hendrik would ask her about the torn dress that night, but he had been oblivious to it. When she came in, he had just come home from his job at the print shop and was sitting at the kitchen table, squeezing the keys of his saxophone, but not blowing it, so their son Hank could get some sleep.

Tino and Nick settled down at a front row table and drank their beers while she played two verses and two choruses of the song. As she finished with some of her best playing, Tino came around to her side of the piano and perched on the bench beside her.

"Well, you missed your chance this time, Al," Tino said and put a firm arm around her waist, squeezing her tightly through her sheer dress. He smelled strongly of cigarette smoke, after shave lotion, and pomade. "Next time, I won't take no for an answer."

A cold shiver passed through Albertine as Tino released her and headed for the stairs. Maybe Tino hadn't actually killed anyone, but he had bragged to her about slamming doors on men's fingers, breaking their kneecaps, and dumping them out of moving cars. Now she understood that the message of such talk wasn't to prove how tough he was. No, he'd been warning her all along: Don't cross me!

As Albertine caught her breath, a tall, dark-haired woman in a tight, purple dress came up to the piano and dropped a few coins into the beer glass. Seeing the silk gardenia in her hair, Albertine recognized her; it was Pearl Cornell, one of the younger girls who had started to frequent the club since the end of Prohibition. "Play 'Makin' Whoopee' for me," Pearl said, "so I can sing along."

"Do I need to play real soft so they can hear you?" Albertine asked as she began the introduction.

"No. Give it all you got. I can hold my own. But I need a lower key?"

"This is G. Which key do you want?"

"I dunno. A lower one."

"Start singing and I'll find your key," Albertine said and listened to Pearl sing, "Another bride, another June…" Then Albertine started playing in E-flat to match the woman's voice, which was hoarse and seductive, the voice of a girl that no other woman could trust. Pearl was too tall, and because of her olive skin and curly hair, Albertine was sure she was part Negro, even though Pearl claimed to have mother from Rome and a father from Cardiff, wherever that was, probably a corner of Africa.

The number was going very well, however, and Albertine sensed that she and Pearl had the right chemistry, so she decided to play through the song a second time to finish out her set. Pearl stood in front of the piano, leaning back into it slightly, and she gripped the attention of every man in the room as she sang about their favorite subject. When the song ended, the audience gave them a gentle round of applause, more than Albertine had received for herself all evening. Pearl bowed and called out, "Thank you! Thank you!" while Albertine quickly retrieved the tip glass and set it on the floor beside the bench.

Pearl leaned over the piano, showing off her brown cleavage. "Thanks, dearie," she said. "We make a good team. We should do this again some time."

"In case you didn't notice," Albertine said, "I normally work alone."

"Well," Pearl laughed, "keep an open mind. You never know…"

"Oh, I know."

"How's that little son of yours? Who's taking care of him?" Pearl grinned at her, as if she were exposing a secret.

"He's not my son," Albertine hissed. "He's my sister's boy, and we're raising him."

"Your sister's boy!" Pearl laughed and gave her a fake look of surprise. "I wonder what Hendrik would say about <u>that</u> fairy tale?"

"What do you know about Hendrik?"

"Didn't he tell you?" she smiled and stared at her with big yellow cat's eyes. "I've started singing with his band."

"That's news to me."

"On nights when you don't have him working at the factory!"

"Hendrik is a printer," Albertine corrected her. "He makes good money at Donnelly's."

As Pearl turned to join the action upstairs, Albertine scolded herself for disowning Hank. He was a great kid, smart and independent enough to be left on his own once in a while. Only she didn't want people at the Top Hat to know she was his mother. How could she pass for 25 when she had a big 10 year-old kid?

Albertine first walked into the Top Hat club in 1932 on the night that Hendrik's combo opened for Bix Biedebecke, the most famous band leader in Chicago. The Top Hat was still a speakeasy then, and the noisy, low ballroom was jammed with gangsters, women in silk dresses, and sports stars she'd read about in the newspapers. Hendrik had paid the manager to let his group set up on the front edge of the narrow stage. Then during the hurried, 20-minute set, the audience ignored the band's tight rhythm and Hendrik's haunting saxophone solos, which poured directly from his heart. That night, Hendrik's music was more disturbing to her than beautiful. He claimed he was happy to be her husband, but a happy man's music wouldn't sound so blue, even if he had come from Germany, "another world," and claimed to see things through "different eyes." Still she recognized that Hendrik had a special gift, greater even than her perfect pitch, and with a lucky break, he could become famous. But in the Depression, only sports stars and gangsters got the breaks. And they were the ones who had money to spend at the Top Hat, buying drinks all around, and tipping the musicians.

Then, as Hendrik's band packed up their instruments to make room for Bix and his octet, Rocko the bass player waved for Albertine to climb up to the piano, and as he called song titles over his shoulder, she played fifteen of them, one after another, in a three-minute medley. When Albertine looked up, she saw a tall man in a tuxedo leaning over the piano and grinning at her. "Neat trick, little lady," the man said. He introduced himself as Lonnie Fulshear, the club manager, and he asked her if she'd like to play the lounge piano for tips, three nights a week. Now, two years later, playing at the Top Hat was just as exciting as it had been that first night.

Before she went upstairs, Albertine collected the money from her tip jar (twelve measly dollars!), and she snapped the money next to her cigarette case in her tiny pocket book that she strung like a bracelet on her wrist from its gold-plated chain. She wondered if Monty would be lurking upstairs. Worse yet, she could meet her brother Larry, who would report back to Ma and Pa, and make them think she was a bad wife and a worse mother.

Since full repeal, the Top Hat on North Rush Street had grown from a basement speakeasy to take over the restaurant above it, and now the club had many tables, a long mahogany bar with a mirror behind it, and an expansive parquet dance floor.

The featured combo played a too-fast number with a syncopated rhythm that sounded forced to Albertine, and maybe that was why so few couples were dancing. But it was only 9:00 o'clock. In another hour you couldn't breathe in here, it would be so crowded. But now you could look around and spot people you knew, and Albertine was lucky enough to see Colby Malone sitting at a big table with two other ballplayers from the Cubs and a couple of girls. People said Colby had a wife back in West Virginia, but he didn't act like it. Colby was out on the town almost every night, and he liked to spend time with her.

If you met Colby Malone on the street, you wouldn't guess that he was one of the best hitters in the National League. He looked like he had just left his job at the steel mills. Instead of being tall and lanky, Colby was five foot seven and powerfully built, with huge arms, a barrel chest and a square, determined jaw. He had tiny feet, size five, so that when he ran the bases or chased a fly ball he had a choppy stride that made you think he was going to fall flat on his face. No, he wasn't a graceful athlete like Lou Gehrig or Pepper Martin, but he got the job done. In 1933, he was one home run short of Babe Ruth's record, he drove in more runs than anyone, and he earned a salary of $50,000, one of the highest in baseball. Already this season he'd hit 20 homers, and it was still early June. But that didn't keep the sports writers from making fun of him, calling him an iron worker, a coal miner, a fire plug, a bull dog, and even a freak of nature.

Albertine knew the criticism hurt Colby. When she looked into his soft blue eyes, she wanted to protect him. He was a star baseball player with muscles like Hercules, but underneath he was shy, sensitive and insecure, amazed that he had made the Major Leagues at all, let alone being in contention for his third World Series. He was also a gentle and caring lover. When Colby touched her, she thought she might melt away. But there were other girls at his table now. He might already have decided to be with one of them tonight.

As Albertine came up to the table, she saw that the other two girls were younger than she was, soft-faced with full lips and beauty spots penciled on their cheeks, false eyelashes and crimped, bleached hair. One was a big gal, with Mae West-sized bosoms, and a long black cigarette holder that she held like a magic wand. The girl who sat next to Colby (in what should have been Albertine's chair) also was very tall and buxom. Even sitting down she was a head taller than Colby. She had a long face and too big, too white teeth. Next time she laughs, Albertine thought, she'll neigh like a horse!

"Hey, look who's here!" Colby called to her. "It's my gal, Al." His voice was deep and mellow, a man's voice, and as he smiled at her with straight rows of small teeth, dimples formed in his cheeks. Oh, she wanted to reach across the table and cup his face in the palm of her hand. But there were two bimbos and two cigar-smoking baseball players in her way.

Billy Herman and Stan Hack were infielders who had the annoying swagger of big leaguers. They were tall and wiry and had cropped and pomaded hair, and clean-shaven faces that were tanned from playing outdoors all spring. They paused to give Albertine the eye, to undress her with a look. But she didn't carry as much flesh as the two bimbos, so Billy and Stan didn't keep their eyes on her for long. Besides, they knew Colby had seen her first. He had the right of first refusal.

"Hey, what are you guys waiting for?" Colby nearly shouted. "Make room for Al. She came over to sit with me. Ain't that right, Albertine?"

"You bet, Colby," she replied and felt her face grow hot. Why was she blushing? Now that Albertine had what she wanted, she was both thrilled and a little ashamed. If Hendrik knew where this evening was headed, he'd give her another big fat punch right in the mouth.

Albertine worked her way around the table, brushing past Billy and making the tall, horse-faced girl switch chairs so she could sit next to Colby, where he leaned toward her. She thought he was going to kiss her cheek, but instead he whispered in her ear. "I was hoping I'd see ya," he said. His breath was warm across her neck, and she wished they were alone together.

"I was playing piano downstairs in the old club," she said and smiled. "I was hoping you'd come rescue me from the gangsters."

"I don't mess with gangsters, you know that," Colby said. "People get ideas. But hey, quit worrying and have some champagne."

"Well, if you insist."

The girl to her right waved her cigarette holder, and then rubbed her cheek against Stan's shoulder like a cat wanting to be petted. Stan ignored her.

"Who are we playing tomorrow, anyway?" Stan asked Billy. Albertine saw how red his eyes were, she heard liquor on his voice like a soggy sponge, and she wondered how he'd be able to get out of bed in the morning, let alone play baseball.

"We're playing Philadelphia, aren't we?" Billy laughed. "They got a new pitcher who throws the knuckle ball. We don't have anybody who can hit a trick thrower like that except for Colby. Don't let him drink too much."

"We're playing Pittsburgh," Colby corrected them. "Phillies don't come to town until Saturday. What's the matter? Don't you read the papers?"

"Why should we read 'em? They only write about you," Billy complained. "Colby Malone, the home run slamming midget."

"The sledgehammer in center field," Stan piled on. "The slugger from the steel mills. The gorilla who shags flies."

"Haven't you teased him enough?" Albertine scolded.

"I guess so," Stan laughed. "We can't think of any more guff to throw at him."

"None we can say in front of the ladies!" Billy laughed.

"Are there ladies here?" Stan asked and grinned drunkenly. "I got the impression they were trying hard <u>not</u> to be ladies."

"Stan!" the big girl said and slapped him so hard his cigar flew out of his mouth and landed on the dance floor. Instead of getting angry, Stan laughed, held the woman's hand in both of his and kissed her hard and long, until she pulled back, gasping for air.

"So that's what a cigar tastes like!" she said and pretended to spit behind her. "Geez, Stanley, your dick tastes better than that!"

"Let's give 'em some room to fight," Colby said and took Albertine's hand. "Let's dance."

Colby led her out onto the dance floor (where he crushed the burning cigar beneath his heel) and then took her in his arms to begin the halting stagger that he believed to be a foxtrot. She didn't care that he was a lousy dancer. His shoulders were almost twice as broad as Hendrik's, and Colby was a full head shorter than her husband, so he seemed just the right size to watch over her. As they danced, they were nearly eye to eye, and although he held her firmly, he didn't crush her body into his. She could tell that he wanted to look at her.

"I'm glad you came tonight," she told him. "I've been thinking about you every day for two weeks."

"We just came in from our road trip," Colby smiled and sighed. "I'm happy not to be cooped up in that Pullman car for a while."

"Were you thinking of me?" Albertine asked and Colby winked at her. It was just the kind of question dames asked to make sure they've got their hooks in you, but he didn't mind.

"Sure, I was thinking about you all the time," he teased her. "I was saying to myself, there's no one like my gal, Al!"

"And there's no one else like you, Colby. There never will be."

"Don't play games with me, Al. I could have lots of girls who aren't married, ya know."

"Everyone knows you're a big star," she said. "Any girl would want to be seen with Colby Malone, the major leaguer. But I want to be with Colby Malone, the man."

"Somehow I believe that mush," he smiled. "Let's get outa here. All right with you? I've got a new place over by Lincoln Park."

"I'd love to see it."

"Let's have one more drink with the gang, and then we can clear out."

When they got back to the table, the infielders and their girlfriends had been joined by a trumpet player named Clyde who'd worked with Hendrik, and by Pearl, the dark-skinned girl who called herself a singer.

"Who's the red dress with Colby Malone?" Pearl called out in her nasal voice. "Why, it's Mrs. Hendrik Kinderman!"

Looking at Pearl Cornell, Albertine knew how it felt to hate someone. Singing with Hendrik's band! She wanted to kick the woman down a flight of stairs, or turn her over to Tino and Nick for a rough time in Cicero.

"Excuse me," Albertine said and smiled odiously at her rival. "Have we met? I don't actually <u>know</u> many colored people."

"Pipe down, Al," Stan the third baseman said. "Everyone knows she's Italian."

"Everyone <u>says</u> she's Italian," Albertine continued. "Hey, don't get me wrong. I've got nothing against Negroes or Italians, either. I just don't like her <u>tone</u>. Not her color, but the way she's talking to me. I never did anything against her."

"I'm so sorry," Pearl replied with a smile that said exactly the opposite. "You're a great little piano player. You should keep it up."

"That's more than I can say about your singing!"

"Oh, my!" Pearl laughed. "I struck a chord, didn't I?"

Before Albertine could respond, Colby whispered to her and poured her more champagne. "You shouldn't let her get your goat. No one pays her any mind. Don't you know that?"

"I'm not turning the other cheek for anybody," Albertine insisted. "Once you give in to people, they walk all over you."

"Boy, you are wound up tonight! What can I do to make you laugh?"

"Get me outa here."

"You gotta laugh first."

"Make me."

"When I get to the ballpark this morning for practice, there's this little boy standing at the gate holding a program and a fountain pen. He says to me, 'Mr. Malone, could ya do me a favor?' And I say, sure, kid, and I take the program and the pen and I sign my name on top of the team photo on page two. When I hand it back to him, he gives me the queerest kind of look and he says, 'Uh, thanks, I guess. But I was hoping you could get me Gabby Hartnett's autograph.' "

Albertine laughed, pleased that Colby could poke fun at himself, though she believed Colby was a bigger star than the Cubs' player-manager. Then she said, "Can we go now?"

"I'll go grab a taxi," Colby said. "Meet me out front in a minute."

Anxious to be alone with her, Colby jumped up from his seat and trotted toward the exit, as if he were running out to center field to start a big game. If things were different, they could have left the table together. If she wasn't married, if Colby didn't have a wife in West Virginia, if that snoop Pearl Cornell wasn't there to tell her lies to Hendrik, if things were neat and tidy, she could walk away from this crowd on Colby's arm with her head held high. But as it was, she had to sneak out when no one was looking. And nobody would notice her leaving by herself, anyway. It was Colby they watched for, Colby the batting king, but not the man she knew.

His new hotel apartment had a small sitting room, a galley kitchen and a bedroom big enough to hold the grandest four-poster bed Albertine had ever seen.

She hadn't been wearing much to begin with, but before she knew it, she was naked between those crisp sheets, waiting for Colby to come out of the bathroom.

On the bedside table she noticed a pewter picture frame lying face down, and curious, she picked it up to see a photo of a young woman with a wide, round face and curly blonde hair. In the photo, her cheeks were rouged with water color and an artist had added blue ink to her eyes. So this was his wife, a sturdy-looking country girl in a simple calico dress and without a hat. The building behind her is probably a barn. Albertine felt uneasy sitting naked in Colby's bed, holding a picture of his wife, so she quickly set the frame down on the table. As she lay back on the pillow, she wondered why Colby and this woman never had any children.

When Colby appeared in the shaft of light, he looked like a statue to Albertine, with powerful arms and well-defined muscles across his chest and stomach. Still, he was shy with her. He didn't take off his BVDs until he had turned off the light.

The way Colby made love was different from Hendrik's way. Hendrik took her for granted. He was always in a hurry and he pressed against her as if he were trying to release a terrible, mindless urge. Sure, it could be thrilling, but Albertine often thought that Hendrik could be sleeping with anyone – that he wanted to have sex and not make love.

Colby, on the other hand, took his time. He massaged her with his small hands, and kissed her neck and whispered her name into her ear, so she was ready for him ages before he came to her. Albertine felt that he really was making love to her.

"Am I dreaming?" she asked him as they lay beside each other in the dark, listening to the sounds of traffic outside their window. "Or do you really love me?"

"Hush," he whispered. "You'll spoil it by talking. Can't we just be together?"

Yes, they could just be together, passionate and restful by turns, but only for a few hours. At 1:30, Albertine was out of bed, taking a shower, and by 2:00 she was down in the lobby with the big Irish doorman, waiting for her taxi.

"Good night, Miss," the doorman said as he held the cab's door for her.

"Thank you, Brian," she said, as she ducked onto the seat. Then she gave her address to the driver and closed her eyes so she could think about Colby on her way home. If only she had met Colby first, before she'd laid eyes on the handsome German musician and heard him play his horn. But when she was 17, Colby would have been a 15 year-old boy in a West Virginia steel town, about to drop out of school to swing a sledge hammer in the mill and a baseball bat in the semi-pro league, until his reputation for slugging home runs reached the scouts for Pittsburgh, who signed him for a year in the Texas League to see if he could hit real pitching. By that time, he was 20 and married, and Albertine was 22 and already had Hank. Having her baby was one thing she did not regret, though sometimes she fudged the truth about his being her son.

The taxi dropped her off in front of her shabby three-flat building on Lexington Avenue. She could see the light in their second-floor apartment, and she shuddered to think that Hendrik had waited up for her.

The wooden staircase creaked beneath her, and she felt ashamed of the musty smell in its rug, the paint worn away from the banister, and the bare bulb that dimly lit her way up the steps.

She took a deep breath before she unlocked the door, and she smiled her brightest smile as she pushed it open, but instead of Hendrik standing in the hallway, it was her younger brother Larry. He wore a dirty yellow shirt and untied brogans with no socks, and he squinted at her angrily.

"It's about time you got home!" Larry accused her.

"What are you doing here?" she demanded.

"There's been an accident."

"What kind of accident? Is Hank all right?"

"Hank is fine. It's Hendrik who's hurt. He lost his thumb in a printing press."

"Is he okay? Can I go see him?"

"He's asleep in the bedroom."

"Why isn't he at the hospital?"

"Dad took him over to Cook County and got him stitched back together. I think he saved his life."

"He nearly killed him, you mean!"

"I don't think Hendrik was meant to be a printer," Larry said. "Christ! I hope he can play his horn without his thumb."

"Oh, Larry, don't even say that! Of course, he can play it," Albertine said, then suddenly felt worried about her son. "How did Hank take it? Did he go back to sleep?"

"He took it all right, I guess," Larry shrugged. "When you weren't here, Dad took him to their house in my car."

"Lonnie Fulshear asked me to play between sets," she said. "I knew Hank would be fine until his Dad got home."

"Did you see any ball players, Albertine?"

"Not tonight."

"Any boxers, Sis? Any mob hoodlums?"

"I don't have to take the third degree from you, Larry!" she said and rushed past him to the bedroom. She turned on the light and hurried to the bed to see her poor, wounded husband lying on his side with his golden hair spread out on the pillow around his flushed face.

"Hendrik, honey? Hendrik? Are you all right?"

Oblivious to her, he snored away. But he cradled his bandaged hand against his chest. She was sure he was dreaming that he would never play his horn again.

A wave of affection and pity came over her. No matter how wonderful Colby might be, no matter how tender and generous and sweet, it was Hendrik who was her husband. It was Hendrik who would always command her love. And while he was being crushed by her father's machines, she was cheating on him with a baseball player who had a wife and a dozen other girlfriends.

"Oh, Hendrik, you poor baby," she said, and as she began to cry, she climbed into bed beside him, careful not to touch his wounded hand, and she kissed his bristly cheek and made it wet with her tears.

Chapter Two

For once, Birdie needed Dr. Bichet as much as he needed her. Nelly Ladoux had been in labor for 12 hours already without dilating much at all, and though strong contractions came every five minutes, Nelly's shape made it clear that the baby's head hadn't dropped to the birth canal. By palpating with her hands against Nelly's abdomen, Birdie could feel that the baby was presenting itself feet first, and a breach birth could be very risky. She needed Doc Bichet's advice to deliver the child safely and with no harm to the young mother.

For the past three weeks, Birdie had been visiting Nelly in an effort to turn the baby. They had walked together in the park, and Birdie had made Nelly lie flat on the teeter-totter with her feet over the handles, while Birdie raised and lowered Nelly's legs every few seconds for a half hour every day, but the baby refused to roll over. She tried to make Nelly skip rope, but she slipped and fell on the sidewalk, so Birdie eased up, not wanting to injure mother or child.

Exercising during labor hadn't helped turn the baby, either. A walk around the bedroom did not convince the child to do a somersault inside Nelly Ladoux. A long, vigorous ride in the rocking chair had not worked, either. Even lying on the floor with her legs up on the bed did not change the baby's insistence on arriving feet first.

Now Nelly was in pain and her child was in distress. But Doc Bichet took his sweet time in coming, even after Birdie had told him it would be a breach birth. Birdie prayed to God that the baby would at least present itself feet first and not leading by the buttocks in jackknife position, a terrible nightmare for mother and midwife. Even a Caesarean delivery would be hard under those circumstances if the baby had traveled too far into the birth canal.

Birdie answered the door to let Doc Bichet into the Ladoux's apartment. He was a rumpled man, past 70, with wild, gray hair and yellowed, bloodshot eyes. For eyeglasses he carried a pince nez on a braided shoestring, and his bag of ancient medical instruments belonged in a museum. He arrived at the Ladoux flat as the expectant mother moaned and sweated in her bed. Nelly's mother and sister had sent her husband away, and for the past three hours these two had been badgering Birdie with questions about the delivery and with suggestions on how to make Nelly more comfortable.

Doc Bichet wore a jacket and trousers from two different suits and a knit tie stained with coffee and food scraps. His straw summer hat was cracked and broken around its crown, as if someone had sat on it. When Birdie caught a whiff of him, she was sure he had been drinking again, but she prayed that he was less drunk than usual.

"So Nelly's time has come!" Doc Bichet concluded with repeated nods. "Two weeks early by my calculation. Does my little Birdie still think it's a breach baby?"

"I told you! I'm sure of it!" (You old fool, she thought.) "I need your help."

"Of course, you do, of course," the doctor sputtered. "Let me go in the kitchen to wash my hands, and then I'll examine the patient."

Doctor Bichet walked down the dim, narrow hallway to the big kitchen, along the rear of the apartment. The prescribed pots of water were boiling on the gas stove, and the windows were opened to the screened porch to release some of the steamy air. The two women in their cotton dresses and ruffled aprons stood up from the table to greet him. Nelly's mother was short and square with dyed-black hair and wire-rimmed glasses. Nora, the younger sister, was plump, soft and friendly. Despite Doc Bichet's disheveled appearance and shaky walk, Nora gave him a big, sweet smile, which encouraged him to ask for what he really wanted.

"Good evening, ladies," he said and grinned with his tobacco-stained teeth. Then he set his bag on the narrow counter beside the stove, opened it and fished out two handfuls of shiny instruments, which he dropped into two of the boiling pots of water. "We'll let these simmer for a good while," he said. "In the meantime, could you lend me a bar of soap?" He spotted one on the sink. "Ah, here's one! And I wonder if you'd have something for my parched throat. A bottle of beer, perhaps? Or half a glass of red wine?"

Nora stepped toward the icebox to see if her sister had any beer left, but her mother spoke up before she could get there. "I'm afraid there's no beer or wine, doctor," she said sweetly, as the old man grunted and ran his tongue over his teeth. "I made a pitcher of ice water for Nelly," she said. "I could offer you some of that. Or I could light the fire under the coffee pot and heat it up for you."

"Well, make it coffee then," he conceded. "If that's all you've got!"

He draped his coat over a chair and rolled up his threadbare sleeves. Then he went to the kitchen sink and leaned his head over the basin where he splashed cold water on his eyes and cheeks and on the back of his neck. Then he shook himself like a wet dog, and rising, he snatched the bar of soap, scraped his fingernails over it and twisted it in his joined fists until bubbles seeped out between his fingers. Then he lathered his forearms to the elbows, rinsed them under the tap and snapped the loose droplets down into the cast iron sink. He turned to Nora who held out a clean dish towel, which he used to dry his hands and arms, face and neck, then tossed it back to her.

"Thank you," he said. "Now to see about your sister."

When Doc Bichet reached the bedroom, Birdie Fontaine was holding Nelly's hand as she rode through another contraction.

"You told them not to give me anything to drink, didn't you, Birdie?" he accused her. "Re-heated coffee is all I'll get!"

"I don't know what you mean, Doc," Birdie shrugged as the contraction subsided and Nelly eased back onto her pillows. "Examine her yourself. See if I'm right."

"Hello, Nelly," Doc Bichet said, smiled at her, and stroked the damp hair from her forehead. "How are you holding up, darling?"

"I'm very tired, doctor. I'm not sure I can make it."

"Of course, you can make it. Birdie's here and so am I now. We'll see you through this and deliver a beautiful baby to your arms."

"I knew everything would be okay," Nelly said sweetly, but Birdie wasn't so sure. She'd had a premonition that there would be trouble today. When she got on the streetcar, she saw a crushed hat on the floor, and people stepped around it carefully, as if it belonged to a dead man. And here comes Doc Bichet wearing a straw hat just like it, in nearly the same condition, and he was oblivious to the fact that it was better suited for a scarecrow than for a doctor. He could have just stepped out of a hobo jungle.

But Birdie felt relieved that Doc Bichet looked in better shape now than when he had first arrived. The hat was gone, the rumpled coat was left in the kitchen, and as he touched Nelly, taking her pulse, checking her temperature, pulling back the sheet to see her tight, round abdomen, and pressing it with his hands, listening with his stethoscope and his naked ear (his whiskers tickled Nelly and she laughed), his engagement with the expectant mother made him seem alert, more like the wise doctor he thought himself to be, and less the broken-down drunk who needed the help of a midwife whenever it was time to deliver a baby.

He used Birdie's gauge to check Nelly's blood pressure, and came up with the same answer that Birdie had already written in the notebook on the bedside table: 145/100, elevated pressure, not a good indication.

"You're right, Birdie," he said and swept her to the far corner of the bedroom. "The baby's not turned at all. Sometimes they stay that way. She'll be having another contraction any second. Once that happens, I want you to check her dilation. Use my light if you need to."

Birdie nodded, and when she turned to Nelly she could see the girl tense up as the contraction clenched her body.

"Oh, my," Nelly cried, and Birdie knelt beside her until the pain subsided. Then she had Nelly raise her knees so she could reach down and feel Nelly's cervix and gauge the opening with her fingertips.

"Progress!" Birdie smiled at Nelly. "Good girl, you're almost there."

When she held up her fingers to show Doc Bichet how far Nelly had dilated, he brought her back into the opposite corner of the bedroom.

"We have to get her out of the bed," he told her. "Fold a blanket in half and put it down on the floor, then put a sheet on top of it. Then we'll help Nelly get up."

Birdie nodded, but needed to go to Nelly's mother and sister for more linen. They were eager to help. Instead of a blanket, they retrieved a padded quilt, and the two stout women knelt on the rug and laid out one sheet, unfolded the quilt on top of, then spread a second sheet on top. Nora stood up first, then helped her mother to her feet.

When the two women were finished, the doctor pronounced, "An old blanket would be better. I'd hate to see blood on that nice quilt."

"I suppose you're right," Thaïs, Nelly's mother, said. "My mother sewed this quilt, you know. I'll see what else Nelly has in her blanket chest." Then she and Nora folded the quilt between them.

In a minute Thaïs returned with a dark gray blanket, which smelled of mothballs but was still shot through with dime-sized holes. Folded in half, it softened the floor as much as the heirloom would have. "Now that's better," Doc Bichet sighed. "Now we can invite the baby home. But I think it's better if you two ladies wait in the kitchen for a while. Birdie and I have our work cut out for us."

Thaïs and Nora obeyed the doctor, and once they had waddled into the hallway, he closed the door behind them.

"Nelly, sweetheart," Doc Bichet said sweetly. "After this next contraction, we're going to help you get down on the floor."

"On the floor?" Nelly asked. "I like my bed, Doctor. Why can't my baby be born in my bed?"

"Your little one wants to come out feet first, Nelly," Doc Bichet told her. "It will be easier on the floor. Once the baby's born, you can get right back in bed."

"Oh, here comes one!" Nelly said, gritting her teeth. "This really hurts!"

"There, there, hang on," Birdie told her, "and don't push yet."

When the contraction passed, Doc Bichet said, "Okay, Nelly, Birdie and I are going to help you get down on the sheet here."

Instead of moving toward the patient, the doctor watched as Birdie stepped across the sheet to hold Nellie's arm as she rose out of the bed. Nelly stood briefly, then moved to lay down. "No, Nelly," the doctor said. "I want you to kneel like you're praying. Birdie, put a pillow on the floor so Nelly can kneel on it."

Nelly nodded, then with Birdie's help, she slowly knelt down on the pillow. Her dark hair was damp, and her nightgown was soaked through with sweat. Although it was a warm evening, she shivered as if it were winter.

"Are you sure about this?" Birdie whispered, concerned that Nelly could not hold herself in a kneeling position for long. "We don't have a labor chair."

"Birdie, could you please get my instruments from the kitchen?" the doctor asked quietly. "I'll watch out for Nelly."

Birdie's mother had taught her the correct vertical delivery position, and it required a birthing chair or two strong women (like Nora and Thaïs) to support the laboring mother. So why had Bichet sent them out of the room? Her mother also had reminded her repeatedly that doctors knew nothing about childbirth. In the past 10 years, Birdie had delivered at least 200 babies with Doc Bichet. In most cases he had done absolutely nothing, and Birdie hadn't needed his help, except in the most difficult cases. But the health department wouldn't renew her license without a doctor's recommendation. Midwives were out of favor, and the medical profession had convinced the authorities that a midwife working alone posed unacceptable risks for women and babies. By collaborating with Doctor Bichet, she'd been able to keep working, and old Bichet – who should have retired years ago – could still charge twice her rate to deliver babies.

As she hurried to the kitchen, Birdie was nervous about leaving Doc Bichet with Nelly too long. What would he have her do next? Hop on one foot? Hang from the door jamb?

"What is it?" Thaïs asked in surprise as Birdie came back to the kitchen. "What's the matter now? Does he want us to come back and help him?"

"No, no, nothing's wrong. I've come for his instruments."

"We'll help you," Nora volunteered.

"No, dear. I'll call if I need you. As you can see, the doctor is very particular."

"You can tell him his coffee is ready when he wants it," Thaïs said, then winked. "We told him we were all out of beer."

"Thanks for that," Birdie said and turned off the fires beneath the two big pots of instruments. Then she took a dishtowel off the rack beside the sink and picked up one of the pots, carefully poured off the water, then carried it to the bedroom.

Doc Bichet was kneeling next to Nelly, and he held her hand as if they were praying together.

"How much longer?" Nelly begged him. "I'm so tired."

"Just a little longer," Doc Bichet assured her. "I'm just as tired as you!"

"How much longer?"

"Until Birdie comes back with all my instruments and a big pot of boiled water."

"Hurry up, then, Birdie!" Nelly cried. "I'm tired!"

"I know dear," Birdie told her and shot Dr. Bichet an accusing stare. "We'll have you set up in a minute." The old doctor knelt there stoop-shouldered and weary, with wild gray hair and watery eyes. He didn't seem to notice Birdie's exasperation.

When Birdie returned from her third trip to the kitchen, Doc Bichet was lying on the bed, and Nelly was on her hands and knees.

The doctor kept his eyes closed as he spoke: "Give her the Novocain, Birdie, and make the episiotomy."

Birdie got the anesthetic needle from his bag, sterilized it with alcohol and found the vial of narcotic. She administered three small injections, waited five minutes, poked Nelly to make sure she was numb, then used a pair of boiled scissors to make the cut.

"Now get her to kneel again," the doctor whispered. "One more time."

"Get up now, Nelly. Get up now. It's time to push."

Nelly raised up, and blood dripped down her thighs. "Now push, darling. Give me a nice push," Birdie said.

Between pushes Nelly rested on all fours, and during each pause Birdie checked to see if any part of the baby was visible. "See anything yet?" Doc Bichet asked every time from the bed, as if he were calling out from his sleep.

Finally, two rose-colored feet poked out from Nelly's vagina. "I can see the feet, Birdie said in an excited whisper. "I see both feet."

"Hooey!" Doc Bichet laughed to himself. "Now we're really making progress! Would those little toes be pointing down at the floor?"

"Yes, doctor, they are pointed to the floor."

"Then we are in luck, little Birdie. Considering the circumstances, things could not be better."

"Can I get back in bed?" Nelly cried. "This is exhausting! I feel like I'm scrubbing the floor and having a baby at the same time."

"Believe me, dear," the doctor said through a yawn. "You are right where you need to be."

On the next contraction, Nelly pushed hard and the baby's legs came out as far as the knees.

"Now don't rush things," Doc Bichet said, guessing correctly that Birdie wanted to grab the feet and pull. "On the next push, guide those feet gently toward the floor until the baby's seat comes out and you can tell if it's a boy or a girl. And have a towel ready. You'll get squirted for sure."

As Birdie reached for a towel, Nelly began another contraction, and while she pushed, Birdie guided the baby's legs downward and the child moved out more quickly than she expected. Then a stream of milky liquid sprayed Birdie as the little girl's buttocks emerged.

"It's a girl!" Birdie laughed and held the baby with her left hand as she dried herself and Nelly with the towel in her right. "You were right about getting squirted."

"Everything gets squeezed out of the baby during labor," the doctor explained. "Usually it squirts back inside mama... Now take a break, Birdie. Things get a little tricky here. The arms have to be birthed one at a time. Turn the little girl a quarter turn to your right. Slow and gentle," the doctor instructed her.

Birdie held the baby's thighs and gently turned her sideways. On Nelly's next push, the right arm was free.

"Turn her back a quarter turn to the left," Doc Bichet said from the bed. "Push again, Nelly, and the left arm will be born."

Again, the old doctor was right.

"Now, wait!" Doc Bichet said before Birdie could order another push. "This is the most important step."

"Okay, we're waiting," Birdie said. "If I let go of this baby, it won't be too good for her neck."

"No, it won't," the doctor chuckled. "What I need you to do now is hold the baby up with your left hand and reach in with your right to grab her chin. When you find her chin, I want you to hold it down against her chest, so she can be born safely. Reach in there and tell me when you feel it."

Birdie held the baby (a six-pounder she guessed), and slid her short, thick hand below the girl's face, stretching against Nelly's straining skin, until she held the baby's chin between her thumb and forefinger, then pulled up and back on it to secure the chin to the baby's clavicle.

"I'm holding it to her chest, Doc."

"Fine. Keep holding it there. One last push, Nelly, and she'll be free."

The baby was free of her mother now, and suddenly Doc Bichet was energized. He hopped off the opposite side of the bed and came around it to clamp the umbilical cord and cut it with some fresh scissors.

The baby's body was white with vernyx, but her face was blue. So Doc Bichet took her from Birdie and quickly dunked her head into the pot of warm water. As he held her, he reached in his bag and pulled out a tiny rubber mask, attached to what looked like a small hot water bottle. He placed the mask over the baby's face and with the same hand he squeezed the small bladder three times. When he pulled it away, the baby was crying and her face was red.

"There you are!" Doc Bichet said to Nelly (whom Birdie was helping back into bed) and laughed with satisfaction. "A beautiful baby daughter!" He handed Birdie the baby so she could clean her up with a dry towel and wrap her in a receiving blanket before letting Nelly hold her while they waited for the placenta to be delivered.

"Have you picked a name?" Doc Bichet asked.

"Eleanor," Nelly sighed. "After Mrs. Roosevelt."

"Do you have a crib, Nelly?" Dr. Bichet asked her.

"Yes, doctor," Nelly smiled at him, as if he were an absent-minded grandfather. "It's in the next room. Birdie knows where. Mama and Nora can bring it in."

"After that maybe they can pull out that bottle of beer they hid when Birdie told them I was coming. While Birdie's stitching you up, I could use a nice, cold drink!"

By the time Birdie could go home, Doc Bichet had drunk two bottles of beer, collected his fee, and had left for his own bed. He waited long enough to check the placenta, and to see that there was no bleeding, but he did not stay for the women's work of cleaning up, changing the sheets, or starting the baby nursing, however weakly. And he would leave the follow up visits to Birdie, too.

It was after two in the morning when the proud young father, Raymond Ladoux, gave Birdie a ride home in his Hupmobile.

"Isn't my daughter the most beautiful baby you've ever seen?"

"Of course, she is," Birdie fibbed. "I've never seen a prettier little girl." Breach babies did have the advantage of being born with round, not elongated heads, and little Eleanor had big blue eyes, a short nose, nice fingers and toes, and a few wisps of dark hair. But having helped at hundreds of births, Birdie had seen many remarkable children. She had held plump ones born with pink fat cheeks and full heads of golden hair. She had delivered twins, born like identical dolls from the toy store, and she had seen boys come out with thick, muscular arms and smiles that said they'd learned something special while inside the womb. One baby was born whistling, and another kept pointing his finger at her and winking as if they were old friends.

Raymond Ladoux drove a delivery truck during the day and had bought the black Hupmobile coupe from his brother who had joined the Army. Raymond had thick, wavy hair, and dimples formed when he smiled, which was most of the time. Birdie liked Raymond a lot and wondered why Albertine had not married a nice boy like him. He even attended the French church, Notre Dame.

When the Hupmobile pulled up to the sidewalk in front of Birdie's three-story house, Raymond Ladoux got out of the car and hurried around to open the door for her.

"Thank you for all your help, Mrs. Fontaine," he said. "I felt a lot better knowing it was you helping Nelly tonight."

"Thank you, Raymond," Birdie said, "but Doc Bichet had something to do with it, too."

"You do more than your share, Mrs. Fontaine," Raymond said. "Everyone knows that."

"Good night, Raymond. Be careful driving."

As Birdie reached into her handbag for her house key, she felt a chill and smelled the strong scent of lilacs. Then she saw a white form take shape beside her on the porch, her mother's ghost like a reflection in a mirror at night, her mother, but not really her mother, and the voice was not so much audible as understood. "Birdie," her mother called to her. "Oh, Birdie!" she was dressed all in white, like a nurse, except for the dark cloche hat that covered her white hair. "I showed the doctor that kneeling trick," she said. "How else would he know?"

"You always insisted on giving support during the upright position," Birdie sighed, a bit disappointed that her mother was still a know-it-all, even from the other side. "You never had a girl kneel on all fours."

"A breach baby is the only exception."

"And why didn't you ever share that with me?" Birdie asked.

"You weren't ready for it until tonight!"

Birdie turned to explain that she was 55 years old and had delivered as many babies as her mother had, and Mére had passed away when Birdie was 43, so she would have been ready then, in any case, if her mother had taken the trouble to tell her. But the vision was gone now, the evening air was warm again, and Birdie was startled by another car pulling up. "At this hour of the night!" She turned and recognized Larry's Model A, but she was surprised when her husband Henry climbed out instead of their son, and then little Hank, her 10 year-old grandson, appeared on the sidewalk, too.

Henry came to her quickly. He wore his gray work uniform from Donnelly Printing Company. "Are you just getting home, Birdie?"

"Nelly Ladoux had a breach delivery tonight. It took a while longer than we expected."

"Was Bichet sober?"

"Sober enough to remember what Mére Elise taught him."

"Mother and baby are fine?"

"Yes, thank God. And why are you showing up so late in Larry's car. With Hank to boot?" Then Hank was climbing up the steps to meet her. "There's my boy, Hank. I'll bet you're hungry! I'll fix you a plate of food before you climb into your feather bed. Would you like that?"

"Sure. Grandma. Sounds great."

They walked through the side mud room, past the family parlor and into the white kitchen, where Birdie could heat up some milk for herself and fix some food for her two Henrys.

Henry turned on the light and explained why he was home so late with the boy in tow. "Around ten o'clock, Hendrik got his hand caught in the Number Three press, and brought all my production to a halt."

"Is he all right?"

"He lost the thumb on his right hand."

"That's dreadful."

"I took him in a cab over to Cook County. And the hospital was full of people."

"On a Wednesday night?"

"There was an explosion down at the rail yard. There must have been a hundred men bleeding or burnt, lying on stretchers in the lobby. It reminded me of France in 1918."

"So what did you do?"

"I took him up to the maternity ward and got your cousin Fay to sew him back together."

"That's a new experience for Fay," Birdie shook her head. "Will Hendrik be all right?

"Well," Henry smiled wearily. "He's a lot better now, anyways. I woke Larry up at his boarding house to drive Hendrik home, and when we got there your daughter was still out on the town!"

"She's <u>my</u> daughter now? And little Hank was by himself?"

"That's why I brought him with me."

They turned and saw that Hank was sitting at the kitchen table, with his head down on his arms, sound asleep.

"I left Larry there to take care of Hendrik until Albertine shows up," Henry whispered. "I was afraid of what I might say when she got there."

"We should never have paid for those piano lessons," Birdie shook her head. "Madame Corbet's music wiped out everything she ever learned from the holy sisters!"

Chapter Three

During the night shift at Donnelly's Printing Company, the rows of incandescent lights on the ceiling cast a dim, yellow glow over the lines of machines forty feet below, and the plant echoed with the roar of the machinery. With production going full tilt, the presses pounded, the electric motors growled, the conveyors squeaked, the cutters chopped, and the jogging baskets vibrated loudly at the end of the line.

The night production supervisor Henry Fontaine wasn't bothered by the noise. He had been an artillery sergeant in France, and he knew what loud noises were all about. The war had cost him the hearing in his right ear, and to preserve his left side, he kept his ear stuffed with cotton. To Henry, the workshop's din was like the soothing natural music of Lake Michigan lapping against the breakwater.

Instead of listening for trouble, Henry watched for it. He watched to make sure the band of paper ran straight through each row of presses and passed true on the center of the overhead conveyors. He looked to see that his pressmen were in place, that the old men who oiled the conveyor chains weren't daydreaming, that the cutting proceeded smoothly, and that the runners from the bindery were there on time to wheel away the full baskets of folded signatures.

He also watched the warning lights on top of each press. If all the green lights were glowing, things were running smoothly, but if even one red light flashed, Henry had a problem to solve, and he had to solve it quickly. He was responsible for printing 300,000 copies of the *Saturday Evening Post* by next Thursday morning.

Henry Fontaine believed he had one of the best printing jobs in Chicago, the United States, or even the world. He had hand-picked each man on his night shift crew. They were all experienced printers, except for the oilcan derelicts and his son-in-law Hendrik, on press number three, the easiest to run, the hardest to screw up. A German immigrant, Hendrik had come to America before the Great War as a boy and somehow got mixed up with Henry's daughter. Hendrik dreamed of being a musician and was a half-hearted worker. But he needed to support Albertine and their son Hank, so Henry had squeezed him in at Donnelly's, for Al's sake and to keep Birdie from worrying. Franklin Roosevelt was working on it, but he hadn't licked the Depression yet. Henry figured he'd have to help his own wherever he could.

But this kid wasn't really one of his. Granted, he had been married to Henry's daughter for eleven years. But you could still hear a trace of his German accent. And his dainty hands were more suited for playing his saxophone than for working in a printing plant. And of all things, Hendrik was a Lutheran and a Republican who stared at Henry with contempt whenever he mentioned FDR.

It was near the end of the run so the roll of paper feeding the presses was shrinking fast, and Henry went to make sure the eight new plates were ready for the next signature. He left the press bay and went into the compositor's room where the three-foot-wide trays of lead type and matted images lay ready on their rolling tables. On the black plates, the columns of reverse letters had been rolled with the proofreader's ink and were still dark from the afternoon's make-ready. The six color plates – two each for cyan, magenta, and yellow – held the headlines, borders, rules, and the dot patterns for the photos, illustrations and advertisements. It wasn't Henry's job to proofread the plates, but he did have to check the paperwork and add his initials to verify they were approved and ready to go.

Every night, John Mahoney, the late-shift linotyper, drank coffee and waited until midnight in case he had to recast any damaged type. Now he sat in the corner with his java mug, and he nodded to Henry, who politely removed the cotton ball from his left ear to hear what John might have to say.

"Get a load of that," John said, nodded down to a black plate, and slurped coffee from his heavy ceramic cup. Henry followed his glance to a halftone photograph of Sally Rand in the middle of her infamous fan dance. It seemed she was wearing nothing but a smile. Her calves, thighs, neck and shoulders were clearly visible, but her vital parts were obscured by feathery wands. The article was about her ongoing performance at the Chicago World's Fair in the "Streets of Paris" exhibit.

"Have you seen her?" John asked Henry.

"Not yet," Henry shrugged and thought of the many burlesque shows he had seen on South State Street. What did Sally Rand have that those hundreds of girls didn't?

"That was the best fifty cents I ever spent," John said. "She's like a goddess. A regular sex goddess."

"That's what they say," Henry said and wondered if the coffee was fresh. Maybe he could take a few minutes to have a cup. But then the rumble of the presses died suddenly, and the alarm bell rang. Something had gone seriously wrong.

Henry stuffed his cotton ball in his pants pocket and walked deliberately back into the press room to deal with the disaster.

All three lines were down, and all eleven red lights were flashing. Someone had already shut off the infernal alarm bell. Then Joe Sobeleski, lead operator on the first line, ran up to Henry, instinctively leaned to Henry's good ear and shouted, "It's Hendrik!"

"You don't have to holler," Henry said, thinking: my whole goddamn plant is shut down. "What about Hendrik?"

"He caught his hand in the press, boss," Joey said. "It's a bloody mess."

"Where is he?"

"He's still up there. We were afraid to move him."

"Christ, get the first aid kit, will ya? Let me see what we've got."

At his station, Hendrik lay sprawled across press number three, trapped in place by the powerful and efficient jaws of the huge machine. Two other pressmen, Rudy Tromblay and Ed Spivak, were standing beside Hendrik. The kid cried like a baby, and Rudy stroked his hair to comfort him. "Mein hand!" Hendrik moaned. "Mein hand."

The rollers and the plate grips were covered with dark liquid, and Henry could see it had soaked Hendrik's gray work shirt up to the elbow, where it had turned a brighter red than the press's magenta ink. To spill that much blood, the machine had to have crushed an artery. It was more than just a finger. His whole hand could be gone.

"Okay, clear out! Gimme some room," Henry said as he slapped Rudy's shoulder and then Ed's. "Clear out. I'll take it from here."

"Mein hand. The machine is eating mein hand."

"Take it easy, son," Henry said in a voice that was just audible over the drone of the ventilation fans. Hendrik was pale as chalk, and when Henry touched his forehead, it was cold and dry. Christ, he's bleeding to death, Henry thought and took a deep breath to calm himself. "First thing," he said, "we gotta get you loose from there."

Hendrik tried to pull his arm out, cried in pain, then collapsed back down onto the machine and sobbed pitifully.

"Steady, Hendrik. Keep still for a minute so I can get you out," Henry said, reassuring himself as much as Hendrik. "Everything's going to be okay."

Henry opened the toolbox at Hendrik's station and pulled out a long, black flashlight, clicked it on and crouched low beneath his moaning son-in-law to peer into the machine. He saw that the leading edge of the impact roller had trapped Hendrik's hand and shirt sleeve and had pulled him into the machine. In a fraction of a second, the kid had been yanked off his feet.

Henry passed the beam of light inside the press and found the chains he had to turn backward to reverse the head, and he crawled back to the toolbox to get the right tool, a 5/8 inch wrench with a two-foot handle.

"Okay, Hendrik, hold still for another minute," Henry whispered to him and patted his shoulder. Hendrik could only moan in reply, with a miserable sound that made Henry tremble. And when he reached between the rollers with the wrench, Henry felt the blood on his arm, still warm but starting to congeal, and he hoped his daughter wouldn't become a widow tonight.

The press was so well balanced that Henry could reverse the head with one push on the wrench, so Rudy and Ed were able to lift Hendrik off the machine and lay him on the floor.

Henry quickly got to his feet and hurried to check the kid's hand. In the shadows of the machinery, Hendrik's forearm glistened with dark blood. Henry knelt above his son-in-law and shined the flashlight on his right hand. The four slender fingers were intact, but most of the thumb was gone, severed at the first joint, and blood spurted weakly from a tube of skin and exposed bone and blood vessel. For a second, Henry felt light-headed, and he clenched his eyes shut and re-opened them to make sure this wasn't a nightmare. But the bloody hand did not go away, and it was up to him to do something about it.

"Hold him there, guys," Henry said. "He needs a tourniquet."

Henry pulled his bandanna from his back pocket, rolled it diagonally, tied it just above Hendrik's elbow, then took a thick pencil from his shirt pocket, slid it into the knot and twisted it tight until the bleeding stopped.

"Thank God," Henry sighed. "Now call an ambulance, will ya, Rudy? We need to get him to the hospital."

"I'm free," Hendrik moaned weakly and tried to smile with cracked and bleeding lips. His eyes were glassy, and his face was extremely pale. "At last, I'm free…"

"That's right," Henry said. "And we'll get you to the hospital as fast as we can."

The ambulance service had no cars available, so Henry had to settle for a taxi. This was okay with him, since the ambulances doubled as hearses and might be littered with discarded flowers and ribbons from the most recent funeral. Taxi drivers drove faster, too, and they knew all the short cuts through the city.

A big, clunky Checker waited at the front door on South Dearborn Street as Henry dragged the semi-conscious Hendrik into the summer night, supporting him by holding the kid's left arm tightly around his neck.

The cab driver jumped out of the car and ran around to help Henry maneuver the kid into the back seat. "Jeez oh man, what happened to him?" asked the cab driver excitedly. He was an elderly man with a snap-bill cap, a white moustache and an unbuttoned vest.

"Hurt his hand in a machine," Henry explained. "He lost a lot of blood. Can you take us to county hospital?"

"Are you sure about that?" the cabbie asked. "I hear it's a mess over there. Hobos started a fire at the rail yard. Kerosene exploded, and a bunch of lumber caught fire. A hundred people were hurt, and they all ended up at Cook County!"

"It's still the closest hospital, isn't it? And I can't afford no place else."

Once Henry climbed in beside Hendrik, the cabbie stepped on the gas, raced three blocks to get out of the printing district, and then swerved around a streetcar on Congress and headed west in heavy traffic. It was nearly eleven, but the streets were full of people gathering in front of shops, walking together or sitting on their stoops talking. On the upper floors, men, women, and kids enjoyed the mild evening near their open windows.

Henry patted Hendrik's cheek to keep him awake, but he couldn't help thinking about the interrupted print run, the blood gumming up his press, and the likelihood that he wouldn't make it back to work before the shift was over.

Then as Henry slapped him harder, Hendrik shivered as if he had a fever, but even in the warm night, he was cold as ice. "I must tell you Henry," he moaned, and smiled grimly to tease him. "Herbert Hoover would never have let this happen."

"Herbert Hoover!" Henry grumbled. "Save your breath."

For a Kraut, Hendrik knew a lot about the Republican ex-president. And he'd been in the crowd in Florida the day Giuseppe Zangara had tried to shoot FDR but killed Mayor

Cermak instead. Henry had thought it was appalling that anyone would try to shoot Roosevelt, but Hendrik was clearly amused, even proud to have witnessed a murder.

The hospital loomed above them in sooty darkness with a greenish glow barely penetrating its filthy windows. After Henry paid the fare, the cabbie opened his eyes wide with sympathy. "You need help getting him inside?" he asked.

"Would you mind?" Henry replied gratefully. Clearly unconscious now, Hendrik was beyond sleep, cold and still, with only shallow, rapid breaths. Henry and the cab driver each took one of Hendrik's arms, and they carried him through the front door into the hospital's low, wide lobby.

"What'd I tell ya!" the old driver exclaimed. The room was full of men on stretchers, on benches and on the floor, men in burned and torn clothes, guys with their faces seared, their hands charred, their hair singed down to red and blistered scalps.

"This kid could die before they even know he's here," the cabbie said. "Jesus! What are you going to do?"

"Help me get him upstairs on the elevator," Henry said. "My wife's cousin Lucy works here. In the maternity ward. She'll take care of him."

"Maternity ward?" The cabbie shook his head. "Are you nuts?"

"Believe me, Pal," Henry assured him. "She's got everything we need."

Instead of Lucy at the night desk, it was Fay, the oldest of Lucy's six daughters, a beautiful red-haired girl who was an inch taller than Henry.

"Oh, hi, Uncle Henry!" she said happily at first, but she frowned when she saw Hendrik's slumping figure, shocked face and bandaged hand. "What are you doing here?"

"Fay, dear, we need your help," Henry told her. "You remember Albertine's husband, Hendrik, don't you?"

"Sure," Fay said. "That's Hendrik? Golly, what happened?"

"He caught his hand in a printing press tonight," Henry said as he and the cab driver lowered Hendrik onto a wooden bench. "I need you to sew him up and transfuse a pint of my blood into him."

"Are you the same blood group, Uncle Henry?" Fay asked him.

"I remember he was O group on his blood test for their wedding," Henry told her. "I'm the same as that. Let's hurry. The kid is very weak, and this gentleman has to get back to his taxi."

Once the cabbie was gone, Henry and Fay lifted Hendrik onto a gurney and wheeled him into a narrow examining room, where Fay packed Hendrik's arm with black rubber bags of ice. Then she stretched a lamp on a flexible gooseneck over his hand and unwound the layers of bloody gauze. She used cotton balls to dab away the clotted blood, and then she gently squeezed his hand between her fingers. Her concentration reminded Henry of the way Birdie examined a newborn baby.

"I don't think there are any other fractures," Fay said as she painted iodine on his hand with a thumb-sized, orange swab. Hendrik flinched from the sting of the cold antiseptic and its sharp smell. "But we really should have his arm x-rayed."

She left the room for a minute and returned with a sterile suture kit, including a curved needle, waxy thread and blunt scissors. Though Hendrik moaned, he hardly moved a muscle as Fay worked to close off the artery and secure the skin and flesh around the severed thumb bone.

Working slowly, Fay closed the wound with 23 stitches. She released the tourniquet and checked for bleeding before she packed his hand with fresh gauze. Then she took Hendrik's blood pressure on his left arm with a heavy rubber strap, pumping the bulb, listening to his arm with her stethoscope, and eyeing the gauge.

"Pretty low," she nodded. "You're right about the transfusion. But I have to check your pressure, too, Uncle Henry, to make sure it's okay for you to lose a pint of blood."

"Come on, I'm fine!" Henry protested but submitted to her attention, her efficient, strong hands, and her quiet, calming voice. All the Carpentier women had that quality to reassure, and Henry loved it.

She led Henry to the adjacent room where she had him lay on another padded table (this one with delivery stirrups) and produced from a cabinet a glass bottle with a stopper that had two long rubber hoses. Each hose was tipped with a hollow needle.

Fay coated Henry's arm with iodine and sterilized one of the needles by dipping it in alcohol and holding it there for five seconds. (He watched her lips move as she counted.) She tied a rubber string around his arm to hold back his veins, and then plunged the needle inside his right elbow. As she released the elastic strip, blood began to drip down into the bottle, which she had perched on a stool just below his arm.

"Relax," she said. "This will take a few minutes."

As his blood flowed into the bottle, Henry thought of the week he had spent in the field hospital in France after his howitzer had exploded next to him during the battle of the Argonne Forest. No one could believe that his only wound was a popped ear drum. Three other men had been blown to bits around him, his boots were blown off, and he was buried in two feet of mud, but he had cheated death. The English nurses wanted to know why a 42 year-old American was serving in France as an artillery sergeant. The answer was simple. He was a member of the Illinois National Guard, and it was his duty to fight. His wife hadn't accepted the explanation, either.

Birdie was only a practical nurse, but she could do as good a job of healing as any doctor he had ever met. She had been a midwife since she was sixteen and had learned the practice from her mother and her aunt. The Carpentiers had come down from Quebec when Birdie was still a child, and all the women were midwives, who doctored the boys and men when they needed to. Birdie had delivered her own grandson Hank while Doc Bichet slept on a chair until it was clear it would take forceps to pull the baby out. Instead of taking up the tongs himself, he instructed her on how to use them. Later she told Henry that she had been afraid she'd crush the baby's skull. It seemed to take so much force. But Hank had come out fine, and he was already ten years old.

"Uncle Henry, I believe you're finished," Fay said as she nodded down to the glass bottle, now filled with red blood to a white line near the top.

She clamped a hose shut with what looked like a metal clothes pin, and then pulled the needle from his vein. She gave him a big ball of cotton (too big to fit in his ear) and told him to hold it against the small red hole inside his elbow. Then she tied a strip of gauze to hold it in place.

"Hold your arm up, Uncle Henry," Fay said and held the pint bottle up so Henry could see its red contents. "I'll go see about Hendrik."

Fay had been gone only a few seconds when Henry climbed down from the gurney and followed her. He felt a little lightheaded, and his arm burned as if a hornet had stung it, but otherwise he felt fine. It was the kid he was worried about.

In the next room, Hendrik lay unconscious on the gurney, and his face was colorless under the harsh light. Fay attached the beaker of blood upside down on a stainless steel pole above him, and she wiped his left arm, first with rubbing alcohol, then with iodine. Then she found his vein with the needle on the unused hose and she released its clamp, so Henry's blood would flow into Hendrik's arm. Fay secured the hose with adhesive tape, then sensing Henry's presence behind her, she turned to him.

"You're sure you're from the same blood group?" she asked him.

"Yes," he nodded. "I'm sure."

"Because, you know," Fay bit her lip, "if he gets a bad reaction, all three of us will be in trouble."

"Don't worry," Henry assured her. "I'm sure."

"Well, you watch him as he takes your blood," Fay said and touched his shoulder. "I've got patients to tend to."

Henry sat on the chair in the corner and watched Hendrik's face gain color as the blood gradually dripped into his vein. When the bottle was half empty, Hendrik opened his eyes and groaned in pain. When the kid began to move, Henry said, "Keep still. You're at the hospital. Getting a transfusion."

"Mein hand hurts!" Hendrik moaned and grimaced from the pain. "It feels like it's still caught in the goddamned machine."

"Sit tight," Henry said. "I'll go find Fay."

When Henry slipped out into the dim hallway, the smell of disinfectant somehow made him crave a cigarette. No chance of lighting up here! He pushed through a pair of swinging doors into a large room with a dozen beds. He guessed these were the difficult cases that could not be delivered at home, the Caesarean sections, the multiple births, the preemies, the mothers with toxemia or syphilis. Their babies would be in the nursery at the far end of the hallway.

He saw Fay by the window shaking down a thermometer, and then placing it under a woman's tongue. Then she held the patient's wrist, simultaneously checking her watch to count the pulse. Fay noticed him, but she went about her work without hurry. These men could wait. These men who had invaded this place for women should not expect priority here. Fay made notes on a chart, adjusted a pillow on one bed, and straightened the sheets on another. She pulled the thermometer from the patient's mouth, made another note, then finally walked toward Henry. "What is it?" she whispered to him. "Is he worse?" It was warm in the maternity ward. Light reflected off the moisture above her eyebrows.

"He's awake now, but his hand hurts a lot," Henry explained. "Can you give him something for the pain?"

"Ice and aspirin are all I can do for him," Fay said, "unless we get a doctor to open the morphine cabinet."

"Where can I find a doctor?"

"They're all downstairs working on the rail yard workers. And the hobos…"

In a few minutes the transfusion bottle was empty and Fay removed the needle from Hendrik's arm. "Aside from the thumb," she whispered to Henry, "I don't think anything else is broken. But please come back to have it checked by a doctor."

"Thank you, Fay. Is there a telephone I could use?"

"If you've got a nickel, there's one on the first floor, at the bottom of those stairs."

"I'll be back shortly."

First Henry called the print shop, and as expected, Joey Sobeleski said that the crew had restarted the presses and would have the second form printed before the next shift began. Joey would punch Henry out. "We'll have to find someone to take Hendrik's place for a while," Henry said. "He'll be sick for at least a week."

Then Henry placed a call to the rooming house where his son Larry lived. Larry had a Model A Ford, which was probably the best means to get Hendrik home to Albertine. He also asked Larry to bring some whiskey for Hendrik's pain, and some ice, too, because he knew Albertine wouldn't have any.

Fay got Hendrik to sit up on the edge of the gurney, and she had him gulp down four aspirins and half a bottle of cough medicine. Then she put the ice packs in a sling and slid his arm on top of them.

"You know," Hendrik smiled as the codeine went to his head. "You are quite beautiful. We should go out dancing some time."

"That's very sweet," she smiled, "but I'm married."

"So is my wife, but that doesn't stop her!"

"You are feeling better!" Fay humored him and watched to make sure he didn't fall flat on his face.

Then Henry came in from the hallway.

"Did you give him those aspirins?" he asked her.

"Yep," she nodded. "And some codeine cough syrup. He threw a pass at me, Uncle Henry. I hope Albertine isn't getting any trouble out of him."

"Those two get plenty of trouble out of each other. No accounting for it, I guess. What makes you love somebody and vice versa? It's beyond me."

By the time Larry arrived, Henry had managed to get the kid (his arm in the sling packed with ice) down the elevator and had perched him on a bench just outside the front door of the hospital. The bench was grimy and smelled of piss, but in his codeine haze, Hendrik didn't seem to notice, even when Henry decided not to sit down beside him.

Larry's tan Model A had patches of rust and a cracked windshield, and its brakes squealed when it jerked to a stop in front of the hospital. Larry shifted into neutral, set the brake, and left the engine running as he came out to help his father. He wore a black derby hat and a beige suit, a yellow shirt with no tie, and two-tone brogans with no socks.

"I got here as quick as I could!" he said and smiled, pleased to play the role of rescuer. He had soft features and crooked teeth in a mouth that just wouldn't quit talking. His dark, wavy hair poured out from beneath his hat and he looked over to Hendrik with gray-green eyes. "God, I love Chicago. Even at one-thirty in the morning there's lots of action out there. Trucks and taxis, even a few streetcars still running. How's Hendrik, Dad? Did he mess up his whole arm?"

"Let's get him in the car first, then I'll tell you all about it," Henry said and tugged Larry by the elbow to one side of Hendrik so he could take the other.

"I brought the whiskey, Pop, but I only had the cheap stuff."

"That's all right, Larry," Henry nodded. "Now let's get him in the car. But be careful. His arm is sore and it's still packed in ice."

They lifted Hendrik to his feet and he wobbled precariously.

"Can you make it, Hendrik?" Larry asked.

"Larry? When did you get here?"

"A minute ago. Can you make it?"

"Sure. Sure," Hendrik said, so Henry tugged him forward and Larry hopped to keep up. The German kid took uneven steps, but he didn't fall. Larry held open the door, tilted the front seat forward, and then helped Henry lift Hendrik onto the back seat.

"You okay back there, Hendrik?" Larry asked him.

"That is a stupid question," Hendrik said and growled bitterly. "Only a banjo player would ask such a thing."

"I play a lot more than the banjo, Heinie," Larry said, but pulled up short of anger. His sister's husband was in pain. And it was true that Larry played the banjo. But he'd also taught himself to play guitar, mandolin, ukulele and standup bass, pretty much anything with strings, and while he wasn't quite Django Reinhardt, he played in a band and three combos, and made almost as much money performing music as he did as an electrician's assistant, which is how he could afford the car.

"Are you okay, Hendrik?" the German mocked him. "You think it will grow back? Will a new thumb sprout from me like a stalk of spargel?"

"Save your energy, kid," Henry said gently as Larry put the car into gear. "You're gonna need it."

"You're not my boss any more, Fontaine. I am free now. I don't have to listen to your noise ever again."

"Where's the whiskey, Larry? Herr Kinderman needs a drink."

"It's in the glove box, Dad, but like I said, I only had the cheap stuff. And nothing to mix it with."

Henry popped open the compartment and found the pint of whiskey, labeled "Knight Owl" with a drawing of a bird. In the dark it looked like a skull and cross bones.

"I hope that shit doesn't kill him," Larry frowned.

"At least it will shut him up."

"That's what we got from your Roosevelt," Hendrik jeered. "Bad whiskey is legal now. You can poison me and blame it on the booze."

"Take a swig," Henry said as he stretched over the seat and held the bottle to Hendriks's lips. He administered a mouthful, watched him swallow, then gave him another belt as the lights of the city whirled over them. "Now that we're blood brothers," Henry said and smiled. "I thought you'd be more polite."

Hendrik opened his mouth to speak, and Henry tipped the bottle and poured another ounce down his throat.

"Hey, Hendrik, you play any gigs lately?" Larry asked. "I know three-four bands what could use a good alto sax, and you're one of the best, you're a natural! The first time I heard you play, I says to myself: that kid plays from his heart, that kid pours out his soul. If you're interested, I could connect you…"

But now Hendrik was drunk, and all he could think about were his ruined hand and his music. How much of his thumb remained? Could he work the stops without it? Would he ever be able to play like before, when the music went straight from his mind into the air? Now all that could be lost with his thumb. Sure, he was free of old man Fontaine, but he might be just like a cripple, too. A broken man, alive but useless.

"I could even get you a job playing at the World's Fair," Larry kept talking. "A friend of mine's dad runs the dance pavilion. He books all the entertainment. A word from me, and I bet he'd add a sax player to one of his orchestras."

Hendrik thought: I can get my own fucking jobs. But he didn't waste his breath by saying it. Hendrik resented Larry: he played his banjos and guitars like somebody doing tricks at a party. See what I can do! Isn't it amusing? And people paid him to do it, to make his infernal noise, but it was no more music than racket from an organ grinder with his monkey. It had no meaning, no feeling, no life.

Hendrik and Albertine lived in the second floor apartment in a three-flat building on Lexington Avenue, a quiet tree-lined street two blocks from the trolley line. Albertine and Hank liked the neighborhood, but it bored Hendrik to distraction.

Henry and Larry carried Hendrik up the narrow stairs to the second floor landing, being careful not to trip on the torn carpet. Not wanting to wake the boy, Henry fished Hendrik's keys from his pants pocket and opened the door.

Henry expected to find his daughter sitting up in her housecoat waiting anxiously for her husband, who was now two hours late coming home. But the small apartment was dark and quiet. Considering everything her husband had been through that night, Albertine should have sensed trouble. Birdie certainly would have felt it if Henry had been hurt. It was her gift. But Albertine hadn't even left a light on for Hendrik.

"Come on, Larry. Let's get him so he's comfortable; then go back down to the car and get the whiskey. He's going to need it."

There wasn't a couch in the sitting room big enough for Hendrik to lie down on. (The black upright piano on casters took most of the space.) So they'd have to go to the bedroom to wake Albertine.

"Hold him steady for a second while I talk to your sister," Henry said, thinking he'd break the news to her before she saw the big bandage around Hendrik's fist. He stepped down the narrow hallway, tapped on the bedroom door, and whispered her name. When he got no answer, he opened the door and realized that she was not at home. He turned on the light to see the unmade bed, the clothes, shoes and magazines strewn on the floor, but no sign of Albertine.

Now he was worried about Hank, and as he turned to the boy's room, its door opened and Hank stood there, fully clothed except for his shoes.

"Grandpa!" Hank said. He was small for his age and always gave adults a look that went right through them, as if he understood a lot more than he let on.

"Where's your mother?"

"She was here when I went to bed." He shrugged.

"You sleep in your clothes?"

"It saves me time in the morning. Why are you here?"

"Your pa had an accident at work. Uncle Larry and I just brought him back from the hospital."

"Is he okay?"

"He will be. But he lost a piece of his thumb."

"Will it grow back?"

"Afraid not. But he'll be back to work in a couple of weeks. Don't worry."

"I'm not worried, Grampa. My dad is a tough guy. He says all Germans are pretty tough," Hank said, then yawned.

"That's one thing in his favor tonight," Henry smiled and mussed Hank's thick brown hair. "Put your shoes on. You're coming home with me."

Henry was upset with his daughter. How could she leave the boy alone while she went out to a night club? Where had she learned to be so reckless? Who had set that kind of example for her? Not me. Not her mother. At least Hendrik was trying to earn their living.

He put his anger aside to take care of Hendrik. He quickly straightened out the bed sheets, then came out to the hallway to help Larry escort Hendrik the few steps to the bed. They sat him down, took off his shoes, his trousers, and loosened his shirt. They stacked the pillows and lowered him down onto them.

"You doing okay, son?" Henry asked.

"Sure. Sure," Hendrik said, then shivered.

"Good, close your eyes."

Henry pulled Larry back into the hallway and asked him, "Did you bring some ice, too?"

"Yeah, if it ain't melted yet. I wrapped it in a towel."

"Can you stay with him till your sister comes home?" Henry asked. "It'll only make things worse if I'm here. I won't be able to hold my tongue."

"Do you think I can?"

"That's different," Henry sighed and shook his head. "Freshen up the ice packs, will you? Then please try to keep him comfortable until Al gets home. I'll take Hank out and see if we can catch a taxi."

"You won't get one at this hour, Dad. Take my car. By the time Albertine gets here, the trolleys will be running again."

"Okay, thanks, Larry. Hank, come on. Let's go see your Grandma Birdie."

Chapter Four

Wait a minute, Hank thought, Ma's wearing that bathrobe for dinner, not the silky Japanese one, but the gray robe that looks like a towel. So she's going out after we eat, and she'll be gone all night!

Albertine stood at the stove with her back to her son. She forked a frankfurter from a pot of boiling water and set it on a plate, then scooped a large spoonful of pork and beans beside it. She took a fork from the dish rack next to the sink, then turned to serve Hank his dinner. At ten, he was small for his age, with his father's big blue eyes and her dark hair. Tonight he looked at her in a way that made her feel guilty. Sometimes she thought the kid could read her mind.

"Here's your dinner, sweetheart," she said as she set the plate in front of him. "I don't have any milk tonight. We're all out of ice, Hank. But you're a big boy. How'd you like a cup of coffee with your supper? With three lumps of sugar."

"Okay."

"Okay? Is that all you can say to your sweet, kind mother? Okay? Why don't you say: yes, please! Thank you very much?"

"Yes, please," he said and picked up the hot dog with his fingers and bit off its end. "Thank you very much. Got any ketchup?"

The ketchup bottle was warm when she pulled it out of the ice box, but she didn't think it had gone bad (no visible mold when she unscrewed the cap), so she set it on the table next to him. Then she filled a cracked mug with coffee from the tin percolator on the stove, dropped three sugar cubes into it and stirred it for him.

"Here ya go, my best fella," she said, set the cup down and kissed his cheek. "Sweet coffee."

"This hot dog is real good, Ma."

"You can thank your grandpa for it, then. He brought us a string of six hot dogs today on his way to work. Wasn't that nice?"

"Aren't you having any?"

"Sure. I'll fix my own plate now. Ya want another?"

"Okay. Just so we save some for Dad."

"Don't worry. The wieners and beans will be setting on the stove when your Dad comes home tonight. I assure you that he never goes to bed hungry."

The kitchen window faced the alley, but even in the fading afternoon a shaft of light shined brightly on Albertine as she prepared her plate and got the sliced white loaf from the breadbox on the counter. The light brought out red highlights in her black, chin-length hair, made her smooth cheeks glow, and it seemed to sharpen the tip of her pointed nose. To Hank, his mother was the prettiest woman in all the world. Compared to her, Grandma Birdie was a bossy old witch, and his aunts were fat and dumpy. And of all the women he saw at church or on the street, he liked the way his mother looked best of all.

When Albertine joined her son at the table, she transferred a long pink sausage from her plate to his, and she ate her own hot dog with a knife and fork, dipping the segments in the sauce around the beans. (She avoided the ketchup, suspecting it.)

"Are you working late again tonight?" Hank asked her.

"That's none of your sweet bee's wax!"

"Mom! Don't tease me like that! How late will you be out?"

"You'll be asleep when I get home, so the exact time can't matter to you."

"And what am I supposed to do?"

"You know what you're supposed to do!" she reminded him. "I am going to lock the door when I leave, and I want you to stay inside and be a good boy while I'm gone."

"Can't I stay out with the other kids until it gets dark, Mom? We were going to play stick ball."

"Not tonight, son. You lost your key, remember! You can practice the piano for half an hour, then read your comic books or listen to the radio. But by nine o'clock, it's lights out, do you hear me? By nine o'clock, it's lights out and to bed with you."

"Get me another key. Take yours to the hardware store and have them make a copy."

"I can't do that now, sweetie. I'll be late to work. Staying inside in your own apartment won't hurt you."

"Mom!"

"Promise to be good."

"Mom!"

"Promise me!" she insisted and gripped his narrow wrist, but she did not squeeze very hard.

"Okay, okay," Hank said reluctantly and his face flushed. "I promise."

"That's better," she said. He sat stone silent for the rest of the meal. He kept his eyes on his plate as he ate all of his beans, devoured the second hot dog, and mopped up the sauce and ketchup with three slices of bread. When he was finished eating he went to the sink and dropped his plate in the basin and ran water over it, then walked past her to the living room and went to the piano (which was on wheels and filled a third of the room). He hopped up on the bench (his feet couldn't reach the pedals), then pushed back the cover and started playing the scales she had taught him. He played slowly and quietly at first, but soon picked up the pace and played louder until he was pounding out the notes. He hoped she could hear how he felt from the way he banged on the keyboard.

Then, he sensed his mother walk behind him to the bedroom to fix her makeup and hang up her robe, and in less than a minute he heard her behind him.

"Hank," she said and he turned to see her in her beautiful red dress with her cream-colored legs and a pocket book (just big enough for her comb and a cigarette case) like a gold harmonica attached to a shiny chain on her wrist. Hank stopped playing and took a deep breath as he looked at her, his music forgotten entirely.

"Hank, I'm going now, sweetheart. Remember what I said," she told him. "Be good and don't stay up past nine."

She didn't kiss him again because she didn't want to mess her makeup, but she did come close enough to squeeze his shoulder. He smelled her perfume like a crushed flower, and he fought back his stupid tears as she went out the door and secured the dead bolt after her.

Then he started his scales again and played as loudly as he could so she could hear him through the open windows as she walked the two blocks to the streetcar line. He played for another five minutes by the clock on the wall above the piano until it read 7:05, when he closed the piano lid, got off the bench and went to the front window to see if his mother's red dress was anywhere in sight. No, she was on her way to the North Side, to the famous Top Hat Club that he would never see.

"Okay!" he said and went to his room for his cap, which he kept on a brass hook on the back of his door. He pulled it on down to his ears so it wouldn't come off, then he boosted open his bedroom window and climbed over the radiator onto the wooden fire escape, looking both ways before dropping down onto the cinders in the alley where he ran between the garages and ash cans to the corner where his friend Dominic stood waiting for him.

"Hank, there you are!" Dominic called to him. Dom was only 13, but he looked twice Hank's size, tall and chunky and red-faced, wearing a vest over an undershirt and long pants instead of knickers. "What took you so long, kid?"

"My ma was going gaga over me again!" he said. "She locked me in like I was in jail."

"Well, forget about her!" Dominic laughed. "The dice game has already started!"

Dominic could sneak through any back door in the city. Using this special talent, Dominic had treated Hank to free movies, boxing matches, baseball games, wedding receptions, vaudeville shows, the circus, the World's Fair, and a lecture on female anatomy at the University of Chicago. His curiosity drove him to see what was happening behind walls meant to keep people out, and he had a strong belief that it was a free country, and so he had every right to see every bit of it for free. Dominic's gift was persistence, and he backed it up with a charming smile, a freckled face, and wavy red hair. He was always polite and never lost his temper, even when he was being thrown out of a show for not having a valid ticket.

Tonight, Dominic would take Hank to the neighborhood crap game in the back room of the Melrose Barber Shop. "They play for real high stakes, Hank! It's exciting to see a guy roll the dice and walk away with a hundred bucks. My dad works two weeks for a hundred dollars, Hankie. Gambling is like magic: it creates something from nothing."

The back way into the Melrose Barber Shop was through an attached garage that faced the alley.

"Remember," Dominic told Hank. "The trick is to look like you belong here. Take my shoeshine brush," Dominic pulled a brush from his pocket and passed it to Hank. It had the strong waxy smell of polish.

"I've got the polish and the rag. Once I get done putting the polish on their shoes, you buff 'em up with the brush."

"Will we get paid?" Hank asked.

"Why not? We'll charge 'em five cents a shine!"

Dominic led Hank into the garage, around the shiny, green Packard with tan fenders, to a narrow door that opened into a mud room right behind the dice hall. When they took the final step into the close, dark room, there was so much smoke Hank thought the place was on fire. All the men inside were smoking and the tips of their cigars and cigarettes looked like red fireflies. The only other light came from a bulb in a green metal cone suspended over the pool table whose pockets were blocked by two-by-fours wrapped in green felt.

Somewhere a radio played, muffled and crackling with static, and Hank heard the sharp rattle of the dice in the cup and the soft bounce when they hit the table.

"Okay! Eight the hard way, Max," someone said, and the men around the table put real folding money in stacks on spots around the table's rim, spots that meant something, but Hank didn't know what.

As in the barber shop out front, where hardly anyone ever got a haircut, the men here were of all ages. Mr. Melrose himself was older than Hank's grandpa. With his white hair, huge stomach, and cufflinks with glass diamonds in them, he sat on a stool at the head of the table, puffing on his cigar and watching the action. He had given Hank bubble gum one day, and when he'd told his grandfather, Grandpa Fontaine had given him a nickel to pay Mr. Melrose back. (He'd kept the money because he was too scared to insult the old barber.)

The youngest man there was Tom Culpepper, a policeman's son. Tom had dropped out of school to run errands for Alderman Donnelly, who kept a bar on Harrison Street. People said Tom had killed a Negro man for coming into the neighborhood, and nobody did anything about it. This evening Tom held a fist full of dollar bills against his vest as if they were a bouquet of flowers.

"Eight!" shouted Max from the end of the table. "The night is young, but it's lucky already! Gimme back them dice, Georgie. I am on a roll!"

Max was tall and thin, his collar and necktie were loose, his sleeves were rolled up to his elbows, and his unbuttoned vest flopped around him as he leaned to take the dice back and drop them noisily into the cup. "Place your bets, gents," he called out to the room. "Some real action is taking place here tonight!"

Hank was fascinated by the real action, the sound of the dice rattling in the cup, the men placing stacks of money along the edge of the pool table, the burning look in Max's eyes as he got ready to pour out his fate on the green felt table. But Dominic was tapping him on the shoulder. He'd already coated his first pair of shoes with polish, and he wanted Hank to brush them. The shoes looked expensive, with wavy decorations over the toe and beside the laces. Hank didn't recognize the man who owned them. He was sitting on a stool with his back to the wall, smoking a cigar and holding a beer bottle. In the smoky room, Hank thought the man had a moustache, though he couldn't be sure, but he could tell he was still wearing a gray felt hat that seemed too heavy for summer. Hank's dad had showed him how to buff shoes with a brush, working his arm with all his might until the dull black polish gradually came to a real shine, first on one shoe, then the other, until they reflected the light from the dice table.

"There ya go, mister," Hank said and smiled because the shoes looked so good.

"Oh thanks, kid," the man laughed and held his cigar between his teeth as he reached into his vest pocket for a coin. Ashes fell down on Hank's shoulder, but they didn't burn him. "Here's your nickel, kid. Nice job."

Wow, Hank thought, if we get a nickel from every one of these guys, we'll be rich! We might even make a dollar each!

The man named Max crapped out, but he stepped back from the table with a nice stack of money, which he rolled into a wad and stuffed into his trouser pocket. Then he went to the bar in the dark far corner to buy a beer from the rough-faced bartender with the scar on his forehead. As soon as Max sat down on a stool, Dominic was at his feet, smearing polish on his shoes.

"Goddamn, you work fast, don't you kid?" Max said and grinned down at him.

"You won all that money," Dominic said, and looked up at him with admiration. "You deserve a good shoe shine. Shows you're a gentleman with style."

"Suppose you want me to pay you?"

"It crossed my mind. A nickel a shine."

"S'pose I could spare a nickel," Max laughed and drank down half a bottle of beer.

Back at the table, men shouted, and Hank stood on tip toe to see what had happened. "Jesus!" a man cried, as the other men took all the money and laughed. "Not a good time to roll snake eyes!" Mr. Melrose laughed and shook his head.

As the dice game resumed, Dominic was tapping Hank's shoulder again. "Come on, get with the program!" Dom said and jerked his head toward Max's brogans. The polish looked like grease on these beat up old shoes.

Hank took up his brush and as he started buffing, he knew he'd have to work hard to make them shine. Hank was still working on the first shoe when Max jumped up and nearly stomped on his hand.

"Hey, watch it, Mister! I'm not finished."

"Gotta get back to the game," Max said. "Oh, yeah, here's your nickel." He dropped a coin on the floor by Hank's knee. But it wasn't a nickel: it was a quarter!

Max left his beer on the rail along the wall, and Dominic moved quickly to grab it and drink the last few swallows while no one was watching. Dominic wiped his mouth with the back of his hand, then looked around for another customer, but all the men had crowded around the dice table to watch Max roll again.

Hank could see that there was more money on the table than ever, clumped in bunches along the rail, signifying bets for or against Max.

"Make it lucky, Sweet Jesus," Max grinned as he rattled the dice in the black leather cup. "Make it lucky!"

He tossed the dice into the shaft of light on the green felt, and twenty pairs of eyes watched them tumble.

"Eight the hard way!" someone called.

"Lucky eight," another man yelled. "Go lucky eight!"

Max had the dice again; he blew on them in his open palm and dropped them into the cup and shook it beside his ear. "Sing to me, babies. Sing to Papa!" he called, then rolled the dice again. This time, Hank caught a glimpse of the two white cubes bouncing off the two-by-four along the table's edge, and when they came to rest someone called, "Eight again. Five and three!" and half the men cheered. "All right, Max! All right!"

Max paused as the men took their winnings, surrendered their losses and placed new bets. Hank saw the sweat on Max's brow, watched him blow on the dice, then drop them carefully one at a time into the cup. "Are we ready, boys?" he asked, rattled the dice and rolled them out.

"Seven! Lucky seven!" a man at the corner called out, and again the bettors reached for their money.

But this time Mr. Melrose raised himself up from his stool and hurried around the table like a bear at feeding time at Lincoln Park Zoo.

"Hold on just one minute!" he commanded. "Everyone hold your goddamn horses while I check this young fella's dice."

"But they're your dice, Bernie," someone protested.

"We'll just see about that," he said and he took the dice from Max and held them up to the light, one at a time, as if they were diamonds and he was looking for a flaw. "You do nice work," he grunted. "Can hardly tell where you doctored 'em."

"What are you talking about, Bernie?" Max asked, and smiled uncomfortably as he tried to sound innocent.

Mr. Melrose lifted his thick hand and bounced the dice onto the table. He didn't look at the dice. Instead, he was staring at Max. "What did I roll?"

Max leaned over to see the dice and whispered hoarsely, "Seven."

"That's what I thought," Mr. Melrose said and scooped them up again. He shook them in his palm and rolled them once more, while keeping his eyes on Max. "What did I roll this time?"

Max didn't budge to look, "I swear…"

"What did I roll?!" Mr. Melrose shouted and clenched his fists.

Max leaned toward the table, hoping for a different number, but he saw the seven dots and mouthed the word, "Seven."

Melrose punched him mightily in the stomach and kicked the side of his shin so Max fell to the concrete floor like a tree in a windstorm. "That's what I thought. Now give me the clean dice!" he demanded.

"I don't have them," Max moaned.

Melrose kicked him full and hard in the stomach. "Then tell me who's got them!"

"I don't know," Max cried. "Please!"

This time Melrose kicked him in the back, then stepped on his hand with his full weight and ground his heel as if he were putting out a cigarette or killing a cockroach. "Tell me who's got the clean dice!"

"I"ve got them," said Tom Culpepper, the policeman's son. "They were lying on the floor." Tom held the dice up with his left hand, but no one failed to notice the black revolver that he held in his right, just above the table.

"That's against my rules, Tom," Mr. Melrose said angrily. "You know I don't allow no weapons in my barber shop."

"You don't allow kicking, either, or gut punching, do you, Bernie?"

"Unless you're a bastard who's been caught cheating."

"Kindly step back from Max there and let him get up, if he can."

Keeping his eyes on the pistol, Mr. Melrose retreated to the dark-paneled wall, and Max pulled himself up, using the end of the pool table for support. Max wasn't bleeding, but Hank saw the stunned look in his eyes and he thought he was going to die any minute.

"Now, so there'll be no hard feelings," Tom Culpepper announced, "Max and I will be leaving all our money on the table and we'll say good night to all you gentlemen."

Tom tossed down the dice and came around the table, and leaving his hat behind, he grabbed Max by the arm and pulled him out the back door, which Dominic and Hank had used as an entrance.

Hank didn't realize it, but once they were gone, he started bawling like a baby. In a second, eighteen men were staring at Hank, and at Dominic, who had rushed to his side.

"Kids?" Mr. Melrose asked indignantly. "What are kids doing here?"

"We're shining shoes, Mr. Melrose," Dominic said without a hint of shyness. "Like we always do."

"What's your name, son?"

"I'm Dominic Lucetti, sir."

"You don't look like no Dago to me."

"Only my dad's eye-talian. Mom's Irish. They used to call her Maureen Clancy."

"And what do they call her now?"

"Mrs. Lucetti, what else?"

Bernie Melrose laughed at Dominic, who was doing his best to entertain the men and stay out of trouble. Then Mr. Melrose looked down at Hank and frowned in disapproval.

"Hey, kid, I know you!" he growled. "You're Henry Fontaine's grandson. The kid that's supposed to stay away from pool halls and barber shops."

"He's my grandpa. Yes, sir."

"He'd tan your hide if he caught you sneaking into a dice game. You know that?" Mr. Melrose asked and squinted so his thick white eyebrows nearly touched his cheeks.

"He said it's wrong to gamble away your hard-earned money."

"Come on, kid! Talk like that will put me out of business!" Mr. Melrose laughed.

"Now get out of here, the both of yas. You were never in my place. You hear me? Get out."

Running on the cinders in the alley, Hank called to Dominic. "Sorry I started bawling in there."

"It's okay. I felt like it myself."

"I didn't know there'd be fighting. I didn't know Tom Culpepper would pull out his gun. I'm sorry I cried about it."

"I said it's okay."

"I can tell you one thing, Dominic," Hank said. "I'm never going to play dice!"

"No?" Dominic shrugged. "Never say never. Hey, let's take the L down to the World's Fair and see what we can see."

They walked under a street lamp, past a clothesline full of women's clothes, including underwear, which seemed to distract the older boy. The garments glowed in the dark, reminding Dominic of the mysteries of sex.

"Hey, Dom, we earned enough money for our car fare," Hank said, prompting Dom to turn back to him in exasperation.

"Come on, get wise, Hank," he snapped. "We don't pay to ride the L. Just do what I told you."

"But we can afford it," Hank announced to him. "Max paid me two bits instead of a nickel."

"He gave me a quarter, too, ya dummy! He was so nervous about cheating, he couldn't tell the difference. He owed us anyway, Hank. Those loaded dice of his got us thrown out of the game. We coulda made a dollar each if he had just played fair."

"That's what I was thinking, too!" Hank said but still felt rich as they came to the iron and wood staircase that led to the L platform three stories above Congress Street. There were only three dim lights at the station –at the bottom of the stairs, at the ticket booth, and one above the eastbound platform – so they would have to climb the stairs through shadows and darkness.

"Okay, remember what to do?" Dominic asked him.

"Yeah, I remember," Hank nodded.

"Let's go."

Dominic hurried up the three flights of stairs and Hank followed close behind, running his hand over the bumpy layers of paint on the iron railing. At the top, they crawled along the wooden platform, ducked under the ticket window and waited in the shadows beside the turnstiles. Within two minutes, they heard the train coming down the elevated track, sending a shock wave through the steel bridge that ran above the street. When the iron screech of the brakes came into the station, the boys sprinted like cats on all fours, bolting under the turnstiles, rushing across the platform, and now running upright into the open doors of the L train. Inside the coach they stopped themselves by grabbing a shiny metal pole, which had been polished from a hundred thousand hands that had held them for balance and support.

Hank saw that this was an old coach with stained wooden floors and cracked wicker seats. Two women in white summer dresses and starched hats sat at one end of the car. At the other end, a pair of colored men in brown suits and broad hats fanned themselves with folded newspapers. Only then did Hank feel how hot it was in the car. The open-bladed fans along the ceiling of the coach had no affect except to make the hot air flow like murky dish water.

"It's hot as a coffin in here," Dominic complained, shouting over the noise as the car pulled out of the station.

Hank looked out the train and caught split-second glimpses through the windows of apartments along the line. A family sat down to a late dinner. A woman in a slip ironed her dress, with a cigarette in the corner of her mouth. A man in his undershirt drank from a whiskey bottle. A Negro woman in a red hat tied a necktie for a small black boy who stood on a kitchen chair. A pretty blonde high school girl looked out the window as she talked on the phone. Hank wondered who she was talking to: her boyfriend, her mother, or another girl?

"Quit day dreaming!" Dominic shouted in his ear. "This is our stop."

Dominic grabbed Hank's wrist and pulled him through the open door onto the elevated platform. This station was clean and freshly painted, with dozens of lights in the ceiling. There was a news stand up there, too, with papers, magazines, candy and cigarettes. A teenage boy, dressed like a bellhop in a shiny gray suit and a pill box hat, was making change for an old guy with a cane. Hank knew he had enough money for a Hershey bar, but he decided to save the full thirty cents until he really needed it.

"Come on, Hankie," Dominic egged him on. "This ain't the World's Fair yet. Time's a wastin', kid. Follow me."

When they came to the bottom of the staircase, Hank felt the cool wind off the lake, he heard the sound of traffic, and he saw the glow of the fair along the shore three blocks away. It was an easy walk to the fair's front gate by the aquarium, but it wouldn't be easy to sneak in under all those floodlights. Instead, Dominic led him over the side of an overpass down a steep slope into the Illinois Central rail yard.

"This is the tricky part," Dominic said and took him by the hand. Hank tried to shake loose, but the older boy held him tightly. "Come on. Stick with me, kid. I'm not gonna let you get run over by no train."

Hank understood that getting killed was a definite possibility. They would have to cross at least ten tracks, and he could see trains on about half of them, but he couldn't tell which trains were moving and which were standing still. Dominic jerked his head back and forth repeatedly to look both ways. They jumped over two sets of tracks then came to a parked railcar. Waiting to plan his route, Dominic gripped Hank's forearm as a fast clattered behind them, creating a gust that almost blew Hank's cap off his head. Hank could see the passengers in the lighted coaches, mostly businessmen in their straw summer hats pulled down over their eyes. By now it must be nine o'clock, pretty late to be going home from work.

When this train had passed, Dominic took Hank's hand and pulled him across several sets of tracks to a slot in the embankment, a drainage gutter in which a ribbon of water reflected the moonlight and the yellow lanterns on the trains. And as Hank looked to the top of this inclined concrete chute, he saw a glowing cloud of golden light.

"Wow, look at that! Is that the Fair?" Hank asked.

"Shut up, will ya?" Dominic scolded him. "That echo will give us away."

Dominic brushed past Hank and surged ahead up the incline, stepping on either side of the trickle of water, breathing heavily and grunting with the effort. The climb wasn't so hard for Hank. He was drawn upward by the excitement of going to the World's Fair after dark. Soon they surfaced through a clump of bushes and landed on a wide brick sidewalk in an entirely different world, a city that was fresh and new and glistening. Hank's eyes were pulled upward to the search lights, six bright beams that swept through the sky, crossing and re-crossing each other in the inky space above the flat and shimmering lake.

"Geez, look at that…"

"Come on, Hank," Dominic hissed. "That's kid's stuff! Tonight we're going to see Sally Rand."

"Who's Sally Rand?"

"Cripes! Where have you been? She's that famous fan dancer."

"Fan dancer?"

Now the boys were strolling with the crowd of hundreds of people along the midway. Women in loose white dresses and hats like inverted flowers walked arm in arm with men in light-colored suits, straw summer hats and white shoes. Some men walked on their own, and ladies strolled in pairs, but Hank didn't see any other kids under 16 enjoying the Fair at night.

Strings of lights were suspended high above both sides of the walkway, outlining a magic ceiling that kept out the night. Hank smelled food cooking in the little restaurants along the way: hamburgers and fried potatoes, onions, polish sausages and pork chops. It had been hours since he'd eaten his beans and franks for dinner, and a stand selling sausages on sticks caught his attention, but before he could buy one, Dominic had rushed further into the crowd, so Hank hurried to keep up.

Dominic and Hank had sneaked into the Fair once before when they stowed aboard a delivery wagon at the entrance by the aquarium. On that day they had seen the Hall of Science where men in white coats conducted demonstrations of static electricity that made people's hair stand on end. The boys sat in a booth where they recorded their voices and played them back, and at another stop they each turned a crank with one hand and lifted a one-ton weight two feet off the ground. Hank and Dominic were carried along on a conveyor belt beside the General Motors assembly line, which started out with loose parts and ended up with a whole car driving out onto the midway. How could the workers keep up with the growing fast-moving car? How could they keep tightening the same bolts over and over again? Hank and Dominic visited the Modern House and saw bread pop out of an electric toaster, heard a radio in every room, opened the door of a refrigerator (not an ice box), and felt cold air blowing through vents to keep the house cool.

Now as the boys rushed through the nighttime Fair, Hank could hear music from all directions. A marching band's horns, fiddles and accordions like the French people play, a banjo like Uncle Larry's, and a saxophone like his father's accompanied by a piano and drums. Dom and Hank passed a pavilion where hundreds of couples danced to the sound of a band with at least twenty players.

They hurried past an airplane that was parked along the midway with stars on its fuselage and a red and white tail. People stood in a line that seemed to go on for miles for a chance to try on goggles and sit in the cockpit. When the boys turned the corner, Dominic and Hank found themselves in a foreign city along the shiny lagoon. Gas lights shone on cast iron posts, quaint buildings were decorated with gingerbread trim, and women in feathered hats and long dresses wore bows of ribbon on their backsides.

"We have arrived!" Dominic announced. "On the Streets of Paris!"

They walked fifty yards more and reached the Follies Bergére Theatre. Flickering gaslights made its façade glow. Giant posters showed a woman who held huge pink feathers that couldn't hide her bare shoulder and neck, the edge of one hip, and all of her legs below mid-thigh.

"Fan dancer!" Hank said to his friend. "Now I get it."

A man in a bowler hat, red vest, and white shirt with sleeve garters waved a cane at the gathering crowd and called out to them: "Ladies and gentlemen, direct from her tour of the capitals of Europe, the Streets of Paris is proud to present, the artiste who dares to reveal the true nature of feminine beauty, the famous, shall I say infamous, Sally Rand will start her show in five minutes. Seating and standing room are still available. So hurry up folks. Step right up. Buy your ticket and step right in!"

There were at least fifty people lined up at the two ticket windows, and Hank saw a big sign over each that said "50¢." Ten times the price of going to the movies!

"Holy cow, Dominic! I don't have fifty cents!" Hank whispered to his friend.

"You sure are a Doubting Thomas!" Dominic laughed and shook his head. "Follow me, pal. We've got a date with Sally."

Dominic walked casually around the lines of ticket buyers and tipped his hat to some girls drinking wine at a sidewalk café. Hank raised his cap, too, getting the women to smile, and he nearly lost track of Dominic who turned suddenly into a narrow alley that fed into the darkness behind the buildings. Hank rushed to catch up and was surprised when they came to a paved lane, twenty feet wide that ran between the Fair's attractions, giving the delivery men access to the loading docks and rear entrances.

Dominic paced down the center of the alley in a stiff walk, turned sharply to his right and vaulted onto one of the loading docks, pivoting on the palm of his hand and kicking his leg up over the edge. Then he reached down and hoisted Hank onto the platform beside him.

"How do you know this is the right place?" Hank asked.

"It's the right place, kiddo. I counted my steps. And see, it's the highest building on the block. That's for the stage mechanics. Come on, we're missing the show."

The back stage door wasn't even shut, and as the boys rushed through it they nearly tripped over the power cord for the electric exhaust fan that blew hot air into the alley. The fan's drone over-rode the music at first, but as Hank came to the second open doorway, he could hear the jazz orchestra, the trumpets and trombone, the clarinet and piano, the chunky guitar and the heavy beat of the drums.

Then Dominic got on his hands and knees and crawled across the dusty floor to the black curtain that had to be right behind the stage. Before Hank followed, he looked up toward the ceiling and saw the grated catwalks and the ropes, sand bags, curtains and scrims suspended overhead, all the stuff that Dominic had called "mechanics."

The music was loud now and Hank heard the rhythmic clicks of tap dancing feet. Then he dropped to his hands and knees and crawled to catch up with Dominic, who was now lying flat on his belly and peering through the space between the black curtain and the stage.

Hank gave this a try, too, and his eyes met the glare of the footlights from straight ahead, and from the spotlights pouring down from above. He blinked for a long time before he saw the eight chorus girls dancing in synchrony, their long, thick legs keeping time with the fast beat in a choppy motion, their arms waving right, then left, like birds flying in formation. The girls wore so few clothes they could have been going to the beach, but no one would go swimming wearing those sparkly headbands with the whispy feathers in front. Hank guessed they'd practiced this dance hundreds of times, because no one seemed to make a mistake, and when they turned their heads a little, he could see they were all smiling all the time.

The dancers linked arms and started to jump and kick all at once, then each girl kicked her right leg in order, so the row of them looked like the hammers inside a piano when someone plays scales. Hank wished he could see them from the audience to get the full effect.

After the kicking display, the trumpeters played a fanfare, the footlights dimmed, and Hank heard the squeak of ropes on pulleys as (invisible to the boys behind the curtain), Sally Rand and her giant feather fans were lowered from the rafters on a gold trapeze shaped like a crescent moon. They spotted her cream-colored torso as she landed on her golden high-heeled slippers, the foot lights were re-ignited, and she was flanked by the chorus, who now seemed overdressed. The chorus girls raised their arms and bowed low, showing Hank the roundness of their back sides, then they scampered off either side of the stage to give Miss Rand space for her tantalizing maneuvers.

And from where Dominic and Hank were watching, Sally Rand wasn't hiding anything at all. Her body was sleek and creamy pink from the blonde hair that just touched her shoulders to the golden shoes on her feet. Compared to some of the chorus girls, she was almost skinny. Her hips were curved, all right, but not padded, and her legs were slender and long like a girl's. Hank could see all the bumps on her spine down the middle of her back. Her shoulders were square, and she didn't have any extra meat on her arms. Hank guessed that was because she had to work so hard to cover her titties and privates with those heavy fans as she strutted and stretched, spun in circles and shook her fanny to the music.

From behind the curtain, the boys couldn't see the audience, but they could hear them, whistling, calling out and howling like wolves. A pretty surprising reaction to a woman who didn't have much of a figure at all.

Dominic was more impressed than Hank. He got up on his knees, lifting the hem of the curtain with him. "Woo-eee!" he exclaimed. "Holy crap! She really is naked!"

Without interrupting her dance, Sally Rand turned her head, smiled at Dominic and winked, so Dom pretended to faint and dropped back onto his stomach on the stage.

Hank was laughing when someone yanked the back of his shirt and hoisted him to his feet right beside Dominic, who was dangling from the policeman's other arm.

"Let's take a walk, gents," the policeman said and carried them along like puppets – feet barely touching the ground – out a door onto a landing beneath a Parisian gas light. Just as Hank thought the copper was going to let them go, he jerked them hard.

"What are you guys?" he growled. "A coupla peeping Toms?"

"We were just trying to see the show, officer," Dominic said and tried to smile, despite by being strangled by his own collar.

"This is a show for grownups, mister," the policeman said and tugged him so roughly that Dominic yelped like a dog. When Hank heard the man laugh, he recognized him. He was Officer Kelly, who had patrolled their neighborhood until the Fair opened last year. Officer Kelly let go of their shirts, but planted himself firmly in front of them so they couldn't get away.

"Hey, what's your name?" he asked Dominic.

"Lucetti."

"I know you. You've got a truancy problem."

"No, officer. You must be thinking of my brother."

"You don't have a brother."

"What do you know?"

"That you've got five sisters and no brothers."

Dominic shrugged, realizing he had nothing to gain by talking back any more. He looked past the policeman for an escape route but found none.

Then Officer Kelly looked down at Hank. "And you, kid, you shouldn't let this one lead you astray. What's your name?"

"Hank Kinderman."

The policeman took off his hat and used his handkerchief to wipe his brow and the back of his neck. (His black uniform was made of wool, not exactly comfortable in summer.)

"Hank Kinderman. You grandfather is Henry Fontaine, isn't he?"

"That's right," Hank nodded and his heart sank. His grandpa would hear all about his sneaking into the Sally Rand burlesque show, and Hank would get a good beating with a razor strap, no matter what his mother had to say about it.

"He's a good man," the officer said. "I served with him in France with the National Guard. He was the oldest soldier in our unit. Can't tell you how many explosions he survived. The Huns couldn't kill Henry. He was an amazing soldier. A man of his age!"

"He told me his cannon blew up," Hank said. "That's all I remember."

"He dragged two men out of a truck that was on fire. Artillery rounds raining down like Armageddon, and Sergeant Fontaine saved those two boys just before the gas tank exploded. Ask him about that day. In the Argonne Forest. Nobody called him 'gramps' after that."

"I still do," Hank said.

"I'll bet you do!" the policeman laughed, raised his arms and resumed his grip on their two shirts. Semi-suspended, the boys were swept down the stairs to the cobblestone alley and then back onto the midway.

As they passed the biplane and its lines of tourists, Dominic asked, "Hey, Officer, where you takin' us?"

"I haven't decided," the policeman laughed, "but wherever it is, you won't like it."

Hank thought of the trouble he'd face when he got home – spankings from his father and grandfather, and worse still, weeks of scolding from his Ma. He should have known better than to go along with Dominic to that dice game where the gun could have gone off and shot both of them, and now to the burlesque show where they'd been arrested and were getting dragged through a crowd of hundreds of people. And what rotten luck, the big copper was pals with Grandpa Fontaine! Hank would probably be stuck at his grandparents' house until Labor Day and the start of school. This was absolutely the last time he would tag along with Dominic!

They came around the Belgian Village, which smelled of fried potatoes and waffles and seemed even more old-timey than the Streets of Paris. Here they found the tall gate of the 23rd Street entrance to the Fair, which opened up on a broad, circular plaza of food stalls and souvenir stands, and men selling balloons and post cards and cotton candy. There were lights strung up in all the trees, like Christmas, but they didn't make Hank feel happy. He had just been arrested and he felt ashamed.

Their destination was a little wooden house with a screened window like a ticket counter facing toward the plaza, with a sign above it that said, "CHICAGO POLICE DEPT." Officer Kelly dragged them between high bushes to a door at the back of the shed.

"Step inside here, boys," the copper said to them. "We'll see if there's room for you at the jail."

Inside the little room a fat policeman sat behind a high desk and sweated profusely despite the effort of a buzzing electric fan that blew hard enough in his face to send his hair flying. Big drops poured down his cheeks as he talked on the phone, holding the conical ear piece to his head with his right hand and gripping the candlestick base with his left.

"Okay, Murdoch, all available men. I heard you. They're on their way!...Oh, there you are, Kelly," the desk sergeant said. "I hoped you'd report back…What you got here? Coupla shoplifters?"

"No, two more kids who sneaked into the Sally Rand show. They got an eye-full, too."

"Tell me boys," the sweaty sergeant asked them with a hoarse Irish voice and an amused twist on his mouth. "Was it worth the effort?"

"We're sorry, Officer," Dominic said, sounding like a sweet little girl. "We were just curious."

"Har!" the sergeant laughed as if he'd heard a dirty joke. "Just curious! Don't that beat all!"

"I thought I'd bring them home to their parents," Officer Kelly said. "They live in my old neighborhood." (The worst thing is about to happen! To be brought home by a cop!)

"No can do, Kelly," the sergeant corrected him, and his cheeks wobbled as he shook his head. "There's been an explosion at the Diversey Street freight yard. There's a big fire, too, and a lot of men were hurt. Murdoch says there are hundreds of hobos looting the railcars that got blown open. Eighth precinct needs all the men they can get. I saw O'Keefe ten minutes ago; he was staring at the tattooed lady. Get him in the squad car and go help out."

"What about these boys?" Kelly asked.

"They were just curious!" the sergeant said and laughed his nasty laugh again. "This time we let 'em go. Next time we'll handcuff them to a lamp post and make their mothers come and get 'em."

A wave of relief made Hank feel like laughing, but he was smart enough to imitate Dominic's sad face of regret and contrition. When the police let him go, he'd head straight home so he could climb through his window before his mother got back from work.

"You boys have money for the streetcar?" Officer Kelly asked them.

Before Hank could say a word, Dominic said, "No, sir."

"Well, here then," the policeman said and opened his palm to reveal two coins. "A nickel for each of ya's. If I catch you sneaking into any part of the Fair again, you won't get off so easy."

Five cents richer, Hank ran across the plaza toward the street car stop. He felt exhilarated and free, but anxious to get home.

"Dominic, let's go home now."

"Home? You heard what they said. There's a bunch of free stuff blown all over the Diversey freight yard. And there's a big fire, too. Don't you want to see that?"

"Yeah, but…"

"Come on. My cousin Brian works the night shift at the yard. If he's around, he's probably stashed away a lot of good stuff. I bet he shares it with us!"

"I can't do it tonight, Dominic. What if my ma comes home early?"

"Suit yourself," Dominic said. "But you can't let opportunities like this slip through your fingers, Hank."

"We just watched Sally Rand when she wiggled her hind end," he laughed. "That was an opportunity, wasn't it?"

"She was naked as a jaybird! But ya know, she didn't look much different from my big sister when I barged in on her in the bathtub last week. Neither one of 'em has got very big jugs. Both are kinda pretty, but nothing to write home about."

The boys walked to 23rd Street to the start of the line for the westbound trolley. There weren't many people out walking, but taxis, cars and trucks zoomed down Columbus Avenue at the edge of the fairgrounds, startling Hank. He felt tired and hungry, and he sensed that it was very late as he struggled to keep up with his friend.

"You think you can hold on if we ride out on the bumper?" Dominic called back to him.

"I don't know," Hank moaned and he grew tense with fear. "I never did it after dark." Dominic had showed him how to jump on the back of a streetcar, put his feet on the bumper, and hold onto the window frame to ride for free, but it was a scary way to travel, and he'd only been able to hang on for two blocks.

"It's even better after dark," Dominic said. "The trolley driver can't see you even if he's looking for you."

"Let's use the money from Officer Kelly to ride inside. For a nickel we can get two transfers. You can go to the rail yard and I can go home."

"I hate to waste a nickel when I can ride for free."

"Ride for free then," Hank said as they heard the screech of the streetcar's wheels and saw its approaching sparks on the lines overhead. "I'm gonna pay a nickel to have a seat."

"You're probably too weak to hold on, anyway," Dominic said impatiently.

"You can't dare me to do it, Dom. I'm riding inside the streetcar."

The trolley pulled even with them and Hank climbed up the steps and dropped his nickel in the box and held out his hand for the transfer slip. A dozen people came on behind him, carrying souvenirs, pinwheels and balloons. They were mostly young men with their dates, holding hands and smooching on each other. Hank saved a seat for Dominic and was afraid for a minute that Dom would fasten himself like some cockroach to the back of the trolley instead of coming inside, but as the trolley pulled away from the stop, the red-haired Italian kid squeezed on board and maneuvered his way through the outstretched legs of passengers to join his younger friend.

"Boy, did you see all these girls getting on?" he asked Hank. "Most of them have better asses than Sally Rand. I had to watch 'em climb the stairs."

"Why do you want to look at girls' butts, anyway, Dominic? Why don't you look at their faces?"

"Wait a couple years and you won't have to ask that question, Hankie-boy. You won't be able to stop thinking about girls from top to bottom."

The streetcar crossed Lakeshore Drive and moved through the park, then came to the cliff-like wall of tall buildings along Michigan Avenue. And then, as if it passed into the interior of a different, contained world, the trolley came under the L tracks on State Street, and the cars and trucks and horse-drawn delivery carts crowded the street, and men and women filled the sidewalks.

Hank wondered whether he'd spot his mother out there in her red dress and pink hat, coming out of the Top Hat Club after playing her music. She probably thought he was fast asleep by now, with the radio playing him a lullaby so he wouldn't be afraid of the dark. She still thought of him as her baby, but thanks to Dominic, he'd seen most of Chicago. He'd explored more of the city than grownups more than twice his age. And how many people on Lexington Avenue or Flournoy Street had been back stage to see Sally Rand in the altogether?

The trolley crossed the metal bridge over the South Branch of the Chicago River, a few blocks from the printing company where his dad and grandpa stayed up late to print magazines. They'd probably ride the same streetcar going home, and make the change at Western Avenue. Everybody in our family are night owls, that's what Ma says. But it looks like half the people in Chicago never go to bed.

Dominic jerked his head toward the front of the trolley, signaling the corner where he would catch the other line. "Time for me to go, Hankie. My other trolley is coming fast. Don't forget to get off at Congress Street."

Half an hour later he was in the alley behind their three-flat house on Lexington Avenue. It usually took a few tries, but Hank knew he could reach the lowest rung of the fire escape by shimmying up the post on the corner of the house, so when he fell the first time, he wasn't discouraged. When he fell the second time, he scraped his hand on the cement foundation. The pain made him angry and he rushed the pole, pulled himself up quickly, swung his foot onto the ladder, then hurried up the rungs to the platform outside his bedroom window. He tugged open the window and slid inside through the curtains. He didn't know what time it was, so he tip toed to the door, opened it and stepped out into the hallway, holding his breath to be quiet. He walked slowly to the door to his parents' room.

The door was open and the room was dark, and he could tell he was alone. So he had made it home before they did! Wow, what a night! I'll never let Dominic get me into trouble again!

He used the toilet and washed his hands and face at the sink, rubbing soap on his scraped wrist. He yawned and smiled at himself in the mirror, but then heard footsteps on the stairway. He ran back to his room then, pulled the door closed behind him, kicked off his shoes, and then got under the covers of his bed. He felt safe in his dark, quiet room, in his familiar, comfortable bed.

Hank woke up when the apartment door opened, and he heard his grandfather's voice telling someone else to be careful. He recognized the sound of the man who answered, Uncle Larry, so he climbed out of bed and opened his bedroom door a crack in time to see his grandfather and his uncle carry his dad into the other bedroom. Dad was so sick or hurt so badly that he drooped unconscious between them. He could have been drunk, too. Hank had seen his Dad pass out before, after he had slugged ma. Then she had whacked him on the head with a flower pot.

Then his grandfather came back to the hallway and spotted him.

"Where's your ma?" he asked.

"Working," Hank said. "She left and told me to go to bed."

"You always sleep with your clothes on?" his grandfather teased him and shook his head.

"It saves time in the morning."

"I bet it does. Well, put your shoes on. You're coming home with me."

"What's wrong with my dad?

"Your pa will be okay," Grandpa Fontaine assured him. "He got his hand caught in a press tonight. He lost a piece of his thumb, but he'll be okay. We just got back from the hospital."

"Can I see him?"

"Yeah, but quietly. He needs his rest."

Hank went across the hallway and peeked into the dark bedroom. He saw his dad's thick blond hair shiny on top of the pillow, and he heard his loud breathing, broken up by snores. His dad rolled over and then jerked suddenly when he bumped the bandaged hand. Hank saw the thick layer of gauze all the way up to his dad's elbow, and he worried that his Grandpa had lied to him, and that his dad might really be dying after all.

When his grandfather stopped Uncle Larry's Model A in front of the big three-story house in Larry's Model A, Hank saw his grandmother standing on the porch, looking up into a tree. His grandpa yanked the parking brake, then popped open the door and jumped down onto the sidewalk as if it were the afternoon and not the middle of the night.

"Are you just getting home, Birdie?" Grandpa called loudly as he moved toward her. His grandparents talked among themselves as Hank climbed out of the Ford and walked around the front of the car to join them. Even in the dark, the big house looked inviting to Hank. There were always aunts and uncles, cousins and friends there. And plenty of food! Grandma Birdie always had plenty of food!

When he reached the porch, his grandmother embraced him. "There's my boy! Hank, I'll bet you're hungry! Why don't I fix you a plate of food before you climb into your feather bed? Would you like that?"

"Sure, grandma," he said and fought back a yawn. "Sounds great."

Chapter Five

Birdie Fontaine returned from 10 o'clock Mass to finish cooking her Sunday dinner. Her nephew Norman, whom she had raised as her son, was coming home on leave from the Navy, and she had planned a family reunion for at least 20 people to welcome him.

Every letter she had received from Norman for the past three years had included his complaints about the bad food aboard his ship. He described the diluted oatmeal, the stale bread, the soggy rice, the salty pork and the unending servings of beans. "Oh, how I miss your Sunday dinners," Norman wrote. "Aunt Birdie, it would be heaven to taste your roast brisket, your turkey, your lamb stew, your carrots and potatoes, your flakey rolls, your fish casserole, your blueberry upside down cake, your maple syrup pie, and your bread pudding. Some days when I am forced to eat this swill, I am sure I would sign over a month's pay for one plate of your food, and I would kill for the chance to sit down at your table with Uncle Henry and your girls." Birdie Fontaine had decided to prepare her best Sunday dinner so Norman could enjoy her food before returning to the U.S.S. Toledo the next morning.

If her daughters had any consideration, they would be in the kitchen already, working on the things that didn't need her special attention, but the place seemed deserted and the only things cooking were the main courses, which were baking slowly in her two ovens, while potatoes sat unpeeled, beans rested unsnapped, and no one had pushed down the yeasty dough for the rolls.

Where was Claribel? Where was Lorraine? They had gone to 8:30 Mass so they could come home and help her, but now they were nowhere to be seen. And Albertine and Elsie may be young married women, but they knew she'd need help with today's special meal. Why weren't they with her in the kitchen already? For that matter, where was Henry? And why hadn't

Larry come early to help her instead of showing up five minutes before she served the food?

She opened the right oven to check on the brisket (not quite finished) and the leg of lamb (nicely browned), and she pushed down the door on the left oven to baste the turkey, and she saw that it had maybe an hour to cook. Nearly everything else needed to be prepared.

Lorraine and Claribel were certainly in the house someplace, but she would have to summon them, so she took her cast iron skillet from the stove top, turned it upside down and then beat it with her largest mixing spoon. The dull, loud ring sounded like a fire bell. In another household this might have brought back memories of life on the farm, the happy signal inviting family and guests to dinner. But in Birdie's house there was no mistaking the meaning of the alarm. If the girls did not come to the kitchen and put on their aprons within two minutes, there would be hell to pay.

As she kept banging on the skillet, Henry called from the living room, where he was napping with the Sunday Tribune in his lap. "Give it a rest, Birdie! Give it a rest!" But she kept up the racket until Lorraine and Claribel came down the stairs from their rooms on the third floor, annoyed with their mother but afraid to disobey her.

Lorraine was twelve years old. She had been Birdie's late-in-life baby. Of all her daughters, Lorraine most resembled Birdie, with her short stature, square figure, and pleasing if not pretty face. Birdie knew what it felt like to be the homely younger sister (her two older sisters had been rare beauties), so she went easy on Lorraine. The other kids accused her of playing favorites and spoiling the baby, but Birdie thought Lorraine needed a little extra attention to balance things out.

Albertine had looked like an angel from the time she was born, and Birdie couldn't help feeling jealous of her good looks as she grew older. Albertine was a wonderful dancer, too, and she had perfect pitch, so she would have been one of Madame Corbet's best piano students if she had just practiced more.

And smart! Why Albertine would sit in her father's lap and read him the newspaper when she was just three years old.

Elsie wasn't as pretty as Albertine, but she turned boys' heads, too. She had a wonderful singing voice, and she could sew her own clothes. As a girl, Elsie had stood in the kitchen with her for hours to learn all the old recipes from Quebec, so that Birdie missed Elsie when she married and left home. (Too bad her husband couldn't keep a job. What a shame they were on Relief, and with two kids to feed!)

Claribel had average looks and average talents. She was nearly eighteen now and she laughed too much (and cried too much, too). Clare had invited a boy to dinner today, which was why she had spent so much time upstairs in her room, primping.

Lorraine came into the kitchen first, changed from her Sunday dress to a pink blouse and a blue cotton jumper. She wore her dark hair in braids with pink ribbons on their ends. Birdie thought her daughter was too old to dress this way, but probably too young to dress as a grownup.

"You don't need to beat on the frying pan, Ma," Lorraine whined. "Clare and I would come if you'd call us like anyone else's mother."

"I can't strain my voice calling up three floors to you lazy things! We've got guests coming, for heaven's sakes, Lorraine. You know I need help preparing the meal."

"You could have just called us," Lorraine repeated.

"And where's your lazy sister?!" Birdie snapped.

"Here I am," Claribel said as she tied her apron around the red dress Elsie had sewn for her.

"You took your dear sweet time, Claribel Marie!" Birdie scolded her. "Do you think that because you've got a boyfriend calling that the food will cook itself?"

"Give it a rest, Ma! I'm here now, aren't I?"

"Give it a rest!" Birdie mocked her. "Your father is an old softy, do you know that? If it was up to him, you'd all sit around on your fat behinds while I work all day and into the night."

"Hush, Ma, we're here!" Claribel laughed and patted her mother's shoulder. "What do you want us to do first?"

In the living room, Henry was sitting in his armchair holding the newspaper and dozing blissfully. A night worker, he had a problem adjusting to Sundays when he was expected to be alert and outgoing with the large gathering of friends and family who converged on their house every week. But by taking cat naps all morning and drinking half a pot of strong coffee just before the guests arrived, he could rise to the occasion and become a lively and gracious host, many times more talkative than he would be by nature.

But now Henry was dreaming. It was a bright summer day and he was swimming on his back in Lake Michigan, looking up into a clear blue sky. He guessed he was about twelve years old. The water in his ears shielded him from the noises of the world, and his cousins had taken the streetcar home already, so he didn't have to exert himself by racing them. He dreamt of a perfect afternoon of idleness.

Then he heard the faint sound of someone crying for help. It was a woman's voice, and as he flipped into a crawl, he could see splashes on the horizon, pale arms flailing, a white spherical bathing cap reflecting the sun, and he swam hard and fast in a panic to save her. The water around him sounded like crumpling newspaper, and when he opened his eyes with a start, his daughter Albertine was standing before him, wearing a white cloche hat and a yellow summer dress, hardly more than a nightgown. She was carrying a large cloth satchel with a flowered pattern and leather handles.

"Sorry, Papa, I didn't mean to wake you!" she laughed.

"Hello, Al," he said and yawned. "Tell me, honey. Do you know how to swim?"

"Of course, Pa," she said and leaned over to kiss his forehead. "You taught me."

"That's right. You said it was easy as dancing."

"After you showed me the moves."

"Where's Hank?" Henry asked.

"Out on the porch. He brought his friend Dominic. Ma said it would be all right."

"Dominic is too old for Hank. He gets the boy into trouble."

"Don't worry about Hank. He can take care of himself."

"Don't wind me up, Al! And what about Hendrik?"

"He's at home practicing his saxophone. It's not so easy since he lost his thumb. If he can't play his horn, Pa, he'll be lost, and I'm not kidding!"

"I hope he comes later," Henry nodded. "Your ma was counting on him being here to see Norman."

"We'll see. He needs his time. Besides, when have I been able to make Hendrik do something he doesn't want to do?"

"Well," Henry grinned at his pretty daughter. "I hope he wants to come, then."

"I guess I'd better go in the kitchen and help Ma before she starts trying to murder the frying pan."

"She tried that already."

"I'm glad I missed it."

"Will you be playing for us today, sweetheart?"

"I thought I might."

"That's wonderful. I'm really looking forward to that."

"You're very sweet, Pa. Even when you're mad at me, I know you love me to pieces."

"Go help your mother," he urged her. "Maybe I can sleep a wink or two longer before the crowd shows up."

Hendrik Kinderman sat on a kitchen chair with his horn in his lap, leaning over the phonograph. Even the tinny sound of the recording could not diminish the power of this music. It was more complete than anything Hendrik's combo had ever played, and it sounded sweeter, more fluid and more natural, too.

Hendrik had once believed that Bix Beiderbecke was the greatest band leader in Chicago. He had taken Albertine to all of Bix's performances that he could afford, nearly one a week, and he had gotten to know Bix and the members of his band.

When it was clear that Bix wouldn't hire him (after a miserable audition when his nerves made it impossible for him to play), he'd shown up with his whole combo an hour before Bix's performance, and they played at the speakeasy for tips as the self-appointed opening act. The great Beiderbecke tolerated this for three nights before the hoodlums who worked for the Top Hat's owner stood in the doorway and kept Hendrik and his boys from going inside. "We don't need your racket," they told him. "Youse guys are scaring away paying customers."

Now as he listened to the Louis Armstrong record, he understood that Bix and his combo were as stiff and mechanical as a marching band. There was no feeling in their music, or rather it had the wrong feelings. Sad songs sounded happy and happy songs had no joy. The singers were flat and stiff. The musicians were all competent, they played the right notes, but not a single player was outstanding. These hacks had been his models. If he attained their skill, he would only be average. He would be able to play at dances or in bar rooms, and he would soon be forgotten.

Playing in front of him, challenging Hendrik to match his music, Armstrong's recording was beautiful and exasperating. The band made the music glow, it seemed effortless, and it conveyed the joy of life and its pain, its playfulness and its misery. Listening to Satchmo, Hendrik knew what it means to miss New Orleans. To him it was a lot like missing Hamburg.

But as he turned off the Victrola, Hendrik resigned himself to the grim possibility that expression might have to wait. Today he would have to teach himself to play his horn with no right thumb. He had fashioned a wrist strap by cutting down one of Hank's belts, and he used it to bind the base of the saxophone to his right wrist. He found that if he kept the horn tight against his palm, he could control the valves. He tried the first few bars of the number on the record, *St. James Infirmary*. But as he began to play, the pain flared up in the root of his lost thumb, and he stopped for a few seconds and clenched his teeth. Then, anticipating the pain, he took a deep breath and forced himself into the song. In a while he didn't notice the pain, and all he could feel was the sad music.

Wearing her bathrobe over her dress, Albertine worked in the kitchen with her sisters for half an hour before her mother asked about Hendrik.

"My, it sure is quiet out there," Birdie said and nodded to the parlor. "It's all right for Hendrik to wake your father up from his nap. The old man won't bite him, you know."

"Hendrik is still upset about his thumb, Ma," Albertine said, afraid to admit that her husband was still at home. "Pa makes him remember the accident."

"You're right, dear, it was a terrible accident," Birdie reminded her, then opened the heavy oven door to baste the turkey. It was beginning to turn golden brown, and it smelled delicious. Albertine wondered how much money her mother had spent on the feast to welcome her selfish, sneaky cousin Norman. More than Albertine spent on groceries for a month!

"And we're lucky," Birdie continued, "your father saved his life by giving him a pint of his own blood."

"Who says he needed Pa's blood? Pa's no doctor. And Fay's only been a nurse for two years. What does she know?"

"Shush. You have no room to talk! Where were you when Hendrik was hurt? Now take your husband something cold to drink. It's too early for beer, but there's lemonade."

"Ma, Hendrik didn't come with us today. He's resting at home."

"He knows he's invited, doesn't he?" her mother asked and frowned at her insistently.

"Ma, he knows he's always invited to Sunday dinner, but the poor man deserves some time to himself," Albertine sighed.

"Any other day would be an exception," Birdie said, "but with Norman coming on his only day off from the Navy, I'll have to send Larry over to fetch Hendrik."

"Ma, Larry's not going to fetch anybody. Leave Hendrik be."

"To the Germans family may not mean anything, but to the French family means everything!"

"We're from Chicago, Ma. Nobody in our family has lived in France for two hundred years."

"Don't sass me! Quebec was part of France a long time after that, and your father served in France during the war."

"Shouldn't we be checking the brisket or something?" Albertine asked her mother. "We don't want it to be all dried out for Prince Norman."

"Don't you start anything with Norman. You grew up in the same house. He's closer to you than a cousin. He's more like a brother."

"I've got two real brothers, Ma, and that's plenty. You took Norman in, and that makes you a saint, but it doesn't make Norman so special, if you ask me."

"I like Norman," Claribel said and sighed. "And he's so good looking!"

"He's been away for five years, Clare. You hardly know him," Albertine reminded her. "You don't remember all the trouble he got into."

"All boys get into trouble!" Birdie corrected her.

"No, they don't!" Albertine challenged her. "What about Larry? What trouble has Larry ever gotten into?"

"Well, Larry's the exception that proves the rule," Birdie said.

"Norman used to buy me candy bars," Lorraine said. "And he took me to the zoo once. Norman was always special to me."

"Lorraine, let me tell you something," Albertine scolded her. "Norman can't be trusted as far as you can throw him."

"Now, stop it," Birdie said and literally slammed her foot down on the linoleum floor. When Birdie had given birth to Lorraine, a malformed fetus had been delivered with the placenta. Birdie's mother, Grandmére Elise, had preserved it in a jar of formaldehyde for further study, but the jar had disappeared, and Albertine blamed Norman. "When Larry gets here, I'm sending him straight over to your apartment to fetch Hendrik, and we'll all be a family together."

Hank sat on the porch swing, kicking his feet to move it back and forth while Dominic bounced a rubber ball on the steps and simultaneously watched out for whoever might be coming after him.

Dominic caught the ball and turned to watch a figure walking toward them on the sidewalk. "Hey," he said. "I recognize this guy. It's Monty Matheson, the middleweight who's knocked out about twenty other fighters."

"Naw," Hank jumped from the swing to stand on the porch and look at the man coming toward them. "It ain't him."

"The hell it ain't."

As the young man in the blue suit and gray hat walked up the block, he paused at every house to read the street numbers. When he got even with the porch, he stopped, popped his chewing gum and asked, "Hey, is this where the Fontaines live?"

"That's right," Dominic said, and started shadow-boxing in front of him. "And who's asking?"

"My name's Monty," he said and held up a bouquet of flowers as an excuse not to spar with the boy.

"Who are you looking for?" Hank asked from the edge of the porch.

"Miss Claribel Fontaine," he said and smiled, enjoying the sound of her name.

"Aren't you Monty Matheson, the boxer?" Dominic asked him. "The kid with the surprise left hook?"

"Nobody's surprised by it," Monty grinned. "They just can't stop it."

"Oh, yeah?" Dominic challenged him. "I bet I can stop it."

"You're pretty young to be going to the fights. Aren't you, kid?"

"I'm old enough to get in. I've seen a lot of fights. I saw you knock out Lightning Alonzo in the third round at Marigold Gardens."

"That was a good fight," Monty nodded. "He was plenty strong, but not quick enough. I jabbed him in the ear, and he went down like a tree."

"Put down them flowers and show me how you did it," Dominic said. "Hank will hold them for you."

"I don't want to hurt you, kid," Monty said and laughed dismissively. "You don't want to mess with me!"

"Ha! A skinny guy like you?" Dominic challenged him. "Put down those flowers and show me your stuff!"

"All right, if it will shut you up," Monty said and handed the bundle of carnations to Hank. "Let's see what you've got."

Hank thought the red flowers with the stiff white ribbon were too nice for Claribel, who mostly laughed like a ninny all the time. The carnations were just right for his mom, though, with her black hair and green eyes.

Dominic squared off toe-to-toe with the professional boxer, squinted seriously and punched the air inches from Monty's chest.

Monty wasted no time. His left hand flew forward and slapped Dominic's right ear.

"Ow!" Dominic cried and swung wildly with his right fist. Monty blocked the punch, and his right hand shot forward and slapped Dominic's left ear.

"Owie!" the boy said and put his hands over both ears. "Son of a bitch! My ears are ringing!" When Dominic raised his head, Hank could see tears streaming down his cheeks.

"Are you all right, kid?" Monty asked. "I didn't mean to hurt you."

"What?" Dominic cried. "What did you call me, you bastard?"

"Take it easy, kid!" Monty said and handed Dominic a handkerchief. "I could have busted your nose. The ringing will go away in a day or two."

"What?" Dominic asked. "What did you say, asshole?"

Ignoring Dominic, Monty turned to Hank and took back his flowers. "Is Claribel inside?" he asked and popped his chewing gum.

"Yeah, she's in the kitchen, helping my grandmother fix dinner," Hank said. "We're expecting more than twenty people."

"How do I get to the kitchen?" Monty asked.

"Right through the living room," Hank said, "but you better spit your gum out first. Grandma Birdie doesn't allow chewing gum inside!"

When Monty came into the living room, he met Albertine, still in her bathrobe, and her father, in his unbuttoned vest, who sat together on the couch.

"Albertine, is that you?" Monty asked. "What are you doing here?"

"Monty," she answered, jumped to her feet and dropped her robe like a damp towel, revealing her yellow silk dress. "Monty. This is my parents' house. How did you know?"

"I didn't. I came to see Claribel Fontaine. The kids on the porch said I'd find her inside."

"My sister? You're looking for my kid sister?"

"If Claribel is your sister, then yes, I'm looking for her."

"Monty, she's only seventeen."

"I'm only twenty-one," Monty grinned. "Not much difference."

"Albertine," Henry said as he buttoned his vest to greet the young caller. "Go tell your sister that he's here."

"What? Fine. I'll get Clare right now." Albertine snatched her robe off the rug, draped it over her arm, then hurried to the kitchen. Why was Claribel going after her boyfriends? And where did she meet him, anyway? She was too young to go to the Top Hat!

In the parlor, Henry motioned for Monty to sit down in the arm chair opposite the couch. The young man grinned nervously. He would have been handsome, Henry thought, except for the broken nose, flattened as if he were pressing it against a window pane.

"So you're a friend of Albertine's," Henry asked, tamped a cigarette against the side of the Camel pack and lit up. "Like a smoke?"

"No thanks," Monty replied, "I'm in training."

"Yeah? What kind of training?"

"The usual boxing routine. Road work, dumb bells, sit ups, punchin' the bag, jumpin' rope, and sparring of course."

"Somehow getting in shape from real work makes more sense to me. They say Colby Malone got in shape by swinging a sledgehammer at the steel mills. That's how he can hit so many homers. The strength in his arms."

"I see him around town," Monty shrugged and smiled shyly. "But I never saw him carrying a sledge hammer."

"I heard he has one at the clubhouse at Wrigley. Have you been fighting long?" Henry asked.

"Since I was sixteen," Monty said. "Went professional in '32."

"Well, I hope you get the fights out of your system before they knock your brains out," the old man grinned.

"I'm a pretty good fighter, Mr. Fontaine," Monty insisted. "I haven't met the guy who could knock my brains out."

Henry's grinned widened. "You will, kid. Sooner or later you'll meet him."

In the kitchen, re-cloaked in her bathrobe, Albertine confronted Claribel. "Where did you meet Monty Matheson?"

"He's here?" Claribel laughed. "He's half an hour early!"

"Answer my question!" Albertine demanded. "Where did you meet him?"

"At the Aragon Ballroom. He's a marvelous dancer."

"And a prize fighter…"

"So?" Claribel said, hung up her apron on a hook beside the sink, and straightened the front of her red dress.

"Do you know what rough people he knows?"

"Hush, Al! You need to help Ma. My boyfriend is waiting."

When Claribel reached the parlor, her father and brother Larry were talking to Monty as if they were old friends. In fact, Larry had known Monty as long as Albertine had, for two years, which seemed an eternity as the Depression dragged on and the Top Hat had grown from a basement speakeasy to a grand night club. And Monty had changed from a kid who liked boxing to an undefeated fighter who might get a shot at the title.

"I hear you're going to New York for the championship," Larry said, his mouth a few inches from Monty's ear.

"I hope so," the boy nodded and smiled eagerly. "But I have to fight Dutch Hansen first."

"The Windmill!"

"That's right," Monty said, then spotted Claribel coming into the room, and he stood up immediately, stepped toward her, bent down and kissed her hand. Then he presented her with the red flowers. "For you," he said and blushed. Clare took the carnations and glowed with happiness.

"Aren't you gallant!" Albertine called over her sister's shoulder. "You never kissed my hand."

"I wouldn't have felt right about that. You're a married lady. If I'd met you when you were Clare's age, I probably would have kissed your hand, too."

"At least when I was her age, I wasn't so empty-headed."

"You met Hendrik when you were my age!" Claribel said and laughed, then she stood on tip toe to kiss Monty's cheek.

"What's Hendrik got to do with it?" Albertine hissed, but knew she had no right to be jealous of Claribel. Hadn't she done everything to discourage Monty so she'd have time with Colby Malone? But it hurt to be upstaged by her kid sister. It hurt that Monty made her feel like an old married woman.

"Hendrik is your husband," Birdie said as she came into the room, shaking water from her fingers, then wiping them on her apron. "Hendrik is your husband and he's not here yet. But Larry's going to fix that right now. Larry, jump in your car and go fetch Hendrik. I want everyone to be here when Norman comes home."

"Ma," Larry moaned, "if he wanted to come to dinner he'd be here already."

"Larry, please do as she says," his father said. "Fay's coming by later to check his thumb. It's only a ten minute drive."

"Will he pay for my gas?"
"Larry," Henry growled, "you heard me."
"Hendrik hardly knows Norman."
"Fetch him," Birdie repeated, "and come straight back."
"Okay!"

Chapter Six

As soon as Larry hopped out of his Ford onto the sidewalk, he heard Hendrik's saxophone. What is he playing? Something bluesy in a minor key, three four time, slow and with feeling. Geez, even with his thumb crushed down to a stub, Hendrik is playing great! Larry pushed open the front door and climbed the rickety steps toward the music. He stood on the landing and listened with his ear close to the door as Hendrik kept playing sadly and sweetly.

Larry shook his head. "That's Armstrong!" he said to himself. He tried the knob, and pushed open the unlocked door. He found Hendrik sitting on the kitchen chair holding his saxophone as he played *St. James Infirmary*. His right hand was ringed with a bright red bracelet of blood. Tears poured over Hendrik's cheeks, and Larry could not tell whether he was crying because of the beauty of the music or the pain in his thumb. Hendrik acknowledged Larry with his eyes and kept playing until he finished the last note of the song. Then he reached down with his left hand to release the bloody strap from his horn.

"Get a rag for me, will ya?" Hendrik asked, and Larry went to the kitchen sink and retrieved the cleanest dish towel. He reached out to daub the blood on Hendrik's hand, but Hendrik snatched the towel from him and used it first to wipe the red smudges off his saxophone.

"That sounded great," Larry said. "You're a natural!"

"Danke."

"When did you start covering Satchmo?"

"When I saw that Bix is full of shit."

"I don't like him, neither, but his band <u>is</u> entertaining."

"Bix is a fake," Hendrik said and nodded to the Victrola on the floor in front of him. "That guy makes music."

"Oh, yeah? I've heard that record! Have you seen Satchmo in person?"

"Not yet."

"Christ, you'd love him in person, Hendrik," Larry said. "Let's go together some time."

"It would hurt too much, I think," Hendrik said and eased his sax into its case and snapped it shut.

"Geez, you gotta let Ma look at your hand!"

"It's not the hand. It's the music. I'll never come close."

"You already have, Hendrik! Today you played better than ever!" Larry told him, and like a boy he followed Hendrik to the sink where the German rinsed the blood off the strap and then took the bar of soap and scrubbed his wounded hand, splashing blood and soapy water over the dishes in the bottom of the tub.

"Christ, you play great already, and it's hardly been two weeks since the accident!" Larry said. "Man, you're just like Django Reinhardt. He burned up two of his fingers so bad he could hardly move them. Now they say he can play the guitar better than anyone in Europe. Those burned fingers made him a genius."

"You're just saying that to make me happy." With his left hand he scooped water on his face to wipe away the tears. He had a three-day growth of beard, and the undershirt he was wearing had holes in its armpits.

"No, I'm not just saying it. You're a frickin' natural, and you know it. You don't play music. You are music."

"No, he is music," Hendrik said and pointed to the record player. "I only try." Hendrik opened the ice box and pulled out a bottle of beer. "Last one. Wanna split it?"

"Sure," Larry said as Hendrik popped the bottle open with a church key and poured some beer into a tea cup on the table.

"That's yours," Hendrik laughed.

"Thanks," Larry said and emptied the cup in one swallow. "You want me to help you shave?"

"Why? It's Sunday."

"My Ma sent me to bring you home for dinner. A special occasion. Norman will be there."

"I knew you didn't show up just to hear me play," Hendrik said, drank from the bottle, and poured some more beer into Larry's cup.

"Normally, I would have left you alone."

"Doesn't matter," Hendrik said. "I proved I can still play… Do I really have to shave?"

"You know my Ma."

"It's good she has standards." Without asking for Larry's help, Hendrik went to the bathroom and taped some gauze over his seeping wound. Working one-handed, he had become adept with the dressings and scissors. Then he took up his shaving brush and mug and started lathering his face.

The dining room was the only space that could hold all the guests, and because they wanted to be together, talking over each other in a stew of conversation, everyone congregated around Birdie's immense table, an hour before she announced that dinner was ready.

"I'll tell you what," Arthur said as he looked suspiciously at the glass of lemonade that his sister Lorraine handed him. "We drank more beer during Prohibition, when we made it ourselves. Now we can't afford it."

"Wait till Norman gets here and I'll break out the beers, son," Henry said.

"Well, I hope the little s.o.b. gets here soon," Arthur grinned. "I'm getting damn thirsty."

"Drink your lemonade, zen!" Olga, his companion, told him in her thick Polish accent. She had only been in America for five years and had moved in with Arthur just two years earlier, after his wife Vivian had killed herself by drinking lye. No one blamed Arthur. Vivian had been strange from day one. "Or you vant I should get you some vater?"

"Jesus, Olga, I'm just kidding! We've been together, what? For two years? And you still can't tell when I'm kidding."

"Vell, excuse me for livink!"

"Don't listen to him," Elsie said. "Art don't have a sense of humor, except for a sick one. He laughed his head off when

John Dillinger got gunned down in front of the Biograph. Only a sick creep would laugh about that. If you ask me, there's nothing funny about a guy getting gunned down on the sidewalk when he's coming outa the movies."

"You wanna know why it made me laugh?" Arthur asked her and grinned eagerly. "John Dillinger was so cocky, he thought he could come right back to Chicago after killing those coppers up in Wisconsin, with the FBI tracking his every move, with even his girlfriend, The Woman in Red, informing on him, and he thinks he's so goddamn smart that he can go to the movies without getting spotted by no one. It serves him right to get shot. It is so right it's goddamn funny, Else. And the funniest part is that Pop was in the Biograph that night, weren't ya, Pop? What was playing?"

"A picture called the *Manhattan Melodrama*," Henry said. "What do you expect? A gangster picture. But I didn't think it was very funny hearing gunshots just as I came out of the lobby. On a quiet Sunday night, you don't expect to see a gangster getting mowed down by a hail of bullets. And the feds in the car kept shooting him even when he was sprawled on the pavement. No telling how many bullets ricocheted down the block. And there were innocent bystanders everywhere. That's no joke."

"You're right, it's no joke that the whole city is a shooting gallery," said Elsie's husband Eugene. "Somebody's getting murdered in Chicago every day, Arthur, and that's no goddamn laughing matter. A neighbor of ours went missing for three days last week, and they found his body on Congress Street under the L tracks yesterday morning. The police think loan sharks killed him because he owed them money…And he was just a kid."

"That was Max Hartman, wasn't it?" Art said and laughed as he shook his head knowingly. "I saw the story in the paper. He was a gambler and a small-time punk. He must've pissed off the wrong gangster."

"That doesn't mean anybody had a right to kill him," Gene said and glared at his brother-in-law with eyes that were magnified by his thick eyeglasses.

"Not Max!" Monty said. "Max was in my class at Crane Tech. Why would they kill Maxey?"

Hank had been stealing walnuts from a bowl on his grandmother's sideboard, tossing them to Dominic and rolling them to his cousins Ricky and Roxanne, who were cracking them with a hammer under the dining room table. When he heard Max's name, Hank looked at his friend in surprise, but Dominic's ears were still ringing, and he hadn't understood the news.

"The kid was a petty criminal," Arthur said. "He would have wound up in jail, anyways."

"He wasn't so bad," Monty said and stroked Claribel's hand. "He just got mixed up in the wrong crowd."

Remembering the dice game, Hank thought of Max's bloody lip, the snot pouring from his nose, and the way Mr. Melrose had kicked him in the gut as he lay in the shadow of the pool table. And now Max was dead.

"They say he was a cheater," Hank said hoarsely. "They say he cheated at dice."

"What are you talking about?" Dominic asked.

"This proves my point, Hank," Henry told his grandson. "You have to choose your friends carefully. If you spend time with hoodlums and gamblers, you'll become a hoodlum yourself. Now Maxey is a dead punk, and he didn't make it to twenty-two."

"Is he talking about Max Hartman?" Dominic asked.

Before Hank could answer, his father and Uncle Larry came into the dining room. Hank's dad was dressed in his good blue suit, but without a necktie. Postage stamp-sized squares of toilet paper were plastered over shaving knicks on his neck and cheeks. Hank was happy to see that his dad was smiling, apparently glad to be there.

"Hey, Hendrik," Claribel called to him, "good to see you. You sure look happy!"

"When I got there to pick Heinie up," Larry explained, "he was playing his horn better than ever. He proved he don't need two thumbs to play like Louis Armstrong."

"Doesn't Armstrong play the trumpet?" Monty asked.

"Armstrong plays music," Larry corrected him, "and so does our pal Kinderman. Pure music is what he plays. And I never heard him play better than he did today."

Hearing that Hendrik had arrived, Albertine hurried in from the kitchen wearing her bathrobe, and she reached up to put her hand around his neck, and she pulled him down toward her so she could kiss him on the mouth. "So you played your horn today, Hendrik? I knew you could. I'm so happy for you!"

"It hurt like hell at first," he said and looked her straight in the eye as if they were alone together, "but then the music found me. It was so beautiful I had to cry."

Tears formed in Albertine's eyes, too. Then she kissed him again. "Gotta go," she said. "We'll never eat if I don't go back and help, but I want you to play for me as soon as we get home."

After Albertine was gone, Monty called to Hendrik, "Hey, Kinderman, I've been meaning to ask you something. Your wife says you were down in Florida the day that Italian shot Mayor Cermak."

"She told you about that?" Hendrik smiled and raised his eyebrow with amusement. "The little Dago stood on a chair and tried to shoot Roosevelt."

"You saw that?" Monty asked. "You personally saw Zangarra shoot at FDR?"

"We were two rows behind him," Hendrik said.

"We?"

"The band and I were waiting in the park for Roosevelt to show up for the rally. Hundreds of people were sitting there on folding lawn chairs. Mayor Cermak was already up on the stage with the governor of Florida, about twenty beautiful women, and a brass band."

"Vhat were you doing in Florida?" Olga asked him. "Taking zee cure?"

"My combo had a gig at the Flamingo Hotel," Hendrik said. "Geez, I love Miami Beach in the winter. No snow, no ice. You can swim in the ocean in February!"

"Did that really happen in February? I remember it distinctly as Christmas time," Olga corrected him.

"It was the fifteenth of February," Hendrik said. "Our last week in Florida. Roosevelt wasn't president yet, he had a couple of weeks before getting sworn in. We heard he had come to town to meet Mayor Cermak, so we thought we'd get a look at this Franklin Roosevelt. What makes him so special, anyway? Nobody ever tried to shoot Herbert Hoover."

"Well, they should have!" Elsie laughed.

"No," Hendrik protested. "You don't know what you're talking about. History will show that Hoover is a great man. He didn't create the Depression…But we were out there on this beautiful sunny day, with hundreds of people in summer hats waiting for the next president to show up, and he comes riding in, sitting up high on the back of an open Packard, and he never even gets out of the car. Instead, his driver pulls up in front of the stage and Cermak hands him the microphone, and FDR makes a little speech, and the crowd is cheering when this little anarchist (he wasn't much taller than my son Hank here), this little anarchist stands up on a white folding chair and he's holding a little black gun. It looked like a toy pistol. He fires off all six bullets. He keeps shooting even when people are dragging the little wop down onto the grass. Me and the boys run up to help, but four big guys are already holding Zangarra down, and the little bastard is laughing like a maniac, trying to bite everybody with his crooked, yellow teeth. One guy has picked up Zangarra's little pea shooter gun and tries to blast him right in the face. But the gun is out of bullets and it just clicks like a toy.

"The anarchist thinks he's killed Roosevelt, but it's Mayor Cermak and a woman who are laying there bleeding on the stage. The big Packard drives away for a minute with Roosevelt in it, but it circles back and they lift the mayor and the wounded woman into the back seat with FDR, and they speed off to the hospital. Roosevelt is holding Mayor Cermak's gray head and I can see he's talking to him. The woman is probably dead already. That's why Roosevelt isn't even trying to talk to her."

"So the President was as cool as they say he was?" Monty asked. "He didn't panic. He came back to pick up the mayor and get him to the hospital?"

"Yah," Hendrik nodded. "He did all that. He didn't seem afraid. But I can tell you I was afraid. What if there were more shooters? What about bombs? Don't anarchists have bombs? Or there could be snipers on the rooftops all around the park."

"But that was it," Arthur said. "There were no more shots. The guy was a pathetic lunatic. A nut case out to kill the next president."

"Didn't FDR say he was sure Zangarra was a Chicago gangster," Henry reminded them. "He said Zangarra meant to kill Mayor Cermak all along because he was fighting the mob. And they electrocuted Zangarra three weeks after the mayor died, so no one will ever know the truth."

"I'm glad he missed Roosevelt," Claribel said. "Without him, we wouldn't have a New Deal, and this Depression wouldn't ever go away."

"It's gonna take something bigger than Roosevelt to get this country back on its feet," Eugene insisted. "I dunno what that is, but the goddamn government hasn't done nothing yet but give me a fifteen dollar relief check and a box of surplus cheese every week."

"Things will get better soon, dear," Elsie told her husband. "Before we know it, we'll be back on our feet."

"The next Ice Age will be here before we know it, too. Right after the Second Coming of Christ," Eugene said bitterly.

"I'll just be happy when Norman gets here," Larry laughed. "Then Ma will let us eat something."

Chapter Seven

As if on cue, the doorbell rang. Lorraine jumped to her feet and hurried to answer it. "He's here!" she called, "He's here!" Hank rolled his eyes in disgust, not wanting to believe that this silly girl really was his aunt. Still, he didn't want Lorraine to have more fun than he was having, so he slipped past the seated family to the front room where he could see Cousin Norman as soon as she did.

Lorraine was anything but graceful. Hank thought she hopped like a chubby dog trying to walk on its hind legs, but she moved quickly enough and nearly left her feet as she grabbed the knob and swung the heavy door open.

There in a shaft of gleaming light stood a tall man dressed entirely in white. Hank thought he looked like a policeman carved out of snow. He wore a white officer's cap with a patent leather bill; his bright coat had two rows of brass buttons; and there were black diagonal stripes on his sleeve and an embroidered eagle on his shoulder. He wore white gloves with flat buttons over his knuckles and white spats over glistening white shoes. His face didn't have much color, either. His eyebrows were blonde, his eyes were light blue, and he had a pencil line of a yellow moustache above his lip. The only reddish mark on him was a straight scar that ran from below his left ear nearly to the point of his chin. Hank guessed it had come from a sword, or a dagger. How could he get such a serious wound during peace time? From pirates?

"Hello, little lady," the man said, smiled and touched the bill of his cap. "You must be Lorraine."

"That's right! How did you know?"

"You're even more beautiful than the picture Aunt Birdie sent me."

"And you're even more handsome than Claribel says you are, Norman. DO come in. Everyone's been waiting for you."

"And who's this half pint?" Norman asked, nodding to Hank as he stepped in on the hooked-rug doormat. "Are you Albertine's boy Henry?"

"My name's Hank."

"Your nickname is Hank. You were baptized Henry. I should know, I was there."

"Why are you dressed like that?" Hank asked him. "Was there a parade that I missed?"

"Almost! Your grandmother wanted to see me in my uniform, so I put on my dress whites. This uniform is just for special occasions."

"It's whiter than a wedding dress," Lorraine said. "You could be the bride."

"Let's not get carried away," Norman grinned. He had a handsome smile, Hank would allow, even though it was a bit sneaky, like Dominic's.

"Come on, kids," Norman said. "Let's go in and say hello to everyone."

Birdie met him as he came into the dining room. Her apron was gone now so she showed off her flowered print dress, and as she hugged him close and hard, tears poured from her eyes.

"Oh, Norman, you've come to see us! Oh, I had terrible nightmares about you being lost at sea, and I can't tell you how many rosaries I prayed for you to come home safely. At least one a month. And how long has it been since you've been back to Chicago? Three years?"

"Just two, Aunt Bird. I was here before the election in '32."

"Only for a few days."

"But I came to see ya's," Norman said and addressed the family around the table. "Hello, everyone! You weren't holding up dinner for me, were you?"

Without taking off his hat or gloves, Norman worked his way around the room, shaking every man's hand and kissing every woman on the mouth.

He held Claribel with a little too much interest, pressing her full, new breasts against the brass buttons on his chest. "Cousin Clare, you're all grown up!" he said as he licked the taste of her lips on his. "And who's this? You've got a boyfriend already?"

"This is Monty Matheson," Claribel laughed, happy to show him off.

Monty stood to show he was as tall and strong as the sailor, and then he clenched Norman's hand.

"Now that's a firm grip!" Norman laughed. "I bet you got that strong at the stockyards. I had a buddy who said there's nothing like slaughtering hogs to strengthen your grip!"

"Monty's a boxer," Claribel explained. "The sports writers say he's the best middle weight in the Middle West. One more win and he's going to New York for the championship."

"Isn't that something?" Norman laughed and slapped Monty's back. "Remind me not to make you angry, okay Pal? I wanna leave the party standing up."

"You're nuts, Norman," Clare scolded him. "Monty won't hurt you."

"Larry," Norman called out and moved to his right. "You're looking super-duper. How's the banjo playing coming along? I hope you stopped wearing the clown suit. It made you seem like a child molester."

"I only had the job one summer," Larry said and blushed with embarrassment. "We were playing for kids' parties at parish halls…Geez, nobody got molested!"

"So you've moved on? That's great, that is great," Norman laughed. "And Art, when did you grow that goatee? Makes you look like Fu Manchu."

"You're as full of shit as ever, Norm," Art said. "Ya know that. You're so full of shit, you stink."

"You still working at Marshall Field's?" Norman asked him. "Counting beans like usual?"

"It's called accounting, Norm," Art corrected him. "We don't sell beans at Field's."

"And Vivian, how are you?" Norman said to Olga and leaned over to plant a kiss on her mouth. "You're more lovely than ever."

"Norm, this is Olga," Art said in exasperation. "Not Vivian."

"Oh, hi, Olga," Norman said and turned back to his cousin Arthur. "What happened to Vivian?"

"Christ, Norman. You know what happened to Vivian."

"Oh my God!" Norman said and looked up at the ceiling. "Now I remember. Aunt Birdie wrote me about the poison and all. I'm sorry, Art. How could I be so stupid?"

"It comes naturally to you, I guess."

"Well, I'm truly sorry, Art. I know how much you loved her. But give me a break. Ghosts don't visit me all the time like your ma."

"Shut up, already!" Larry insisted and threw a walnut at him.

"Truce!" Norman said. "I haven't seen you guys in two years! Give me a break… Hello, Elsie, how's my favorite cousin?" He kissed Elsie's mouth and worked his lips to smear her lipstick.

"We're making the most of the Depression," Elsie told him and flipped the rim of his hat so it shifted to the back of his head.

"You know, Elsie, you're the best kisser of the bunch," Norman said. "You enjoy it the most."

"Not with you, Norman," she said. "You kiss everybody, but you don't mean it. You do it to tease us."

"No fair, Elsie," Norman protested. "I learned to tease from your Pa…You taught me, Uncle Henry, didn't you?"

"I tried to teach you a lot of things, Norman," Henry said and shook his head in bemusement. "That doesn't mean you learned anything from me, though. Like respect for my daughters. You didn't learn that."

"Geez," Norman laughed, "and I didn't get a kiss off of Albertine yet. Come on, Al, you owe me."

"I don't owe you anything, Norman, but a smile and a nod." She gave him both.

"I'll take what I can get," Norman said. "Al, you never looked better. Staying out late agrees with you."

"What happened to your face, Norman?" she asked him. "Did someone cut you?"

"Oh, this," Norman paused and traced his gloved index finger over the long scar on his cheek. "I fell down a ladder during a typhoon. Everything onboard ship is made of steel. There are sharp edges everywhere."

"On knives in dark alleys, too," Albertine said and shook her head. "The world's not a safe place for drunken sailors."

"Or Chiefs," Henry said. "When did you make Chief Petty Officer, Norman?"

"On May first. There was a big celebration on deck. Flags. The ship's band. A Commodore. They did everything but kiss my ass…You were right, Uncle Henry, the military changed me."

"Aside from the scar, you haven't changed one bit," Albertine said.

"Now, wait a minute, everyone!" Birdie said, raising her hands as if she were quelling a riot. "Don't gang up on Norman! We haven't seen our Norman in two years, so please make him feel at home. Now girls, help me serve the wonderful meal we've fixed together."

It took twenty minutes for the women to carry all the food from the kitchen to the dining room table. First, they brought an assortment of relish trays, laden with radishes, celery, green onion, olives, pickles, and sliced cucumbers. Next came the bread, rolls, muffins, corn sticks, pretzels and crackers. The women carried in the cooked vegetables, boiled spinach, corn on the cob, zucchini casserole, string beans in bacon fat, carrots glazed in maple syrup, steamed broccoli and asparagus. The next wave delivered the mashed potatoes, candied yams, boiled new potatoes, flat noodles, macaroni and cheese, and rice pilaf. Then the parade of meats began. Albertine carried in the platter of sliced ham under brown sugar and canned pineapple. Claribel brought in the beef brisket baked in onion and garlic. Lorraine balanced the leg of lamb with fresh mint high on one hand. And Birdie came in last with the golden turkey on her large yellow platter, ready for Henry's carving knife.

Three or four gatherings of this size could not have eaten this much food, but Birdie expected it all to be consumed, or taken home as leftovers by guests with empty pantries of their own.

"Birdie, you've outdone yourself," Eugene said as he drove his fork into a thick slice of brisket and flopped it onto his plate. "This feast is bigger than Christmas!"

"Look at all this food!" Norman said as he rubbed his hands together. "It's enough to feed the whole crew of the U.S.S. Toledo. Aunt Birdie, can I say the blessing?"

"Of course, you can, Norman," Birdie said as she took her place at the opposite end of the long table from her husband. "I do believe that's the first time you've ever volunteered to say grace."

"When you ride through a typhoon in a destroyer, you get religion real fast. Now I even keep a set of rosary beads under my pillow," he grinned widely.

"Don't mock the rosary, Norman," Elsie scolded him.

"I'm not mockin' nothing," Norman said and pulled off his gloves, folded them neatly, and slid them into the side pocket of his white tunic. "Let's bow our heads, everyone, and thank the Lord for this wonderful bounty. Outside this warm and loving house we face the hollow cheeks and sharp jaws of the Depression. When I left this comfortable home, I joined the Navy with its rigid discipline, hard cots, and food they wouldn't serve in a prison. And instead of cruising the calm waters of family life, I've been tossed by waves, buffeted by winds, and cut by other seamen who were jealous of my success. So Lord, look down on my Aunt Birdie, my Uncle Henry, and all their family and friends, because they have built a tradition of welcome, a life of kindness that, yes, feeds us today, but which has literally kept my spirit alive through my ordeals over the past three and a half years. I guess that's a long-winded way of saying thanks to the Lord for this food and thanks to my aunt and uncle for keeping this Sunday dinner tradition alive."

"That malarkey sounds good, Norman," Arthur teased him. "Can we eat?"

"Not until Aunt Birdie says it's okay."

"Eat, for cripe's sake!" Birdie laughed. "And thank you for the nice speech, Norman. If you meant half of it, it would be enough to make me blush. Now who wants to pass their plate for some of this brisket?"

When the dinner plates were carried away, and the guests began eating their desserts, Lorraine carried Norman's hat around the room and began collecting donations.

"Cousin Norman needs money to buy a train ticket back to Philadelphia," she said to her brother Arthur, and held the inverted cap under his chin.

"Where is the little coward?" Arthur asked. "Is he too afraid to ask for money himself?"

"Come on, Arty," she scolded him and shook the loose coins inside the hat. "Sailors don't make much money. Norman just needs thirty-five dollars."

"Where is he?"

"In the kitchen helping Ma make more coffee."

"Okay, I'll give him a buck, if only to get rid of him," Arthur said and dropped the paper money on top of the change that was already in the hat.

"What about you, Larry?" Lorraine asked. "You don't want Norman thumbing a ride back to Philadelphia, do you? He might get mud on his nice white uniform."

Larry shook his head and reached into his pocket and fished out a green wad of paper. To Lorraine's surprise, he unfolded a five dollar bill, smoothed out the creases and dropped it into the hat.

"Five bucks!" Lorraine exclaimed. "Larry, where did you get five dollars?"

"I work for a living, little sister," Larry said and smiled with satisfaction. "Don't let anyone believe I'd hold out on my family."

"Come on, Elsie, what about you and Gene?" Lorraine asked her sister.

"Sorry, sweetie. We've hardly got car fare to get home, let alone buy a ticket to Philly!" Elsie laughed. "I'll wrap up a nice turkey sandwich for Norman. He can eat it on the train."

"Not even a nickel?" Lorraine asked and pushed out her lower lip unhappily. In response, Eugene tossed a handful of coins into the hat, as if it were a collection basket at church. "There! We helped the kid out. Never too poor to help a relative."

"He's not <u>your</u> relative!" Elsie said and swatted his shoulder.

"We're all family."

"What about you, Clare?" Lorraine said and carried the hat to the corner of the table where she sat with Monty. They were sharing a bowl of bread pudding and cream. "Can you get your <u>professional</u> boxer to put in a few bucks?"

"What about it, Monty?" Claribel asked him sweetly and stroked his cheek. "For Cousin Norman."

"I suppose I could put in the same as Larry," Monty said.

"Only the same?" Clare asked, and looked at him sadly.

"Okay. Ten bucks," he said and reached for his wallet. "Ten bucks, it is."

"Thanks! And Pa promised ten, too," Lorraine said, "We've almost got the whole fare collected, Albertine." She jiggled the hat in front of her eldest sister. "Can you and Hendrik make up the difference?"

The coins rang, the bills jumped, and Albertine squinted down into the hat as if it were crawling with cockroaches. "Of all the nerve," she snapped. "Sending a <u>child</u> to collect money to replace the pay he wasted on tarts and booze!"

"I am not a child!" Lorraine protested. "Norman said I'm practically grown. He said I kissed just like a woman."

"He kissed you, too, did he?" Albertine asked indignantly.

"What's wrong with that?"

"Wait a minute! Wait one goddamn minute!" Albertine said and reached into the hat to push the coins and bills out of the way so she could read the name stenciled in the lining. "KOWALSKI," it said.

"Kowalski?" Albertine called out. "It's not even his goddamn hat!" Then she snatched the cap from her sister and ran with it into the kitchen.

Her mother was there with the coffee, the sink full of dishes, cousin Fay and old Doctor Bichet, but there was no sign of Norman.

"Where's Norman?" Albertine asked. "Where's that liar, Norman?"

"Hello, Albertine," Doc Bichet said. "You're quite lovely when you blush."

"How are you, Doctor?" she smiled.

"'S allright," Bichet muttered. Instead of coffee, he was drinking one of Henry's homemade beers from a pint milk bottle.

"Sorry for the commotion, Doctor," she said. "I need to clear something up with my stupid cousin…Hiya, Fay. You're not the cousin I was after. That would be Norman."

"So I gathered," Fay grinned. "Home from the Navy two hours and you're fighting with him already?"

"Take a moment to compose yourself, dear," Birdie told her daughter. "What are you doing with Norman's hat?"

"Lorraine was passing it around to raise his train fare back to his ship."

"Good idea!" Birdie said and the doctor nodded.

"Using a child to raise money he squandered in some bar room?"

"The Navy doesn't pay much," Fay reminded her. "When my brother Joe signed up, they only paid but thirty dollars a month. A dollar a day."

"I don't care if they pay him a penny a day," Albertine shook her head. "Where did he go, ma?"

"If I tell you, do you promise not to stir up any more trouble?"

"I promise."

"He's on the front porch, smoking a cigarette with your pa."

"Norman!" Albertine hissed and ran to confront her cousin.

"I'm glad you got your promotion, Norm," Henry said to his nephew as they blew smoke into the afternoon breeze. "It shows you've matured. It shows you're not afraid of hard work. That you can be a leader, too."

"If I keep it up, the captain says I might be eligible for officer's candidate school, if not Annapolis itself."

"Well, you look the part, Norman," Henry said. "Over in France I didn't see anyone who <u>looked</u> as good as you do in uniform. And Christ! White shoes! Spotless white shoes. They wouldn't last five seconds in the trenches!"

"Lucky there's no trenches in the Navy. Not on the Toledo, anyway."

Then Albertine burst through the door and stood with them on the porch. But when she was met by her father's "you'd-better-relax" stare, she took a deep breath and spoke in a quiet, if strained voice.

"Norman, is this your hat?" she asked.

"Yeah, of course it's my hat," he said and took it from her. "And wow, Lorraine did a great job of collecting my train fare, didn't she?" In seconds he had scooped out the money and pocketed it.

"No, really, Norman, is this your hat?"

"Yeah, it's really my hat. Why are you asking me if it's my hat?"

"Because it has somebody else's name stenciled inside of it. Somebody named Kowalski. You're still Norman Fontaine, aren't you?"

"Of course, Al, what do you think?"

"Then, why are you wearing Kowalski's hat? Does the whole uniform belong to this Kowalski? Did you borrow it from him to impress us? You don't have to impress us, Norman. We're your family."

"Come on, Al," he said, but he looked toward Henry to gauge his uncle's reaction. Yet, as was often the case, Henry's kind expression concealed what he was thinking. "Uniforms are expensive, see. We gotta pay for them ourselves. When I got my promotion, I bought some of it second-hand. This jacket. This hat. Kowalski was mustering out, and he was about my size. I bought a few things from him before he went back home to his mother in Duluth."

"They let you buy somebody else's uniforms? With those patches and all?"

"The insignia are mine, Al. You believe me, don't you?" Norman begged her. "I made Chief on May the first, so I needed a new dress uniform. You believe me, don't you, Al?"

Albertine looked at her handsome cousin, with the new scar on his chin, the tears welling up in his pale blue-green eyes, and the white uniform, still spotless even after he'd eaten like a truck driver and a lumberjack combined. He was pleading for her to believe him, but she did not believe him, how could she? He had lied to her every time they'd been together. But she loved Norman anyway, the poor lost soul, she wouldn't hurt him any more today. "Sure, I believe you, Norman," Albertine said. "Do you think you've got enough money for your train fare?"

"Yeah. Your pa just gave me twenty bucks."

"Let's go see if the fresh coffee is ready," Henry said and flipped his cigarette butt into the bushes.

"Good idea," Norman said and smiled in relief.

"Do me a favor, Norman," Albertine said.

"What's that?"

"Keep your hands off Lorraine. If you kiss her again, I swear I'll cut your nuts off."

When Albertine came into the parlor, Fay and Birdie were examining Hendrik's wounded hand.

"You did a nice job of stitching," Birdie told Fay, "but it still looks banged up. What have you been doing with this thumb, Hendrik? Pounding nails?"

"I played the saxophone," Hendrik shrugged and smiled at his wife as she at on the chair next to her mother. "It sounded better than before. It sounded like Louis Armstrong."

"I don't know who that is," Birdie said and shook her head. "One of those colored players, I suppose. Not like my French music…Let me see. I'm going to leave the stitches there for another few days, Hendrik. But I'm going to put one of my mother's healing plasters on it and give you a can of herb tea. You drink a cup right before you go to bed every night for one month and a day."

Birdie went into the kitchen, and Fay washed Hendrik's hand in a basin of warm, soapy water, then daubed it with a cotton ball soaked in peroxide.

"Geez, that smarts," Hendrik complained. "You like to hurt me?"

"Oh, no!" Fay reassured him. "I want you to get better."

Then Birdie returned carrying a white towel with a four-inch square of cloth resting on top. The plaster was saturated in yellow liquid and smelled like ginger and alcohol. She picked it up by the corners and wrapped it over his stump, his palm, and the back of his hand. The plaster imparted a glowing warmth that soaked through his flesh to his bones and made him want to sleep. As he leaned back onto the couch, Birdie wrapped his hand in gauze and fastened it tight with two small safety pins.

"Feels better," Hendrik said, nodded and teased her. "Will this plaster make my thumb grow back?"

"No, I'm sorry to say," Birdie shook her head. "But it will keep the infection away. And I'll show Albertine how to make a healing plaster for you. And you'll wrap his hand in one every night, won't you, dear?

"I'll do anything to make his hand heal faster," Albertine said and hopped over the couch to sit beside him.

At the piano, Albertine began the sing-along with a flourishing introduction that swept from the bottom to the top of the keyboard. Then she nodded to her sister Elsie, who sang, "Blue moon. You saw me standing alone, without a dream in my heart, without a love of my own."

Henry, who stood ready to turn the pages of Albertine's music, joined in with full voice. Hendrik sang too, as he sat on the bench next to his wife, his back to the piano. Larry accompanied his sister on his curved-top Gibson guitar, with chunky chords and a few tuneful riffs.

Though out of tune, both Arthur and Olga joined in the singing. Birdie didn't sing, but she did feel happy. The gathering was like the days before radio, when you had to create your own entertainment. She wished they had a fiddle and an accordion like the French people played in Kankakee, but this music was pleasant enough. Her son and daughter were playing, and everyone sang along, even Hendrik with his clear German tenor, Elsie's kids mumbled the words and tried to keep up, while Lorraine mouthed the lyrics without uttering a sound.

Only Clare and her boyfriend seemed untouched by the music. They sat in the corner hand in hand, whispering in turn into each other's ear. (If Albertine could have seen them, it would have driven her mad, but she had her back turned as she concentrated on playing the piano.)

Norman had hung up his second-hand tunic and hat on the coat tree in the hallway, and in his white shirt sleeves he looked smaller and younger than before. His blonde hair was mussed on top as he nodded his head in time with the music and sang in harmony with Elsie's Eugene, who had a pretty fair baritone voice himself.

And so the guests entertained themselves for an hour, occasionally dancing to the music if the song was right, until Albertine needed a break from the piano and all the singers grew thirsty.

"I think your playing is better than ever," Henry told his daughter. "Yours, too, Larry."

"Thanks, Pa," Larry said, but Albertine turned to her husband for a nod of approval. And though Hendrik had been an enthusiastic singer, he seemed withdrawn now that the music had stopped. He sat still on the bench and didn't turn to face her.

"What's the matter, Hendrik?" she spoke close to his ear, but he stood up without answering, waited a second, then extended his left hand to take hers.

"Nothing's wrong," he said. "I like to hear you play."

Pleased now, she kissed him, and put her arms around him. "See," she said, "Sunday dinner's not so bad."

"No, it's not," he whispered and squeezed her backside with both hands.

"Don't," she laughed but didn't try to pry his hands away.

In the dimly lit kitchen, Birdie put the last pieces of silverware in the drawer and hung the last pot on the hook beside the stove. She had hoped that Norman would spend the night, but he had left at nine to catch the ten o'clock train to Philadelphia. At least, the dinner had been a success. Everyone had plenty to eat, the conversation was pleasant, and all the guests enjoyed the music. She had sent most of the leftover food home with her daughters and sons and Doc Bichet. Aside from a few arguments with Norman, there was no ugliness today, no conflict that broke the family's good will.

She was pleased that Norman was doing so well in the Navy, that he had been promoted, that he looked so handsome in his uniform, and that despite his complaints about the food and discipline, he looked healthy and fit and relatively happy. The younger girls doted on him. Lorraine and Claribel were thrilled to see him and flirted with him. Why not? A handsome young man in uniform, six feet tall, with blue eyes and golden hair!

Albertine was jealous that Norman had left Chicago and was seeing the world. They always had been rivals. Even though Albertine was nearly four years older, she resented the attention her mother paid to Norman, Henry's nephew abandoned by his parents when their farm went under and they moved back to Quebec without him. A lonely boy. No wonder he exaggerated the truth sometimes. No wonder he wants things to be better than they are.

As Birdie filled the bucket to mop the kitchen floor, her mother appeared to her as a white, glowing column beside the ice box. The kitchen grew cold, and Birdie could see her breath on the air.

"Why do you fawn over that horrible boy?" Mére Elise haunted her. "I'm embarrassed for you!"

"Mother," Birdie scoffed, "don't be silly. Norman has his faults, but he's a good boy at heart. He loves our family."

"He's a snake!" another voice called out, and Birdie saw her dead brother, Louis, standing in the sink. He was still a boy, wearing short pants.

"How do you know?" Birdie laughed, "You were dead twenty years before Norman was born."

"I have been watching out for you ever since."

"Pish! You've been hounding me, Louie. Why don't you rest in peace like a good soul?"

"Don't speak to your brother that way!" Mére Elise scolded her.

"You may be able to read minds," Birdie told her, "but you don't understand Norman."

"What is it that I don't understand?" her mother's spirit asked.

"Norman is practically an orphan," Birdie explained. "He'll always be unsure of himself. He will always pretend to be somebody he thinks we want him to be. Somebody important. Someone exciting."

"You mean he's a congenital liar," the voice was her father's. He appeared as a bright cloud above the stove. "But he's not as bad as the German. How could you let my granddaughter marry a Kraut?"

"Albertine stopped listening to me when she was eleven years old," Birdie said as she lifted the bucket and set it on the floor. Then, as she went to the broom closet to get the mop, Henry was already there holding it.

"I'll mop up for you," he said.

"I thought you were asleep already," she said.

"I'm a night owl, you know that," Henry said. "Let me finish up for you."

"If you insist," she said and winked at her mother, who shook her head before she disappeared.

"I like the fighter, though," her father's ghost said, and his voice lingered after he was gone. "He will be champion some day!"

"As if I care!" Birdie scoffed.

"What?" Henry said as he mopped in front of the stove.

"Nothing."

"Ghosts again?"

"My family," Birdie said. "Three of them this time. Mére, Pére, and my late brother Louis."

"Late for what?" the ghost boy asked with a laugh that made him fade away.

"Everyone enjoyed the party today, dear," Henry nodded and raised his voice so the ghosts could hear him. "Today was one of your best. It puts Mére Elise's dinners to shame. Your food was better. The table was prettier. And the guests had more fun."

"Hush," Birdie said. "I just got rid of them. Do you want them to keep me up all night?"

"Go to bed, dear," Henry said and waved her from the kitchen. Then he dunked the mop into the bucket, wrung it out in his bare hands, and began to wipe down the linoleum floor.

Chapter Eight

For once Dominic and Hank didn't have to sneak into Wrigley Field. Dominic had talked Alderman Donnelly into giving him two tickets for the upper deck. And once the boys made it through the gate, there was no law that said they had to sit in those seats for the whole game. Wrigley Field was a great place for exploration, and Dominic knew every corner of the ballpark including the passageways that would bring them close to the players on both teams.

"You want Colby Malone's autograph?" Dominic asked Hank. "Well, I'll get you Colby Malone's autograph."

"That's what I want," Hank said and gripped the top of his hat. "I've got his baseball card inside my cap."

"Well, don't get it all greasy with pomade."

"We don't waste our money on pomade!" Hank lifted his cap and pulled the card down so he could look at it. He studied the square-jawed photo and read the name "Colby Ronald Malone" beneath it, then waved the card in front of Dominic's eyes. "See, it's like new. Besides, Dad says pomade makes you look like a grease ball, anyway. Like one of those Dago wise guys."

"Watch your mouth!" Dominic said. "I'm half Italian, you know."

"Come on, they're hitting batting practice already. I hope we don't miss Colby."

The boys pushed through the turnstiles into the dim space inside the stadium. The ballpark had an incomplete look, like the underside of the L, with gaps where the light shined through the upper deck.

Immediately Hank smelled popcorn and hot dogs, and he felt a knot in his stomach. He hadn't eaten anything since the toast and coffee his mother had given him for breakfast. "That smells good," he called out to Dominic. "Let's eat!"

"Let's get our autographs first. There's plenty of time to eat."

When they walked up the ramp and through the portal behind home plate, the vibrant green field came into view. Under the open blue sky, the ballpark's heightened colors were thrilling to Hank, better than fireworks. For batting practice the pitcher had a bushel basket of baseballs next to the mound, and his fresh white uniform was so bright his movement from the stretch could have been a flame at the center of the diamond. The pitcher let go of an easy fast ball, and the batter cracked it into center, where the fielder stood right under the ball and made an easy catch between his open hand and stubby mitt. Scanning the field, Hank counted five outfielders, so no one needed to run very far to snag a fly or retrieve a grounder.

"What are you staring at?" Dominic asked him. "If we want Colby's autograph, we need to find him before it's his turn at bat."

Before he let Dominic pull him back under the grandstands, Hank looked around the ballpark to see how many people were there. He guessed Wrigley Field was more than half full that afternoon, over 20,000 people. Not bad for a Tuesday. The men wore light colored suits with straw Panamas or gray or tan fedoras, and the women wore loose summer dresses and hats with wide rims and fake flowers. It was a warm day, but there was a nice breeze coming off the Lake, which meant that no one but Colby Malone would be able to hit a homer today.

Back in the darkness below the stadium, Dominic led Hank past the concession stands and the souvenir kiosks around to the left-field side, about even with the Cubs' dugout. Then Dominic turned to his left, toward the outside of the park, to an unmarked door that looked like it belonged to a broom closet. He tested the doorknob and found it unlocked.

"Okay, Hank," he whispered, "when I count to three, I'm going to open this door, and we're going through it as fast as we can. Got it?"

"We're going in there? A closet?"

Dominic pulled open the door, tugged Hank ahead of him, and shut the door after them. To Hank's surprise, it wasn't totally dark in the small space they shared. Light came from below, and Hank saw that they were at the top of a staircase that would bring them down to the field.

"Geez, Dom! How did you know?"

"Shut up," his friend hissed. "We don't want to get thrown outa here before we get his autograph."

The brick staircase was so steep Hank had to hold onto the metal handrail as he followed Dominic's slow descent. When they reached the bottom, they stood at one end of a narrow hallway that was interrupted by a shaft of light coming through a doorway. And in the brightness only a few yards away, they saw Colby Malone standing very close to a lady in a yellow dress and a small white hat.

Then the baseball star leaned down to kiss the woman on the mouth and squeezed her bottom with both hands. As Dominic held his hand over his mouth to keep from laughing, Hank had a feeling that made him dizzy. He recognized this woman. And as she broke off the kiss and turned her face into the light, he was sure it was his mother.

Hank dropped his baseball card to the floor, and off balance he hurried up the stairs, gripping the steps with his hands to keep from falling backwards. Back in the hallway beneath the upper deck, Hank felt his heart race with confusion. His Ma had said she had seen Colby at the Top Hat Club, but this was something else! How could she let him kiss her and touch her that way? It wasn't just a friendly kiss; it was like the way she kissed his dad. But why would the best player on the Cubs want to kiss his mother? It didn't make sense. So maybe it wasn't his mom, after all. There must be a hundred ladies in Chicago with the same dark hair and the same dress who are the same height as his mother. But he knew his own mother, and she had been standing right in front of him. There was no mistake. That was his mother kissing Colby Malone!

He sat on the floor and leaned against a steel pillar. People were still coming into the ballpark, hurrying to find their seats before the opening pitch, but Hank didn't even want to see the game now. Why did he want to watch the jerk who had just touched his mother that way? And she had skipped work to come here! What if she loses her job? He couldn't go home now, either. What would he say to her? And what would his dad do if he found out? He'd probably punch her even harder than before.

"Hey, Hank!" Dominic's voice scolded him, and the older boy loomed overhead. "What's wrong with you? I practically get you into the Cubs' clubhouse, face to face with Colby Malone, and you run away! What gives? Are you some kind of chicken?"

"I'm not a chicken!"

"Then why did you run away?"

"Did you see his girlfriend?"

"Yeah, I saw her. So what? You're scared of girls now?"

"Did you recognize her?"

"I only looked at her legs," Dominic said. "She left as soon as you did."

"Weren't you embarrassed?"

"Why? All them ball players have girlfriends. It comes with the territory. Why do you think they want to be in the major leagues? To play baseball? Nuts! They're in it for the women. A great center fielder can get all the tail he wants."

"Thanks for telling me," Hank smiled, relieved that Dominic hadn't recognized his mother. Maybe she didn't see me, Hank thought. And outside the neighborhood, she probably didn't recognize Dom, either, if we're lucky, anyway. "I guess we should be practicing our game."

"I'll never be good enough," Dominic conceded. "My talents lie elsewhere. That's what my Ma says."

"Did you get the autographs?"

"Yes, I did, numb-nuts. I should charge you a dollar for yours, though. You dropped your card on the cement."

"What did he write?" Hank asked.

"His name! He wrote his name. What do you think an autograph is?"

"Did you get him to write 'To Dominic' or 'To Hank'?"

"If you wanted something fancy, you shouldn't have run away like a scared cat."

"It would make it more personal if he had written our names, too."

"Well, he was in a hurry, Hank. It was his turn to hit batting practice."

"He didn't look like he was in a hurry to me," Hank said and thought of the star's hands squeezing his mother's behind. For such a strong man, he had really short fingers.

"Well, he left in a hurry… Come on. Let's see what's going on. They're playing the national anthem."

A brass band on the left-field line played the Star Spangled Banner, and everyone in the stadium stood to sing the words. It was all a blur to Hank, the bright light, the sound of the band, and the off-key voices. He was not sure any of this was real. He hoped the whole day was a bad dream, and he wished he would wake up from it soon.

Albertine took her place behind the Cubs' dugout, in a row of empty seats. It was a great spot to watch the game, but it was in the direct sunlight. How would she explain a sunburn to Hendrik? There wasn't even a window in the switchboard room at Swanson's Tea & Coffee. But there was nothing she could do about the sun now, so she might as well enjoy the game, drink a beer, buy some Cracker Jack and get a prize.

When the players trotted out for the first inning, Colby ran backwards into center field and tipped his hat to her. She stood and waved back to him with both hands. Then she called to the beer man and waved to the kid with the Cracker Jacks, who was right behind him.

The Cubs were playing the Boston Braves today, a scrappy, base-running team, which could make a pretty boring afternoon for the Chicago outfielders. The leadoff batter bunted the first pitch and beat out the throw by one step. Then the runner stole second while the pitcher, Guy Bush, took his time with his delivery and Hartnett, the catcher, didn't even try to throw him out. The second batter hit a chopper to the first base side that bounded high and pulled Charlie Grimm off the bag. They got the kid out, but the runner advanced to third without even having to slide. The next hitter, instead of swinging away, laid a slow bunt down the first base line, luring Hartnett away from the plate, and Bush away from covering it, too, so the man scored from third and the Cubs had to settle for the easy out. "Death by a thousand cuts!" Albertine hissed and took a sip of beer from her paper cup. They were smart not to hand out the bottles, Albertine thought. We'd be throwing them at the Bostons just to see how brave they are!

The fifth batter cracked one into the gap between right and center, and Colby put the speed on, pumping his short legs like a miniature locomotive. "Get it, Colby!" she called out along with 20,000 others. The ball looked like it was going to fall in for a single, but Colby snagged it just above his ankle to retire the side.

"That's my Colby!" Albertine cheered and hoped the Cubs would tie it up in the bottom of the inning.

The band in left field played "Ain't We Got Fun" as Ed Brandt warmed up for the Braves and their fielders shot their practice ball around the infield like a big white bullet.

Albertine went to work on her Cracker Jack box, turning it upside down to peel off the foil and cardboard to get to the prize right away. There it was, a shiny little whistle on a red ribbon. She held the box between her knees to keep it from spilling, put the whistle to her lips, and blew. It had a strong, sweet sound, and the little ball inside it rattled nicely. Hank would have fun with it. As she blew the whistle a second time, a shadow passed over her, and she turned to see a woman in a flower-print dress and a floppy hat sit down just one seat away. Albertine quickly snapped the whistle into her pocket book and smiled uncomfortably to greet her new neighbor. "Hello," she said. "It's a nice day for a ball game."

"It shore is!" the woman said and although Albertine could tell she wasn't from Chicago, she looked familiar. The woman was very pregnant, clearly uncomfortable in the wooden seat. A big-boned girl to begin with, she had gained too much weight during her pregnancy, and it showed on her chubby arms and her ankles that made her silk stockings bulge out like balloons. By the size and position of her straining belly, Albertine guessed she had already passed her due date. What in hell was she doing at the ballpark all by herself? Albertine moved a seat closer to speak with her. "Would you like some Cracker Jack?" she asked her. "All I wanted was the prize."

"Sure, thanks! As you kin see, I'm eating for two."

"When are you due, honey?" Albertine asked, imitating her mother.

"Any day now, I guess," she said. "The doctor's not sure."

"Do you have other kids?"

"No, no, no!" she shook her head and laughed. "This is our first."

"I hope you're not planning to sit out here for the whole game," Albertine said and looked into the woman's smiling face. She was clearly a country girl, with big, widely spaced teeth, a few freckles and blond hair hanging down on her forehead. But her hat was a nice one, and her dress was expensive and new.

"Why shouldn't I stay for the whole game?"

"You look so uncomfortable," Albertine said, "and you'll get a sunburn."

"The sun will drop behind the stands by the fourth inning," she predicted. "I'll do just fine!"

"You must be one of those devoted Cubs fans!" Albertine laughed and touched her shoulder.

"You could say that," the pregnant girl smiled and nodded. "Have you ever heard of a ball player named Colby Malone?"

"Of course, we're…"

"He's my husband."

"Your husband!" Albertine echoed and knew she was the woman in the photo beside Colby's bed, quite a bit heavier now, but the same person. "Gee, what's it like to be married to such a big star?"

"Everybody asks me that!" she shook her head. "Flora, what's it like being married to the best hitter in the National League? Well, it's really not that great! I hardly see Colby more than half the year. I spend most of baseball season with my mother down in Morgantown."

"Morgantown? Where's that?"

"West Virginia. That's where we're from. Colby was playing semi-pro ball down there when the Pittsburgh scouts saw him hit four home runs in the same game. The rest is history."

"You don't like it here in Chicago?"

"I don't know anyone here," Flora told her. "All my folks are down in Morgantown. What would I do by myself while Colby's on the road? And when the team's in town, he's busy all the time, anyways."

"But you're here today."

"I couldn't help it," Flora said. "I just had to surprise him! I'll go home next week to have the baby."

"Good for you," Albertine said. "Don't let him forget you."

"That's what my Momma tells me!" Flora laughed. "By the way, my name is Flora Malone."

Flora held out her hand and as Albertine shook it, she noticed it was cold and clammy. "I'm Alice Carpentier."

"Nice to meet you, Alice."

As the two women talked, the Braves put out the Cubs' first three batters in order, and the home team took the field again. Flora stood to wave to her husband, as Albertine kept her seat, trying not to call attention to herself. Colby back-pedaled into center field and turned to wave to his girl, and he was surprised to see which girl was waving back to him. Recognizing Flora, he tripped, fell to one knee, and then turned to run to his position.

To Dom and Hank, a ticket to Wrigley Field meant nine innings of wandering around the ballpark to watch the game from every possible perspective.

As the first inning began, they were looking through the screen in deep right field on a walkway just beyond the seats. They could see the backs of the fielders and the pitcher, and the shapes of the batter, catcher and umpire in the distance. How can they hit the ball all the way out here? Hank wondered. When he played stick ball, he could barely hit it across the alley. The Braves weren't trying to hit it very far, though. The lead off player bunted.

"Bunting should be illegal," Dominic complained. "It's sneaky. They trick you to get on base."

"Yeah," Hank agreed. "Why don't they just smack it?"

"Have you ever seen Colby Malone try to bunt it? He's too much of a man to do that. He doesn't have to trick anyone."

Hank looked out at center field to the baseball star. Colby Malone was shorter than the other outfielders (Kiki Cuyler in left, Babe Herman in right), but he had a lot more muscle. He wasn't just standing there, either. He was moving constantly. He'd run in place for a few steps, or stretch his arms high over his head, or take off his cap and wipe his forehead with the back of his hand, or make a pretend throw to the plate with an imaginary ball. The Braves' running game made him restless. Hank thought about what Dominic said, that Colby never tricked anyone, and he decided that Dom was wrong. Maybe Colby never tricked anyone on the ball field, but he did play tricks with peoples' feelings. Why was he kissing my Ma? Hank wondered. What would dad do about it if he knew? There would be a big fight, and Hank didn't want to be around to see or hear it.

"Dom," Hank asked him, "did she remind you of my Ma?"

"Did who remind me of your Ma?"

"The lady who was kissing Colby Malone."

"I told ya I only looked at her legs…They were okay, but nothing to write home about."

"I think she looked like my Ma."

"Geez, what a goof ball! Is that why you ran away?"

"Maybe."

"Come on, Hank! Why would a star like Colby Malone want to kiss anyone's mother, let alone your mother! That's disgusting."

"My mother's not disgusting!"

"But a ball player kissing her? That's nuts, Hank. You've got to be out of your mind."

"I guess you're right…But even her clothes were the same."

"Hank, it's 1934. Most clothes are manufactured now. You know what 'manufactured' means? They have factories where women who just got off the boat sew hundreds of the same dresses all day long."

"How do you know that?"

"My sister works at one of those factories. On Halsted Street."

"She's not right off the boat."

"No. But most of the girls are. The point is, lots of people wear the same clothes. That broad was wearing a yellow dress. Your Ma has a yellow dress. That don't make them the same person. It's a coincidence."

"I think I know my own mother."

"You saw her for five seconds!" Dominic scolded him then pointed to the field. "Look out! That's gonna be a hit!"

The line drive shot out into the gap between right and center, but Colby Malone was sprinting toward it with quick, short strides. He scooped the ball out of the air just before it hit the grass.

"He's out!" Dominic yelled. "He's outa there!" He laughed, slapped Hank on the back, and said, "Let's move!"

Albertine studied Flora very carefully. She was nearly twice Albertine's weight, with the baby, those chubby arms, thick ankles and broad hips that barely fit into the seat. She did have pretty features, and even under the hat, Albertine could see that she had loads of thick, golden hair. But the expensive dress, the diamond ring, and the golden locket around her neck, none of that could make Flora anything more than just an ordinary country girl. Why did Colby have to be chained to such a plain and boring woman? No wonder he hadn't breathed a word to her about the baby. He probably didn't want her to know that he was caught in such a miserable trap.

"How are you feeling, dear?" Albertine asked her.

Flora was waving with both hands to the outfield, trying to get Colby's attention. He tipped his hat to her, then crouched low and pounded his mitt to bring himself back into the game.

"Oh, me?" Flora yawned. "I feel a little sleepy, and my back aches pretty bad. Must be this hard chair."

"Want something to drink?"

"No thanks. I'll just eat these Cracker Jacks, if you don't mind sharing."

"They're all yours," Albertine giggled. "I've already got my prize."

"Do you have any children, Alice?" Flora asked her.

"Yes. My son Hank is ten years old."

"I've wanted a kid for a long, long time," Flora said. "I've felt a big hole right in the center of my life because I've wanted a baby so bad. Colby doesn't understand how I feel. Once this child is born, we'll have us a family. Even when he's traveling on the road, I will have a part of him with me always." Then she stuffed a handful of Cracker Jack into her mouth and chewed it noisily.

"That's very sweet, Flora," Albertine replied, but thought that getting pregnant was a trick Flora had played to hold onto Colby. What other reason would he have to stay with a cow like her?

Albertine looked down on the field and could see that the Braves already had men on first and second. How had this happened? Elbie Fletcher was up, a left hander, choking up on his bat and slashing it across the plate as if he were chopping down a tree. Guy Bush pitched from the stretch and the runners sprinted down the base paths. Fletcher cracked the high fast ball and sent a wobbly pop fly into short center field. A great chance for a double play, Albertine thought, but Colby reacted too late and had to sprint to reach the ball, and when he got to it, the baseball ricocheted off the heel of his glove and dribbled into center behind him. Two runs scored and Fletcher ended up on third. The crowd actually booed Colby, the way they had yelled after he'd lost the ball in the sun and dropped an easy fly during the '29 World Series against Detroit. Albertine could see his anger by the way he ground his fist into the pocket of his mitt, and the way he scraped the outfield turf with his spikes, like a bull getting ready to charge.

"It's okay, Sweetheart," Flora called to him. "You'll get them next time!" Then she ate the rest of the Cracker Jacks and tossed the box under her seat.

The boys had worked their way into the upper deck, right behind home plate and had parked themselves in some unclaimed seats just four rows back from the rail.

"Ain't this the life, Hankie-boy?" Dominic asked him, as he tore a hot dog in two and gave half to his friend. "Sitting behind home plate like a coupla capitalists. Only thing we don't got are a couple of Bernie Melrose's big fat cigars."

It only took Hank a few seconds to eat his share of the hot dog. His mother had fed him a slice of toast with sugar on it before she'd left the apartment that morning, telling him she was going to work. He felt as if he could eat two more hot dogs by himself.

"Dominic, do you have any money left?" he asked. "I'm still hungry."

"That broke the bank for me," Dominic said. "Hey watch! Colby's up."

Hank looked down and saw Colby swing three bats together in the on-deck circle, pounding the air as if he wanted to kill someone. His hat was cockeyed, too, and as he dropped the two extra bats he turned to the mound and glared at Big Ed Brandt, the pitcher. Before he entered the batter's box, Colby kicked up a cloud of dirt that reached over the plate, then spat into each of his hands in turn and gripped the bat at the very end of its handle. The papers said he never used anything lighter than a 50-ounce bat.

The first pitch was a curve and Hank could see the ball dodge low past Colby's ankles, but he swung level and hard anyway and the bat's momentum nearly pulled him off his feet.

"Stee-rike!" the umpire cried, and Colby kicked more dirt onto the plate.

The umpire raised his arms to call time out and lifted his mask to tell Colby to "quit it with the dirt." Then the ump took out his whisk broom to clear home base. In a few seconds, the umpire was bent low behind Shanty Hogan the catcher, awaiting the pitch from Brandt.

Hank noticed that Big Ed had an extremely high kick – he brought his spikes up to his teeth – and his left arm whipped over his shoulder like a catapult. The ball flew so fast it was a blur to Hank, and it made the catcher's mitt jump back when Colby's bat made another full circle to bruise his right shoulder blade.

"Stee-rike two!"

Colby backed out again, kicked dirt away from the plate this time, and looked toward the crowd behind the Cubs' dugout on the third base side. He spat into the dirt, straightened his cap, hitched up his belt, turned and stepped into the batter's box, closer to the plate than usual.

Brandt read the signals from his catcher and shook off two calls before he nodded, swung his mitt and the ball to his chest, then performed his exaggerated windup and threw the ball so hard that he stumbled down the front of the mound.

Colby connected with this pitch and hit it with all his frustration and power. From the sound of his bat, everyone in Wrigley Field knew he had nailed it, and from the hollow crunch that echoed it, they knew the line drive had smashed into Ed Brandt's face.

"Holy crap!" Dominic said, and both boys ran down to the rail to get a better look. "I bet he killed him!"

The pitcher lay on his back, his bare head on the slope of the mound. He'd been flipped completely like a pancake by the force of Colby's drive. Forgetting the game, Colby was the first man to reach the pitcher, and he knelt on the grass trying to revive him as a thin trail of blood dripped from the left side of Brandt's mouth. The infielders hurried in, tugged Colby away from their man, and the Braves' manager McKechnie appeared as if from nowhere. All eyes were on the unconscious pitcher until Colby turned to face Hogan the catcher, who held the ball between his thumb and forefinger. He tagged Colby lightly on the Cubs' logo above his heart.

"You're out!" the umpire called and stroked his fist with its pointed, judgmental thumb. No one had remembered to call time out.

Behind the dugout, Flora was standing to ease the pressure on her back when her husband's furious liner nearly killed the Braves' pitcher.

"Oh, my God!" Flora cried as she saw Brandt fly backwards as if he'd been shot. "Oh, my dear sweet Lord!" She brought her hands down quickly to brace her abdomen and then she began to cry. Albertine heard a trickling sound and looked down to see that Flora was standing in a growing pool of water.

"Oh, I hope that man is all right," Flora moaned. "I hope Colby didn't kill him!"

"Don't worry," Albertine consoled her. "No one dies in baseball. It's against the rules."

"And wouldn't you know it!" Flora sobbed. "I've wet myself. I've peed my pants!"

"You haven't wet yourself, Flora," Albertine assured her. "Your water just broke."

"My water broke?"

"You're in labor. The baby is on his way."

"It can't be. Not here. Not now. Not at the ballpark."

"You'd better go down and lean over the dugout to tell your husband," Albertine told her. "He'll want to get you to the hospital."

"I can't do that! He just found out I came to town."

"You said you wanted to surprise him."

"I did. But not like this! My dress is soaked."

"You want me to go tell him?" Albertine asked, but hoped Flora would say no.

"You can't do that, Alice! Colby doesn't know you. He'll think you're playing a joke."

"You're right here, for Chrissakes! All he has to do is look at you, and he'll know it's not a joke."

"He's got a game to play, Alice. They're already losing four to nothing."

"Gabby Hartnett will let him leave the game to take care of you!"

"How long will it take? How long before the baby's born?" Flora asked with a pleading tone.

"For a first baby, eight hours of labor at least. Maybe twelve. I think yours started with that back ache."

"So can't you get me to the hospital first, then call the clubhouse to tell Colby I'm there?" Flora asked her. "The game will be over before the baby is born."

"Do you have a doctor here? A hospital that's expecting you?"

"No. What would I need a doctor for? I thought I'd be back in Morgantown with my mother when the baby got here."

"Well, you're sure in a pickle then, aren't you, Flora?" Albertine said and sighed dismissively, which made Flora cry again, even louder. People in nearby seats stared at them, and whispered to each other. Standing, the two women blocked their view. For a moment Albertine wanted to make Flora even more miserable. Flora was Colby's wife, and in a few hours she would bear Colby's child, and they would surely be drawn closer together. What chance did Albertine have of seeing Colby after he had started his family? And Flora was so fat and clumsy, so unsuitable for the great Colby Malone! He deserved someone beautiful, someone graceful, someone with musical talent, and not some tubby backwoods girl who was too stupid to stay home when she was nine months pregnant. But Albertine knew Colby, so she understood that he would never desert his wife now that they were having a child. And she saw how frightened Flora was, and it was clear that Flora had no idea what she should do next. So her fate was up to Albertine, the last person Flora should be trusting to help her.

"Oh, Alice, what am I going to do? My Momma told me not to take the train to Chicago, but I couldn't stop myself, you see. I missed Colby too much! I'm a fool for love, I always have been. Oh, what am I going to do?"

"My God, Flora, why are you asking me?" Albertine cried and thought: I'm an even bigger fool than you!

"You're the only one I know here!" Flora sobbed.

"No, I'm not, goddamnit!" Albertine hissed. "No, I'm not. You sit down and wait right here!"

Albertine nearly shoved Flora down into her ballpark seat, hurried to the aisle, then clattered down the three rows toward the dugout wall.

While the Braves' trainer worked to revive Ed Brandt, Hank and Dominic climbed to the top row of the upper deck to walk along the vacant bench seats and get a bird's eye view of the field and the neighborhood around the ballpark.

"How high are we, Dominic?" Hank asked, feeling slightly dizzy as he looked down the steep grandstands to the sharp drop off the lip of the upper deck.

"I dunno," Dominic said and looked through the screen behind him, straight down to the street. "Over a hundred feet, I guess. Way taller than any tree. Twice as high as an L platform."

"Colby's not himself today," Hank said. "First he dropped an easy fly, and now he nails the pitcher and gets tagged out to boot. I think it's because of my Mom. She recognized me and told him I was here."

"You're crazy, kid," Dominic said as he walked along the stadium's rim toward the right field side. "That wasn't your Mom. It was just a bimbo…or maybe it was his wife. Did you ever think of that?"

"It wasn't his wife," Hank said. "Nobody does that to his wife. Not in public."

"They weren't in public," Dominic said. "They were behind the scenes. You think your parents act the same way when you're not looking?"

"The same way as what?"

"As when you <u>see</u> them, numb nuts! At dinner or in church. What do you think they do in their bedroom together? Shake hands?"

"Don't they sleep?" Hank asked his friend.

"Jesus, Hank, don't you know anything?"

Then the boys heard the applause from the crowd, and they peered down to the distant field to see two coaches slowly escorting the dazed pitcher toward the Boston dugout. Hank saw a player standing stock still between home plate and the pitcher's mound. Was it Colby? From so high up, Hank couldn't tell. But why was he just standing there? Hank heard an airplane buzzing out over Lake Michigan and he looked up to the sky and spotted the yellow double-winger before it disappeared into a cloud. When he turned back to the field, a new pitcher was warming up and Colby was nowhere to be seen.

As Albertine reached the wall, the crowd at Wrigley cheered and applauded. In front of the mound, Ed Brandt was on his feet, being guided off the field by two coaches from the Braves. He was slouched over and stumbling, staring at the grass below his feet. Albertine looked down to her right to search for Colby in the dugout, but then she realized that he must still be out on the field. She turned to see him standing in front of home plate, staring at Brandt as he limped to the visitors' locker room. Colby shook his head abruptly, as if to wake himself from a nightmare, then trotted toward the dugout.

"Hey, Colby!" Albertine called to him. "Colby! Your wife's in labor!"

Colby looked up, saw her, and ran close to the wall so he could hear her. "Al, what is it?"

"Your wife is in labor. Get up here and take of her."

"What?"

"You heard me. Flora is having a baby! Get up here. Now."

Colby backed up about 20 yards from the wall and took a running start so that when he jumped his head and arms were atop the bricks, and he easily swung his feet over the edge to land in the aisle next to Albertine.

"Where is she" he demanded, with a desperate look on his face. He barely noticed Albertine; she could have been a stranger, just another baseball fan.

Breathless, Albertine ran up the stairs to the third row and pointed to Flora, who had turned toward Colby and had raised her arms to greet him. She had tears in her eyes and could not lift herself from her seat.

"Flora!" Colby hurried down the row to his wife, and when Albertine paused in the aisle, the batboy squeezed past her to follow him. He must have climbed into the stands to help the star center fielder.

So Flora would be taken care of, and Albertine didn't have to stick around to make sure she and the baby would be okay. They were Colby's problem now. He had married Flora and had decided to stay with her. So Colby was stuck with her and their child. They might live happily ever after, if they were lucky. They might have more kids, a house with a yard, a long and loving marriage… Albertine tried not to care, but she couldn't help crying as she made her way up the aisle and through the stadium to the streetcar stop. If only they had met earlier, in a different time and place, it might have been Albertine who was with Colby; that baby might have been hers. She and Colby would have been just right for each other, for a while, anyway.

Chapter Nine

At the Marigold Gardens arena, a cloud of cigar smoke hovered over the ring, making a yellow fog in the shaft of light over the canvas. The standing room crowd was loud and restless because the two boxers, instead of fighting full tilt, had seemed to avoid each other for the first two rounds of the fight.

Monty Matheson came out of his corner for the third round and met a flurry of punches from the red gloves of Dutch "The Windmill" Hanson. For the first two rounds, Monty had managed to keep away from Dutch's powerful combinations by circling, parrying and ducking. He hadn't been hurt by any of the stuff that hit him, but he had landed only two good punches on Hanson so far. Monty had to get closer to score, dancing around wouldn't do any damage to the Windmill, and it wouldn't tire him out, either. After round two, when he had returned to his corner, his coach, Mac McMurtry shouted in his ear, "When the fuck are you going to start the fight?"

So now in the first five seconds of round three, Monty walked into a quick succession of left jabs and straight rights, so fast and so hard that they knocked his own left glove back into his face and flattened his nose. Geez, Hanson's trainer must have told him the same thing!

Monty circled to his right, made Dutch think he was going to land a right uppercut, then let loose a left hook that hit him squarely on the eye and snapped his head back. Then Monty stepped closer, punching the whole time, playing the Windmill's own game, driving him back against the ropes. But somehow Hanson found an opening and pounded one into Monty's jaw. It made his ears ring, so he raised his gloves to his face and backed off.

From the fourth row, Albertine called out, "Stick it to him Monty! Nail him!" Just as the crowd reacted to his retreat with a chorus of boos.

"Why are they booing?" Claribel asked.

"The crowd paid to see a fight," Hendrik explained. "Anyway, he can't let up or Hanson will kill him."

Monty was as lean and graceful as a track star, a man who could work a punching bag until it was invisible and skip rope for hours without breaking a sweat. Dutch Hanson was a square block of muscle whose fists dealt swift punishment and crushing pain. His thick shoulders glistened with sweat, and he kept his chin down low against his collar bone as if he was about to knock his head through a door. Monty circled fluidly, taking four steps for every one of Hanson's, but his punches didn't seem to have any effect on the Windmill. Even when he had him on the ropes, his punches could have been drops of rain.

"I don't think I can watch any more," Claribel said. "That guy wants to hurt Monty!"

"Well, Monty better hurt him!" Hendrik laughed. "That's why they call it a fight, Clare. They are supposed to hurt each other."

"Well, I don't like it!" Claribel moaned.

"Just shut up, will you?" Albertine scolded her. "You'll spoil it for everyone else!"

But the way the crowd was screaming, she and Hendrik were the only ones who could possibly have heard Clare's concerns. The Gardens were full of 2,000 people, and the roar was overwhelming. Contained by the roof, the noise seemed much louder than any crowd at Wrigley Field.

Hanson gave Monty a determined pursuit, lowering his shoulder, plodding ahead, driving heavy punches toward Monty's stomach, head and chest. Monty was able to knock most of the shots away, but he took a hard one in the ribs before he wheeled to the right and landed a left jab on Hanson's stomach and a right cross to the side of his head. Hanson staggered then, and when Monty came closer, trying to land a series on Dutch's body, Hanson fell into him and hugged him in a clinch. Then he banged Monty's temple with the sharp edge of his head and rubbed the laces of his glove over Monty's eyes.

"Break clean! Break clean!" the referee called to the fighters and reached in to pull them apart. As they separated, Hanson landed a merciless right uppercut to Monty's diaphragm, and Monty's mouthpiece shot out onto the canvas. On reflex, Monty brought a fist down hard on top of Hanson's head, but the stocky fighter took advantage of the opening and pounded Monty's ribs with three hard blows. In another ten seconds, Hanson might have finished him off, but the bell rang to end the round, and Dutch's late right scored a glancing blow on Monty's nose, so blood sprayed over his face. The crowd roared for more blood, even as the fighters retreated to their corners.

"Poor Monty," Claribel said. "He's hurt. His nose is bleeding!"

"That's the least of his problems," Albertine said. "He has to keep that sonofabitch away from his body."

With a word from Alderman Donnelly, Dominic's cousin Brian had gotten a job as an usher at Marigold Gardens. His arm, which had been broken in the rail yard explosion, was still in a cast, but the burns on his face and scalp weren't so raw and ghastly any more. Dressed like a bellhop at the Parker House, he let Dominic and Hank through a door on the loading dock so they could crowd in the aisle with the standing room spectators to see the fights from the balcony. "Not the best view," Brian admitted, "but beggars can't be choosers."

"Don't worry, Bri," Dominic assured him. "We'll work things out."

"Come on, Dominic! Stay put, will ya? If somebody decides to throw you out on your ear, I can't help you! Stay up here in the rafters and enjoy the fights."

"We get the message," Dominic said, and Hank could tell that Dom still hadn't made up his mind not to look for a better spot. "Thanks for getting us in."

By the time the boys worked their way to places on either side of a pillar where they could get unobstructed views of the ring, the first round was already half over. They saw Hanson charging with his head down and fists swinging and Matheson skipping around him, dodging his punches, throwing his own jabs that barely made any impact on the square, steady fighter.

"I hope the Dutchman cleans his clock," Dominic said. "I hope they carry Monty outa here on a stretcher."

"Why do you say that, Dominic?" Hank asked in surprise. "Monty came to my grandpa's house. My Aunt Claribel is his girlfriend. He ate dinner with us. And that includes you, Dom!"

"Did you forget what he did to me?" Dominic demanded. "He practically popped my ear drums. After he hit me, I couldn't hear for two days."

"You asked for it!"

"And besides, everyone expects him to lose, anyway. The line at Melrose's barber shop is four to one in favor of Hanson."

"People bet on boxing?"

"Geez, Hank! People bet on everything. Where have you been?"

"I've been following you."

"All right, then. I'll bet you a quarter that Hanson cleans his clock."

"I don't have a quarter."

"How much ya got?"

"A nickel," Hank said, mentally holding back the other nickel, for his streetcar ride home.

"Okay, I'll bet you five cents that Hanson beats Matheson tonight."

"Okay, it's a bet."

"Geez, Kinderman! It sure is easy to take your money."

During the break before the fourth round, Tino Traficante and Nick Capoletti walked down the aisle to say hello to Albertine and Hendrik. They came to the fights dressed the way they might have been for Easter Mass or a wedding, in their best, shiny chalk-striped suits with silk ties and matching handkerchiefs. They had new haircuts, too, and their narrow moustaches were carefully trimmed. The only disturbing aspect was the white bandage that encased Nick's right ear.

"Hiya, Sweetheart," Tino said to Albertine, and then reached over to shake Hendrik's hand. "And how's Chicago's best sax player?"

"Never been better," Hendrik said and extended his left hand to grip Tino's right.

"I guess nobody's at the Top Hat tonight," Tino laughed.

"Everybody's here!" Nick echoed.

"Larry's there," Albertine said. "He's playing with the house band."

"They could always use another banjo!" Tino laughed again.

"Guitar," Albertine corrected him. "Rhythm guitar."

"And who's your lovely young friend?" Nick asked and leered past Hendrik to Claribel.

"My sister Clare. She's dating Monty Matheson."

"Too bad," Nick shook his head. "My bet says he only has one round to go."

"Don't jinx him!" Clare said.

Both Tino and Nick laughed derisively and slapped each other's shoulder. Then the bell rang and the fighters rose from their stools.

"Well. Gotta go. See ya at the club later, huh Al?" Tino said and waved to her as he went up the aisle back to his seat.

"Who are those guys?" Claribel asked.

"Hoodlums," Hendrik said. "Knee breakers."

"Stay away from them," Albertine told her sister. "They're a couple of small-time crooks who hang out at the Top Hat."

"Those guys mean trouble, Clare," Hendrik told her. "They have both been to prison."

Albertine would have explained that half the people who came to the Top Hat had gone through some trouble with the law, but the fight had resumed, and so had the roar of the crowd.

In the fourth round, Monty (with wads of cotton stuffed in his nostrils) changed his tactics. Instead of avoiding Dutch's punches, he seemed to run into them, taking blows to his chest and stomach for the chance of landing his own punches on Hanson's ears and jaw and forehead. Then Monty would sidestep to recover enough energy to go back for more. When the bell rang at the end of the round, Monty seemed exhausted, and Hanson stepped slowly back to his corner like a plodding machine.

"That hoodlum was wrong," Claribel said. "Monty's still in the fight."

"He needs to stay back from him," Hendrik told Claribel. "Hanson is stronger. His only chance is to go in quick and slide away."

"That's good," Claribel said, obviously encouraged. "That's just what he's doing."

Instead of watching the fight, Albertine turned to look at her husband. It was sweet of him to try to protect Claribel, first from the gangsters and now from her worry over Monty. Somehow his temper didn't seem such a big deal now. And handsome! He had a profile like a statue's, and his hair was thick, wavy and golden. His blue eyes seemed to concentrate the dim light that fell on the floor seats, which were in darkness compared to the shaft of spotlight on the ring. Hendrik was a handsome man, and a kind one, too. Why had she ever strayed from him? She felt a longing now to hold onto him, to make sure he didn't lose interest in her, even after the rumors he'd heard from that Negro singer. Maybe it was time to have another baby. It had certainly worked for Flora. Now Colby was a family man, home with his wife and child, while the rest of the Cubs were here in the first row watching the fights.

Albertine took Hendrik's hand, his damaged right one, and brought it to her lips and kissed it. When Hendrik looked at her, she winked. A warm feeling passed over her, and she was convinced that she could make him slow down and think about her, and only her, the next time they made love. She kissed his hand again and remembered how Flora had said she was a fool for love. But how foolish was she? She had managed to use that love to turn Colby into a family man and hold onto him for life.

Just beneath the rafters, Hank watched the fight proceed. Hanson was a steady boxer with slow footwork and fists that were hard to see because he threw them so quickly. He didn't seem to be bothered by the silent punches that Monty landed on his chest and shoulders as Matheson shuffled around him.

But Hank could hear the Windmill's punches from the upper tier. They hit Monty like a slamming door, and his body recoiled from them. Toward the end of the fifth round, Hanson trapped Monty against the ropes where his footwork was useless. Hank heard a dozen loud thuds to Monty's stomach and then a crack to his jaw. Monty fell forward and hugged the Dutchman, squeezing the Windmill's arms against Hanson's body so they would stop hurting him, even as Hanson thrust and butted with his head like a trapped animal, and worked his laces across Monty's face. The referee had just managed to pull them apart when the bell rang to end the round. Hanson was quicker to return to his corner, and Hank thought this was a bad sign.

"What did I tell ya?" Dominic said as he leaned around the pillar to shout in Hank's ear. "The guy is cleaning Monty's clock!"

"Nobody's won the fight yet," Hank reminded him.

"Your boy won't make it through the last round!"

After five rounds, the violence affected Claribel so much that she started to sob, then cry openly. Her moans were drowned out by the noise of the crowd, but both Hendrik and Albertine could sense that she was deeply upset.

Hendrik put his arm around her, but learned immediately that this was a mistake.

"Don't you touch me, Heinie Kinderman!"

"Sorry, I thought you were crying."

"Why didn't you tell me it would be like this?" Claribel demanded.

"Like what?"

"Like two men trying to murder each other!"

"It's only a fight," he said. "The blood will wash off."

"Hooo," she cried. "All you men! You're all alike! You're all brutes and liars!"

"That's not true," Hendrik insisted. "What about me?"

"You?"

"Well, What about your father, then?"

"Don't you talk about my father!"

Albertine tapped her husband's shoulder. "Let's trade places," she said. "I'll take it from here."

As Monty's trainer worked on him in the corner, Albertine sat next to her sister and lent her a hankie.

"I never knew it would be like this!" Claribel moaned. "It's so brutal. So mean."

"Come on, you baby. Get a hold of yourself!" Albertine scolded her, but held her hand gently, too. "You're the one who wanted to date a fighter, aren't you?"

Claribel nodded and wiped her nose. "Uh-huh."

"And didn't I warn you? Did I tell you how rough these people are?"

"You never said it would be like this!"

"Well, I couldn't describe it, Clare. You just had to see it for yourself!" Albertine shook her head in exasperation.

"Well, I've seen enough!"

"Not yet, you haven't. You're going to watch the rest of this fight. And win or lose, you're going to go down and wait for him outside the locker room so he knows that you're here."

"Al, I don't think I…"

The bell rang and the trainers pushed their fighters off their stools and into the ring for the final round. Hanson seemed to move even more slowly than before, like a bulldozer plodding forward to knock down a tree.

Monty's left side was hurt, so he moved lopsidedly, shuffling to the right, then back left, until the Windmill reached him and started punching. His blows pounded Monty's arms, handcuffing him so he could hardly return a punch. Then Hanson raised his aim and landed three quick punches on Monty's mouth so that his lower lip split and a stream of blood poured out. The crowd roared at the sight of blood, and half the audience jumped to their feet.

Monty spun away, throwing ineffective punches to make Dutch keep his distance, but the Windmill stepped in again with a left and a right and another left, all to Monty's face. His right eye swelled quickly in a purple balloon, but he managed to lower his shoulder and slam the Dutchman hard in the ribs so Hanson backed off and raised both fists to protect his face.

As he circled to his left, Monty turned his head and spat a mouthful of blood and mucus onto the canvas. (Albertine could see the thick, red clot in the ring.) Then Hanson stepped on the clot, and as he thrust a punch at Monty, he slipped backward and raised his head.

As if by instinct, Monty drove his right fist into the cleft of Hanson's chin. Instantly, the Windmill collapsed and he hit the floor face-down without trying to break his fall.

Monty staggered back to his corner as the surprised referee leaned over the Dutchman and counted slowly to ten. Hanson never moved a muscle.

In a few seconds, the referee was holding Monty's right arm straight up in the air, and the crowd was on its feet, screaming. The wrong fighter had won the bout, and most people in Marigold Gardens did not like it.

"Holy crap!" Dominic yelled. "What a lucky punch!"

Monty was already wearing his black satin robe, waving his gloves at the crowd, when Hanson's trainer finally revived him enough to lift him to his feet and prop him up as they left the ring. The crowd booed Hanson instead of cheering Monty. Apparently, Hank was one of the few people there who had bet on Matheson.

"Lucetti!" Hank yelled to Dominic. "Time to pay up. You owe me twenty cents."

"Twenty cents?" Dominic complained. "You bet me a nickel."

"You said yourself that the odds were four to one."

"I didn't give you no odds!" Dominic insisted.

"Then pay me my nickel now," Hank said and held out his palm. Dominic slapped the coin into his friend's hand, hoping to make it sting. But Hank just said, "I'll collect the rest later."

"Like hell you will!"

"Come on, Dominic. Let's go. I gotta be home before my Ma gets there."

"But we'll miss the heavyweights."

"So what?" Hank said. "We saw the fight we came for."

"Okay, okay, but only for you!" Dominic grumbled as they ducked through the crowd and headed for the stairway.

Hendrik went into the locker room to check on Monty while Albertine and Claribel waited on a bench under a yellow light bulb in the concrete passageway.

"Check on him, Hendrik," Claribel had called after him. "Make sure he's okay."

No crowd of reporters stood around the victor, no fight promoters vying to represent Monty Matheson. Instead, Monty lay face up and naked on a rub down table as his trainer and coach ministered to his wounds and bruises. It occurred to Hendrik that Monty looked nearly dead, with his arms hanging over the edge of the table, freed of gloves but still taped around wrists and knuckles. Both of his eyes were swollen shut, his nose was clogged with bloody cotton, and his lips were split in numerous places and still dripping with blood. His ribs and abdomen were marked with fist-sized bruises, purple and red and yellow. Only his legs had gone unscathed. Hendrik did not believe that Monty could ever be healed: the fight had maimed him for life.

"I told ya I'd win," Monty said to McMurtry, his coach. "Not many people gave me a chance against the Windmill, but I showed 'em."

"Lie still for a second, Champ," McMurtry said. "I think we may need to put a coupla stitches in that lip."

"Nah, just put ice on it," Monty shook his head. "I'll be okay."

"We need to save the ice for your eyes," McMurtry said. "Can you see yet?"

"Yeah, I can see," Monty told him. "Looks like we got a visitor." He waved his hand, wrapped in sweaty tape, toward Hendrik. "Hey, are you from the newspapers?"

The two grisly, sixty year-old trainers turned to look Hendrik over. In his brown, double-breasted suit and yellow necktie, he looked too fresh and young to be a reporter.

"He ain't no reporter. They're out front watching that colored fighter in the heavyweight match," McMurtry said and chuckled. "This guy probably just wants your autograph."

"I am Hendrik Kinderman. Claribel Fontaine is my wife's sister."

"You're Albertine's husband?"

"Yah. We have met before. We came with Clare to see your fight. Congratulations."

"Thanks."

"Shut up, kid," McMurtry said. "Leonard is going to stitch up your lip.

"Claribel is outside in the hall waiting for you," Hendrik said.

"That's nice," McMurtry waved to him. "Why don't you go out there and keep her company. We got about half an hour of work to put the kid back together. Then he'll be ready to see his sweetheart."

When Hendrik went back out into the hallway, Claribel rushed to him and grabbed his arm. "Where's Monty?" she asked frantically. "Is he all right?"

"He'll be fine," Hendrik said without meeting her eyes. "They're working on him a little more. He'll be out in a few minutes."

"Is he in pain?"

"Nothing serious," Hendrik lied. "When fighters win, they forget the pain."

"Brace yourself, honey," Albertine told her. "Monty took a beating tonight. He's going to look like hell."

"Well, I hope he's finished with boxing now," Claribel whispered. "Pa said that if he took a good beating, it might knock the fights right out of his system."

"Don't count on it, honey," Albertine warned her. "Men don't think the way we do. It takes them longer to figure out what's best for them."

"What do you think, Heinie?" Claribel asked him. "Do you think Monty has had enough of boxing?"

"Maybe he has had enough," Hendrik said and squeezed her shoulder. "But don't expect him to quit tonight. He probably won a hundred bucks for knocking out the Windmill."

They waited in the hallway for 45 minutes and listened to the echoes of the crowd as they cheered the heavyweight fight between Buck Everett and a young colored fighter named Joe Louis. That fight was in its eighth and final round when Monty emerged from the locker room, with his left eye still swollen shut in a purple and yellow lump and with thick black stitches down the center of his lower lip. He breathed shallowly, too, because of the bruises on his ribs.

Claribel moaned in pity as she stepped close to Monty, but then she pulled back before she hugged him. Would it hurt if she touched him?

"Oh, Monty!" she said. "Does it hurt a lot?"

"Geez," Monty said, tried to smile, but stopped when the stitches in his lip pulled and hurt him. "Ow! Man, I'm fine, Clare! It don't hurt that bad. You should see the other guy, I knocked him out, you know."

"I know, I know," Claribel said, "but you look like…"

"Like what?" Monty asked.

"Like you've been in a fight!" Albertine said and laughed, but Claribel glared back at her.

"Shut up, Al!" she said, and Hendrik took Albertine's hand and pulled her down the hallway.

"Let them talk," Hendrik told his wife. "They don't need us."

"She's my baby sister!"

"Let's give them some time to themselves," Hendrik insisted. "It's hard enough on Clare."

"You want to just leave her?"

"Let's just wait over here. But look the other way, Albertine. Don't stare."

Standing before Monty, Claribel held back her tears. "I had no idea it would be like that," she told him. "You'd get arrested if you fought like that in the street. It's assault. It's attempted murder."

"Not in the ring," Monty explained. "In the ring it's what's called a fair fight. With rules and a referee. A fighter can't get arrested even if he kills someone. We all sign a paper."

"That's just dreadful!" Claribel said. "Why do you want to hit anybody, Monty? You don't have to prove anything."

"I'm good at it, Clare. A couple more wins and I'll be fighting in Madison Square Garden."

"That man nearly killed you, Monty," she told him. "Look at you! If someone told me a streetcar ran over you, I'd believe them. And you only won because he slipped. You made one lucky punch!"

"Sometimes that's all it takes!" Monty laughed. "One lucky punch and the chump is out cold!"

"Okay, okay, you proved you can win," Claribel conceded. "So now you can quit while you're ahead. Promise me you'll stop fighting, Monty. Please stop before you get hurt even worse than tonight."

"Are you crazy? I just beat the toughest middleweight in Chicago. By a knockout."

"With a lucky punch!"

"Come on, Clare. You don't understand. I'm a boxer. This is my job. I can't quit now. I could get a shot at the title!"

"Well, I'm not going to watch you get killed, Monty! Make up your mind."

"My mind's made up," Monty said and smiled in a kind of dazed triumph. "My next fight's in two weeks. Right here."

"Then good night, Monty," Claribel said and broke down in tears. "Good night and good luck. I'll pray for you, but I'll probably never see you again." Clare wouldn't let Monty comfort her. Instead, she turned to her sister. As she and Albertine made their way out of the arena, Claribel was sorry that she had come to the fight to see Monty take such a beating and then act happy about it. The arena was hot and smoky, and just sitting there had made Clare feel dirty from head to toe. Now she wanted to forget about Monty and go home to take a long, hot bath.

Chapter Ten

There was something about Pearl's voice that fascinated Albertine and infuriated her. Pearl didn't have a pretty voice or a sweet one. Yes, she could carry a tune and was a pretty good alto singer. Sticking to the middle range as she sang, she might have been talking through her nose while trying to be heard in a crowd. Her voice wasn't exactly husky, but it sounded a little hoarse, as if she'd been smoking and shouting and laughing at a party late into the night before, and her vocal chords hadn't had time to recover from the strain. What made Albertine jealous of Pearl's singing was that it caught your attention and held it. You couldn't help listening to her, because the song had been paid for with some prior misery, so she trapped you with a captivating sadness. And this melancholy tone was a perfect match for Hendrik's saxophone, with its haunting sense of otherness and loss, its voice the voice of a stranger crying out to be understood. So when Pearl sang in front of Hendrik's five-piece combo, she was really just singing a duet with Hendrik, and that's what upset Albertine most of all.

Even from the back of the room, where she concealed herself at the worst table in the Starlight Club, Albertine could feel the chemistry between them. A cheery song like "I Can't Give You Anything But Love" became a romantic lament, as Hendrik stepped forward -- in his worn blue suit with its shiny knees and elbows -- to introduce the melody, breaking the rhythm with pauses that made you feel sad, and with a plaintive tone that said that he existed for love, too, and that if Pearl did not accept his love, he would die.

Pearl wore a tight black dress with long sleeves (an odd choice for July) and she had a silk gardenia pinned over her left ear. She held the big square microphone with both hands, as if it were a man's face that she was about to kiss. She repeated Hendrik's slow cadence, singing the simple words, conveying that simple message, that she would give him her self, which was inseparable from the love that consumed her.

As Pearl sang, she never laid eyes on Hendrik or the rest of the band. They were just background noise to her. Instead, she made eye contact with a succession of men in the audience, hoping they would connect with her feeling, hoping that love mattered enough to them so they would keep listening to her song.

From her spot beside the pillar, Albertine could tell that Hendrik was listening to Pearl, but she guessed that the women in the smoky room were the only ones who understood that Pearl was giving them more than a song, that she was really offering up her heart.

After a bridge, it was Hendrik's turn to pour out his emotion, and he did it by turning the music inside out, speeding it up and sharpening it, so that some of the notes actually hurt Albertine's ears, but it didn't seem to matter to the audience. They listened to him and nodded. Between the two of them, Pearl Cornell and Hendrik Kinderman, something was really cooking, and everyone wanted to taste it.

Albertine couldn't understand how this could be happening. When did those two have time to rehearse their act to make it seem so natural? She'd thought Hendrik was working late at the insurance company, trying for a promotion to sales manager. But it was clear now that he was doing the minimum at his job so he wouldn't lose it, and spending every spare moment with Pearl…or rehearsing with Pearl and the band, anyway. She hoped that they hadn't made progress on the love part, that they hadn't made that other kind of music, between the sheets. Still, anything was possible. Why else would he have come to see her at Swanson's Tea & Coffee to tell her about their combo's big gig at the Starlight (several rungs down the ladder from the Top Hat, in her opinion)? But in the next breath he was begging her to wait until the second weekend of their run. "I want it to be perfect for you, Al. Give us a few days to get the kinks out of our act."

All the other girls in the office had stopped working to look at him. In a light summer suit that complemented his golden hair, he was handsome and clean-looking. He smiled with his straight, square teeth and nodded to them, and they giggled in response, before Albertine could pull him out into the hallway for their quick conversation. In the end, she had promised to wait until their fourth performance, and he had kissed her, then hugged her with such force that he lifted her off her feet.

But here she was anyway at their opening night at the Starlight, and she hadn't seen a kink in their act yet. Aside from Jake, the piano player who had bricks for hands and finished late on every song, the band and the vocalist were pretty tight. The audience loved them and applauded for Pearl after every number until she gave them a little bow. And it was all driving Albertine crazy.

She could only bear to listen to one more number. Pearl waited at the microphone as Hendrik played the introduction to "I Can't Believe You're In Love with Me." He played quickly with a syncopated rhythm, but when Pearl sang, her voice was slow, hoarse and imploring. "Your eyes are blue, your kisses, too. I never knew what they could do."

Then Hendrik played a solo before the chorus, quickly again but with Pearl's plaintive tone. Albertine knew it was just a song, but it touched her, pushed her to nausea.

"I always put you far above me," Pearl sang, "I can't believe that you love me." And as she finished the chorus, Hendrik played in harmony, as if he were equally grateful that Pearl loved him.

Albertine could see the drops of sweat glistening in the spotlight's glare on the top edge of Pearl's lip, and she could see how flushed Hendrik was as he played under her vocals. It was more than Albertine could stand. She left her drink, sweating in the humid club, and hurried out to Wabash Avenue where she found a taxi waiting. She gave the driver her Lexington Avenue address and felt sick, abandoned, alone. How could he choose Pearl over her? How could Hendrik be so stupid?

As Albertine got out of the cab, it was only 9:30, and she thought that Hank would be happy to have her home earlier than usual, but when she unlocked the front door to the apartment, she found the rooms dark and quiet, without even the sound of the radio, and she knew immediately that Hank had disobeyed her and stayed out on the street with his friends.

She hung up her wrap and put her hat on the shelf in the closet, then changed out of the green dress into her housecoat. Then she went to the kitchen to make some tea and to wait for Hank and then Hendrik to come home. As she filled the kettle with water from the tap, she felt a powerful urge to play the piano, to make the song that Pearl had sung come to life. "And after all is said and done, to think that I'm the lucky one," she sang quietly. But it was a Thursday night and the neighbors would be in bed. She had promised them not to practice after 8:00 pm on weekdays.

She made some toast to go along with her tea and sat down at the small kitchen table and looked blankly at the front page of the newspaper she had purchased on the way home from work.

There had been another strike at the U.S. Steel plant, and Roosevelt had proposed a new civilian jobs program. There had been a murder just south of the stockyards, someone had robbed a bank on North Kedsey, and a man had ridden backwards on a bicycle from New York to Chicago using a shaving mirror to see where he was going. And the Cubs had won again because Colby had hit a home run in the eighth inning with two men on.

"I wonder if he thinks about me," she said aloud and put the newspaper aside. It didn't seem right that Hendrik was cheating on her now that she had finally given up Colby Malone. It was no way to reward her sacrifice.

And she would have to deal with Hank, too. She would have to punish him for staying out past dark without her permission. He was only ten years old, too young to be out at night in the city. Pa was right about Dominic being a bad influence. The kid was 13 going on 40. He'd have Hank smoking cigarettes and drinking beer before he was twelve. She should probably tell Hank that he was forbidden to see Dominic again.

On the other hand, who could blame Hank for not wanting to be locked up in the apartment all evening when his friends were outside playing? Would she have stayed inside all alone to please her mother night after night? No, of course not, even if her Ma had threatened to spank her with the back side of a hair brush, or make her do all the dishes after the next Sunday dinner at Grandmére's. And Hank took after her, didn't he? He was independent, adventurous, and not afraid to get into a little trouble now and then. He was the kind of kid she had wanted to be, but she didn't want him to take so many chances. She had to make it clear that he had to do as she said. It was for his own good.

It was fun when Hank was a baby, and as a toddler, too, when she would dress him up in cute outfits and keep him close to her. Sometimes, she'd even thought of him as a living doll. But now he had a mind of his own, and it was impossible to really control him. And she didn't like imposing her will, because what if she was wrong about it? What if Hank needed friends like Dominic to survive in the neighborhood? What if it were okay for him to spread his wings a little bit, even at the age of ten, on a summer night? There was no way of knowing until it was too late. The thought frightened her.

So what had possessed her to get pregnant again? She didn't think she was well suited to be a mother, and Hendrik had next to no interest in being a dad. Having kids was what married couples did, especially if you were Catholic. But of course Hendrik was Lutheran and encouraged her to douche after sex, and he used a French letter when he thought of it, saying that one kid was plenty, especially during the Depression when every cent was hard to come by. His parents had nearly disowned him when he'd married her, a Catholic you see, and from the French church, to boot. His father had been angry with him, anyway, for not going to work in the garage with him, when business was steady as people tried to keep their old cars running as long as possible. Hendrik didn't like to get dirty, and he hated the greasy fingernails, the oil dripping in his face, the smell of gasoline that stuck to his father no matter how much he bathed. At some point his father promised to make him a partner and give him a share of the profits, but after he married Albertine, he had offered to pay Hendrik just two dollars a day, to keep the business solvent. How could he support a wife on that? And so he had tried to make it on his own as a musician and hotel bellman, then as a musician and a haberdashery salesman. When Hank was born, he tried driving a taxi, and then got the job as a coffee taster at Swanson's Tea & Coffee, but after six months he got sick, his legs turned purple and swelled up to twice their normal size, and Doctor Bichet diagnosed the condition as caffeine poisoning. After Hendrik stopped drinking coffee, things cleared up and his legs went back to normal, and Mr. Swanson felt so guilty about Hendrik's illness that he gave Albertine the job on the switchboard, even though she'd had no experience as a telephone operator. When Hendrik had fully recovered, her Pa got him the job at Donnelly's for $1.50 an hour, and if it weren't for the accident with his thumb, he'd still be working there, the three of them would have plenty of money, and Hendrik wouldn't be performing three nights a week at the Starlight Club with Pearl Cornell.

A little before eleven, Albertine heard the squeak of the window in Hank's room and the thud of his feet as he vaulted over the radiator and landed on the floor. Instead of going in to confront him, she waited for Hank to come into the hallway to use the toilet. When he opened the door on cue, he noticed that the lights were on, and he realized immediately that he'd been caught, so he tried to retreat back into his bedroom.

"Wait, Hank," she said, and he stopped, his hand still on the doorknob. "Go ahead and pee. Then come out and have some tea and toast with me."

Hank took his time in the bathroom, flushed the toilet twice and washed his hands for nearly a minute before he flung open the door and reluctantly walked back to the kitchen.

His plaid shirt was untucked, his tan shorts were smudged with soot, and his socks drooped. His sneakers were so worn and dirty, it was hard to tell what color they had been when they were new. Hank's dark hair was mussed, and he needed a haircut. He looked at her apprehensively with his light blue eyes, clenching his teeth as he anticipated his punishment. Although his hands and face were clean (still moist from washing up) his elbows and knees were dirty. She wondered where in the neighborhood he had been crawling around all night.

"Hank, where have you been?" she asked.

"Out," Hank shrugged and squinted at her, "out in the neighborhood."

"I see," Albertine said. "Have a seat. I'll fix you some toast and jam."

"All right," Hank agreed, but was still suspicious of her as he sat down on a creaky chair and put his elbows on the stained wood table.

She placed the slices of bread on a small metal tray and slid it into the toaster, and she felt his eyes follow her as she relit the stove under the tea kettle. She took the jam out of the icebox and a knife from the drying rack and she placed them on the table in front of Hank before she eased herself back down into the chair beside him.

"And where in the neighborhood did you go?" Albertine asked him.

"I don't know," he shrugged. "A bunch of places."

"Hank, you're a very intelligent boy with an excellent memory. You can be more specific than that."

"Well, we played stick ball in the alley until too many kids had to go home and we had to call the game."

"Did you get any hits?"

"I got on base most of the time. We were ahead 23 to 18 when we stopped playing. I made a coupla good catches, too. Not bad for someone who has to play bare-handed."

"I didn't know you liked baseball so much, or I would have…"

"I don't need no baseball mitt, Ma. I bet Colby Malone didn't have one when he was my age. What do you think?"

"Who can say?" she said and hesitated and gave him a concentrated look. "I hear he was poor growing up. So he probably didn't have one."

"No. Probably not," Hank said and yawned. "You should know."

"Why should I know?" she asked, and her heart fluttered nervously. What did he know? The toaster clicked and the tea kettle whistled, and she got up too quickly to fix Hank's snack. She placed the slices of toast on a small, cracked plate and put a teabag into a cup, and as she poured the hot water some of it spilled over into the saucer. "Why should I know?" she asked again and studied his face before she set the dishes in front of him.

"Because you know him."

"I know him?" So I did see him at the ballpark! Hank was the boy who ran away!

"You said you saw him at the Top Hat Club," Hank said but looked down into the tea cup so he couldn't see her blushing.

"I saw Al Capone once, too," she said and went to the sink to wash her hands unnecessarily. "That doesn't mean I know Al Capone."

"So you couldn't get his autograph if I wanted it?" he asked her. "You don't know him well enough for that?"

"No, honey. I've only seen him at the Top Hat a few times."

"Okay, you don't really know him. I was imagining things," Hank said, sorry that he had come so close to confronting her. "I'm glad we got <u>that</u> straight."

"I'm glad, too," Albertine said and felt very tired. Lying to her son was exhausting. Now she wasn't sure she had the strength to lay down the law with Hank tonight, but she guessed she'd better give it a try. She didn't want him getting run over by a streetcar while she was working at the Top Hat or out checking up on Hendrik.

"Where did you go after the stickball game?" she asked.

"Dominic and I went up on the roof of his uncle's building to watch his flock of pigeons come back to their coop for the night," Hank said. "They came in like a big gray cloud moving together in the sky, like the shadow of a whale…that's how Uncle Freddo described it. He has two hundred and fifty pigeons. Up close some of them are nice-looking, Ma. Their feathers are like flakes of colored glass. Uncle Freddo let us help feed them."

"And where is this pigeon coop?" Albertine asked as she watched her son bite into his toast, then lick the peach preserves from his lips.

"It's over in the Italian neighborhood. On top of a five-story building. I don't know the address. Dominic took me on the streetcar."

"So the pigeons flew home at sunset, I'm assuming," Albertine said and sipped her tea. "That was at least three hours before you climbed in your window here…What were you doing for three more hours?"

"Uncle Freddo fed us spaghetti with meatballs and then we went to the Biograph to see if there was a good movie playing, but Dominic had already seen the show."

"Where did you get money to go to the movies? From your grandpa again?"

"No. Dominick's big sister works as an usherette there. We were going to ask her to sneak us into the balcony."

"Oh, Hank!"

"They're allowed to do that, Dominic says."

"Well, don't believe him! You'll get arrested!"

"We won't get arrested, Ma. We're just kids. The coppers just give you a lecture and tell you to go home."

"You know this from experience?" Albertine demanded.

"Well, not exactly…Dominic told me about it."

"I'm sure!" Albertine laughed and shook her head. She took another sip of tea then said, "Hank, I don't want you going out at night by yourself."

"I wasn't by myself! Dominic was with me."

"You know what I mean. Dominic is not an adult, and you're only ten years old," she reminded him. "It's not safe for you to go out without an adult. There are bad people in this city. Someone could hurt you. You could get run over by a taxi, or a streetcar or a milk wagon. I thought you were minding me and staying in the apartment after dark."

"Mom!"

"So you can understand why I'm disappointed in you. I'm very disappointed that you disobeyed me. And I assume from the way you climbed in your window that this isn't the first time you've sneaked out against my wishes."

Hank didn't answer. Instead, he ate his last crust of toast and slurped his tea. He was waiting for her to take out the belt to spank him, but instead she kept talking.

"I know what you're thinking, Hank. I know what you're thinking," she said. "You think I'm a terrible mother for leaving you home alone at night. Even though you're plenty old enough to keep yourself occupied and go to bed on your own, you just can't resist the temptation to sneak out with Dominic. It's not humanly possible for you to resist that temptation, is it?"

"Nobody likes to be locked up by themselves every night," Hank said. "You go everywhere you want. You go to nightclubs and leave me here. You skip work to go to the ballpark. And what about Dad? He doesn't care if I sit here and rot so long as he can play his horn."

"Listen, Hank. We're adults. Believe it or not, we have lives of our own. We love you very much, but we are musicians, too, and that means we have to perform at night."

"I could come to the Top Hat with you," Hank said, knowing that the idea was out of the question. "I play the piano, too, you know."

"That's sweet, Hank. You may be ready to play at a night club in ten or fifteen years, but the Top Hat is no place for a ten year old," Albertine said. "We'll have to make other arrangements."

"What other arrangements?" Hank asked.

"On nights when both your Dad and I are working, you'll be going to Grandma and Grandpa Fontaine's house."

"What difference does that make? Grandpa works nights, and Grandma does, too, if she's delivering a baby. I'd be all alone there, too."

"Lorraine and Claribel would be there to watch you, Hank. At least on the nights when Grandma is busy."

"Mom! Grandma Birdie treats me like a baby!" Hank protested. "And your sisters boss me around."

"One more word out of you and I'll get the belt out, young man," she said, without enough outrage to frighten him. "Now go in the bathroom and wash your knees and elbows, then go to sleep, honey. You've had a long day."

Relieved that he had avoided a beating (and didn't have to tell her about their visit to the pool hall), Hank hurried to the bathroom to use a little more soap and water before he went to bed.

By midnight Hank was asleep and the apartment was unbearably quiet. No wonder Hank hated to stay here all by himself. And with him sleeping in the next room she couldn't turn on the radio. She wondered whether she should just go to sleep and deal with Hendrik in the morning when they'd both be dragging themselves out of bed to go to work. But there would be no time for a conversation then, and neither of them would have a clear enough head to make any real decisions. For that's what she wanted: to resolve things with Hendrik, to make him choose her once and for all.

She made some more toast, ate it quickly then sat back down at the table to wait for Hendrik. On a Thursday night, their last set may have been over by one o'clock, so he could be home soon. But if they played until closing time, 2:00 a.m., she'd be in for a long wait, and neither of them would feel like going to work in the morning.

She tried to read more of the newspaper, but the words wouldn't stay in focus. The news didn't seem to matter, anyway. There were a lot more important things going on in her life than the Depression, politics and sports. Her family was at stake, and her marriage. She had to hold onto Hendrik, to keep him from cheating on her with Pearl Cornell. She decided to put her head down on the table, just for a minute, and the next thing she heard was Hendrik's key in the door, and his quiet steps on the hall runner. She forced herself to her feet, hurried to meet him, then hugged him before he could put down his saxophone.

"Hello, darling," she said, kissed his cheek playfully and inhaled deeply so she could smell him. Tobacco smoke, sweat, but no scent of perfume, and no smell of liquor, either. He had come home to her, chaste and sober, or so it seemed. "How was your first night at the Starlight?"

Hendrik nodded, stepped around her to the piano, set down his saxophone case next to it, then reached back to her with his left hand.

"The audience liked us," he said, "but we were very rough. You should have heard Jake on the piano. It was as if he was rolling down a flight of stairs."

"I'm sure the rest of the band sounded fine. Especially the saxophone."

"I had my moments," he grinned. "I played and I flew above the stage. I can't describe it. If I can keep it up, we are going places."

"That's wonderful, Hendrik," she said and pulled him over to the table. "Are you hungry darling? Can I fry you an egg?"

"That would be nice," he said and sat down on the sturdiest chair.

She went to the stove to light the fire and heat up the cast iron skillet. Albertine was glad that she still had three eggs left, and she decided to cook one for each of them and save the last egg for Hank's breakfast in the morning.

As she worked at the stove, she asked him, "What about the new singer? Sapphire? Is she any good?"

"Oh, you mean Pearl," Hendrik said and shook his head. "I don't know what to think about her. She's got the looks, and the audience loves her, but she always sounds frightened and sad. And she gets lost sometimes and doesn't know when she's supposed to come in. She's waiting for me instead of the piano, I guess."

"But you think she has talent?" Albertine asked as the toaster clicked and she turned the eggs without breaking the yolks.

"Yah. Pearl has talent," he nodded. "And something <u>makes</u> her sing. That's why I put her in front of the combo, Al. Her singing reminds me of the way I feel when I'm playing my horn."

"Oh, geez, Hendrik," she said and pretended to laugh. "Should I be worried? Are you sweet on her, darling? Or is it just the music you have in common?"

"Just the music," he grinned and winked at her. "Why would you ask that question?"

"I guess I'm a little insecure," she said and served his plate.

"Well, don't be!" he said, then began eating, quickly devouring the egg, then mopping the yolk with the toast.

"I have an idea that might help you, Hendrik," she said as she sat down next to him with her plate.

"Oh yeah? What's your idea?"

"Fire Jake and let me play piano in your combo."

"I can't do that. Jake has stuck with me from the beginning."

"But you just told me that his playing stinks, Hendrik. You know I could do better than he does!"

"But you've never played in a group."

"I can't hide behind anyone else when I play at the Top Hat, Hendrik. I <u>have</u> to be good."

"What about Hank? Who will stay with him?"

"I'll send him to Ma's house the nights we're both out, Hendrik. I should have done that all along."

"Do you really want to try it, Albertine?"

"Yes ,of course I do, Hendrik. I want your combo to be the best it can be."

"Okay. But give me a week, Al. I've got to teach you the music."

Chapter Eleven

To make sure Albertine learned the combo's music, Hendrik insisted that she practice with him every night the band wasn't playing. So on Sunday, they left the Fontaine's house as soon as dinner was over, and they came home to start working through the songs on Albertine's piano in the living room. Curious, Hank followed them and sat on a dining chair in the kitchen doorway to watch and listen.

Hendrik seemed happy, enthusiastic and interested in playing with her when he untied his cardboard portfolio, set the sheet music on the piano, and opened it to the first number, Gershwin's "Someone to Watch Over Me."

"Oh, I love this song, Hendrik," she said. "But we don't have to practice it. I know it by heart!"

"You'll have to learn it all over again," he laughed at her. "This is a completely new arrangement."

"How different can it be?" she shrugged and smiled at his trace of a German accent. She hardly noticed it anymore, but from the beginning she'd thought his German tenor voice was exotic and sexy.

"It's for the whole band," Hendrik asserted and touched her gently on her hand where she held open the over-sized music chart. "You need to study your part."

"Let's see," she said and scanned the bands of notes across the sheet. It took her a minute to find the familiar tune on the crowded page. After the introduction, the piano stayed in the background most of the time, supporting the soloist and vocal, but she noticed a nice piano solo in the middle, and her part came back to the foreground at the song's finale.

"Play it through," Hendrik instructed her, "and I'll conduct you."

Hendrik's way of conducting was to interrupt her every few bars to tell her to emphasize a phrase, speed up the tempo, or not to skip a passing chord. She had to admit he had great intuition for music. Albertine could name every note that she heard, but Hendrik could tell you how the whole piece should sound.

"And remember," he coached her, "you've got the drums to keep time and a bass and trombone to play under you. I'm playing solos, and Pearl is singing. You're the rhythm section. You're the only one who can play chords, so you have to fill the space between everyone else."

"So you can't live without me!" she concluded happily.

"I can't live without a piano player," Hendrik laughed. "And you'll be pretty good once you learn the music."

"Pretty good? Geez, Hendrik, I'm better than pretty good already! Let's play it together."

This time Albertine listened to Hendrik's playing. He had a natural, rich sound that could make you cry. But on principle, she stopped him twice when he hit wrong notes: a flat A in the chorus and a sharp D in the bridge. Hank laughed, pleased to see her correct his dad.

"Just don't do that on stage!" Hendrik complained but worked his fingers on the valves, mentally correcting his errors. He had an ego, all right, but he had a right to one, Albertine thought: he was so handsome and cut such a fine figure even in his most worn-out suit that the girls in the neighborhood had talked about him months before she'd met him at the parish dance, and when they were finally introduced, she guessed there might be a few good reasons for all the sighs.

On the next pass through, they performed the number smoothly, and Albertine sang quietly to fill in the vocals between Hendrik's solos. "There's someone I'm longing to see, I hope that he, turns out to be, someone who'll watch over me."

The lyrics were sweet, but Hendrik's solos were absolutely hypnotizing. He turned the simple melody into an aching river of sound that made her hope for, to truly desire a love, his love, that would protect her for a lifetime. It was the same feeling she'd had for him when they'd first met and he came so close to her that she'd felt his breath on her cheek, and he gazed at her with the bluest eyes in the world, smiling with pure happiness to meet her.

But tonight, instead of drawing Hendrik closer to her, his playing pulled him in on himself. He closed his eyes and created the flow of music by combining his private emotion with his memory of all the ways he had played this song before, twisting and bending the original melody to the shape he wanted, and bringing his solo to a close exactly in time for her to play the progression of chords leading to the last vocal section, which was designed to be a duet between Pearl's voice and Hendrik's saxophone. Albertine sang the words, but her soft voice was smothered by the finale's loud piano chords and Hendrik's beautiful, throaty horn conclusion.

From his chair in the doorway, Hank could not catch his mother's voice, but he could see her lips in profile mouthing the words. When his parents finished the song, Hank jumped to his feet and applauded. It was great to see and hear them play together. The music and his pride in them were better than seeing the Sally Rand Revue or spending Christmas at his grandparents' house. This special moment belonged just to the three of them.

"So you liked that?" Hendrik asked his son and squinted as if he weren't happy with the third attempt at bringing Gershwin's song to life.

"Yeah. That was great!" Hank said and grinned with approval.

"It was okay for starters," Hendrik said and shrugged. "We need to make it better, but it's time to work on the next number."

Albertine knew that Hendrik was a perfectionist, and her mother had warned her that all Germans were demanding and stern, and she disapproved of Hendrik because he was not Catholic and liked to keep to himself. But Birdie's reservations drove Albertine to want him even more, and Hendrik's aloofness only made him seem more mysterious to her. And over time, he had revealed himself to her. He told her about his cousins in Hamburg, especially the twin girls with golden braids who sang Christmas carols with him, and the boy who seined eels from the river and roasted them on a stick for breakfast. Hendrik told her about his kind grandfather who had taught him the harmonica and had given him a Swiss pocket watch the day Hendrik and his parents climbed aboard the ship to New York. Hendrik had known many girls before Albertine, but he claimed that she was the only one he loved enough to bring her flowers or buy her a gold chain necklace.

Albertine mastered the next piece, "My Blue Heaven," more quickly because she now sensed what it meant to play in an ensemble, and she understood how to shape her playing to match Hendrik's maneuvers through the song. As they worked on the third number, "The Man I Love," Hendrik sensed that she was following his lead like a good dancer, and that her chords rang in whenever he needed her to fill the gap. She wasn't just a girl who could call out any note he played. She understood the music's structure and could adapt to his pace, so that she responded just in time to accompany him as he improvised with his horn. He sensed that Albertine's piano would greatly improve his band, and as he realized how much better the group would sound with her on stage, he loved her for it. Why hadn't he thought of adding her to the band earlier? He had heard her play a thousand times before, but he had never really listened. He had never appreciated her technical skill or how versatile she could be on the keyboard.

After four hours of practice, when they paused to begin another song, a series of dull thuds hit the floor below them, reverberating through the piano and making its strings vibrate. "What time is it?" Albertine asked and looked up at the wall clock above the piano. It was already nine o'clock. Another quick series of blows shook the room and made the piano hum. "That would be Mrs. McIlhaney," Albertine said. "I promised her I wouldn't practice after eight on work nights."

"That's too bad. We were just starting to roll. But I guess we've done enough damage for one day," Hendrik smiled.

"Damage?" Albertine protested. "What did we break?"

"I've spoiled you," he said. "Now we know how well you can play!"

"Thank you, Hendrik!"

"You were hard enough to handle already," he laughed. "How am I going to deal with you now?"

"With respect," she said, "and maybe with some tender loving care." She smiled at him, gripped his hand and licked the corner of her mouth.

Getting her message, Hendrik smiled back at her and quickly unfastened the strap from his saxophone. But then they both remembered that Hank was watching them, and they turned in unison to see him perched on the edge of his chair, waiting for their next move.

"Isn't it time you got ready for bed?" Albertine asked him.

"No, I'm not sleepy," Hank insisted.

"Well, we have to be quiet now, anyway, so go wash up and stretch out until you fall asleep."

"Can't I stay up a little while longer?" Hank pleaded. "A few more minutes?"

"It will take you that long to get ready," his mother said. "So please don't press your luck! Go to bed like a good boy."

"Geez!"

"You got to hear the music," Hendrik told him. "The fun is over. Now get your rest."

Hank frowned bitterly. If only they knew all the places I've been! Then they wouldn't try to boss me around! If they knew how I can take care of myself, they'd treat me with respect, too! But there was nothing he could do to challenge them. If he told them his about the World's Fair, the boxing matches, or the dice games in the pool hall, he'd only get into more trouble. "Oh, all right! Good night."

Hank took his time in the bathroom, brushing his teeth and washing his face (two things he usually did in a hurry) as slowly as possible, but in less than five minutes he was bored, and he stood on tip-toe to yawn at himself in the mirror above the sink. After he said good night to his parents again, Hank went into his room, closed the door, got under the covers, and was glad to know that his Mom and Dad would hurry home tomorrow after work to practice. It was something to look forward to.

With Hank out of the way, Hendrik stepped close to Albertine and kissed her gently. "You have a nice touch on the keyboard," he said.

"I'm glad you finally noticed," she said, kissed him back, then ran her hand over his cheek. This was the man she loved, a handsome man whose blue eyes understood her, a brilliant musician whose trained ear recognized her talent, her friend, her partner, her lover, whose heart was her heart. "Why don't you shave and meet me in the bedroom?"

"I had the same idea," he whispered and slid her hand over his lips and kissed her palm. "I won't be long."

Albertine and Hendrik had been married for eleven years. They knew the meaning of each other's looks and could decipher the tone and inflection of each other's voices, and they could even interpret each other's posture and walk as they came into a room. They knew each other's bodies, too. Albertine liked the feel of his breath on the back of her neck, and it thrilled her when he kissed the spot at the base of her skull. She craved the way he stroked her hips and massaged her hands with his musician's fingers. She liked the solid feel of his shoulders and arms, the warmth of his body next to hers, the smoky smell of his hair, and the slight roughness of his cheek even after he had shaved. Hendrik loved her small shoulders and thin neck, her fragile ears and fragrant hair. He loved her full mouth and the sharp feel of her teeth as he moved his tongue over them. He loved the contrast between the hard edges of her hip bones and the softness of her flanks and buttocks. He loved her firm breasts and the smooth insides of her thighs. He never stopped being amazed by her vagina, its mushroom taste, and the way it swelled with moisture.

After they made love, Albertine and Hendrik knew how best to lie together side by side, and even after they drifted off to sleep they rolled over and turned in unison, as if they shared the same dream.

For the next few weeks, as they practiced their music together, Albertine and Hendrik made love as frequently as newlyweds, but without the awkwardness. Albertine felt sure that if she weren't pregnant already all their lovemaking would create another baby that would hold them together forever, no matter what. For his part, Hendrik enjoyed the sex and he felt at home with Albertine, but his mind kept racing back to the band and its music. Paying so much attention to Albertine now was an investment in the combo's future. With a piano player as good as she was, the band would come together and people would take notice. And the better Albertine played, the better his saxophone would sound, and the more captivating Pearl's voice would become.

On the next Saturday night, Albertine realized that it was great fun to play in Hendrik's combo. The full sound they made together, piano, sax, trombone, bass and drums was joyous to her, even on the sad tunes, and she felt that her playing made all the difference. She was thrilled at the connection with the other players, and at how their music filled the ballroom. It was only when Pearl stepped up to the microphone that Albertine's stomach tightened into a knot.

Hendrik played the introduction to "Ain't Misbehavin' " and Albertine laid down the chords, Rocko tugged the beat on his bass, but the audience did not pay attention until Pearl slinked forward in her black dress, held the microphone in both hands and sang, "No one to talk with, all by myself. No one to walk with, I'm happy on the shelf."

If she's not colored, my name isn't Albertine, she thought as she played rhythm, the progression of minor chords that kept Pearl's hips in motion and enabled her voice, husky and bitter sweet, to tempt all the men and taunt all the women in the Starlight's low-ceilinged and smoky ballroom. "I'm saving it up for you!" I bet! Albertine thought as she played, you're not holding back one damn thing!

But playing in the band, Albertine was too busy to focus on Pearl. She had practiced their music with Hendrik, but she'd only had one rehearsal with the band so she had to concentrate to keep the pace, and listening to the drummer was different from counting in her head all the time.

Although Pearl sang on almost every number, Albertine didn't get annoyed with her again until Pearl began singing, "You're the cream in my coffee…" and Hendrik entered into a rhapsodic duet with her on that stupid little song. "You're the salt in my stew…" Ridiculous! Why is he playing as if Pearl is his dream girl? "You're the sail on my love boat…" God, I could throw up!

But Albertine had to take her turn playing a solo of the vapid tune, right after Hendrik paid Pearl such sickening homage. So she played the first few bars as sweetly as ever, but then finished her run with some diminished chords and some downward scales when the audience was expecting a flight of fancy. But she made a good transition to the short duet between the bass and drums that brought back the bounce for the dozen or so couples who were dancing. The song's finale placed Hendrik beside Pearl and he played harmony to her trite warbling. It was too cute for Albertine, too silly for words, but the audience applauded them enthusiastically, confirming Albertine's assumption that people who went to the Starlight had no taste at all.

Between sets, Albertine walked down the narrow hallway to the ladies' room and met Pearl just inside the door. Pearl leaned on her hip against the edge of the sink, smoking a cigarette.

"Oh, hiya" Pearl greeted her.

"Hello," Albertine said and tried to squeeze past her to the stall.

"Thanks, by the way," Pearl said and smiled slyly.

"Oh, yeah?" Albertine asked suspiciously. "For what?"

"For getting Jake off the band," she nodded. "You can actually play the piano. It makes it a lot easier for me. I don't have to change keys in the middle of a number."

"I do my best," Albertine said. "I want Hendrik's band to be a success."

"I'll bet you do!" Pearl said and turned to douse her cigarette under the faucet. "I'll bet you do."

"Have a drink of water," Albertine suggested. "You were sounding a little hoarse out there."

"I'll work on it, sweetheart," Pearl laughed, then applied some very red lipstick. "I'll have myself a champagne cocktail."

"Don't overdo it," Albertine said. "We don't want you to forget the words."

"The band only knows twenty songs!" Pearl laughed as she pushed back out into the club. "Don't worry about me, dearie!"

After she fixed her own lipstick, Albertine went out into the club to find Hendrik. She was pleased that Pearl had noticed her playing, but felt annoyed that Pearl was acting like she was the star of the show when it was really Hendrik's band. And there was something snooty about Pearl's attitude, too, as if she had something on Albertine and was just waiting for the right time to use it.

Hendrik was leaning on the bar, drinking a short beer, and listening to Rocko, the bass player, who spoke at close range into his ear. They both laughed as Terrell Jones, the drummer, walked up to them in a cloud of smoke and with a big, smelly cigar between his teeth. Billy, the trombone player, came up next and put his arm around Hendrik and kissed his cheek. The boys were a little too chummy, she thought, but at least Pearl wasn't hanging all over Hendrik. Rather than break into the huddle, Albertine turned back to the bandstand and saw the other woman sitting at the piano. Pearl was sipping a wide glass of champagne and looking at the sheet music.

Albertine strolled over the dance floor and stood beside the singer. "Want to trade places?" Albertine asked her.

"Naw, I can't play," Pearl said with a smile, and shrugged. "But you sorta spooked me. I was refreshing my memory. I don't want to forget the words on the next set!"

Albertine laughed, took the champagne glass, and drank the last few sips. Before the men came back, Pearl stood up and surprised Albertine by hugging her and holding her tight.

"Oh, dearie," Pearl said, "I always thought you were so beautiful."

Albertine wondered whether this was what Hendrik felt when he hugged Pearl, if he hugged her. She was softer than Albertine expected, and her embrace was tender and not a formality. Albertine smelled cigarette smoke and crushed flowers, and the sour smell of cheap wine. But there was something sweet about Pearl in the end. Even after all the dark things they had said to each other, Albertine was beginning to like her. She made a mental note to ask Larry what he thought of Pearl's singing. Larry was always a good judge of talent, even if he was wrong half the time about a person's character. He knew Hendrik was a natural musician, and he had been the first to notice that Albertine had perfect pitch.

Hendrik had been brave to add the Armstrong medley at the beginning of the next set. Everyone was copying the colored players as it was, and for weeks Hendrik had played the tunes over and over again, saying Satchmo this and Satchmo that, as if the colored man was following Hendrik around telling him what was wrong with his music. And at the rehearsal that afternoon, he brought the charts for "Old Rocking Chair", "St. James Infirmary", and "St. Louis Blues", and he planned to play the trumpet parts on his saxophone. It could have been a disaster, but with Albertine at the keyboard, the bass and trombone had a structure to build on and the drummer filled in nicely. There wasn't much singing for Pearl, and most of the piece was devoted to Hendrik playing what he remembered from Armstrong's records.

Hendrik opened by playing "Old Rockin' Chair" the Hoagie Carmichael tune with its slow, sad melody, and whose lyrics didn't make sense, anyway. The drummer played softly with his brushes, and Albertine played chords in the background, pleased that there were no vocals for Pearl. For her part, Pearl didn't seem to mind; she stood in the shadows just off the stage, smoking a cigarette and nodding in time with Hendrik's playing. Albertine wondered why Pearl had suddenly started to treat her nicely. Maybe she had a guilty conscience.

Albertine played a bridge of chords to bring the combo into "St. James Infirmary," which Hendrik played again as an instrumental. As Albertine hammered the rhythm, she mouthed the words, "Let her go! Let her go! God bless her, wherever she may be. She may search the wide world over, and never find a better man than me."

The thought of a woman lying in a hospital made Albertine imagine not a corpse, but Flora at Cook County with her newborn infant beside her. The baby must have been beautiful, but Albertine resented the fat young cow. But their fate had been decided the moment the baby had been conceived. There was no chance that Colby would leave Flora once the child was born, and Albertine couldn't bring herself to do anything to separate him from his only child. And Albertine knew she couldn't do anything that would separate her from Hank, either.

"So that's the end of my story," she sang to herself. "Let's have another round of booze. And if anyone should ask just tell them I've got the St. James Infirmary blues."

After Albertine played another bridge, Hendrik started up on "St. Louis Blues" and Pearl pranced up to the microphone. From the piano, Albertine couldn't see Pearl's face, but she resented a certain slink in her hips, exaggerated by the way she raised her right heel in time with the music. "I hate to see the evening sun go down, because my baby, he done left this town," she sang, and Hendrik and Albertine played the interlude together and then Pearl echoed it with her mournful voice, crying out about the woman with the store-bought hair who stole her man away. Immediately, even as she kept playing, Albertine stole glances at Pearl's hair to see if it might be a wig. If she really was a Negro, she might have her hair cut short and that black wavy hair could be a wig for sure. And she had changed her hair style a couple of times since Albertine had known her. Pearl might have several wigs, a whole closet of store-bought hair.

Pearl sounded genuinely angry that her man had gone so far away from her. She leaned toward the microphone and threw her arms into the air, as if flying in pursuit of her lover.

Then Hendrik ended the medley with a solo that played through all three melodies at a quick pace, so quickly that Albertine couldn't keep up with him, so she waited for the end and caught up with him when he got back to "St. Louis Blues."

When the number concluded, only two couples were on the dance floor, and there was only a trickle of applause. Albertine felt sorry for Hendrik. He's playing his heart out, and these people are ignoring him. They don't recognize how talented he is!

But she turned the page on the sheet music to a more popular tune, "Red, Red, Robin," which Hendrik launched into without hesitation. Albertine knew it well. She had played it for years at the Sunday afternoon sing-alongs at her parents' house, and she played it at the Top Hat, too, as filler when she couldn't think of anything else to play.

It was a great tune for the saxophone, too, with the notes bob-bobbing along, and its cheery energy lured the couples out onto the dance floor. Once Hendrik played through the first verse as an instrumental, Pearl tilted the microphone stand, leaned over it and sang happily. The hoarseness was gone, her voice grew younger, and she sounded as if she meant it when she sang, "Live, love, laugh and be happy!"

The song progressed into a duet, like the one Albertine had witnessed last Thursday night, between Pearl's voice and Hendrik's saxophone. Albertine was an accomplice this time, playing the chords and giving it the rhythm that held it all together. But there was more to their music than a Sunday sing-along at the Fontaine's. Albertine recognized a strong chemistry here. Why did Hendrik step next to Pearl, unless he wanted to be near her? You could hear his horn well enough from his place in the band. Maybe he would say that the number called for him to share the spotlight, but he hadn't moved forward during their rehearsal that afternoon, because he had known that Albertine was watching. Now in the heat of the show, he had forgotten that his wife was playing piano behind them, and he was drawn to Pearl, his new fascination.

Albertine told herself that it was all part of the act. The band leader should come front and center. And there was only one microphone and only a single spotlight. Where else was the vocalist supposed to stand? And the crowd loved them. Any reservation they'd had over the blues medley was gone. Here was something they could dance to.

Without pausing, Hendrik nodded for Albertine to begin the next number, "All of Me," which started with a piano solo, soon joined by Hendrik on his saxophone. For the first time that evening, Albertine and Hendrik were playing a true duet, and as Albertine played through the chorus, she heard her husband's plaintive horn, and she believed for an instant that they were begging each other to reaffirm their mutual love. It was a brief, magical moment. But then Pearl caressed the microphone and sang, "All of me, why not take all of me?" with such longing that she became the voice for everyone who wanted to be loved. And as Hendrik's saxophone joined her, it was obvious that she was pleading with him. To everyone in the audience, the conversation was between the tall, thin vocalist and the blond band leader on saxophone. The petite girl on the piano was just playing chords in the background. Don't give her a second thought!

The applause at the end of the number was too enthusiastic for Albertine. It had not been a difficult song. Anyone could sing that tune. Maybe that was why it was so popular.

"Thank you, everyone. Thank you so much!" Pearl cooed into the microphone, and Albertine wanted to strangle her.

The next number started with Pearl's vocal going straight into the chorus: "You do something to me, something that simply mystifies me…" And she turned to look at Hendrik when she came to the line "Do do that voodoo that you do so well." She finished her chorus and stepped aside so Hendrik could come forward with his saxophone, strapped to his damaged hand. He belted out a brilliant solo to Pearl's obvious delight.

Albertine told herself that this public love making between Pearl and Hendrik was just part of the act. Practically every number was a love song, and it would seem unnatural if the vocalist didn't flaunt her sex appeal. But as she played the piano part, Albertine felt that she had been captured in the voodoo spell of that dark woman, locked there to the keyboard while her husband pranced in the spotlight with this siren. Somehow this thought made her music better: Albertine played with a vengeance. She thought she heard applause after her brief solo, and she lost herself entirely in the final, loud conclusion. When she looked up, both Terrell, the drummer, and Rocko, the bass player, were waving for her to stand up and take a bow.

After this, Hendrik wouldn't be able to dismiss her as an amateur. He would have to recognize her as an important member of his band, at least as important as Pearl, who couldn't play an instrument, and only used her body to attract attention.

The next song started with the trombone playing ironically, accompanied by Albertine's piano underneath. She mouthed the words over the instrumental before Pearl repeated them. "Another bride, another June, another sunny honeymoon. Another season, another reason, for making whoopee…"

This sly song was designed for Pearl, the home-wrecker, who would be only too willing to sing about the entrapment of married life. She would understand how easy it was to manipulate men with sex, at least until you tried to obligate them in any way, tie them down with a family. And Pearl sang it perfectly, even before Hendrik joined in on the saxophone.

And the lyrics, of course, reminded Albertine about her recent nights with Hendrik, making whoopee as much as ever, and she knew it had taken effect, just as in the song, and she was carrying his second child. And no matter how much voodoo Pearl tried, Albertine knew that Hendrik was tied to her now, the way that Colby was tied to Flora. Nothing could split them apart. The morning sickness was worth it; the fact that her own body would grow fat and be stretched out of shape; that she would not be able to wear any of her pretty clothes; and that she would be tied down again with an infant; none of those things would matter as long as she could keep Hendrik. And as long as she kept him, she'd never stray from him again.

But in the spotlight, you'd think that it was Pearl and Hendrik who had been making whoopee together. Albertine couldn't see their faces, but even as she played the piano, she could glance over and see them lean together like two stupid love birds: she with her wiggly hips and Hendrik bowing toward her with the shiny brass saxophone, like an ancient love offering. There was no room for a piano solo here. The trombone, bass and sax all flirted with Pearl, who intended to make fools of them all. Why couldn't Hendrik see how Pearl was trying to wrap him around her little finger? Because he was a man. Because men are oblivious. Because men don't understand women at all.

The band closed the evening with "Bye-Bye Black Bird." Musically, this was the most satisfying number of the night. After the saxophone lead-in, and Pearl's prelude, the band came to life, with Pearl's vocal as part of the ensemble. "Pack up all my cares and woe, here I go, singing low. Bye, bye, black bird."

There was plenty of room for good licks from the trombone, a nice solo from Albertine, and a triumphant improvisation on the chorus from Hendrik. In the middle of the number, Pearl asked the audience to sing along with her, which they did enthusiastically. The band finished with an instrumental version of the chorus, which kept the dancers moving until the final chord.

"Thank you, thank you so much!" Pearl announced to the dispersing crowd. "Come back here to the Spotlight Club next week to hear the Kinderman Combo. Our leader on the saxophone is Hendrik Kinderman. This is Pearl Cornell. We wish a good night to you all!"

There's nothing quieter than a night club after the music has ended, Albertine felt. For a part time band, they had sounded pretty good, and Albertine felt satisfied to have been part of it. There was something more complete, something magical about performing in a group, and she understood how Hendrik craved it. It was more than just parlor music: when the whole ballroom came to life, you knew you were doing something special. The excitement was over now, and she felt tired and let down.

The Starlight's owner, a German named Freddie Heinz, shook Hendrik's hand, disregarding the missing thumb.

"Zat was some show," Heinz said as he nodded rapidly. He was taller than Hendrik, bald and much heavier. His black, unkempt moustache protruded two inches over his mouthful of stained teeth. He wore a tan summer suit and a red tie painted over with pink roses. Heinz reached into his coat pocket and pulled out an envelope. "Here ya go, mein freund," he said. "Tommy vill wait for you to load up and he'll lock the doors behind you. See you next week."

"Danke, Freddie. We appreciate the gig," Hendrik said.

"Forget about it," Freddie said as he picked up his straw hat. "Güten nacht."

Terrell had a panel truck (he worked as a plumber during the day), so they loaded the drums and the bass into the back of it.

Pearl and Albertine sat at a table and waited as the men loaded the truck. Albertine didn't want to be near the singer, but she felt too exhausted to move. She might have fallen asleep if Pearl didn't keep talking to her.

"Now <u>that</u> was a performance, dearie," Pearl said. "We had them eating out of the palm of our hand."

"It could be better," Albertine shrugged. "We could use more practice."

"It's night and day with you on the piano," Pearl told her. "It's like a different band. A good piano player makes all the difference. A gal can sing with just a piano behind her. Everyone else is gravy."

"Even the saxophone?"

"Yeah, what do ya think? When I'm up there I gotta compete against the goddamn Pied Piper. I know how to sing, but I'm no match for that."

"You're okay," Albertine said through a yawn. "Everyone was listening to you."

"They were paying attention to me because I'm young and wearing a tight dress."

"That's show business," Albertine said and smiled. "At least you don't have to take your clothes off."

"Oh, I do that too, when I have to," Pearl nodded. "I'm no fool."

Chapter Twelve

Through the fall Albertine played piano in the Hendrik Kinderman Quintet at a series of small joints around the city. Over time their 20-song repertoire became second nature to them, and performing was exciting and fun for Albertine, in spite of her constant suspicion that Pearl and Hendrik had more going on than their musical act. She learned to like Rocko, the bass player, who worked in the relief warehouse during the day handing out food staples and children's clothing. He told her the Depression was bound to go away, but the lines at the relief center were getting longer every week.

Terrell, the drummer, complained all the time about the "dumps" where they were "reduced to performing" for a "measly eight bucks a night." He didn't like Hendrik's choice of music, either, covering popular tunes that didn't take full advantage of "the element of percussion." He had the disgusting habit of eating sunflower seeds all night and spitting the shells onto the floor behind his drum set.

Billy, on trombone, shoveled coal from delivery trucks during the winter and delivered ice the rest of the year. He had gone to high school with Albertine's brother Larry at Crane Tech. He played the trombone so expertly that with the right material he could have upstaged Hendrik. Albertine was sure that he would lead his own band some day.

Pearl seemed to go out of her way to ingratiate herself with Albertine. "I need to keep you in the band," she would say. "Behind every good singer is an even better piano player." Pearl knew that Albertine was hungry all the time, and she brought her sandwiches, saltines, cookies and lemon drop candies. She hugged her every night after the show and thanked her for another great performance. But there was something false about the way Pearl talked to her, and the clinging way she touched her made Albertine feel that Pearl was trying to distract her from the truth.

Hank's mother had brought him to the Fontaine house just as his grandfather was leaving for the night shift at Donnelly's Printing Company. The old man carried some sandwiches wrapped in newspaper and a big red apple.

"This is for you," Henry told his grandson and handed him the piece of fruit. "You need the vitamins to grow."

Hank took the apple and immediately took a big bite. It was crunchy, juicy and sweet, as good an apple as he'd ever tasted. "Thanks," he said as he chewed.

"Hank!" Albertine scolded him. "He meant for you to save it for later."

"Not at all, not at all," Henry said and squeezed Hank's shoulder. "Enjoy it right away! You never know when the next apple will come along."

"Whatever happened to 'save for a rainy day'?" Albertine asked him. "That's what you always told me."

"You're his mother," Henry laughed. "That's your job."

"Don't be late for yours."

"I won't be. How's the music going? Larry says the group is sounding very professional."

"We're making progress. And a little money, too."

"Larry says Hendrik found a hot new singer. A regular chanteuse."

"Larry knows talent," Albertine said, trying not to let her dad get her goat. "I just play the piano."

"Well, he told me that you make the band, Albertine. He said you hold it together."

"He has to say that," she smiled. "He's my brother."

"You know better than that," Henry said, kissed her cheek and strode out to the sidewalk. "Play well," he said.

Albertine walked inside briefly to make sure her mother saw Hank and that she took custody of him. Birdie, in a flowered apron, stood at the kitchen stove stirring a pot of ham bone soup. A fresh loaf of bread was cooling on the counter beside the stove.

"Hi, Ma. Here's Hank."

"Oh, there you are. How was your day at work?"

"Slow, Ma," Albertine said and shook her head. "If you ask me, Swanson's will be out of business by Christmas."

"Don't say that," Birdie shook her head. "It's bad luck. If they can just hang on for a few more months, we'll be out of this Depression."

"Don't hold your breath," Albertine sighed and placed a pillow case on the table. "Here's some clean clothes for Hank. I'll come and get him at nine tomorrow morning." She stepped toward the door.

"Don't be in such a hurry, Albertine. Sit down and have something to eat. In your condition, you need your nourishment."

"In my condition?" Albertine shrugged. "I'm not even four months gone."

"Nutrition is important. Rest is, too, you know. I wish you wouldn't…"

"Ma!"

"All right, all right. I've said it all before. At least sit down and eat a bowl of soup and a slice of bread. And I'll pour you and Hank a glass of milk each."

Hank took another bite of his apple, licked the juice off his lips and looked at his mother and grandmother. His mother was wearing a blue dress with sleeves down to her elbows and a white-flowered pattern over her stomach, which was beginning to bulge out with the new baby. She was still as pretty as ever, with her green eyes, black hair and beautiful hands. But she seemed tired these days, with dark circles under her eyes, and a short temper.

Birdie was an inch or two shorter than her daughter and her body seemed twice as wide as Albertine's. She wore heavy black shoes and white socks with lace fringes around her ankles. Her hair was gray and crimped, and she wore glasses with steel frames and black nose guards. She grinned at Hank, and he guessed she was watching him so he wouldn't do anything bad. He felt a little scared. His mom had a temper, but his grandmother could really get mad!

"Come on, young man," she said to him. "Take off your hat and sit down at my little table here and have a bowl of soup with your mother."

Hank hooked his cap over the back post of a chair and climbed up as his grandmother placed a glass of milk and a soup spoon at his place, then gripped Albertine by the shoulders and pulled her down onto another chair.

"Okay, okay, I'll eat!" Albertine said. "You'd think I was starving."

"You look like you're starving! You're responsible for that new baby, remember! When are you going to get some meat on your bones?"

"Ma, I don't want to get fat. If Hendrik wanted a fat wife, he'd have married a German girl."

"Look at me," Birdie said to her daughter, raised her arms, and turned around in a little dance. "Sooner or later you're going to look like this. You can't escape turning into a little fireplug of a woman. It's your heritage, your fate."

As Hank tasted the too-hot soup, he thought it would be a horrible thing for his mother to be transformed into Grandma Birdie. It was the reverse of the ugly duckling story: someone beautiful being transformed into a person that no one wanted to look at.

"Ma, I don't know where you get your theories," Albertine said and shook her head in disbelief. "From Doc Bichet, I suppose."

"Hush now and eat," Birdie scolded her. "I thought you were in a hurry."

It didn't take Albertine long to eat a big bowl of soup and drink two glasses of milk with cream on it. Hank's soup was barely cool enough to eat when his Mom was getting up to leave.

"Bye-bye, sweetheart," she said and kissed his cheek. "You be good for your Grandma. I'll see you in the morning."

After working another full week, Albertine had to make quite an effort to get Hank to her parents' house and then take the streetcar through a sudden downpour to the L to meet the band for Friday night's performance. They had been playing two or three nights a week for four months now, and they had four good sets that they performed very well. Albertine thought her piano playing was better than ever, but the schedule and her pregnancy were wearing her down so that she ached for rest. The baby was showing a lot, too, and her loose dresses made her look dowdy on stage. She was hungry all the time, and her big stomach made her feel more distant from the keyboard, so she had to adjust the way she played.

Tonight they were performing in a basement club called Harvey's Moonglow off North Clark Street. The place reminded Albertine of the Top Hat when it was still a speakeasy. It was dark, cramped, smoky and full of patrons who didn't pay attention to the performance. She arrived in a hurry nearly running from the L station in flat shoes, a baggy flannel dress, and a cloth coat that she had borrowed from Elsie. She knew she'd make it through the night, and the music would be fine, but she didn't know how long she could maintain this routine. And when she would eventually have to leave the band in a month or two, how could she trust Pearl and Hendrik together?

As Albertine took off her coat in the small dressing room beside the stage, Pearl came in behind her carrying a brown sack and a paper cup. "Hiya, Albertine," Pearl said. "I brought you a coffee and a corned beef sandwich. I figured you probably didn't have time to eat a thing before rushing over here."

"Thanks," she said, "but I could have bummed something from the kitchen."

"In this dive?" Pearl laughed. "I wouldn't risk it, if I were you."

In spike heels and a hat with feathers, Pearl seemed taller and more slender than ever. She pulled off her gray raincoat to reveal a sleek, emerald-green dress.

"Have you already eaten?" Albertine asked her.

"I had some corned beef hash with an egg on top," she said. "That's why I thought of that sandwich for you. Now, eat up! What good is a piano player who's starving? I should let you faint in the middle of a set?"

Pearl was right: Albertine was ravenous tonight. She sat down on the musty couch, unwrapped the sandwich in her lap, and took a big bite. It tasted great. The rye bread was fresh and full of caraway seeds. The meat had plenty of juicy fat and was spiced with brown mustard. The coffee was just right, too, with plenty of milk and sugar.

"Is Hendrik here yet?" Pearl asked as she pinned her silk gardenia in her hair.

"I don't know," Albertine said as she chewed, "I just got here myself."

"Better keep track of that husband of yours," Pearl teased her. "He's got a lot of fans in this city now."

"Come on, Pearl, get real!" This came from Terrell, the drummer, who carried his drumsticks and brushes in a long, leather-covered box with a shoulder strap, like a flute case. "We're playing in a dump called 'Harvey's Moonglow.' How many fans can we have?"

"I wasn't talking about <u>your</u> fans, Terrell," Pearl said and pressed her fist to his cheek until he swatted her hand away. "The fans belong to Hendrik and me, and to Albertine…I wasn't talkin' about no drummer."

"In the real jazz clubs, drummers get credit for what they do," Terrell insisted. "But we're reduced to playing in joints like this for next to nothing."

"Last I checked," Pearl reminded him, "you were never the headliner at the Palmer House. What exactly are you reduced from?"

"I'm playing drums in a basement club with a band that's going nowhere."

"We're a band that's working, Terrell," Pearl corrected him. "That means we're a success, kiddo. We're a success!"

"Dream on, Sweetheart," Terrell said and hurried back out into the club.

Rocko, the bass player, leaned into the dressing room to hang his leather jacket and snap-bill cap on the coat tree.

"Evening, Ladies," he said and smiled at them. "Nice fall weather we're having."

"It'll be cold soon," Albertine said. "Then that rain will turn to snow."

"We got a shipment of blankets at the Relief center today," Rocko said. "Government issue. Heavy wool. Too bad they smell like moth balls."

Rocko worked a day job at the armory on Division Street, which had been turned into a distribution center for the Relief program. He doled out flour and surplus cheese, canned milk, powdered eggs and dried beans to hungry families, and he passed out boxes of clothes and shoes for kids who couldn't afford them. He wasn't paid much himself, but he was always in a good mood. Rocko saw suffering every day – and nowadays, who didn't? – but he was happy that he could do something about it. And with the extra he made with the band, he could help his mother get by.

"Those blankets will air out just fine," Albertine said. "And people will be grateful to have them."

"Albertine," Rocko asked her, "would you mind helping me tune up? With all these changes in temperature, my bass gets a little off."

Since Rocko had discovered Albertine's perfect pitch, he had relied on her to help get his bass in tune before each performance. He could match the notes on the piano fairly well, but he found that Albertine could get him perfectly synchronized.

The double bass looked like an antique, and its tuning pegs hardly seemed strong enough to hold its rope-like strings. Rocko was only a few inches taller than the instrument, and he handled it like a living creature, a very large exotic bird or a nervous horse.

To tune the first string, Albertine played the lowest E on the piano, then listened as Rocko adjusted the bridge and slowly tightened the string. When the two notes matched exactly, she nodded to him, then played the A. She was pleased that the lower end of the keyboard was well-tuned: she could get Rocko's bass right on the money from the beginning. The way he slapped it and tugged the strings to be heard, they'd have to re-tune between sets, but if they got it right now, they'd only have to make minor adjustments later. They repeated the process through the D and G strings, and then Rocko played some chords (plucking and using his bow), and Albertine helped him make the final adjustments so that all the strings sounded right together.

As soon as they finished, Billy began warming up on the trombone. As usual, he started with Beethoven's "Ode to Joy," and then he played a section of the Alleluia chorus from Handel's Messiah, before sliding into "When the Saints Go Marching In."

Albertine thought Billy was a truly gifted musician, and she wondered why he stayed with Hendrik's band. He was talented enough to play with anyone. He could play notes faster on the slide trombone than many trumpeters could play by pushing their valves. But when he put down his horn, Billy seemed more tired than usual. He sat down on a chair in the first row of tables and yawned.

"What's the matter, Billy?" she asked him. "Didn't you sleep last night?"

"Naw, I switched back to shoveling coal this week," he said. "For the cold weather season. That's a lot harder than delivering ice. First I shovel it onto the truck, then down the coal chutes, all day long. Holy Cripes, it's killing me, but I'm lucky to have a job."

"Tired or not, your horn sounds great tonight, Billy," Albertine encouraged him.

"Thanks," he said, and yawned again. "But youse guys better play well enough to keep me awake, or I'll be sawing a log by the second set."

Then Pearl came out of the dressing room with a glass of water and stood beside the piano. "Come on, Al, play a few scales for me to warm up with. I need to loosen up my pipes."

Albertine played through scales starting at middle C, and working upward, and Pearl kept up with her, singing all vowels, "eee-ooo-eee-ooo-eee." Next Albertine played the scales downward, and Pearl's voice grew lonely and turned husky. Then Pearl drank her water and asked, "Where's Hendrik? It's time for the show."

The dinner crowd had begun to come in, and they sat in clusters at the rear tables, near the bar. The bus boys came out with long wicks to light the candles on all the tables and someone turned the house lights low. By eight o'clock, when their first set was supposed to begin, Hendrik still hadn't arrived. The manager, dressed in a shabby old tuxedo, came out from the kitchen and spoke to Pearl, and she in turn came back to the piano and leaned over to Albertine. "Play them some cocktail music until Hendrik gets here," Pearl said.

Thinking back to the songs she had played at the Top Hat, she played "Tea for Two" straight through without sheet music, and when Hendrik still didn't come, she played "Button Up Your Overcoat" and "Let a Smile Be Your Umbrella." She was halfway through "Who's Sorry Now?" when Hendrik hurried into the club, tossed his overcoat on the floor of the dressing room, and rushed to the front of the room, simultaneously struggling with the straps on his saxophone to secure it around his neck and against the heel of his right hand. But instead of seeming pressured, Hendrik was smiling, and as Albertine cut to the end of the song, the rest of the band took their places. Then Hendrik started the evening's opening number, "Ain't Misbehaving" with a contagious energy that lifted the band to one of their best performances.

Much later, after closing time, Hendrik grabbed a bottle of Seagram's from the bar to pour everyone but Albertine a drink. They sat around the first table in front of the bandstand, and Hendrik smiled wearily as he filled their glasses. Rocko had already opened a can of condensed milk for Albertine and poured it over a glass of ice.

"Geez, what's the occasion? Terrell asked. "Did your horse come in?"

"In a way, yes," Hendrik said. "I've found us a gig in Florida for the whole winter."

"We're going back to the Flamingo?" Billy asked. "Out of the cold?"

"Out of the cold, yah," Hendrik said and smiled as he nodded happily. "But this time it's the Coconut Grove. A new hotel, a thousand guest rooms, three night clubs. We will be playing in the Balinese Room. Very exotic. Real deluxe."

"Will we get to live there?" Pearl asked.

"We get to share a cottage on the beach," Hendrik explained.

Albertine whispered to him frantically. "Hey, wait," she protested. "I'm having a baby! I can't go to Florida!"

"I know, and I'm sorry," Hendrik said and walked her around the bar away from the band. "But this is a big break for the combo. All the New York people go down to Florida. This could lead to big things!"

"But why this year, Hendrik?" she pleaded. "Don't you want to be here when your baby is born?"

"I'd take you with me if it made sense. But it don't make sense. You need to be close to your mother."

"You need to be close to your wife!"

"You can't turn down an opportunity like this one. If you say no, they will never ask you again. A hundred bands in Chicago could take this gig. Do you think the booking agents will save us a place in line for next year?"

"But you told me yourself that my piano-playing had given new life to the band, that getting Jake out of the equation made all the difference."

"All you say is true. And I appreciate it," Hendrik admitted. "But look at you, Albertine: you'll have to leave the band soon, anyhow."

"You could have discussed it with me first!" she hissed. "Why didn't you talk to me first?"

"There was no time! He needed an answer on the spot."

"I don't believe you!" she moaned. "You could have asked for more time."

"Do you want me to call him tomorrow and tell him to forget the whole thing?"

"Yes!" she insisted. "Tell him you'll find a gig in Chicago."

"No!" he growled. "We are going to Florida, whether you like it or not."

Then he spun away from her and went back to the others. Albertine felt like crying, but she didn't want to give him the satisfaction of knowing how badly he had hurt her. She watched as Hendrik sat down at the table between Rocko and Billy and put hs arms over their shoulders. But as Hendrik acted buddy-buddy with his musicians, Albertine could see that Pearl's eyes were fixed on Hendrik and she was smiling the whole time.

What could Albertine say now? What could she do? Her husband was going to run away to Florida for the winter with another woman, and she would be alone with Hank when the baby was born. Her plan of having a baby to keep Hendrik with her had backfired. Not only did he resent having to support another child, but he saw her now as fat and unattractive. He could play around with the slinky, twenty-four year-old colored girl all he wanted. The thought made Albertine sick at heart, and she felt extremely stupid. For months she had worked to make Hendrik's band an act that people noticed, and her reward was to be abandoned when she needed him the most. She should have been angry, but instead she felt worn out, dizzy, and defeated.

"Geez, Al, you look a little peeked," Rocko called to her. "Come sit down and finish your milk."

She took one step and collapsed onto the floor. It wasn't Hendrik who rushed to help her first, but Pearl. "Honey, are you all right?" Pearl asked as she knelt beside her.

Albertine couldn't answer as Pearl stroked her hair and patted her cheek. "I think you're just tired," Pearl said to her gently. "Rest for a minute before you try to get up. And forget about riding home in the back of Terrell's truck. We'll make sure Hendrik gets you home in a taxi."

Doesn't this beat all? Albertine asked herself as Pearl helped her up, guided her across the room and eased her onto the chair in front of her glass of milk. My worst enemy is helping me while Hendrik is too busy getting drunk with his friends to even care that I fainted! It's like me helping Flora, while all the time I wished I could steal her husband. Except Flora never knew what I was up to, and I can read Pearl like a book. She acts like a nice girl when she takes care of you if you're hungry or sick. But she can't take her eyes off what she really wants, which is Hendrik Kinderman, who happens to belong to me.

Look at him, the cocky German, drinking and laughing with his friends. He's totally forgotten that we've just had a fight, and it's eating me up inside. He's just happy that he's going back to his tropical paradise where he can play his horn for a living without working a day job. Maybe Pearl isn't even part of the equation yet, but without me watching she'll find a way to fox her way into his bed. The last time Hendrik was down there, when Mayor Cermak was killed, he didn't have a singer with his band. He said that's why they only played there for three weeks. With Pearl they'd gotten a gig for the whole winter, so Albertine wouldn't see Hendrik for months.

The condensed milk was too sweet, even in the melting ice, and Albertine could only swallow a few sips. She felt very sleepy now, and all the cigarette smoke made her queasy, and although she wished she could go home right away, she didn't want to beg Hendrik in front of the others. So she sat in the chair and dozed off, opening her eyes every few minutes to see the blur of four men and a woman drinking whiskey, smoking cigarettes and celebrating at a time of night when all sane people were at home and in bed. Thank goodness that's where Hank was: sound asleep in the feather mattress on the roll-away bed in the hallway at her parents' house. At least she didn't have to worry about Hank.

Chapter Thirteen

After Hendrik left for Florida, Albertine gave up the apartment on Lexington and took a spare room at her parents' house, where Hank slept in the hall outside her door on the roll-away bed. (Her piano was the only piece of furniture she kept. Her father wedged it into the corner of the dining room.) She continued to work on the switchboard because Mr. Swanson knew that Hendrik had left her alone with Hank, so he waived his policy against pregnant women on the job. She also needed to keep busy, and with her advancing pregnancy, she couldn't go back to play at the Top Hat or anywhere else. Answering phones all day gave her something to do, and it kept her away from the house and out of her mother's way.

The Fontaine house was within walking distance of the Notre Dame Church and Grammar school, where Hank was enrolled in the fourth grade and Lorraine was in the seventh. Though he tried to avoid it, Hank couldn't help walking Lorraine to and from school every day. She was a picture of neatness in her braided hair with shiny barrettes, her starched and pressed white blouse, and her pleated skirt and wool knee socks. When it got colder, she wore her new lamb's wool coat every day with her red beret and beige kid gloves. (Most of Hank's clothes had come from the Relief center.) One November afternoon Lorraine was so talkative that Hank wondered when she was going to take a breath so he could get a word in edge-wise.

"If you ask my opinion," she said, "I'd say that boys and girls should go to separate schools. The way boys act is rude, crude and totally inappropriate."

"Well, girls are too fussy," Hank reminded her. "Grandpa says they're fastidious."

"Pa just likes to use big words. He likes to go camping and doesn't understand why girls hate to go to the bathroom in the woods. When he says 'fastidious', he means 'civilized.' "

"You'll get away from the boys when you go to high school, won't you?" Hank asked her. "Aren't there only girls at Providence?"

"That's two years away for me, Hank," Lorraine told him. "It's an eternity! I hope I can survive to the fall of 1936!"

"You never know," Hank teased her. "You could be struck by lightning, or hit by a stray bullet from a gangster's machine gun."

"I'm more worried about flying spit balls," Lorraine scolded him. "And the fart noises you boys make by jamming your hands under your armpits."

"Geez," Hank sighed. "I wish I knew how to do that!"

They had been walking down Congress Street past the green grocers with the stands of fruit and vegetables, the butcher shop with a whole pig hanging in the window, the bakery with its pyramid of loaves, the dry goods store with its bolts of fabric, and a barber shop where you could really get a haircut and there were no dice games in back.

They turned the corner and walked the two blocks to the Fontaine house. At the curb in front, Larry stood beside his Ford, loosening a monstrous green armchair that was tied to its roof. Hank ran up to him, but Lorraine talked first, calling out from a distance.

"What's up, Larry?" she yelled to him. "Don't tell me you're moving back in!"

"This stuff belongs to Elsie and Gene," Larry replied impatiently. "They got evicted today. I'm trying to get everything inside before it starts raining."

"They got evicted?" Lorraine asked him and screwed up her face into a particularly ugly expression. "Why did they get evicted?"

"Listen, sister," Larry barked. "I don't have time to draw you a diagram. It's gonna rain in a minute, and Gene's waiting on the sidewalk on the other end with the rest of their furniture. So why don't you and Hank help out by unloading the back seat while I try to lug this chair inside without killing myself?"

Hank ran to the house and set the books on the porch and hurried back to the car to see how he could help. Something large and made of cast iron was practically falling out of the open trunk. Then Hank saw that it was secured with ropes.

"What can I do?" Hank asked. "How can I help, Uncle Larry?"

"You can get Elsie's fabric out of the back seat," Larry told him. "That is, if your hands are clean."

"Yeah, they're clean," Hank said. "I just came home from school. Why shouldn't they be clean?"

"Just checking. Your Aunt Elsie will kill you if you get fingerprints on that cloth!"

Hank wiped his hands on the thighs of his trousers, then held them up for Larry's inspection. "See. Clean enough?"

"Clean enough." Larry said and stood aside so Hank could lean into the car to pick up the first bolt of cloth, which was yellow and printed with green stems and blue and white flowers. The roll of fabric was stiffer and heavier than Hank expected, and it smelled of dye – like ink or laundry soap. He stepped carefully with this special load up the brick sidewalk to the porch steps. The front door opened just as Hank walked up to it. His Aunt Elsie stood on the threshold.

"Hello, young man," she said with a forced smile. "Are you helping unload the car?"

"Yes, Aunt Else. Where should I put this?" he asked her.

"On the dining room table, dear. Let's put all the fabric on the table."

"Okay," Hank said and walked to the dining room and set the bolt on an empty space on the table, which was nearly covered with dishes, pots and pans, and stacks of folded linens. Hank guessed that this was Larry's third or fourth trip with his Ford. When Hank got back outside, Elsie was untying the ropes that held her sewing machine in the trunk, and Grandpa Fontaine was helping Larry slide the bulky chair off the roof of the car. Grandpa's left hand was wrapped in a white bandage of gauze and adhesive tape, and Hank wondered how he had hurt himself. Grandpa wasn't the kind of person who got hurt: he was the guy who helped everyone else when they got hurt.

"Easy now, easy," Grandpa said as they set the chair down on the mud beside the sidewalk. "What makes that chair so damn heavy?" he asked.

"Springs," Larry guessed. "Steel springs."

"I think it's packed with sawdust," Henry laughed. "Wet sawdust."

They carried the chair to the porch and set it down under the eave, next to where Lorraine sat on the porch swing.

"It can sit here for a while," Henry said and unconsciously cradled his bandaged hand. "Out of the elements."

"Geez, Dad. What happened to your hand?" Larry asked.

"Got an alignment pin jammed through my palm," Henry shook his head. "Just like Christ on the cross."

"Has Mom looked at it?"

"Who else?"

"Then it should be all right," Larry slapped his shoulder as Hank hurried past them with another bolt of fabric.

"Hello!" Elsie called to them from behind the car. "I think I felt a rain drop. Could you help me get this sewing machine inside before it gets wet and rusted? It's the only source of income we've got."

"Sure, Sis, we'll get it in for ya," Larry said. "But what happened? I thought you were the most popular dress maker on the North Side."

"Everyone's watching their money now," Elsie explained. "The orders dried up. We missed two months' rent, and all of a sudden our furniture is out on the sidewalk!"

"And still nothing for Gene?" Henry asked his daughter.

"As a day laborer once or twice a week," Elsie said. "Things are bad out there. He has worked for as little as a dollar a day, Pa. He has walked home for two hours just to save car fare."

"Hey, Elsie," Lorraine called, "where's Ricky and Roxanne."

"I hope they're with their dad. They were in school when we got evicted. Gene's guarding our things so no one steals them before we get them all over here."

"I guess the kids will be upset when they find out your family's been thrown out of your apartment," Lorraine said.

"Probably about as upset as you'll be when you find out that you'll be sharing your room with Roxy."

"I'll be what?"

Ignoring her baby sister, Elsie stepped down the porch stairs to supervise her dad and brother as they lifted the treadle sewing machine from the jump seat-trunk and hefted it precariously to the sidewalk, where it landed too hard for Elsie's liking. "Hey, easy there! Don't bend it!"

"We won't bend it!" Henry scoffed.

"And it's got to go all the way inside," Elsie told them. "It can't take any moisture whatsoever, or it will seize up on me."

"That's what oil is for," Henry teased her. "I've got an oil can in the shed with my motorcycle."

"Can we please bring it in the parlor and set it next to the piano?" Elsie asked.

"We'll try to make it fit," Henry winked at her as Hank came down the steps to get another load. Hank quickly retrieved a basket from the back seat and set it down on the porch steps as his grandfather and uncle carried the sewing machine through the front door.

"What's in the basket?" Lorraine asked, ran up to it and lifted its lid. "Buttons and thread! Scissors and needles! A cushion full of straight pins! Square pieces of chalk!"

"What did you expect?" Hank asked her. "Buried treasure?"

"For once, I hoped our family would have something interesting. Some rare jewels or a basket of snakes like Cleopatra's."

"Where would Elsie get a basket of snakes like Cleopatra's?" Hank asked her.

"I'm just imagining, silly," Lorraine teased him. "Where's your imagination, little Kinderman?"

"You can quit razzing me, Lorraine," Hank told her and clenched his fist, "unless you want a fat lip!"

"Punch me and see what my Pa does to you!"

"I'm not going to punch you!" Hank shook his head. "Where's your imagination, Little Fontaine?"

He picked up the basket and followed the men back into the living room, where Elsie sat in front of her sewing machine, working its pedal and making its needle reciprocate. "Well, it still works, anyways. That's one small blessing."

Hank walked through to the dining room, and when he couldn't find an empty space on the table, he set the basket on a chair. When he came back to the living room, he met Larry and Grandpa squeezing the big armchair in the corner next to his mother's piano.

"It'll be safe here," Henry said, "until Elsie and Gene find another place."

Larry turned to Hank, "Well, kiddo, do you have the car all unloaded?"

"Just one package left," Hank said, eager to please. "I'll bring it in."

The last package rested on the front passenger's seat. It was a long, flat bundle, surrounded by shiny brown cardboard and tied up with soiled pink ribbon. From what Hank could see it looked like a crumpled stack of butcher paper all wadded together. It wasn't heavy, but it took him a while to maneuver it out the car door without banging its edges. As he bought the bundle free, the rain began to fall, and Hank hurried to shelter it under the eaves before more than a few drops could fall onto it. He wiped them dry on the sleeve of his sweater before he opened the door and tugged the bundle inside.

"Thanks, dear," Elsie said to him. "You've saved my dress patterns from ruination. I'll be back in business in no time."

"The rain's starting to fall," Larry said. "I'd better go back for the last load before Eugene gives up on me."

After Aunt Elsie, Uncle Gene, Ricky and Roxanne moved into the Fontaine's, the old house didn't seem so large any more. Albertine moved in with Claribel to make room for the couple, Roxanne shared Lorraine's room, and worst of all, Hank had to sleep with Ricky on the feather bed in the hallway. Now ten people had to share one bathroom, and Birdie was forced to put more water and cabbage into the stew.

Albertine had almost forgotten what it was like to carry a baby inside her. The balance of her body had shifted, and her strength had turned inward to nurture the new life. Her uterus was hard and growing, expanding more and moving higher each week. Her breasts grew larger and more sensitive, and because she was hungry all the time, she ate too much, and her hips widened with more padding.

She had mixed emotions when she felt the baby flutter inside her, first like a minnow, then a goldfish, and then like a little person with arms and legs. Sometimes she felt wonder that there was a new life inside her. And she sometimes felt tenderness toward the baby, her second child, the product of her love for Hendrik. But when she was tired, or when she felt fat and ugly, or when she considered herself abandoned by her husband, she blamed the creature that was growing inside her, and she deeply resented the baby. Why was she suffering the consequences? Why was she trapped when everyone else was free?

And she was back in her parents' house because of the baby. It was worse than being a child again because she knew what it meant to be a married woman, an independent adult. And even though her father assured her that this was a temporary condition and that she would be released from it when the baby came and Hendrik returned in the spring, she sometimes felt that she had irrevocably lost him, not only to Pearl, but to Florida and to his wandering life as a musician.

Birdie was a tough person around the house, an impatient task mistress who banged on her frying pan, a bossy old woman who did not rest until you bent to her will. Yet, as a nurse and midwife, a caregiver, she was gentle and calm, healing and infinitely patient. There was nothing more reassuring than the touch of her hands. In her two roles, Birdie could have been two different women.

In November, Birdie had Albertine lie on the big double bed in her second-floor room and stood beside her to touch her abdomen and feel the baby. She used her palms and her fingertips, cupping the top, sides and bottom of her belly, then pressing, first gently, then more firmly to find the baby's head, his bottom, and to estimate his length and weight. She used a cloth tape to measure Albertine's uterus, and she made careful notes in her leather-bound midwife's log. She used her stethoscope to listen to the baby's heart, and after a minute, she wrote down its rate. Then she carefully examined her daughter, checking her blood pressure, listening to her heart and lungs, checking her breasts with the same motions she'd used to examine her stomach, and then feeling inside to check the consistency and size of her cervix.

As Birdie lathered her hands above the wash basin on her bureau, she asked Albertine, "And when was the last day of your last period?"

"Some time in the first week of June."

"Are you sure?"

"Ma, you know I've always been irregular."

"Was that a light period? A heavy one?"

"Light. Lighter than usual, I think. But I wasn't worried about it. Should I have been worried, Ma?"

"Well, I think you're at least a month further along than that," Birdie told her. "Now I think you're due in early February, not March."

"That can't be right, Ma," Albertine insisted. "I had a period in June."

"You might have had some spotting, dear, but I think you were already expecting."

"That can't be right!"

"Dear, you wouldn't be this big if you were only five months gone."

"That can't be right!" If she was right, Colby Malone could be her baby's father.

"What difference does it make if you conceived in April or May instead of June?"

"That was before I was trying to get pregnant."

"Oh my, girl, if women only got pregnant when they were trying, half the people in the world would have never been born. More than half."

"That means I'll have to stop working sooner!" Albertine said. "Mr. Swanson said I'd have to quit when I started showing too much."

"You keep working as long as you feel like working," Birdie told her. "You're just sitting down at the switchboard all day. If he wants you to leave, make him fire you."

"But the rules are that pregnant women have to leave…"

"So pregnant women have to starve?"

"You'll feed me, won't you?"

"That's not the point. Men don't have babies! They shouldn't set the rules for women who carry them and give birth to them. Where do all their sons and daughters come from? Jesus, Mary and Joseph!"

"I can't play at the Top Hat looking like this."

"Just forget the night clubs for a while! You need your rest. You need to keep regular hours. Do you hear me?"

"I hear you."

"And you wouldn't be stranded here if that German hadn't run away to join the circus!" Birdie scolded her and shook her head.

"You know he didn't join the circus!" Albertine snapped back. "He's a musician. He has to go where the work is."

"I see. And there's no work for musicians in Chicago?" Birdie asked sarcastically and scowled at her. "I notice that Larry has jobs every weekend."

"That's right," Albertine argued, "but there's no money in it. Larry has a day job, too."

"And I suppose your Heinie makes plenty of dough down in Florida? Enough to support you and Hank?"

Albertine paused to choose her words carefully. "Well," she said, "Hendrik does his share."

"He does his share. Is that it?" Birdie shook her head and then pushed her eyeglasses back in place. "I saw that you got a letter from him this morning. The first one in quite a while."

"Two or three weeks," she admitted, though it had been closer to four.

"And how much money did he send you this time, dear?" Birdie asked and folded her arms across her chest.

"I'd have to check," Albertine said and began sobbing. The letter had been two sentences long and arrived with a money order for just twenty dollars. "He knows I still have my job," she moaned. "He knows I don't have that many expenses, now that we're staying with you."

"I didn't mean to upset you," Birdie said, sat down beside her on the bed and held her hand. "But if you'd only listened to me about that Heinie in the first place…"

"Enough, Ma! Enough," Albertine cried. Suddenly, she felt she had to deny that this could be Colby's baby, so she shouted at her mother. "Isn't it hard enough on me already? Aren't I being punished enough? Are you going to keep criticizing everything I do?"

"Hush now. No one's criticizing you."

"Like hell you're not!"

Birdie stood up quickly and went to the basin where she hurriedly washed her hands again. "Don't forget that I'm your mother," Birdie said as she fought back tears. "Now put your clothes on and help me see about dinner."

Albertine now regretted having given up the apartment, but she knew she couldn't work much longer, and living with her parents was her only option. If Hendrik was going to be away until the baby was born, she would need her parents' help. So she would have to put up with all the family togetherness, the crowding, the complaining and the total lack of privacy. Now she'd have to endure her mother's judgmental lectures. And to keep the peace, she'd have to bite her tongue with her mother and ignore Eugene whenever he opened his mouth. But there were times when she just couldn't keep quiet.

"If it weren't for the Jews, do you think we'd be in this mess?" Eugene asked the family as they ate a dinner of lamb-bone soup with fried potatoes and onions. "It's the goddamned Jews who caused the Depression."

"Where did you hear that tidbit of so-called information?" Albertine challenged him.

"It's well known that the Depression was caused by Jews manipulating the money supply, starving real Americans of credit."

"What Jews are you speaking of, Eugene? All the Jews we know just got off the boat from Russia and Poland. They're all as poor as dirt, the same as we are!"

"The New York bankers are all Jews. The financiers on Wall Street and in London are all Yids. They pulled the rug out from under the market so they could buy everything cheap and rake in even more money."

"The stock market crashed," Albertine asked him, "how can they make money on that?"

"The Jews know how to make money when the market's on the way up, and when it's on the way down. Just like lawyers. They're vultures, hyenas profiting on the misery of others."

"Who are these mysterious vultures?" Albertine asked him. "What are their names? Herbert Hoover? Al Capone? Frank Nitti? John Dillinger?"

"These people are careful to remain anonymous," Gene pointed out. "They control things from the shadows where no one can pin it on them."

"What have you been reading?" Birdie challenged him. "Is that what you're getting from those pamphlets you got from Father Coughlin? Those rags full of hate and lies?"

"The truth hurts sometimes," Eugene reminded her. "But if you ignore it, it hurts even more."

"Well, there are children at this table," Albertine told him and waved toward Hank, Ricky and Roxanne. "I don't want them hearing you talk like a Fascist, telling ugly lies based on nothing but jealousy, frustration and hate. Next thing you'll be blaming unemployment on the Protestants and the dust bowl on the atheists. Or maybe you'd like to spread more rumors about midwives and put Ma out of a job, too?"

"Can you deny that there's an international conspiracy of Jewish bankers?" Gene demanded. "A conspiracy that intentionally manipulated the financial markets to hurt the working man?"

"That's enough, Eugene," Elsie corrected him, and shaking her head, she apologized to the family. "Sorry, Gene's not usually like this. He listens to Father Coughlin's radio show every week. I can't get him off the Jews and the Communists, or FDR, either. I wish he'd find a job so he'd quit blaming the bogeyman for ruining his life."

"Maybe I should blame you for ruining it!" Eugene stood up and threw his napkin into his empty soup bowl. His heavy eyeglasses slid down to the end of his nose.

"We're in this together, aren't we, Gene?" Elsie said and tears welled up in his eyes. "Aren't we?"

Her voice was like an embrace that held him and kept him from storming out of the room. It calmed his anger and made him want to take back the words he had just spoken. But how could he sit back down without seeming like a jerk?

"Okay, Gene," Birdie told him. "You got that out of your system. Now sit down and have some more soup."

"Oh, all right," Eugene said and took his chair as Birdie stood to take his bowl and napkin. "Sorry to fly off the handle."

"It doesn't help to be so resentful," Elsie reminded him. "We're all family here. We love you."

"Yeah, I know. I appreciate that," he said. "Only…"

"Only you'd better lay off those radio diatribes," Birdie said as she set another bowl of soup in front of him. "Lorraine, pass some bread, will you?"

"Thanks," Gene said as Lorraine handed him the bread basket and squinted at him in disapproval.

"Why don't you take Pa's advice and visit the alderman tomorrow?" Elsie encouraged him. "He says they may be hiring for the snow removal crews."

"Do I look like a road worker?" Eugene asked, cradled his pot belly in his two hands and smiled at the absurdity of the idea.

"It's a job," Elsie said. "You'd be bringing some money home."

"Awright. Awright. I'll go see him. Along with a hundred other guys. Maybe this time I'll get lucky."

"Sometimes we make our own luck," Albertine said. "That's what Pa always says, and he's the one who's working overtime."

"I saw you got a letter from Hendrik today," Claribel said. "What's the news from Florida?"

"He wrote that it was sunny and warm every day and that his combo is a big hit," she said. "They're playing the grand ballroom over Christmas, he says."

"You mean Hendrik won't be home for Christmas?" Lorraine asked.

"He knew that when he left," Albertine said sadly. "The contract is to entertain the rich people who go down to Miami for their winter vacations. And that includes Thanksgiving, Christmas, and New Year's, too."

"Why did you let him go?" Lorraine asked.

"You know Hendrik," Albertine sighed, "and you're asking me that question?"

"My dad does what he wants," Hank told his young aunt. "And this winter he wants to play his horn in Florida."

"What's so special about Florida?" Lorraine asked and screwed up her face so her nose wrinkled.

"It's warm and sunny. The beach and ocean are right there, and he gets to play in a fancy hotel."

"So why aren't you down there with him if it's so nice?" Lorraine pressed him.

"Because my Ma is expecting a baby. I need to stay in Chicago to look after her."

"You?" Lorraine laughed to tease him.

"Yes, I need Hank with me," Albertine said. "He's my only loyal friend. I can depend on Hank, can't I, son?"

Hank smiled and nodded at his mother, glad to be recognized as her special one. Even when the baby came, he would be there to help her. He looked across the table at her and reminded himself that she was the most beautiful woman in the family. All these others were chubby and plain compared to his mom, who was a rare beauty even with her swollen stomach.

"Well, it's time for school kids to do their homework," Birdie said, "while the rest of us do the dishes."

Hank handed his grandfather another nail as Henry braced the wooden box on the kitchen table. Then Henry held the nail in place, raised the hammer, and drove the nail into the wood with three quick strokes.

"There! That should do it," Henry said, held up the one-foot cube, and examined it from all sides. It was open in front and had a round hole in its back wall.

"So you think this box will heal up your hand, Grandpa?" Hank asked.

"That's the theory," Henry said as he set the box on the table, open side up, and began unwinding a sheet from a roll of tin foil. "Usually I don't read the articles we print in the Post, but just as I was noticing how swollen my hand was getting, I spotted a story on the healing powers of electric light and heat. Hospitals in Switzerland use light boxes like these to treat wounds that won't heal and to prevent blood poisoning. I figured, what the heck, nothing else seems to be working, I could make one of those boxes."

Henry wrapped the foil around the inside of the box, pressed it deep into the corners and creased it over the outer walls. Then he carefully punched a hole through the foil at the bottom of the box and folded it neatly around the rim.

"Why is your hand so sore, Grandpa?" Hank asked and touched the edge of his bandage.

"Because for a second I was really stupid," Henry said, smiled and shook his head.

"Grandpa, you're not stupid."

"I was stupid when I put my hand in the machine and got an alignment pin poked through my palm. Lucky it missed my bones."

"But it got infected?"

"Yep. I squeezed it to make it bleed as much as I could, and then I doused it in peroxide and painted it with iodine. But it's still full of pus!"

"And none of Grandma's herbs or ointments would help you?"

"Not this time," Henry sighed. "It's the first time she couldn't cure me."

He took a porcelain light socket and used a screw driver to attach an old lamp cord with fabric insulation to it, then pulled the cord through the box and through the hole in the bottom. Then he fastened the socket over the hole inside the box with two long screws and twisted a light bulb into place.

"It looks finished, Grandpa. Are you going to give it a try?"

Then Henry stood by the sink and used a pair of Birdie's medical scissors to cut away the bandages. Hank saw the raw and swollen hand, with its red, yellow and purple skin and the brownish discharge from the winking, open wound. It smelled terrible, too, like rotten meat. Hank wanted to cry out, but he covered his nose and mouth instead and stepped back as his grandfather washed the hand with soap and hot water, then dabbed it dry with fresh gauze. Then he opened a jar on the counter, which Hank guessed held one of Birdie's ointments. Henry grit his teeth and smeared his wounded palm with the thick paste that smelled like vinegar, garlic and cloves.

"All right, young Henry, let's give it a try. Fifteen minutes should be enough for the first treatment."

Henry took the roll of gauze and loosely wrapped his injured hand, then went to the table and stretched the cord to plug it into the wall. Hank saw a blue spark when the plug entered the outlet, and the box filled with an intense, white light. Henry sat down at the table, leaned toward the box, and inserted his hand, palm up, beneath the glowing bulb.

Hank saw that his grandfather closed his eyes and waited for the radiance to have its healing effect. It must have been very hot in the chamber because in less than a minute sweat appeared on his forehead and above his lip. After a little while longer, the kitchen began to smell like the clove and garlic ointment. The aroma intensified until Hank thought he smelled smoke. In the next instant, his grandfather pulled his hand out of the box and shook the flames on the burning gauze until they went out. Then he hurriedly unraveled the strip of cloth and checked to see if he had been burned.

"Wow, Grandpa! Are you okay?" Hank asked. "Do you need some water?"

"I'm fine," he nodded and checked a couple of small, white blisters on his wrist. "The thing is hotter than I imagined."

Hank heard quick footsteps rushing toward the kitchen, and he assumed it was someone coming to make sure no one was hurt in the fire. But it was Uncle Gene, dressed in his gray work clothes, with his head tilted back to sniff the air.

"Oh man," Gene said, "what's cooking? Smells like baked ham."

"It's just Grandpa's hand!" Hank said and couldn't help laughing.

"He's cooking his hand?"

"Never mind that," Henry said and went to the sink to rinse his hand in cold water. "It's time to get ready for work."

"I <u>am</u> ready," Gene said and patted his chest with both hands to remind him that he was wearing his crisp new work shirt. Henry had finally been able to get him a job at Donnelly's in the bindery, well away from the presses.

"Good, we'll go in a minute," Henry told him, and as he rinsed his hand, Hank could see that he was in pain. The old man moved his stiff fingers as if he were playing a scale on the piano, and Hank could see that his Grandpa was squinting because every movement hurt him.

"Unplug the light for me, will ya, Hank?" he said, as he applied more of the salve to his wound.

"Sure thing, Grandpa," Hank said and watched for the blue spark as the brass prongs came out of the wall.

Three girls worked the switchboard at Swanson's Tea and Coffee in a long, narrow room adjacent to the warehouse. Albertine and her co-workers wore harnesses around their necks that held the conical transmitters, which were like ear horns that they spoke down into. The big black earpiece was attached to the aluminum head braces. Both were connected to the wooden cabinet by cloth-covered wires. When a call came in, a switch would open and then the operator would connect the call to her earpiece and transmitter by inserting her wire's jack into the open hole and flipping a toggle switch to close the circuit. Once she asked the caller for his party's name, she would insert the jack into the socket for the right sales agent's line and turn the crank to ring his phone. At one time there were more than fifty sales agents in the front office, sitting at long rows of desks. The operators often connected the sales agents to each other as they worked on orders. Now there were only eighteen salesmen left. Still, that was plenty of names and extensions to keep track of, and there were dozens of customers and suppliers to remember, too. During her first week on the job, Albertine had cut off a call for Mr. Swanson from his main importer in New York, and she thought she'd be fired for it. But the old man was a good sport. When he'd come back on the line, he'd said, "That's okay, dearie, I've been trying to get Rothstein to shut up for twenty-three years."

After a while Albertine's true talent was revealed. She could recognize anyone's voice after hearing it only once, so she not only knew all the sales agents by sound, but she also could greet every wholesale buyer and import supplier by name as soon as they said 'hello.' She became their favorite operator, and Mr. Swanson kept her on as business declined, and as her figure grew larger, when he could easily have gotten by with one or two girls.

Mr. Swanson was a big, tall Swede, six-feet-four and over 300 pounds. His thinning hair was wispy as flax and his long, white eyelashes and washed-blue eyes made him seem like an albino. Despite his unusual (and at first scary) appearance, Mr. Swanson was soft-spoken and gentle. Albertine had never heard him say a cross or angry word. He had come from Scandinavia as a boy, but stayed in Chicago when his parents took the train further west to Minnesota. He'd started his tea and coffee business almost by accident when he was just 16 years old. He was driving a team of horses for his uncle's local delivery business. He was curious about everything in the big city, and he soon learned that wholesalers paid a lot less at the lake front or railroad depot for the commodities that they later sold to local merchants. He started trading coffee one sack at a time until he was able to rent a small warehouse and become a wholesaler full time. Thirty years later he was one of the largest tea and coffee dealers in the city. He roasted beans from South America and East Africa, and he imported tea from China, India, Java and Ceylon. In 1928, he had 208 employees and he tried to treat them all like members of a big family.

By the end of 1934, there were only eighty people left working at Swanson's Tea and Coffee. The Depression had taken its toll, and worse still, canned coffee like Maxwell House was being advertised on the radio, and cheap teabags became more popular every year. "People don't take time to enjoy a hot drink," Mr. Swanson would say. "They don't know what they're missing."

When Albertine got to her PBX console on the third Tuesday in November, she found an index card on its counter with a note in Mr. Swanson's secretary Helga's handwriting: "Mr. Swanson is not taking any calls this morning." The switchboard girls got notes like this one regularly, so Albertine didn't think much of it. But when the first call came in at 9:00 o'clock, she sensed that it was not going to be a good day.

"Eric Swanson, please," a man's voice said flatly. Albertine recognized him as Franklin Curtis, one of their largest Indian tea suppliers.

"Good morning, Mr. Curtis," Albertine greeted him warmly, but his voice was cold and flat in response. "Could you connect me to Mr. Swanson now?"

"I'm sorry, Mr. Curtis, but Mr. Swanson's not in the office this morning. May I take a message?"

"Tell him I need to talk to him. This is extremely urgent."

"Yes, sir. I'll make sure he gets the message."

"Did you hear me?" Mr. Curtis insisted. "Urgent!"

For the rest of the morning, the only calls that she, Mary or Corinne answered were from Mr. Swanson's suppliers, and they all said they needed to speak to him urgently. All seventeen of them.

When the noon bell sounded, Mr. Swanson, who'd been working in his office all along, sent word around to all employees to gather in the warehouse amid the burlap sacks of coffee and wooden barrels of tea, so they all could hear what he had to say at the same time.

When everyone had gathered in the long, high bay, Mr. Swanson climbed up onto one of the tea barrels like a politician about to give a speech, or a preacher about to deliver a sermon. His bow tie was undone, he'd left his jacket in his office, and his navy blue vest was unbuttoned to show his stomach bulging against his starched, white shirt.

"Before I say anything else," he said in his reedy voice, which didn't match his very large body, "Before I say anything else, I want to thank all of you for your loyalty, hard work and years of dedication to Swanson's Tea and Coffee. The company gave you the opportunity to earn a living, but for years you've done more than that. For years, you have made this a growing concern. But since the Crash, things have made a turn for the worse. Our customers are spending less and less, my debts have gone higher and higher, the suppliers want their money, and the banks refuse to renew my credit. Mr. Albertson here, in all his accounting wisdom, will point out that a business can't operate indefinitely at a loss. Though I refused to believe him at first, the figures in his ledger are proof that I have been losing money since July of 1931. For more than three years I have been keeping the company afloat by selling investments, running through my personal savings, and last month you may have noticed that I sold off my Duisenberg automobile. But I regret that none of these actions have enabled me to keep the company in business. Mr. Albertson and I met this morning with the manager of the LaSalle Bank and my attorney, Mr. Dietrich. We have come to the only solution possible in this dire situation. We are forced to liquidate our inventories and let this property revert to the bank."

There was a collective sigh from the crowd, a few shouts of disbelief, and at least three women, including Albertine, began to cry.

"The most painful thing I have to tell you is that Swanson's Tea and Coffee is no more, so I can no longer offer you employment."

Again the former employees sighed, but this was the Depression, and people expected the worst. No one really protested.

"But there is one small consolation," Mr. Swanson shrugged and tried to smile, but the effort only brought tears to his eyes. "Under the terms of our closing, I am able to pay you in full for what you would have earned through this coming Friday. If you will line up here to receive them, Mr. Albertson will distribute your pay envelopes from his valise. It has been an honor and a privilege to work beside you all. With that, I must say good-bye and good luck with all my heart."

Awkwardly, Mr. Swanson dismounted the barrel and the stunned crowd of workers opened a pathway so he could stumble through their midst through the side door to the old Ford that had replaced his limousine.

Albertine continued to cry quietly as she stood in line for her last few dollars in pay. Mr. Swanson was such a good man, he didn't deserve to lose his business. He never pressured her about the baby. He would have let her work as long as she wanted if he hadn't gone bankrupt first.

"I didn't think I'd be out of work for the holidays," Mary said as they waited in line. "I don't know if we'll be able to afford a turkey."

"I won't be able to even look for work until after my baby is born," Albertine complained. "No one will hire me looking like this."

"At least they'd feel sorry for you," Corinne said. "They won't even talk to us."

"Sure, they will! You two are the best PBX operators in the business. And you're willing to work for thirty-five dollars a week."

"I'll work for twenty-five," Mary said.

"Twenty," Corinne underbid her.

"Cripes," Albertine sighed. "I'm glad I gave up my apartment. At least I don't have rent to pay."

"You're lucky."

"I don't feel lucky," Albertine moaned. "Now I feel like the Depression has finally caught up with me. With all of us, really. How lucky is that?"

Chapter Fourteen

Elsie had converted the front parlor into a sewing room where she could work on the dresses that she had been commissioned to make, mainly for women and girls from the Notre Dame parish, but also for others who had heard about her skill and reasonable prices. She also had an inventory of nice fabrics that her customers could see and touch when they came for their fittings, or which she would bring with her to their homes when she visited to take their measurements.

Elsie was equipped with an excellent Singer sewing machine, a folding table where she cut the cloth, and three fitting manikins that she could adjust to the dimensions of her clients. Within a few weeks after she and Eugene had moved in with the Fontaines, Elsie's business had picked up, with orders for new dresses for the winter season and the holidays. And once Albertine had lost her job, she tried to help her sister for a few hours every day.

"Today I want to finish up the matching frocks for the Pottinger sisters," Elsie said as she came into the parlor in her blue cotton sewing apron, which was decorated with ruffles around its edges and had eight pockets to hold her scissors, pinking shears, measuring tape, a cushion with pins and needles, thread, a wedge of chalk, and a little notebook that had a stub of a pencil attached to it with eighteen inches of red yarn.

The four Pottinger sisters ranged in age from nine to 16, and their father was a fish wholesaler and lumber yard owner, who was reported to be worth millions. Mrs. Pottinger was head of the Altar and Rosary Society at Notre Dame, and because Elsie volunteered at the church every Saturday, she knew her well and Mrs. Pottinger had hired her for the past three years to sew her girls' matching holiday dresses. This year's design had a flowing skirt of red and black plaid wool, a high waist marked by a patent leather belt, and a black velvet top with balloon shoulders and white lace collar and cuffs. The fabric was beautiful and of high quality and would last forever if you could keep the moths away. Albertine guessed there was five dollars of material in each dress, and she wondered why Mrs. Pottinger was spending so much on clothes that her girls would outgrow in a few months. Of course, the sisters may be passing their clothes down to their younger siblings, the way the Fontaine girls did when they were growing up, but somehow that didn't seem to be the Pottingers' style. These dresses were for one season and one season only.

Albertine stroked a piece of the black velvet, brushing out some of the chalk that remained where Elsie had traced the pattern before cutting the cloth. The velvet was as smooth as the fur of a spoiled cat. "How can I help you, Elsie?" she asked.

"Could you pin the silk inside the skirts?" she asked her. "I'd like to sew in the lining first, then attach the lace. They're expecting me to come over this evening for a fitting."

"Do they have a big house?" Albertine asked.

"A beautiful house that looks out over Garfield Park. Three floors for one family. We've got three floors for <u>three</u> families the last time I counted," Elsie pointed out.

"We used to be one family," Albertine said with a sigh. "We're all still related."

"We've got five adults living here, six if you count Clare, and four kids from three sets of parents. The Pottingers have one set of parents and four spoiled little girls. With beautiful furniture and rugs in every room. A chandelier above the dining room table, and a baby grand piano in the parlor. They hired a painter from the Art Institute to do an oil portrait of the entire family, six feet across."

"And they hire Elsie Fontaine every year to make their daughter's holiday dresses."

"Harding," Elsie corrected her. "I've been Mrs. Harding for nearly ten years, Al. And I suppose they could afford to pay me ten dollars apiece for the finest dresses in Chicago."

"You should charge them twenty dollars each," Albertine said, as she fastened a pin to hold the shiny black silk inside the smallest skirt. "They wouldn't even notice an extra forty bucks."

"That's how much <u>you</u> know," Elsie laughed as she threaded her machine. "Rich people don't stay rich by throwing money to people like me. They hold onto every penny they can."

"They'll go to Marshall Fields and spend more on the petticoats to wear under these dresses than they're paying you, Elsie."

"Not on your life!" Elsie said. "Their underwear is a disgrace! When I go there for fittings, their slips are all patched, and they've got holes in their drawers. Mrs. Pottinger says that if no one sees it, how can it matter?"

"What if one of them gets run over by a streetcar?" Albertine laughed. "All the nurses at Cook County will know her Ma was too cheap to buy them decent underwear!"

"Mrs. P. is above all that. She doesn't care what working people think. She has dinner with Cardinal Mundelein four times a year."

"Well, that don't impress me," Albertine said as she started pinning the second lining and Elsie straightened out the pins on the first. "I was more impressed by Al Capone in his pin stripe suit than that old man in his red dress."

"You would be! I hope you live long enough to repent!" Elsie scolded her, only half teasing.

"Repent!" Albertine scoffed. "What do I have to repent for?"

"Only you can answer that question, big sister."

"Only I can answer it!"

"Working late in those night clubs, I guess it would be hard to resist the temptations of all that liquor and all those handsome men on the make."

"I'm a married woman with a ten year-old son," Albertine insisted. "Everyone knows that. And look at me. I'm seven months pregnant. No man's going to come near me."

"Well, seven months ago, you weren't pregnant. Seven months ago, you were having a pretty good time."

"And what's wrong with that? Do I have to repent because I like to go out at night and hear good music? I played in

Hendrik's band for three months, too. Does that make me a sinner?"

"I don't understand how you could have left Hank on his own so much. I never leave Ricky and Roxanne without adult supervision."

"I was wrong to think he would stay home on his own, I admit it," Albertine said and pricked her finger. "Ouch! All those months I played in the band, Hank was here every night, wasn't he? I made sure he was safe, Elsie. Don't accuse me of being an unfit mother!"

"I wasn't accusing you, Albertine," Elsie said as she ran the skirt through the sewing machine. When the first lining was in place, she turned to her sister with tears in her eyes. "I guess I've always been jealous of you, living the way you damned well pleased ever since we were little. But I guess you're paying for it. I guess you're doing your penance for it now."

"In a few months things will be back to normal," Albertine told her and began to cry, too. "In a few months Hendrik will be back and we'll have a new baby. We'll get our own place again and make a fresh start. Spring isn't that far off, Elsie! Why did you have to make us both cry?"

One Saturday morning it was too cold to play outside, but Birdie insisted that Hank, Ricky and Roxanne stay out of the house, anyway, so they kept warm by raking leaves and burning them in an oil drum in the alley.

"Stay back," Hank ordered his cousins. "I'm the only one who's big enough to put fuel on the fire."

He did stand a head taller than Ricky, who was a year older than Roxanne, and their hands would have come dangerously close to the hot and rusted steel if they tried to reach over the rim with their armfuls of leaves. And even if they didn't burn themselves, they'd get soot or their new green and red plaid coats that their Ma had sewed for them before Halloween. Soot would even show up on Hank's black overcoat that he got from Rocko at the Relief distribution center. It was a couple of sizes too big, but Hank didn't care. It gave him plenty of room for two or three sweaters underneath.

Hank scooped up a pile of leaves between the wooden rake and his left hand and raised it over the oil drum, and then he let them fall into the fire before the wind could blow them away. The flames shot up and Hank hurried to his right to avoid the plume of white smoke that had rushed in his direction. As he got back in position to scoop another load, he noticed that his cousins had lost interest in the fire and were trying to pet a stray cat that lived in a culvert under Grandpa Fontaine's driveway. Hank didn't care about the cat, but he was bored with the fire, too, since he didn't have any marshmallows or weenies to cook. He was wondering what he'd do next when Dominic appeared in the alley. He was bareheaded and his ears and nose were just as red as his hair.

"Dominic," Hank asked, as if he had seen him yesterday and not a whole month ago, "where's your cap?"

"I lost it in a dice game, if you have to know."

"So what brings you all the way over here?"

"I've got some news for ya," Dominic said.

"Like what?"

"I heard your grandfather is moving back to Germany."

"He never was in Germany. He fought the Germans in France."

"Not this Grandpa, numb-nuts. I mean old man Kinderman. They say he's leaving on Monday. I thought you might want to go over and say good-bye to him."

"I've only been to their house one time that I remember, Dominic. I don't even think I could find it if I wanted to."

"Geez, Hank, it's right behind their garage with the gigantic sign that says 'Kinderman Auto Repair' big as life right on Division Street. A moron could find it."

"Are you calling me a moron?"

"I didn't, did I?" Dominic slugged Hank's shoulder, but it didn't hurt through his overcoat. "I just thought you might want to see your grandparents before they went back to the old country. Family and all, you know what I mean? And if they feel guilty about neglecting you, they might want to make amends with a going away present, which could be worth a few bucks for you, Kinderman."

"I'm not going to beg them for money. Geez, I'm not a dirty moocher like you, Lucetti. Some people have some pride left, you know. And that includes me!"

"Come on, it's only a short streetcar ride over to their neighborhood. If they go back to Germany without seeing you, you'll regret it for the rest of your life."

"My Ma would say that they should come to see me!" Hank insisted. "They're the grandparents. I'm just a kid."

"Your Ma's right," Dominic said. "But you're bigger than that. You have <u>respect</u> for your elders."

"What if they don't recognize me?"

"I'll introduce you, then," Dominic said. "Come on, let's go. I got other things I need to accomplish."

"Well, all right," Hank said. Then he called out to his cousins, who were still pestering the stray cat. "Ricky! Watch your sister."

"What for?"

"I'm going with Dominic. I'll be back before dinner."

"Aren't you gonna tell your Ma?" Ricky asked him.

"Don't worry about my Ma!" Hank said, to prove to Dominic that he wasn't a baby. "I'll be home before suppertime."

The trip took longer than Hank expected as the streetcar moved across the dreary November city under low clouds and through a bitter wind. As usual, Dominic talked the whole time.

"I wonder why your grandparents want to move back to Germany. Their lot is full of cars. They must be making a mint! And what's left in Germany? We creamed them in the Great War, didn't we? What's left? Sauerkraut and beer? And there's so many Germans in Chicago now, there probably aren't any Heinies left over there."

"It's a big country, Dom. Bigger than Italy. And we're still getting Italians coming over. And maybe they aren't going back, after all. Just because you heard it doesn't make it so."

"Well, you can ask them yourself," Dominic said. "You can hear it from the horse's mouth."

His grandfather's garage was only two blocks from the streetcar stop on Division Street. The big sign that extended over all three bay doors read: "KINDERMAN AUTO REPAIR. SPECIALIZING IN TRANSMISSIONS. ALL MAKES AND MODELS." Dominic had been right about the volume of business at the shop. Cars and small trucks were parked two-deep in the lot in front of the garage, everything from Fords and Chevrolets to De Sotos, Studebakers and Hupmobiles. Each car had a number written in soap on its windshield.

Unlike many auto shops that Hank had seen, the Kinderman garage was freshly painted, the driveway was clean and swept of loose gravel, and when the boys came close to the open garage doors, they could see the mechanics working in their crisp gray uniforms with caps and cotton gloves. The garage floor was painted light gray, and it was shiny, reflecting the bright lights in the many fixtures above. The cars in the bays were parked over concrete trenches in the floor, and mechanics worked beneath the vehicles to extract the gear boxes that needed to be repaired.

Hank recognized his grandfather immediately. He was the same height as his dad, a little heavier, in suit pants and shirt sleeves, suspenders and a flowered necktie. He was polishing the chrome on the side mirror of a huge purple Chrysler that took up the middle bay of the garage. To Hank, it didn't seem that Grandpa Kinderman was planning a trip back to Europe.

"You wait here," Hank said to Dominic, then stepped into the garage toward the old man. His pink scalp showed through his white hair, but his moustache and small beard were still golden brown. He spotted Hank's reflection on the chrome, then took a step back to look at him in the mirror before he turned to face him. "Yes, vhat do <u>you</u> vant?" he asked, sounding a lot like Hank's dad but with a thick German accent.

"Ve don't need any more newspapers, if zat is vhat you are selling."

"I'm not selling anything," Hank told him. "I'm your grandson, Hank Kinderman."

"Ah," the man said and reached to squeeze Hank's shoulder as if to prove that he was real. "Wie geht's?"

"I don't speak German, Grandfather, but I hope you and Grandmother Kinderman are well, anyway."

"Humph," the old man grunted and raised his voice to assert his authority. "You have grown since two years. Did your mother send you for a reason?"

"No, sir," Hank said. "I came on my own. A friend from the neighborhood said you were moving back to Germany. I wanted to see you before you left. To say good-bye, I guess."

"Is zat so?"

"With my Dad away and all, I thought I could say good-bye for him. Maybe even get your new address for him."

"I see, I see," the old man nodded. "And how old are you, Hank?"

"Ten, sir. I'll be eleven in January."

"Vell, you are quite ze young man," the old man said. "Now tell your friend to come in out of za cold and vee can talk a little."

Hank was surprised that his grandfather had even noticed Dominic out on the lot among the cars. He must have known I was coming up behind him all along, Hank thought. He just pretended to be surprised to see me.

Hank went to the front of the garage and called out, "Hey, Dominic. Come on in."

Dominic had been sitting on the running board of a big Buick, blowing on his fingers to take away the numbness. He stood up and walked slowly to meet Hank, not wanting to seem in a hurry.

When Dominic came into the warmth of the garage, his ears and nose glowed red, and he wiped the snot from his upper lip onto his coat sleeve.

"Grandfather, this is my friend Dominic."

Grandpa Kinderman nodded.

"Nice to meet you, Mr. Kinderman," Dominic said.

"Come through to the house, boys," the old man said and waved with both hands toward a door at the back of the garage. The boys followed him into a hallway lined with windows and doors that passed through another narrow lot full of cars and led to the back door of a two-story brick house.

"With my breezeway I can get from my house to my business in any weather condition," the old man explained loudly. "This project was one of my best investments ever."

When they reached the house, the old man led the way up a few steps and through a door into a mud room, where many coats and raincoats hung on hooks, and pairs of shoes, boots and galoshes lined the baseboards.

"Leave your shoes, coats and hats here, bitte," he instructed them.

Hank was happy he was wearing the new wool socks that Grandma Birdie had given him last week. They were clean and had no holes. He noticed that Dominic was wearing one black sock and one gray one. His grandfather exchanged his shoes for a pair of red house slippers. (His socks were black silk with a checkered pattern.)

They passed into a big white kitchen with a giant blue stove and a dozen copper pots, the color of new pennies, hanging above the sink. The parlor was alive with the sound of ticking. There were four cuckoo clocks in a row on one wall, a large round brass clock on the mantel, and a grandfather clock in the corner. Hank scanned them quickly and saw that all their times matched, agreeing that it was five minutes past eleven in the morning.

An old woman sat on the overstuffed couch, sewing a flowered pattern on a needlepoint frame. Grandmother Kinderman was a large woman with bluish hair and steel-rimmed glasses. She leaned back on the couch and crossed her puffy ankles on the rug in front of her. Before she looked up, she finished her stitch, snipped the thread with scissors on a ribbon around her neck, and parked her needle in a red felt pin cushion next to her thigh.

"Who's there?" she asked and looked hard at Hank and almost recognized him.

"The short one is your grandson Henry," the old man said. "He believes we are moving back to Deutschland."

"Henry, you've grown, haven't you?" she said. "Come give your grandmother a small kiss."

Hank crossed the padded rug and approached this strange woman as she pushed her cheek toward him. The only thing he could do was lean forward, close his eyes and plant a kiss on her cheek. She smelled of perfume and talcum powder. She didn't try to hug him, and he kept his hands to himself. When he opened his eyes, she was patting the couch beside her. "Sit next to me a vhile," she said. "Vee are pleasantly surprised to see you."

Dominic helped himself to a wingback chair by the window, while Grandpa Kinderman sat in the big leather throne beside the grandfather clock.

"Vee are only goink to Germany for a visit," she explained. "The relatives in Hamburg invited us for the Christmas season. Your grandfather is taking his Chrysler on zee ship viss us. So his brothers can she how fine zee automobiles are here in America."

"I have three brothers," the old man said, "and I offered all of zem a chance to come to America and be partners in zee business. But zey all said no, they loved Germany too much. I'll show zem my car, and zey vill see vhat zey missed."

"It <u>is</u> a pretty nice car, Grandfather," Hank said, trying to please him, but the old man's thoughts were elsewhere.

"Your father, mein only son, turned me down, too. And he could see it all the time. He could see what a good life I had made. But he was too stubborn, too proud to vork viss his hands."

Old Kinderman held up his hands and Hank could see the black grease embedded in the cuticles around his fingernails and in the rough creases on his knuckles. Hank had heard his Dad complain about the old man's greasy fingers and that he was "always breathing down my neck" when he had worked in the pits at the garage.

"Now, Claus, you know Hendrik has dreams of his own," Grandma Kinderman said. "His band is making a big success for him down in Florida."

"It is a farce!" the old man declared and pounded the armrest on his leather chair. "This music is a game. It doesn't pay anything, and it vill never pay anything!"

"He mailed us those post cards," she said. "He wrote that they were playing to huge crowds."

"I predict, Elizabeth, I predict that your son vill be writing for money soon. Blowing a horn is no vay to make a living."

"My dad sent you post cards?" Hank asked. "Can I see them?"

"Yah, sure," she said and with a great effort raised herself from the couch and limped to a small table with a telephone on it. She opened a shallow drawer and pulled out a small stack of colorful post cards. She walked back, obviously in pain, sat beside Hank and showed him the picture on the top card, a beach with umbrellas, palm trees and a tall white building behind it.

"That's the Coconut Grove Hotel," she said. Hank took the card and studied it carefully, and he noticed that there were no people in the photograph. It seemed like a deserted place in a dream. He turned the card over and recognized his father's handwriting, but he couldn't read a word of it.

"Oh," his grandmother laughed at his confused expression. "You can't read Deutsch! He just writes that his band is performing at this beautiful hotel six nights per veek."

There were four other cards, showing flamingos, an alligator, the hotel ballroom, and a sunrise over the ocean. The short messages were all in German and none of them mentioned his family. Hank's grandmother translated the last one. It said, "With luck we can play here all year."

"He must have sent you cards, too?" his grandmother asked.

"Yeah, sure, a bunch," Hank lied. "I just wanted to see if he sent you something different on yours."

"And did he?"

"No. The pictures are the same, but on ours he told us how much he missed us," Hank pretended. "And how he couldn't wait to get back to Chicago."

"He's a good father, then?" she asked him.

"The best."

"Fine. You can keep these cards with your collection," she said.

Then at a quarter past the hour, the four cuckoo clocks, the mantel clock, and the grandfather clock all sounded at once, each with its own distinct alarm. This was a house that ran on a tight schedule, Hank could tell. It was more regimented than the Fontaine's house, and probably had a lot more rules.

"Well, it may be Saturday for the rest of you," Claus Kinderman announced, "but this old man has to get back to vork! If you'll excuse me…"

The old man stood up and padded across the rug in his slippers and left without saying good-bye.

"Before you go," the old woman said to the boys, "come into the kitchen for a glass of milk and some strudel. We leave for Germany on Monday, so please eat the strudel so it won't go bad while we're away."

The boys followed her into the kitchen and sat at a white enameled table and ate huge pieces of strudel off blue and white china plates.

"And in vhat grade are you studying now, Hank?" she asked him.

"Fourth grade, Grandmother."

"And are you a good pupil?"

"I get good grades when I study."

"Then you must study," she said and refilled his glass. She ignored Dominic, but he didn't seem to mind as long as she gave him something to eat. "And what school do you attend?"

"Notre Dame grammar school," he said. "It's attached to the French church."

"Ah, yah, the French church," she said, frowned in disapproval and made a little clicking noise with her tongue. "Your mother sends you there, does she?"

"That's right. And my Grandma Birdie, too. We're staying at her house while Pa's away."

"And how is your mother?"

"All right, I guess. As good as she can be. She's expecting a new baby."

"Is that so?" she said, sounding surprised. "When is it due, boy?"

"I don't know, Grandma. Some time in the New Year. We hope Pa will come back before he's born."

"Let us pray for it," she said. "And let's pray that mother and baby are vell."

"I'll pray for that, too," Dominic said, "especially if I could get another piece of this strudel, Mrs. Kinderman. It tastes like it was made in heaven."

"Yah, of course," she said and shook her head impatiently. "But you must eat it quickly, and then you boys must run along. It's time for me to fix lunch for Claus and his men. The girl who helps me has Saturdays off. The meal must be on the table precisely at one o'clock so as not to disrupt za business."

Hank didn't have room for another piece of strudel (it was flakey and filled with sweet juicy apples, spiced with cinnamon and nutmeg), so while Dominic ate, he watched this strange grandmother as she started washing potatoes at the sink with a vegetable brush and hot water from the tap. She didn't turn around to look at him, and he knew that she would be happy when he was gone. When Dominic finished his strudel and drained the last of his milk, Hank nodded toward the mud room. "Time to go," he whispered.

"Thanks for the strudel, Grandmother. And the post cards," he called to her as they got up from the table. "Have a safe trip."

"Auf Wiedersehen," she said without turning to look at him. "Be a good boy to your mother. And keep yourself clean."

Hank hurried to put on his shoes, coat and hat, while Dominic snooped through the coats on the wall and reached into the pockets looking for money. All he found was a dirty handkerchief and a box of matches.

"Come on," Hank said. "Let's go!"

"Just trying to make the most of things," Dominic hissed as he tied his shoe. "Usually people are able to get something besides food from their rich relatives."

"Let's go," Hank repeated and led the way out the door and through the passageway to the back of the garage. His grandfather was standing at the counter in the corner wearing eyeglasses and going over papers under a lamp with a green glass shade.

"Goodbye, Grandpa Kinderman," he called to him.

"Vhat?" the old man grunted, and looked over the glasses to squint at him and Dominic.

"Good bye," Hank said. "Have a nice trip."

"Of course, vee vill have a nice trip."

"And I'm glad you're not moving back to Germany, after all."

"Not to vorry," he said. Hank thought the old man was going to smile, but he didn't. Instead, he said, "If you want to learn to become a mechanic, come back when you turn sixteen. At sixteen, I can put you to work in the business."

In his heart, Hank knew he would never take his grandfather up on this invitation.

Chapter Fifteen

Early on Thanksgiving morning, Henry prepared his hand for another heat treatment as Hank screwed a new bulb into the therapeutic light box.

"You know, Hank, things may be hard on you with your dad down in Florida," Henry told him, "but I really enjoy having you around here with us."

"I like being with you, too, Grandpa. I just don't like being surrounded by so many women. It's like I've got five mothers bossing me, including Lorraine."

"Don't let it get to you," Henry said as he pulled the gauze tightly around his hand and fastened it with a pair of safety pins. "Some kids don't have anyone who loves them, and you've got a whole house full of people who do."

"I know that's supposed to make me feel better," Hank shrugged, "but it's not working…Is your hand getting any better?"

"It's not getting any worse," his grandfather said. "Now plug her in so I can have my treatment before the girls come down here to start cooking. Look at that turkey. It fills up the whole sink! I've roasted whole pigs that were smaller than that."

Hank stretched the cord to the wall socket and plugged it in, taking pleasure in the blue spark in the dimly lit kitchen and then delighting in the square shaft of light that beamed from his grandfather's cube.

The old man slid his palm under the light bulb and sweat appeared immediately on his forehead and upper lip.

"Grandpa, how can you stand the heat?"

"It's hot all right," he smiled through his pain. "But after fifteen minutes of lamp therapy, I get relief for six to ten hours before the swelling starts up again. I've lanced it with sterilized needles a couple of times to get the pus out, but it comes right back like a stubborn boil."

"Why don't you let Doc Bichet try to cure you, Grandpa? He's a real doctor, isn't he?"

"He used to be. Now he lives off the work your Grandmother brings him. To speak true, I trust Grandma Birdie more than I trust that old buzzard. I use her salve every day, and it's protected me from blood poisoning. And if I go to the hospital, you know they'll want to operate, and before you say boo they'll be sending me home with a steel hook in place of these good fingers, like the poor boys back from the war. Have you ever seen a printer working with a hook in place of his right hand?"

"Well, no."

"And how many people are depending on the work of this right hand?"

"About ten of us, I guess."

"That's why I'm relying on science from Switzerland…to give my hand a modern cure that keeps me all in one piece."

"My Pa plays the saxophone pretty well without his thumb," Hank reminded him.

"A man can do without one digit," Henry nodded. "But losing my hand? I'd hate to think what that would mean to all of us."

"You won't lose it, Grandpa," Hank said. "I heard Lorraine praying for your hand to heal by Christmas."

"Then it has to get better, doesn't it, Hank?" the old man said and pulled his hand out from under the bulb. He pulled off the gauze and went to the sink, but saw the turkey there preventing him from washing up. His hand looked as bad as ever – a ghastly wrinkled glove of black, purple and bright yellow. It could have been crushed by the printing press, not just pierced by it. Henry didn't seem to mind that his hand looked so horrible, so dead. He moved his fingers, with about half their normal agility, but he was clearly pleased with the treatment's results.

"See Hank, it'll be fine until supper time. Now let's clear out of here before the kitchen gets invaded by women."

"Good idea!"

Birdie didn't have to bang on the cast iron skillet to get her daughters to help prepare the Thanksgiving meal. By eight o'clock she had opened her hand-written cookbook and had Elsie rubbing spices into the turkey, Albertine chopping celery and onion for the dressing, Claribel peeling potatoes, and Lorraine washing the cranberries and grinding them with the oranges, peel and all.

Birdie reserved for herself the duty of making the pies, all four of them: apple, cherry, pumpkin and maple syrup. As she stood at the counter and rolled out her crusts, she continued to issue instructions to her daughters.

"Elsie, when you get done with the bird, will you sauté the onion and celery for Albertine? She shouldn't be on her feet too long."

"Okay, Ma, I'm almost done here," Elsie said.

"And, Albertine, you can start peeling apples for the pie," Birdie instructed.

"You got it," Albertine said, "but one thing at a time, please."

"You've always got to think a step or two ahead," Birdie reminded her, "or else all the food won't be ready at the same time."

"We know, Ma," Albertine said. "You say that all the time."

"Hush," Birdie smiled, knowing that Albertine was teasing her. "And Clare, you can move straight on to the carrots and turnips."

"Oh joy!" Clare said as she dropped a quartered potato into a pot of water.

"Clare, you're very good with the paring knife," her mother told her. "You hardly waste any of the vegetables, your peels are so thin."

"What a compliment!"

"And Lorraine, I need you to sift three cups of flour for the dinner rolls."

"Can I finish the cranberry-orange relish first?" Lorraine asked impatiently.

"Don't use that tone with me, young lady!" Birdie scolded her. "You can keep more than one idea in your head at the same time. You're not feeble-minded!"

"I might as well be!" Lorraine said, "The way you boss me!"

"In the interest of keeping peace in the family," Birdie said. "I'll ignore that."

"Thank heaven for small favors, Ma," Albertine said. "Lorraine's working hard for a change, ease up on her, will ya?"

"For a change?" Lorraine complained.

"I think she is feeble-minded," Elsie laughed as she poured the chopped vegetables into the skillet.

"I am not!" Lorraine said and banged her spoon on the rim of the ceramic mixing bowl.

"Please start sifting the flour, dear," Birdie smiled. "So we can get the yeast to rise in time to bake the rolls."

"Well, excuse me!" Lorraine shook her head. "Happy Thanksgiving, too!"

"Your sisters are right, Lorraine," Birdie said. "I must have spoiled you if you'd sass me like that."

"If I weren't the youngest, I might get some respect."

Lorraine's mother and sisters laughed at her and kept preparing the food. In a few minutes, they heard the phone ring in the hallway and then Larry came into the kitchen. "Ma," he said. "It's Marie Dubois. She sounds upset."

"Oh dear," Birdie said as she put down her rolling pin and untied her apron. "Are her twins coming today? Of all days!" She hurried across the kitchen to the hallway where the phone sat on a small black table.

"There goes Thanksgiving!" Claribel said and tossed another potato into the pot, splashing water onto the counter.

"What do you mean?" Elsie asked. "We haven't even put the turkey on yet."

"Larry," Clare asked her brother. "Did Marie Dubois say she's in labor?"

He nodded. "I think that's why she called."

"So Ma will be gone till midnight!" Clare concluded.

Birdie came back to the kitchen doorway, put her hands on her hips and leaned toward her daughters.

"I'm sorry, girls, but I have to go help Marie Dubois. She's having twins, and this could take a while."

"What did I tell youse?" Clare said quietly.

"You'll have to prepare the meal while I'm gone. You know what to do. Put the stuffing in the turkey. Bake it on low. The pie crusts are made. You know how to fix the filling. Albertine, you can make the dinner rolls, can't you?"

"Of course, Ma," Albertine said. "Don't you worry, the four of us will make sure everything's fine. We'll have a beautiful meal on the table when you get home."

"Thanks, love. That's what I want to hear. Tell your Pa where I am. Larry, could you please give me a lift to her apartment?"

"Sure, Ma," Larry said. "Are you ready?"

"Let me get my coat, my scarf and my birthing kit, and I'll be right with you," Birdie said. "I don't know when I'll be back, so don't hold up dinner for me!" Then she and Larry hurried down the hall together.

"You'd think Marie Dubois would have the courtesy to hold off her labor at least until tomorrow!" Lorraine said, twisted her lips and shook her head. "She's spoiling Thanksgiving at her house, too!"

"Geez, if she's carrying twins," Albertine groaned, "then she probably doesn't care about anyone's holiday. She just wants to get those babies out of her." She rubbed her large, taut abdomen through her purple rayon dress and felt her own child shift inside her. Is it an unwelcome visitor in there, Albertine wondered, or a wonderful new life? Should she feel sorry for getting pregnant and driving Hendrik away, or should she be thrilled that a beautiful new baby was growing inside her?

"Well, maybe it's good that Ma's gone," Claribel said. "At least now we can speak our minds. If she's not listening, we can talk about anything we want!"

"What is it, Clare?" Elsie asked her. "Do you have a guilty conscience?"

"No, of course not."

"Then what is it that you don't want Ma to hear?" Elsie pressed her.

"Come on, Else," Albertine said. "Lay off of her. You know there's a million things you don't want Ma to hear...What are you thinking about, Clare?"

"Albertine, I wanted to ask you about..."

"About what?"

"Love."

"Love!" Elsie laughed.

"Hush," Albertine said. "Don't tease her! I'm no expert, but I'll try. What do you want to know?"

"How do you get all the men's attention? When you come into a room, if there's a man or boy there, he looks at you, and he keeps checking to see what you're doing, hear what you're saying, and to see if there's anything he can do to help you."

"Really?" Albertine smiled. "If I had known that, I would have taken advantage of it!"

"You do take advantage of it every day!" Claribel insisted. "Doesn't she, Elsie?"

Elsie nodded as she mixed the dried bread cubes with the sautéed onion and celery.

"Doesn't she, Lorraine?" Claribel asked again. "Doesn't she take advantage?"

"She's the queen bee, all right," Lorraine said and nodded vigorously.

"I am not!" Albertine protested. "Queen bee? That's Ma, not me."

"You're the one who flirts with anyone in long pants," Elsie said. "And the poor dopes flirt back."

"There's nothing wrong with being friendly," Albertine said. "That's not flirting. Nobody's going to flirt with a big fat pregnant lady, anyways."

"They'll be flirting with you at Thanksgiving dinner today," Claribel said. "My question is: how do you make them do it?"

"Smiling helps," Albertine said with a shrug as she stood up from the table to check the flour that Lorraine had just sifted, and to begin making the dough for the dinner rolls. "You have to make people feel that you're comfortable with them and that you enjoy their company. And you ask them questions about themselves, their work, their life story, the music they like, and their hopes and dreams. Nothing gets a man to like you more than the opportunity to talk about himself."

"But it happens before your have a conversation with them," Claribel told her. "They're attracted to you. But why?"

"Maybe because I'm attracted to them…I mean, I like men. Not like Elsie here, who considers them a necessary evil."

"Not that necessary!" Elsie laughed.

"You see," Albertine said. "Elsie is just as pretty as me, she's two years younger, and she's got a beautiful singing voice, and a nice big bosom, bigger than mine, but she broadcasts that kind of attitude. How inviting is that?"

"I also happen to be a married woman," Elsie said, "a fact that you seem to have forgotten about yourself."

"Look at me!" Albertine laughed. "How can I forget?"

"But surely it's more than being friendly! Even I'm friendly," Claribel said. "There's more to it than that."

"Your appearance matters, too," Albertine nodded. "You have to keep your hair nice, and your makeup just right, and you have to make sure your clothes are snappy—fresh and ironed and cut so they flatter your figure. And you wear stockings when you're supposed to and pretty shoes that let you show off your ankles. And you don't eat dessert. Those extra pounds show!"

"But that's not why you're Pa's favorite."

"I'm not Pa's favorite!"

"Yes, you are. And Hank adores you."

"He doesn't 'adore' me," Albertine laughed.

"He does so. Have you ever seen a 10 year-old boy who thinks his mother hung the moon?"

"Is this my son you're talking about?" Albertine asked and grinned. "The boy who climbs out his window and stays out all night?"

"That's the one," Elsie told her. "He worships you. Heaven knows why."

"He's a good boy," Albertine said. "He loves his mother. The way Ricky loves you."

"Ricky is afraid of me," Elsie said. "That's the sum total of his affection for me."

"That's not so, Elsie," Claribel said. "It's easy to see that both of your kids are fond of you. Ricky just doesn't have a crush on you the way Hank does for Al."

"So that's all I know about attracting men," Albertine said. "Be nice to them, seem interested, and look as nice as you possibly can. But why are you asking me? You're cute. You're eighteen, and you've got a new boyfriend. What's his name? George?"

"That's right, George," Clare nodded but didn't sound very pleased. "George the transit cop."

"Taste this," Elsie said as she held a fork of uncooked dressing in front of Albertine's mouth. "Did I use enough sage?"

Albertine tasted the moist bread. "Enough sage, but you need a little more salt and pepper…What's wrong with George? He seems nice enough. And he has a steady job."

"But I don't really care for George," Claribel said. "He's a terrible dancer, and he's not interested in having fun. Whenever I say I want to go out, he says he's saving his money."

"Sounds like a keeper to me," Elsie laughed.

"But you see, he chose me, and I would never have chosen him. That's the truth of it," Claribel said. "Albertine, you can pick whatever man you want. That's the kind of magic I'd like to work."

"And my man is down in Florida with his band and a girl singer," Albertine shook her head. "I don't call that working magic."

"And now Monty wants me back, too," Claribel cried in consternation.

"So now you have a choice!" Albertine laughed.

"But I don't want him, either!" Clare cried.

"Beggars can't be choosers," Elsie teased her.

"Is Monty still boxing?" Albertine asked and waved for Elsie to shut up.

"He lost his last two fights," she said. "He told me he would give it six more months. He doesn't want to become one of those zombies who get paid to get beat up by stronger fighters. But he still goes to the gym to box every day."

"Do you think he wants to marry you, Clare?" Lorraine asked her.

"Not Monty. George wants to marry me. Monty wants to sleep with me!"

"Lorraine, leave the room," Elsie ordered her baby sister and pointed to the dining room.

"No, let her stay," Albertine said. "She's gonna need to hear it soon enough…Have you had your period yet, Lo?"

"Not yet, but I expect to real soon."

"You need to learn how to take care of yourself. You might as well start today."

"I say go ahead and marry George," Elsie said. "He'll save you a lot of grief."

"But you'd rather sleep with Monty, wouldn't you?" Albertine asked Clare.

Claribel blushed bright red all the way down her neck, and Lorraine stared at her with an open mouth.

"I don't know," Clare said. "I mean, I was tempted. He's so attractive and athletic, but I was afraid."

"Afraid of getting pregnant?" Elsie asked.

"Yes, I guess so. But I was more afraid of the sex act itself…Is it really as animalistic as the nuns say it is?"

"Nuns!" Albertine scoffed. "What do nuns know about the sex act?"

"Well," Clare paused. "Is it?"

"Yes," Elsie insisted. "Sometimes it is."

"But usually it's not," Albertine corrected her. She felt light-headed and thought she should sit down, but Clare kept her questions coming.

"Then what is it like – usually? Does it hurt?" she asked, and tears of embarrassment welled up in her eyes.

"It can be a little awkward at first," Albertine reflected. "But it has never hurt me. You can experience an incredible closeness with your lover; at the very least it's an intense pleasure when things go right. Waves of pleasure is how I'd describe it. It's a feeling that takes you away from the world, but makes you happy to be alive so you can enjoy it. For a few minutes you are owned by this man, and you own him. And you don't care about anything else, for a few minutes anyway, until those waves a pleasure fade away, and he wants to get out of bed."

"You could get the same feeling with George," Elsie informed Clare. "It's all the same with the lights out, I imagine. And George won't get his brains knocked out before he's 25."

"But don't men expect you to do dirty things?" Claribel asked, her eyes wide open. "With your mouth and all?"

"I think I'm going to be sick," Lorraine said, but it was Albertine who felt dizzy. She braced herself on the counter and took a deep breath, but it was hot and close in the kitchen, and the air didn't make her feel any better.

"You don't have to do anything that you don't want to do," Albertine told her sister. "But sometimes you surprise yourself."

"That's disgusting," Elsie said. "She won't say it, Clare, but men can be pigs, and they want to drag you down into the dirt with them. They pester you for sex and when you finally give in, it's never enough. Here comes Willy Peter for a second helping. They're goats if you ask me, randy, hairy billy-goats who drink too much beer."

"My goodness, Elsie. You must have picked the wrong man!" Albertine sighed. "I married a gentleman. For all his faults, Hendrik never once treated me like that in the bedroom."

"But he doesn't mind giving you the back of his hand in the kitchen or the parlor!" Elsie reminded her.

"That's all in the past," Albertine said, but felt faint, and this time she did sit down on one of the kitchen chairs. "We've worked out our differences."

"And what about your other boyfriends?" Claribel asked her. "Were they gentlemen, too?"

"I don't know what you mean," Albertine said and felt a terrible headache coming on, too. "I've been married for twelve years this month."

"Monty said you flirted with all the men at the Top Hat. They were drawn to you like moths to a flame, he said."

"He's exaggerating. They liked to hear me play the piano."

"Monty said that even <u>he</u> had a crush on you for a while. That you liked to dance with him and the other guys. That you encouraged them all to love you."

"I danced with some of them. You know yourself that Monty's a very good dancer. There's no crime in that, is there? To dance when the music is good and you have a partner who knows the steps?"

"I didn't say there was anything wrong with it," Claribel said. "I have to hand it to you, a woman past thirty who could have her pick of the swells at the Top Hat!"

"I enjoyed myself when I worked there. That's all there was to it."

"And he said that you would drive over to Cicero with a couple of gangsters who used to work for Al Capone and Bugs Malone."

"I did not!"

"He says they threatened to hurt him if he didn't stop dancing with you."

"He's imagining things."

"Then, who were those men who spoke to us at Monty's fight against the Windmill? The two tough guys who had bet against him. One of them had a bandage on his ear."

"Those were friends of Hendrik's…From the German clubs where his band played."

"Then why did Hendrik tell me to stay away from them?"

"He must know something about them that I don't," Albertine said and leaned her chin on her palm as she slumped over the table, suddenly feeling exhausted and very heavy.

"And what about the baseball player, Colby Malone?" Claribel asked her.

"What about him?" Albertine asked and tried to shrug, but the sound of Colby's name made her feel that she had lost something important, that her life would never be quite right again.

"Monty says that you were with Colby Malone whenever he was at the club, that you were his favorite girl."

"He's married isn't he?" Albertine sighed. She had hoped that Larry would keep his mouth shut about Colby, but it was Monty who had betrayed her, trying in a sick way to get Claribel to love him again.

"You're married, too," Claribel insisted. "But you've got enough of whatever it takes to attract the biggest baseball star in Chicago."

"That's not so," Albertine said. "We talked sometimes, so what?"

"But I want some of that," Claribel declared. "I want some of that power to choose whoever I want and make him come to me. I'm so jealous!"

"You'll have your turn," Albertine told her slowly, then closed her eyes.

"Don't be ridiculous!" Elsie interjected. "Why should you be jealous of a married woman who risks throwing away her reputation by dancing with mobsters in a speakeasy?"

"My reputation!" Albertine cried weakly. "No one cares about my reputation."

"You won't believe it," Claribel said with wide-eyed delight, "but Monty says the rumor is that the baby you're carrying isn't Hendrik's at all, but Colby Malone's. And that's why Hendrik ran off to Florida with that Negro girl who's passing for white. Isn't that crazy, Al?"

But when Claribel turned to get a response, she found that her sister had collapsed from her chair onto the linoleum floor, and that Albertine couldn't hear a word she was saying.

When Albertine regained consciousness, someone was carrying her up a staircase, cradling her head in the crux of his left elbow and bracing the back of her knees with his right. At first she thought it was Hendrik, and she even called out his name, imagining that he had come back home to take responsibility for her and for their children. But she heard the familiar click of an ankle, and she knew that her father was carrying her, had rescued her from illness and retrieved her from the prying, impertinent questions of her sisters. And yes, she knew she was his favorite. They had known each other the longest, after all. "Pa," she said weakly. "You don't have to carry me. I can walk by myself."

"We're almost there, Sweetheart," he said as he came to the third floor landing, maneuvered around the boys' feather bed (where Ricky was still sleeping), and nudged open the bedroom door with his foot. Then he lay her down on the bed as tenderly as he had lain his babies in their cradles. He reached for the comforter to cover her, but she shook her head. It was so warm in that attic bedroom that she was beginning to feel nauseous.

"No, don't cover me, Pa. Could you please try to open the window to let in some fresh air? It's jammed shut. Clare and I haven't been able to even crack it since Elsie and Gene got here."

"I'll see what I can do," her father said, and she noticed the bandage on his right hand.

"Don't struggle with it if it hurts your hand," she said. "I'll be all right."

"You look pale as a ghost," he said. "A light green one at that! You need fresh air, and I'm not carrying you back down those stairs."

The stifling air was making her feel sicker every minute. As her father went to the dormer window, she crawled to the edge of the bed within puking distance of the waste basket. Ma would say it was too late in her term to be having morning sickness, but she couldn't help being out of sorts. Maybe the soft boiled egg she'd eaten for breakfast was bad, or all the questions from Clare that she couldn't quite answer had turned her inside out. It couldn't be Colby Malone's baby; the timing was off, wasn't it? And she had done everything to prevent it then. But with Hendrik, she did exactly what the Church expected. She'd spread her legs and let the will of God take over.

Her father couldn't budge the window on his first few attempts, which grew successively more intense until his face turned red, and purple veins appeared on his temples and across this bald head.

"Boy, that bastard is stuck!" he said breathlessly. She followed his eyes as he examined his palm. A red spot of blood, ringed with yellow pus, had risen to the top layer of his bandage.

"That's okay, Dad, you don't have to," she said.

He took out his pocket knife, opened its blade, then ran its edge through the gaps on the sides and bottom of the window, periodically wiping paint chips from the blade with his handkerchief.

"Pa, you never give up, do you?" Albertine asked him.

"Over the years," he replied, "I have found that no matter how big the problem is, you can usually solve it by staying with it long enough. When brute force doesn't work, there's usually another way."

He closed his knife, put it back in his pocket, pulled up on the window and opened it all the way. The cold wind blew in, making the curtains flap, and Albertine breathed deeply on the cool, crisp air. "That's more like it!" she said. "I don't think I'll die after all."

Henry leaned on the windowsill and looked across the neighborhood of colorless bungalows and three-family houses. He noticed a few patches of blue sky between the leaden clouds. "I think we'll have a nice Thanksgiving," he said, grinned over his shoulder to her, and winked.

The window fell then, as swiftly as a guillotine, and it slammed with great force on his bandaged hand. Somehow his left hand was spared.

"Holy Jesus!" Henry cried when he saw the splash of blood and pus that covered the lower half of the window pane. He lifted the window to free himself from the trap, then took a book from a shelf to prop the window open for his daughter.

"Let me get a rag to clean up the mess," Henry said. And as he tried to re-wrap his hand with the saturated gauze, he noticed that it had lost its intense color and become pale now, more like his normal hand. Could he have been saved by this accident?

"I'll clean it up," Albertine said.

"You'll rest," her father corrected her and turned to see Hank standing with bare feet in the doorway. "Hank will help me."

"What's wrong, Grandpa?" Hank asked and hurried to his side.

"Your mom's not feeling real well," Henry said, "and I got blood all over the window. Let's get a wet rag and clean it up."

"But you hurt your hand, Grandpa. It looks all bloody."

"Believe it or not," Henry said, "my hand feels better than it did before the window fell on it. The pressure's gone." He nodded to the bloody windowpane. "I got rid of all that poison."

"You're sure you're all right?" the boy asked.

"I'm fine," Henry laughed. "You're supposed to be worried about your Ma."

"Oh, right," he turned to his mother, who was lying on her side watching them curiously. "How are you feeling, Ma?"

"I'm feeling better now that I've got some fresh air," Albertine said and took another deep breath. "Now please put your shoes on before you start traipsing after your grandfather all over the house."

When Birdie came home after helping Marie Dubois give birth to her twin girls, Larry was playing the guitar as Elsie sang "You Are My Sunshine." Everyone else in the room (Claribel, Lorraine, Henry, Eugene, Arthur, Olga, Ricky and Roxanne) was too full to join in. "You'll never know dear how much I love you," Elsie concluded. "Please don't take my sunshine away."

With ten family members seated on the couch, love seat and overstuffed chairs – amid the sewing machine, manikins, bolts of fabric, and the second piano – the room was crowded. Elsie had made a Pilgrim's hat and two white bonnets (and rag heads to hold them up) for her manikins to keep things as fun as possible for the children. For a second, Birdie thought they were the ghosts of her grandparents, but soon realized that they gave off no energy or light, so they could not be from the past. Birdie felt exhausted and hungry herself, and she resolved not to criticize her daughters' cooking, even if the turkey was dry, the stuffing was spiced incorrectly, or the pies were scorched.

She applauded when Larry finished the guitar solo at the end of the song, and she noticed that Albertine was not in the room with them. "Happy Thanksgiving, everyone. Is everything okay? Where's Albertine?"

"Resting upstairs," Henry said and yawned. "Are mother and babies fine?"

"They couldn't be better. Everything went smoothly. Marie had an easy delivery. The two little girls are about four pounds each, but well formed and with good color. And Doc Bichet was clean and sober today and didn't even beg for a drink. That's why I made it home before midnight. Marie and her new arrivals are resting peacefully."

"I guess the old doctor took your last warning seriously," Henry said.

"He has his good days even when I don't warn him, dear. Marie Dubois and her family have something to be thankful for anyways…I'm starving. Did youse save any food for your poor old mother?"

"There's plenty in the kitchen, Ma," Elsie said. "We'll heat it up for you."

"Is Albertine all right?" Birdie asked her husband. "She looked a little green around the gills when I left this morning."

"I don't know whether she's got a virus or whether her sisters said something to upset her," Henry said and puffed on his cigarette. "But she was out cold when I carried her upstairs at nine this morning. She hasn't come down since. Hank brought a tray up to her, but she didn't eat much. I got the impression that she was hiding from everyone."

"I'll go up to see her after I have something to eat," Birdie said.

"Don't scold her," Henry reminded her. "It will only make her more resentful."

"We've done nothing but help that girl! She has no reason to be resentful."

"Reason has nothing to do with it, dear. Our number one daughter is very unhappy right now."

Then Larry put his guitar in its case and stepped over to kiss his mother's cheek. "Gotta go, Ma. I have to work tomorrow. The older guys are taking off so we have to carry the load."

"Work will do you good," she said and patted his shoulder before he turned to go.

In the dining room, Birdie sat at the big table, whose linen cloth was sprinkled with crumbs and stained with gravy and cranberry-orange relish. Elsie had served up the warmed plate with the sliced turkey breast, dressing, mashed potatoes, yams, candied carrots and green beans simmered in bacon fat. Claribel had saved her mother two of the misshapen dinner rolls (which still tasted fine) and Lorraine poured her a large glass of red wine.

The rest of them – Claribel, Lorraine, Eugene, Elsie, Arthur, Olga, Hank, Ricky and Roxanne – joined Birdie with their second slice of pie, and no matter which flavor they chose, Elsie topped each slice with a dollop of freshly-whipped cream. They all drank coffee, too, even the children.

"My, this looks good," Birdie said and she shook salt onto her turkey, then smothered it and the dressing with a thick layer of steamy giblet gravy laden with chopped eggs. With her first mouthful she said, "Not bad for being reheated, dears. The dressing could use a little more sage, and the turkey is a little dry. But all in all, you did a marvelous job."

"Don't act so surprised, Ma!" Elsie scolded her. "I cook every day, you know. Look at my kids! They don't look starved, do they?"

"No, of course not. They're chubby as piglets. But Thanksgiving dinner should be special, and that's just what you've made it. A very special meal."

"We're glad you like it, Ma," Claribel said. "Wait till you taste the pie!"

"After eating this big plate, I won't have room for pie," Birdie laughed and proceeded to eat her whole meal without saying another word. And as she enjoyed the food, she took pleasure in seeing her family around her. They had all started as fresh, smooth newborns like the Dubois twins. She remembered how Elsie had dimples the day she was born, how Claribel had a full head of dark hair, how Lorraine was born along with her stillborn twin, and how she had pulled Hank from Albertine with forceps and then dunked his head in a bucket of water before he began to cry. Arthur had been her hardest delivery, his head was so big, which scared her own mother until she could maneuver the baby free. Ricky and Roxanne were small babies, under five pounds each, but now look at them! They were so chubby, they made Hank look undernourished. And her poor beauty Albertine. She was her first child, in a way her most precious baby, the child she had conceived after two and a half years of marriage, after she had convinced herself that she could never have children. Be careful what you wish for, her mother had teased her. And Mére Elise had recognized Albertine's beauty, her talent and her temperamental nature. "A delight when she wants to be," she declared, "and a holy terror the rest of the time."

Birdie thought of her mother's words when she climbed the stairs to check on Albertine. Albertine was her most beautiful and most gifted daughter, but she also wanted more than the others, so she was the unhappiest.

The light was on in the back, third-floor bedroom. Albertine, with the bedspread pulled up to her neck, lay on the single bed along the right wall, beneath the etching of the Eiffel Tower that Henry had brought back from France. There was a tray on the small desk, and the plate on it was full of cold, untouched food. The window was propped open by a book, so the room was quite cold.

"You'll catch your death with the window open like that," Birdie said and went to close it. "It's like winter in here."

"Be careful, Ma," Albertine said, "if you pull that book out, the window will fall like a rock."

"We'll see," Birdie said and held the window up with her right hand and pulled the book out with her left. Then she snapped her hand back from the window and it stayed up for a second before it fell suddenly and landed with a thud. "My, you're right!"

"I enjoyed the fresh air until it got dark outside," Albertine said. "But I was a little afraid that the window might crack my knuckles if I tried to close it. I decided to crawl under the covers instead." Albertine pulled back the blankets to reveal her gray terry cloth bathrobe. A long flannel night gown showed beneath it, and when she turned to sit with her feet on the floor, she was already wearing her slippers.

"How are you feeling, dear?" Birdie asked her. "Your Pa said he carried you up here and that you've been in bed all day."

"I had some bleeding this morning, Ma," Albertine said and her eyes opened wide in fear.

Birdie asked her daughter for details then went to the bathroom to wash her hands before examining her. When she was finished, she said, "I don't think it's serious dear, but to be on the safe side, I think you should have bed rest for the next few days."

"So it <u>is</u> serious!"

"I didn't say anything of the sort," Birdie said and sat down on the bed beside her, put one arm over her shoulders, and stroked her cheek. "We just don't want it to get serious by over-doing things."

"So I'm trapped up here?"

"Unless you want to camp out on the sofa downstairs."

"Could I still help Elsie sew?"

"If you stay put and don't lift anything. And someone will need to help you up and down the stairs."

"What a nuisance I've become!"

"Nonsense. Are you hungry? We can bring you up some warm food."

"No thanks. I'm ready to sleep!"

"Well, I'll take this tray out of your way, and I'll tell Claribel to be quiet when she comes to bed."

All day Albertine had emerged from the bedroom only once, at six o'clock when Hendrik finally telephoned from Florida. As she lay there on top of the comforter, she had tormented herself with thoughts that Hendrik had abandoned her for Pearl and wouldn't even try to wish her and Hank a happy Thanksgiving. Hank had given her the post cards Hendrik had written in German to the Kinderman grandparents, proof that Hendrik was enjoying himself, but they were incomprehensible to her, evidence that he would never let her completely understand him.

The thought of Hendrik spending his time with Pearl, sharing a cottage and probably a bed, made her stomach even more upset. Didn't he respect the fact that she was carrying his child? How could he prefer that half-Negro tramp to her? She remembered how Pearl, a tall, soft woman with full breasts and strong perfume, had pretended to be her friend and hugged her with almost a sexual enthusiasm. Albertine imagined that Pearl had been hugging Hendrik the same way after each performance, pressing closer and harder each time until he got the message and came to her bed after their last show. If she were Hendrik, she probably couldn't resist Pearl, either, because she offered too much pleasure, too much relief from the loneliness. So Albertine knew that Pearl and her husband must be lovers. That's why he wrote such short letters, because he didn't want to reveal too much about his time with Pearl. He sent money wrapped in a blank piece of paper with only 'Love, Hendrik' written on the outside flap. And it was no wonder that he had put off calling her long distance on Thanksgiving because he was spending every free moment with Pearl.

Then around six o'clock, Lorraine came to the bedroom door and rapped on it, "Albertine! Albertine, can you get up?" she shouted. "A phone call for you. Long distance!"

"I'm coming!" she called and her heart jumped to her throat. He loves me after all! Of course, he loves me!

"Help me, Lo," she said to her sister. "Please help me get downstairs to the phone?"

They took the staircase one step at a time as Lorraine held her sister around the waist and kept saying, "Steady, easy, watch your step!" until they reached the bottom, and Albertine felt so weak that she had to sit down right there on the last step.

When they got to the telephone, Hank, dressed up in his Sunday clothes, was talking into it. "Hi, Pa!" he shouted. "How's Florida? We had four kinds of pie today. I hope you had a good Thanksgiving, too. U-huh, I miss you, too, Pa." Hearing his mother's slow footsteps, Hank looked over his shoulder and saw how tired and worried she seemed, and he spoke again to his father. "Okay, Dad. Here's Ma. Come home soon."

Albertine took the receiver and felt afraid and lonesome, and even more helpless than a kid like Hank, her little boy, a kid who was brave enough to ride on the outside of a streetcar, a boy who missed his Pa but could cope without him. But Albertine knew that she needed Hendrik now, she needed a husband to provide for her and this new baby. She wanted to sleep in a double bed with him, to regain her place as his wife and lover. What would she do without him? How could she live if he never came back? She couldn't stay in her parents' house forever.

The phone burned her ear with an electric vibration, more of a bite than a tickle, before she heard a word from Hendrik.

"Hendrik? Is that you, Honey?"

"Yah, it's me." His voice was crackly with static, like a radio program that was barely tuned in. "How's my Albertine? How are you feeling?"

"Not the best today, Hendrik," Albertine sighed. "We've missed you so much."

"Did you get the money I sent you?"

"I got the money, Hendrik," Albertine said, "but why didn't you write a letter to go along with it?"

"We're very busy, darling. We play three shows a night. And we have rehearsals every morning. You may think we're having fun down here, but we are working all the time."

"And how's the music, Hendrik? Is it any good without your best piano player?"

"Ramos doesn't hold a candle to you, baby. He fakes it sometimes and drinks too much rum. But we're still the best band in Miami. We bring huge crowds in for every show."

"Don't sound so happy, Hendrik!" Albertine said, because she could tell he was enjoying himself, even through the hiss and crack on the line. "Don't you miss me?"

"Yah, sure, I miss you," he said. "This is hard on me, too."

"Then come home to Chicago," Albertine said. "I need you with me."

"We play until Valentine's Day, you know that. We have a contract."

"I don't care about your damn contract. We need you, Hank, me and the new baby. Come home, please."

"If we leave now, we are finished," Hendrik laughed with a tone that dismissed her. "Berg will make sure we never play in Florida again."

"You can make a fresh start in Chicago."

"Let's talk about it later, Al," Hendrik said. "I gotta go now. Our first set starts in five minutes."

"Hendrik!"

Then the line went dead, and Albertine dropped the phone so the receiver swung like a pendulum over the edge of the table. Hank hurried to catch the receiver before it hit the table leg again, and he replaced it in its cradle.

"So, is Pa coming home early?" Hank asked her. "Is he?"

"Not yet, Honey."

"He told me that he misses us, too," Hank told her. "So why doesn't he come home?"

"He'll come home, Sweetheart. Just not for a while. Now help me back to bed, will you, Sweetie? I'm not feeling too well. Lorraine, will you help us, too?"

Later, after the last dishes were washed and order was restored to Birdie's kitchen, she and Henry sat down at the small kitchen table to share a pot of chamomile tea. As the tea brewed, Birdie used a pair of scissors from her delivery bag to cut the bandage off Henry's hand so she could examine his wound. The swelling was gone, the wound had scabbed over, the bruising had subsided, and for the first time in weeks, he could move his fingers without pain.

"It's healed in 12 hours," Henry said and grinned happily. "All the poison was released when the window came down on me so hard. It's a miracle, if you ask me."

"My, it <u>is</u> better!" Birdie said and smeared some of her garlic and clove ointment over his palm and then wrapped gauze around his hand. "Keep it covered a few days longer," she said. "Looks like I can stop worrying about you, and start concentrating on Albertine."

"Isn't she just tired and lonesome?" Henry asked her. "Or is there something new to worry about now?"

"She had some bleeding this morning," Birdie told him. "Not too much, but enough to be concerned about. And she's in such a blue funk with her husband away, I'm afraid she's not taking care of herself and the baby the way she should. She's wallowing in her misery, and that's not good for anyone."

"You're the expert on expectant mothers," Henry said. "But she has every reason to feel sad and lonely, doesn't she?"

"There's a right time for everything," Birdie told him. "And she should be taking care of that baby and herself. She has to realize that all that gallivanting around at the night clubs is over. She's a grown woman with serious responsibilities now. That's the only blessed thing I've been trying to get through her thick skill."

"I think Hendrik is the one with the thick skull," Henry said. "He turns down a chance for a steady job at Donnelly's, then he runs off and leaves a beautiful wife and a wonderful son to play night club music in Florida. It's just stupid, if you ask me. It doesn't make an ounce of sense. He thinks he's an artist, but he's just selfish, if you ask me."

"You're onto something there," Birdie said. "I'd have to say that he and Albertine were made for each other in the selfish department. Interested primarily in number one."

"Well," Henry shrugged and slurped his tea, "when you get down to it, that applies to all of us."

"Don't make excuses for them, Henry! You know I'm right!" Birdie said. "This morning I was sitting with Marie Dubois, keeping her comfortable until it was time for her to deliver, and I couldn't help thinking how different that girl is from Albertine. Marie doesn't have any possessions. She lives in a small apartment with her husband and two other kids. But she was thrilled to be delivering twins. She had an absolute glow about her. I've never seen a woman in labor seem so happy. And when the two babies were born, she was proved right. Two perfect little babies. What a joy! And Albertine is treating her pregnancy like an illness. She hasn't said it in so many words, but I don't think she wants this baby. Deep down, she thinks this baby is a mistake."

"It's not surprising that she'd be having doubts," Henry said. "But don't read too much into it, dear. Once the baby's born and Hendrik's back home, she'll be herself again."

Half an hour later, Henry was asleep in his chair, leaning back against the kitchen wall, for he was a night worker who was accustomed to napping in any position.

And Birdie knew the coast was clear for her mother Elise to pay her a visit. As Birdie poured herself another cup of tea, the room felt cold, and there was a yellow-white glow in front of the pantry, and Birdie saw her mother standing there in a long night gown. Her gray hair swirled down over her shoulders, and her feet were bare and white as marble.

"Hello, Mére," Birdie said to her. "I thought you'd come."

"Have I ever missed a Thanksgiving?" Elise whispered, as if trying not to disturb Henry.

"No, Mére. You always remember the holidays."

"I remember the children, Birdie," she said. "The children need help."

"Which children, dear?"

"All of them. They'll all face trouble. They'll all feel pain."

"That's real cheerful, Mére!" Birdie laughed. "You should have seen the beautiful twins I delivered today. They were something to smile about!"

"And your daughter abandoned by her German? Is that a joy to your heart?"

"Her baby will be born," Birdie said. "Her husband will come back."

"But that won't be the end of it," Mére Elise said as her image began to fade. "Not for Albertine."

Once her mother had dissolved into a puff of steam, Birdie stood beside Henry and shook his shoulder. "Come on, Mr. Fontaine. It's past midnight. Time to go to bed."

Real winter came early that year. By mid-December the rooftops and parks were blanketed in snow and the streets and sidewalks were coated with dirty ice. The wind blew incessantly from the lakefront across the city, chilling everyone who stepped outside and pouring a frigid draft through every crack around every doorway and every window and through every crevice in all the floorboards throughout Chicago. Car batteries died, the switches froze in the trolley tracks, quart bottles turned to ice on the milk wagons, the drunks committed petty crimes so they could spend a few nights in a warm jail, and children and old people froze to death in the hobo jungles. No matter how much coal Henry shoveled into the furnace, the Fontaine house never got warmer than 64 degrees, so the family wore sweaters and knit caps indoors, as if they were on a camping trip in Minnesota or on the Upper Peninsula.

Hank was the only one who ventured outside after school because he found opportunities in the cold. He could run errands for his grandmother, his aunts and their neighbors, each for a few cents. He filled buckets with loose coal left on the sidewalk by the delivery men who shoveled it hastily down the basement chutes before hurrying to their next stop. Hank could sell the coal for a nickel a pail to the deaf mute who roasted chestnuts on the corner of Kedsie and Jackson Boulevard. He made a few cents spreading sand on porch steps, scraping ice from car windows, and sweeping snow off the sidewalk in front of the church and grammar school. He worked so hard that he was able to buy a real pair of gloves to replace the mittens Aunt Elsie had knitted for him, and twice he treated Ricky and Roxanne to Saturday movie matinees. Hank found that he liked the cold, as long as he had wool socks, two sweaters on under his coat, a handkerchief to blow his nose, and a hat with ear flaps to keep his head halfway warm.

And the cold could be fun, too. On winter Sundays between Mass and dinner, Henry would take his box of ice skates from the closet under the staircase and carry it to the lagoon in Garfield Park, where he would let kids and adults borrow a pair for an hour or two on the ice. His collection included 32 pairs of skates, from blades that strapped over your shoes to white figure skates and a pair of size 13 speed skates that had belonged to a Fontaine cousin in Quebec. With this orange crate overflowing with leather, steel and shoe laces, Henry regularly attracted a crowd, and on most Sundays he lent out every pair except for the shiny brown hockey skates that he wore himself and mostly used to skate backwards – like a referee, with a whistle on a shoelace around his neck – through the crowd of skaters of varied skill, who were gliding about on the blades that he had lent them.

Hank, Ricky and Roxanne learned to skate during the winter of 1934-35, using a different pair of skates each week. By January, Henry organized races among the boys and girls of various ages, and Hank and his cousins usually finished first or second.

And the pond was full of motion and activity. Boys used brooms for hockey sticks and a block of wood for a puck, as they made slap shots at goals marked by slats pried from fences. Girls ice-danced, singly and in pairs, and sang the Blue Danube Waltz to provide their own music. Every few minutes, someone fell on the ice, sometimes very hard, but nobody got discouraged. The three hours of skating every Sunday marked an escape from the cares of a life of work and doing without. Skating took such concentration that it was impossible for children, teenagers and adults to worry about anything else. And the swift motion across the ice was as close to flight as most humans would experience, so their adrenaline kept them from noticing the cold, the blisters on their heels, or the pain of falling.

Then promptly at 1:45, Henry put his chrome whistle to his lips and blew it to signal that it was time for him to collect up all his skates and return home for Birdie's Sunday dinner.

Hank wondered why his grandfather didn't just give the skates away to the kids who wanted to use them. Wouldn't that be more generous than just lending out the skates for a few hours on Sundays? But Hank noticed that, while a few of the kids came to skate every week, there were a lot more who skated every other week, or only once a month, so the 32 pairs of skates were shared by at least 80 or 90 people. And by keeping ownership of the skates, Henry could see the pleasure and fun his collection brought to the neighborhood. And maybe, lending out skates made him feel important, too. People looked up to him for making the Sunday skate-times possible without asking for anything in return, except the skates themselves.

Chapter Sixteen

People freezing in Chicago must have thought Florida in December was paradise, but Hendrik's days at the Coconut Grove were more difficult and complicated than the ones he described on post cards and the scraps of paper folded around the money he sent to Albertine.

Soon after they had arrived at the resort, Hendrik saw that there were two classes of people at the Coconut Grove: those who could afford to stay at an expensive hotel for weeks on end, and the people who catered to them. Obviously, the Kinderman sextet was in the second category, the servant class, and that was difficult for them to accept. In Chicago, the band had played at clubs where everyone was equally downtrodden, or at least had the recent memory of being broke, so the audiences treated the musicians with polite appreciation and sympathy.

In Miami, the hotels were full of fancy people from New York, Philadelphia and Boston who had been unaffected by the Depression, or gangsters who had grown wealthy because of it, and who were trying to prove to the old rich that they could act as arrogant and snobby as anyone. They treated the band members no better than the colored porters who lugged their bags.

And the hotel manager who had hired them was a cigar-smoking tyrant. He expected them to play three 90-minute shows every night but Monday, at seven, nine and eleven, and they had to be on call for afternoon parties and receptions. He would not allow any improvised jazz, either. "These people wanna dance to every goddamn tune!" he had shouted at Hendrik after their first show. "I can't have you go off the charts, do you hear me?"

Carl Berg wasn't the first idiot that Hendrik had worked for, but he was the only one who had signed his band for a 20-week contract. Such a steady engagement was probably worth the aggravation, but just barely. Hendrik had to calm Rocko, Billy and Jake so they wouldn't lay hands on the fat old Jew.

"We can't let that sonofabitch dictate to us how to play our music!" Jake the drummer argued. "I'll jam his cigar right up his keister, that's what I'll do!"

"Calm down," Hendrik said. "We don't get paid without him. He won't be listening to every show." But for the first two weeks, Berg was lurking in the back of the room whenever they looked up to check for him.

Valerio Ramos, the Cuban piano player who had joined them in Miami, seemed more interested in rum than in learning the band's repertoire. He was a tall man with black hair hanging down over his collar and a hooked nose. Valerio's hands were his most striking feature. They were immense, with long fingers like the legs of tropical spiders. He could play the band's songs well enough with the sheet music in front of him, but he put no life or spontaneity into the songs. After the last show each night, however, Ramos would play his Latin music, and the piano would come to life with sambas, rumbas and cha-chas. Rocko learned the bass parts to most of Ramos's songs, but Jake always went to bed after their final set, and Billy was so good on the trombone that he could play almost anything after hearing it once.

Pearl wanted to learn the Spanish lyrics by memorizing them phonetically (bess-a-may, bess-a-may moo-cho), but she couldn't bear to sit close to Valerio on the piano bench for more than a few minutes. His breath reeked sourly of alcohol and his clothes stank because they hadn't been laundered for weeks. And it seemed that he could keep the piano going perfectly well with only one hand while the other tried to explore her breasts and the insides of her thighs. Hendrik would pull Pearl away as soon as he spotted her next to him. He resented Ramos' musical influence. In Miami, Latin music was reserved for the Puerto Rican band playing at the Flamingo, and Hendrik was determined to keep Pearl's favors for himself.

Given their accommodations, it was proving difficult for Hendrik to get much time alone with Pearl. Their contract included the use of a two-bedroom bungalow with a living room and kitchenette, perched on the edge of a gully behind the hotel. This cottage had been built twenty years before the hotel opened, and in the tropical climate it had fallen into disrepair. The slatted siding was green with moss and soft with rot. The roof leaked into tin buckets, the porch boards sagged, and the warped doors did not close properly. Mice, ants and roaches had the run of the kitchen pantry, and the furniture was damp and musty. The small house was meant to provide accommodations for four men and a single woman. (Ramos had a room at a boarding house in town.) The most logical arrangement was to have the men share the two bedrooms and let Pearl sleep on the living room sofa, but this didn't give her any privacy, so the men let her have one of the bedrooms and set up a cot beside the sofa in the parlor along with dirty dishes, empty beer bottles and stacks of suitcases and musical instruments. The close quarters made everyone irritable within the first week, and Hendrik had been unable to sleep with Pearl even once. Things weren't working out as he had imagined. There must be a better way. But what was better for Pearl would turn out to be even more frustrating for Hendrik.

Carl Berg may not have enjoyed wild jazz, but he took a liking to Pearl Cornell. He was fond of her voice, her tall, trim figure, and her dark beauty. At 64, he wished he was young enough to act on his urge to embrace her and screw her for four or five hours without letting up. But Berg's dirty fantasy made him understand that it wasn't a good idea for her to spend any more nights in a tiny bungalow with four sex-starved musicians. After the band's first week at the Coconut Grove, Berg came up to the bandstand before the first show on Tuesday night with his necktie undone and his cigar sending out a plume of noxious smoke. He walked straight toward Pearl as she stepped to the microphone in her black velvet dress and pinned a silk gardenia above her right ear. Hendrik saw him coming and hurried to get to Pearl first. He had already attached the leather strap to his right hand and his saxophone, so he wielded the horn like a club to protect the girl from the overbearing Jew.

Berg brushed Hendrik aside with one puffy hand and became a perfect gentleman when he addressed Pearl.

"Excuse me, miss," he called to her, "may I have a word?"

"Why not?" Pearl replied, squinted at him, and folded her arms across her chest.

"Listen, Berg," Hendrik tried to intercept him, but the hotel manager would not be put off.

"Excuse me, I'm speaking to the young lady," Berg said and smiled with calm authority. "Is that all right, miss?"

"I'm listening, aren't I?" she said and nodded as she smiled stiffly.

"Fine then," Berg continued. "I wanted to inquire as to whether you were comfortable staying in the bungalow with the band."

"Comfortable isn't the word for it," she replied. "But the rent is cheap, and it's better than sleeping under a tree."

"I know it's not the best arrangement for a nice young lady like yourself to be sharing such a small place with four men, and I have a more civilized alternative if you're willing to consider it."

"If you've got a suite overlooking the ocean reserved for me, I'm all ears!"

"I wish I could be so generous," Berg said and shifted his cigar to his left hand. "But there's a room available at the boarding house where some of our dancers and cigarette girls stay. An old widow, Mrs. Greeley, runs the place. I can let you have it free of charge, a room to yourself and breakfast, if you get up by nine o'clock."

"You dear man!" Pearl said and leaned forward to kiss him on the cheek, leaving her red lipstick on the frost of his gray stubble. "You have saved my life."

"I'll send a cab after your first show to get your things over to Mary's. It's less than a mile away."

"Thanks, Mr. Berg," she said, smiled happily and jumped like a little girl.

Pearl's obvious joy made Hendrik feel abandoned and angry. Now she would be staying away from him at night, chaperoned by an old widow, and the only way he'd be able to make love to her tonight was metaphorically with his saxophone. After Berg returned to the back of the ballroom, Hendrik growled into her ear, "You didn't have to act so goddamn happy!"

"Why shouldn't I? To get out of that pig sty? Who wouldn't be happy about that?"

"But when can I see you?"

"You're seeing me right now!"

"You know what I mean!"

"We'll work it out, Sweetheart," she said. "We'll be in Florida for months."

"Christ, Pearl. You're driving me crazy."

"That's the whole point, isn't it?"

Their three shows that night were especially torrid. Even without "going off the charts" their duets were charged with tension and longing, and the small Tuesday crowds were caught up in their spell, dancing passionately and drinking a lot. By the time Berg's cab came to fetch Pearl at 1:00 a.m., Hendrik was beside himself with desire. He chased Ramos away from the piano and sat at the bar to have a whiskey with Rocko, Jake and Billy.

"Listen, you guys," he told them, "this is driving me crazy. I have to get some time alone with Pearl, do you hear me? Give us a couple of hours together by ourselves in the cottage tomorrow afternoon."

"So you can screw her?" Jake asked.

"What do you think, Jake? Am I going to give her singing lessons?"

"You shoulda said something earlier," Billy told him. "I knew you liked her, but hell, you're a married man."

"Yeah," Jake said, "you should be giving one of <u>us</u> a chance."

"Shut up, both of yas. It's nobody's business what we do. You hear me? I just want two hours with her tomorrow afternoon."

"But think about what you're doing, Hendrik!" Rocko said, nearly pleading with him. "You're married to one of the prettiest girls in Chicago. She's having a baby in a couple of months. Do you want to throw that away?"

"A man can love more than one woman," Hendrik said. "And we're a long way from Chicago."

"If I were you, I wouldn't risk it," Rocko said, looked down into his beer, and puffed on his cigarette. "You've got too much to lose."

"Well, you're not me," Hendrik grunted.

"Besides," Jake said, "we all know Albertine is no saint, either. I suppose she'd let you have some fun, too."

"What are you talking about?" Hendrik growled and grabbed the front of Jake's jacket.

"It's no secret that she played piano at the Top Hat for at least three years, Hendrik, starting when the place was still a speakeasy. She had a good time, to put it mildly, with the punks from Cicero, a couple of boxers, and the ball players who hang out there, especially Colby Malone. Everyone thought he had a thing for her."

"That's all water under the bridge," Hendrik said. "She doesn't play at the Top Hat any more."

"And Malone's wife showed up from West Virginia one day, so he suddenly became a family man. He disappeared from sight. That's a shame, too, 'cause he was always buying rounds of drinks for everyone in the club."

"Well, the book's closed on him," Rocko said, trying to change the subject so Hendrik would settled down. "I heard the Cubs were trading him to the Giants."

"And Albertine's in a family way herself," Jake carried on drunkenly. "Lucky thing you know you're the father!"

"Shut up, will ya, Jake?" Rocko said. "Just close your goddamn trap for a change."

"I know I'm the father, Jake," Hendrik said, punched him solidly in the chest and knocked him back into the bar. "Just stay away from the house tomorrow afternoon like I said. Ya hear me?"

Jake smiled sarcastically but didn't try to hit Hendrik back. He paused to look at Rocko and Billy, who had jumped between him and Hendrik. "I wouldn't think of intruding," Jake said at last. "Not me."

"Then let's have one more drink," Hendrik said. "Let's make the most of this gig while we're here."

The next day Hendrik met Pearl for brunch at 1:00 o'clock at the coffee shop in the hotel. The room had a tropical theme, with artificial palm trees and a mural showing a beach scene with wading flamingos, leaping dolphins, sailboats and coconut trees. They sat in a booth under one of the papier mache palms, and they spun the lazy Susan that held the syrup, butter, powdered sugar and jam for their pancakes.

"Why are we eating pancakes for lunch?" Hendrik asked Pearl and watched her lick a drop of syrup from her upper lip.

"Because I like them," she said, "and aside from plain toast, they're the least expensive thing on the menu."

"And they're quick, too," Hendrik said and nodded. After he ate the pancakes, he wanted to devour her, too. First her mouth, then her tits, and all the rest of her, too. He wanted to feel the smooth insides of her thighs against his ears. He wanted to taste her crotch and push his tongue deep into her heat. He wanted to drive into her as far as he could go and make her cry out with pleasure. And he wanted to do it all right away. "Hurry up and eat," he told her, "so we can get out of here."

"Oh, yeah?" she said and put another forkful of sweet pancakes between her lips. "Where are we going?"

"You know where we're going. I gave strict instructions for the boys to stay out of the cottage the whole afternoon. Finally, we'll have some time to ourselves."

"You mean…?" she asked and her eyes opened wide.

He thought she was making fun of him, but he knew that anger would have the wrong effect on her, so he smiled as nicely as he could, even as he craved the opportunity to reach up her dress. "I need to make love to you, Pearl. We've been apart for so long!"

"Well, I'm sorry, Sweetie," she whispered, "but you'll have to wait a few more days."

"Wait?" he moaned and nearly knocked over his coffee, "I told you, we have the cottage all to ourselves."

"Please, Buster," she sighed, using her new nickname for him. "Do I have to draw a diagram for you? It's that time of the month. I've got terrible, miserable cramps, and I guarantee you don't want to get that close to me for a few days, anyway."

"But I do. I do," he said. "We can make out, anyway, can't we?"

"And get you all hot and bothered for nothing?" she shook her head. "No thank you, Buster."

"It doesn't have to be for nothing," he reminded her. "You know how to help me. That mouth does more than sing."

"You know I'm not that kind of girl."

"What do you mean? You've done it before. Remember? It was wunderbar!"

"Maybe for you, but it was not so good for me. Maybe it's all psychological, but it gummed up my voice. I couldn't sing right for a week."

"You sang perfectly, even that night, when I took you home, you sang to me."

"It wasn't perfect for me. To me, my throat sounded gummed up. Unnatural like. You'll just have to wait, Hendrik. You've waited this long. What's another few days?"

"You're killing me, Pearl," he moaned. "Killing me."

"Well, then die already! I thought it would be nice to take a walk along the ocean. But if that will kill you, I guess you can go back to the cottage and die by yourself."

Hendrik concluded that if he wanted to get her in the sack after her period, he'd have to entertain her today. He knew this truth from experience with Albertine over the last 12 years. Albertine remembered the times when he'd ignored her or hurt her feelings, or said something bad about her mother, and if she was upset enough, she would cut him off for two or three weeks at a time. Mistresses weren't supposed to act that way, but Hendrik guessed that all women felt the same, that sex was a reward for treating them right, and holding out was a way to punish you for stepping out of line. He wondered if their mothers had told them about the power they had over men and instructed them on how to use it. It might be their only advantage. He couldn't blame them for using it, but he resented being under their power… And when he and Pearl performed their music, she really sang to him; it was obvious how much she teased him and led him on.

"Okay, let's go for a stroll by the sea," he invited her.

As Hendrik walked down the boardwalk by the Atlantic with Pearl on his arm, he worked hard to seem happy and to hide his frustration at not being able to carry out his plan to make love to her. He felt the warm breeze coming off the water, and he turned to see the turquoise sea and the knee-high waves breaking on the white sand a hundred yards below them on their right. Pearl looked pretty enough in her tilted felt hat and her dark green dress with the wide patent-leather belt showing off her trim waist and accentuating her breasts, but today she was essentially untouchable, so his eyes wandered to the women who sunned themselves on lounge chairs a few yards from the waves. It wasn't quite warm enough for swimming, but the sun was strong, and the sky was clear enough to entice these young women from the North to bare their shoulders and legs to gain some color. He spotted a shapely redhead lying on her stomach and displaying the freckles on her neck and shoulders, her rich, pinkened thighs, and her young hips that had not yet begun to sag.

A blonde spread coconut oil on her calves and ankles, and Hendrik could see her full breasts swing with her sweet, rhythmic exertion. Two black-haired teenaged girls played catch with a red and white beach ball, jumping happily on the sand as a golden Cocker Spaniel puppy barked between them. Sure, they were just kids, too young for Hendrik, but he loved to watch their fresh young bodies, with newly sprouted breasts and hips that hitched back and fourth as they jumped on the sand. Even these girls seemed more inviting than Pearl right now, more tempting than Pearl the Untouchable.

The ocean and the clear sky were beautiful, and the palm trees and oleander bushes were lush and seductive. This time of year Lake Michigan would be cold and gray as steel, the leaves would be gone from Chicago's trees, and the beach would be windswept and deserted. People would be expecting an early snow, and soon the waves would form a lacy rim of ice on the lake's perimeter. Chicago would have no bathing beauties in November or December, only women bundled in hats, scarves, coats and galoshes. Their red noses, flushed cheeks and chapped lips would be the only flesh in sight.

Yet, when she wasn't pregnant, Albertine always managed to look appealing, even in winter. Her clothes were always neat and wrinkle-free. She wore silk scarves in bright colors to accentuate her dark hair and green eyes, and she carried herself smoothly so she didn't bounce around while she walked. Though both Albertine and Pearl could be temperamental, Pearl was a lot less predictable. On some days in the afternoon she'd be dressed beautifully, and on others it seemed she didn't care what people thought of her looks. Sometimes her face would seem pale and colorless, and at others, she'd wear more makeup than a stage actress or a whore. Pearl wasn't a good dancer, either, not like Albertine. Pearl's strength was her voice, and Hendrik could swear that he played his saxophone twice as well when he had to compete for attention with her singing.

They stopped at a kiosk on a section of boardwalk, which overlooked the marina with its hundreds of sailboats and motor yachts, where he bought ice cream cones. They were like teenagers on their first date, Hendrik thought. He was licking vanilla ice cream instead of her creamy breasts! He wondered for a moment how Albertine was managing in the cold, living under her mother's shadow again, seeking sympathy from her Dad. He remembered a time they had taken Hank on Navy Pier and bought him ice cream. Albertine wouldn't ride the Ferris wheel with Hank, so Hendrik had to climb into the gondola with him. Hendrik never told anyone how much he liked being up so high, with the wide open views of the city, the lake and the sky. Compared to Chicago, Miami wasn't much of a town, but the southern ocean sure had Lake Michigan beat. In mid-November, Florida was a much nicer place to be.

This was even truer a month later as Christmas approached and northern Illinois entered the Ice Age, while southern Florida still basked in the tropics. The hotel filled up with rich people from up North who were taking extended holiday vacations, and the band's shows were full every night. After a while, Carl Berg, the hotel manager, got too busy to come to every set, so they were able to ease up and improvise during bridges and interludes, and the dancing public did not seem to mind.

The combo was in particularly good form on December 23rd, playing to a full crowd of New Yorkers, in a smoke-filled room accented by the sounds of conversation and the ring of plates and glasses. Enough people were dancing (or just paying attention) to make Hendrik feel that they had a devoted audience.

The band launched into what Jake sarcastically called their "happy set," which began with "Sunny Side of the Street," in which Pearl sang of a love that would make her rich as Rockefeller, and both Hendrik and Billy had lively solos. And because it was too early for the rum to overtake him, Ramos provided a good rhythm and color from the piano. Pearl didn't exactly dance as she sang, rather she hopped like a tall, happy wading bird, as she celebrated a life that could be so sweet if she stepped out of the shadows of Widow Greeley's boarding house and into the sunlight with Hendrik. He tried to match her enthusiasm with his saxophone, but it was an instrument designed to express longing and lust, and tonight he was incapable of making it sound sweet or innocent or happy.

When she stepped up to the microphone again, Hendrik remembered how she made love, and he wondered again if he had been her first lover. She was active enough when they kissed and hugged, but when it came time for the real sex, she became still and let him move her legs and body as he wished while she hardly responded. Maybe her mother or her sisters had told her that she should let the man do all the sex work, but Hendrik didn't know how to make her act more interested. It was pleasant enough to make love to a beautiful, firm young woman, but it would be a lot better if she would make love to him, too. That was something Albertine understood. She had certainly proved she could make sex fun during the three months she had played in his band.

They finished up "the happy set" with "Bye-Bye Blackbird", one of Hendrik's favorites, and he came to life as he joined Pearl up front for the finale. She seemed to be thrilled in the spotlight with him, and he thought he had never heard her sing better. "Bye-Bye Blackbird, bye, byyyyyye!" He ended with a solo that came from a deep place inside him. When he was finished the audience cheered, and Pearl threw her arms around his neck and kissed him on the mouth.

Then a little bellhop in a white uniform, pillbox hat and white cotton gloves rushed to the bandstand holding a telegram.

Chapter Seventeen

Albertine was playing Christmas carols on the piano when her labor began as a dull pain at the base of her back. In the middle of "Joy to the World," she guessed that the ache wasn't just a cramp caused by sitting on the hard piano bench. But she kept playing until her sisters finished singing the carol even as her back and stomach tightened unbearably. "Ma," she said at last. "I think my labor is starting."

"What do you feel?" Birdie asked her daughter, and Albertine described her back pain and the sudden, pulling tightness around the baby. "You'd better rest here on the couch," Birdie said. "Let Elsie play for a while…or Claribel. It may be a false alarm, but it could be your time."

Albertine knew that if this was real labor it was coming at least five weeks early. She worried about the poor baby – the stress he must be under, to be forced out of the warm, safe womb more than a month ahead of schedule. And she felt too tired to go through labor all night. Why couldn't it start in the morning instead of after dinner? Her mother always said that life is inconvenient, but this was more like a mean trick being played on her. Or it was God's punishment for trying to have too much fun. She sat down on the couch with the flowered slip cover, scooted to one end, then lifted her legs to stretch out, but lying on her back felt just as bad as sitting up straight, and lying on her stomach was out of the question. Somehow she managed to curl up on her side. She looked across the parlor at the Christmas tree, decorated with popcorn and cranberries, tinsel and glass balls, and the pine scent made her sneeze. Elsie's three manikins wore Santa Claus hats.

"Geez, Albertine, you look really uncomfortable," Lorraine said. "Can I get you a glass of water?"

"No thanks, Lo," Albertine said. "I don't think water will help. Oh, God, I think I have to go to the bathroom."

"Then go!" Lorraine said.

"I can't move."

"Of course, you can move, you lazy thing," Birdie said. "Claribel, help your sister get to the toilet. And stay with her, please. We don't want her falling down and cracking her skull on top of everything else!"

"Thanks, Ma!" Albertine complained. "Thanks a lot!"

"Hush now and go make yourself comfortable," Birdie scolded her. "If this child is really coming tonight, you'll need to conserve your strength."

Elsie turned the sheet music to "O Little Town of Bethlehem" and began to play haltingly as she parsed out the notes.

Birdie watched Clare help Albertine to her feet and made sure she was steady as they went down the hall toward the first floor toilet. They were both bundled in sweaters because the house was so cold. Lorraine, like a shadow, was right beside her mother.

"When the baby comes, can I watch?" Lorraine asked.

"No, dear," Birdie shook her head.

"Why not?" Lorraine pressed her. "You let everyone else help you."

"If the baby comes tonight, it will be at the hospital."

"The hospital? Since when do you need a hospital, Ma? You're a midwife! And Doc Bichet will come, too, won't he?"

"Use your head, will you?" Birdie snapped and Lorraine nearly cried. "When is Albertine's baby due?"

"January."

"The end of January."

"That's not too far off."

"For a baby in the womb every week is important. How many times do I have to tell you?"

"You don't have to pick on me, Ma!" Lorraine moaned. "I'm only trying to help."

"Well, do you see any incubators around here?" Birdie asked her daughter.

"No," Lorraine shrugged. "What's an incubator? One of those glass boxes at the World's Fair where they hatched chickens?"

"Hush," Birdie said then turned to Elsie at the piano, "and Elsie, please quit that racket. I need to make a phone call."

"Who are you calling?" Lorraine asked.

"Leave me be for five minutes!" Birdie said. "Go find the other children."

"I am not a child."

"You're my child."

"And those kids are your grandchildren."

"Go find my grandchildren, then."

"Oh, Ma!"

Birdie ignored Lorraine and went to the telephone in the hallway beside the kitchen, called Cook County Hospital, and asked to be patched into the maternity ward. She felt relieved when her cousin Lucy answered the phone, but she was not pleased with what Lucy told her.

"Let's pray that it's false labor," Lucy said. "Our ward is completely full tonight, Bird. I've got three mothers out in the hallway. Two babies in each incubator. And three of my nurses did not show up this shift. Merry Christmas!"

"But if Albertine gives birth to a preemie, I won't be able to take care of him, Lucy."

"You may have better luck at home. And have you looked outside? It's snowing so hard now, I don't know if you could get here."

"Jesus, Mary and Joseph!" Birdie muttered. "If we have to, we'll get there."

"Just keep Albertine and the baby warm. That's all we'd be able to do. Call Doc Bichet. Get him to help you."

"I hope we don't need to come to the hospital," Birdie sighed. "But you may be seeing us before long."

Birdie stepped to the kitchen window and saw that the inside pane was laced with ice. She opened the back door for a second and a tornado of snow blew in around her. She looked out to the alley and saw the drifts up to the rims of the ashcans, and halfway to the roofs of the garages. "This is not good," she said, but knew that Bichet would come through a worse blizzard to help her.

At first he didn't answer his telephone, but after the twentieth ring, he picked up. From the sound of his voice, she knew that he had been sleeping.

"Oh Birdie," he yawned. "Are you calling to wish me a Merry Christmas?"

"Merry Christmas," she said. "But it's three days away. And you know you are invited for dinner."

"I know. It's grand of you to think of me."

"I wish this was a social call, Doc, but I'm afraid I'll have to ask you to come out into that horrible weather."

"Oh? What's wrong? I didn't think any of your mothers were quite ripe yet."

"It's Albertine!" Birdie said and was happy that he sounded sober. "She's going into labor. And we're not ready. If that child is born prematurely, I won't be able to protect him, Doc. I don't have an incubator. And if Albertine's milk doesn't come in, I won't have any formula to feed him."

"When should I be there?" Doc Bichet asked.

"I'm not sure she's going to deliver. Four hours maybe?"

"If you weren't sure you wouldn't have called me," he grunted.

"Be careful, Doc," Birdie said and suddenly felt more confident, knowing that her old friend would come to help her. "I'll call you back if there's any change."

Albertine made it back to the couch and Claribel got her situated in the fetal position again, then covered her with a quilt to keep her warm.

"It's so cold in here," Albertine said to her sister. "Tell Pa we need more heat."

"Pa's at work, Al. I think the furnace is going all out. He stoked it before he left."

"And Hendrik's down there in Florida within sight of the warm beach," Albertine sighed. "If I hadn't been pregnant, I'd be down there with him instead…"

"Don't borrow trouble, Al," Claribel said. "You've got enough of your own."

"Where's Hank?" Albertine asked. "Is he at home?"

"He's in the dining room," Claribel said, "playing cards with Eugene."

Eugene (who now worked the day shift in the bindery at Donnelly's) had a coffee can full of pennies that the family used for poker chips. In a game called "poverty poker," Eugene would begin each game by dividing the coins equally among the players, so that each got a one dollar stake. When the game was over, all the pennies went back into the can. This evening he was the dealer for a tough game between him, Ricky, Roxanne and Hank. To no one's surprise, Hank had amassed three dollars' work of pennies, and was the night's big winner so far. He had learned a few things about poker from Dominic and from the men in smoky rooms who had been their shoe shine customers.

It was easy to beat Ricky and Roxanne (they barely understood poker rules) so Hank had to concentrate on winning pennies off of Uncle Gene. Hank had the advantage because from his low height he could read his uncle's cards in the reflection off his thick eye glasses.

Hank could see that Eugene held a pair of nines, the jack of clubs, and a couple of other number cards. On the first deal this was a better hand than Hank's, with the jack, ten and four of hearts, and the six and seven of spades. He knew Gene would keep the nines and the jack and try to match them with his two fresh cards. The best hand Gene could get was four nines, or a full house, which seemed unlikely because Hank held one of the jacks. Hank could beat him with a straight or a flush. Any way he played it, he'd need two matching cards. There were ten hearts out there (maybe in Ricky's or Roxanne's grubby little fists). To make a straight he could hold onto the jack, ten, seven and six, and hope for an eight and a nine, but Gene had two nines already. He decided to bet five cents and to go for the flush. Like lambs to the slaughter, Ricky and Roxanne matched his bet, and Gene actually raised him two cents, trying to scare him off. But Hank matched him, anyway. Then, as Hank predicted, Gene kept the jack and the nines. Hank held his three hearts and said to himself, "Oh Jesus, grant me two more!" As usual, Ricky and Roxanne each asked for three cards, which hurt the odds for everyone, but he couldn't worry about that now. Hank waited until all the new cards were down on the table before he picked his up. His heart sank when he saw that they were both black, but when he looked more closely, he saw that he held the ten of clubs and the four of spades, which made two pair, jack high. Now for the moment of truth: he watched Uncle Gene until he tilted his head at the right angle. Hank couldn't be sure, but it looked like Gene's new cards were an ace and a king, not good enough to beat him.

"All right, Hank, what do you bet?"

"I'll bet ten cents, Uncle Gene," he said and smiled. "I'm feeling lucky."

"Not as lucky as I do!" Gene said, with the stupid grin he always showed when he was bluffing. "I'll see your ten and raise you five. What about you kids? Are you in?" He asked Ricky and Roxanne.

"We don't know, Pa," Ricky said. "Would you bet on this?" he leaned toward his father and held up his cards.

"Pretty good, but I've got you beat."

"Okay, I'm out," Ricky said and tossed down his cards.

Roxanne fanned her cards for her father's approval, and he shook his head seriously. "I'm out!" she said and dropped her cards face up. There were no pairs, but three of the cards were hearts.

"Hey, no fair," Hank joked. "I could have had their money!"

"It's gonna be mine, anyway," Eugene teased him. "Let's see what you got."

"Tens and fours," Hank said, turning over his cards. "Let's see yours."

"Nuts," Gene said. "I thought you were bluffing. A pair of nines, ace high!"

As Hank swept the pennies into the pile in front of his chest, he told himself that seeing Gene's cards wasn't really cheating. His uncle's own glasses gave him away. And besides, all the pennies were going back into his Maxwell House can. The game was just for fun. Still, Hank wondered if he could win without seeing Gene's hand.

Uncle Gene had just announced that the next hand would be seven-card stud when Lorraine burst into the room. Was it bedtime already?

"It's Albertine!" Lorraine cried. "Ma thinks she's going into labor. She might need to go to the hospital."

"Is my mom okay?"

"I'm not sure!" Lorraine said breathlessly. "Clare practically had to carry her to the bathroom so she wouldn't wet the couch."

Hank got up and hurried out to the parlor to find his mother sitting precariously at the edge of the sofa, holding her green and black dress against the sphere of the new baby. Her eyebrows were knitted and her mouth was twisted as if she had just seen something terrible. Her sweater was inside out so the seams showed. Her hair was messy, and her face was red and splotchy. It scared Hank to see her this way.

"Ma," he asked her, "are you all right?

"I'm fine dear," Albertine said, but Hank saw tears in her eyes. "Don't worry about me."

"Is the baby coming?" he asked.

"We'll see," she said and smiled at him, sadly he thought. "It feels like it now, but that may change, Sweetheart. The baby may not be ready yet. We'll just have to wait and see."

"Will you be all right?"

"Of course, I'll be all right! Your Grandma Birdie is with me. And if we need her, Cousin Lucy is waiting at the hospital. They deliver babies every day. We're in the best of hands, so don't you worry."

"I won't," Hank said.

"How's the card game? Are you winning all of Uncle Gene's pennies?"

"Yeah, but I'll have to give them back. They're just for fun. But it would be more fun to keep them."

"You wouldn't want to take Gene's life savings, would you?" she smiled. "Come over here and give me a hug, will ya?"

Since she had gotten so big, he had avoided hugging her because he didn't want to hurt the baby. Now he squeezed her carefully because he didn't want to hurt her. He was surprised at how hard her stomach felt. It didn't give a bit when he pressed against her. No wonder she was so uncomfortable: her whole body was swollen up like Grandpa's hand had been.

"Oh, Ma, I hope you and the baby will be okay," Hank said, and he was truly worried. He had never seen his mother in so much distress and discomfort.

"Now, now, Sweetheart, everyone will be fine, you'll see. And you'll have a baby brother or sister! That will be our reward for all this trouble. A brand new baby!"

"That'll be great, Ma. I always wanted a little brother," Hank said, but admitted to himself that he never really wanted a brother or a sister. It was hard enough to get by with one kid in the family. Who needed the competition? Ricky and Roxanne were only a year apart, so they could play together, but it seemed to Hank that they fought more than half the time and couldn't get away from each other. What was the advantage to that? If he wanted someone to play with, he could go out in the alley and find someone in five minutes. Why did he need a baby brother? He didn't! It was something his mother wanted, and even then she didn't seem very happy about it.

"I'm glad you're looking forward to having the baby, too," his mother said. "I'll need your help in taking care of him. Do you promise to help me?"

"Sure," he said and kissed her cheek then stepped back from her and saw more tears in her eyes and on her cheeks.

"Okay," he said and returned to her quickly to kiss her cheek again before hurrying back to the dining room.

When he reached the table, his uncle was sweeping the pennies over the edge into his coffee can, and his cousins had gone upstairs to see if Lorraine would give them candy.

"So the game's over?" Hank asked his uncle.

"That's right," Gene said and paused to slide his glasses up his nose. "You were beating us pretty hard. The kids decided to call it a night. It's almost their bedtime, anyway."

"I thought you'd want to win your money back," Hank teased him, "instead of just scooping it back into that tin can."

"We'll play again soon, kiddo," Eugene said and mussed Hank's hair. "I'll have plenty of chances to beat you."

Not if you wear those glasses, Hank thought and headed upstairs to read his comic books until it was time to go to bed.

As Albertine felt what she recognized as a real contraction, her mother brought her a mug of herb tea that smelled like wet earth after a rainstorm.

"What's this?" she asked.

"One of my mother's herbal remedies," Birdie said. "Rich in minerals. It should slow down your labor. And Claribel is drawing you a nice warm bath. That should relax you and convince baby Ronald to stay where he is."

Ronald was the name Albertine had chosen for the baby if it was a boy, after her favorite movie actor, Ronald Colman. (It was Colby Malone's middle name, too.)

"It smells vile," Albertine complained. "Like mud."

"It's a very soothing potion," Birdie told her. "Sip it slowly and let it relax you. Then I'll help you upstairs so you can take your bath."

The tea tasted like salty medicine with a metallic edge. Not a bad taste, but a strange one, and her mother was right, it had an immediate soothing effect, as if the concoction was a mixture of liquid sleep and forgetfulness. She held the hot mug in both hands and raised it to her mouth and slurped its contents like an earthy soup.

"Now, doesn't that help?" Birdie asked her, and Albertine nodded as she continued drinking until she drained the whole cup. Birdie took the mug from her, set it on the table beside the lamp, then took her daughter's arm. "Come. Have your bath."

After the exertion of climbing the stairs, the bath was a small wonder. The hot water soothed her tender breasts and soaked through the tightness of her body. The air was full of steam, but she still could feel the sharp divide between cool air and hot liquid where her knees emerged from the plane of the water. Her nipples were twice their normal size and her abdomen looked huge with her navel popped inside out. And as she thought, "How could this be me?" she felt the baby kick upwards into her diaphragm. "Alive and kicking," she whispered. "Alive and kicking." Somehow the phrase seemed to describe her, too. It would take a lot more than a baby on the way, an absent husband, a cold winter and the Depression to keep her down.

And she guessed that the bath and the witch's brew had done the trick. Her back felt loose again, and the labor pains had subsided. It seemed like the worst was over for now. The baby will have more time to grow, she thought in relief, as she dozed off in the bath and the water splashed over the edge of the tub. When she woke up, her mother was calling to her. "Okay, that's great, dear. Time to dry off and go to bed. You can get some real sleep under the covers."

Real sleep. Albertine yawned and wondered if there was any other kind. She had slept a lot since Hendrik had gone down to Florida and she had lost her job, partly because her pregnancy made her tired, but mostly because she was bored and wanted to make the time pass more quickly. As her mother patted her with a towel and helped her put on her long flannel nightgown, Albertine felt wide awake. The labor pains were gone for now, and maybe she could relax, but sleep seemed out of the question. When Birdie ushered her to the bedroom, Albertine saw what a mess it was, and she wanted to clean it up. She picked up one of Clare's dresses from the floor and started to hang it up.

"What do you think you're doing?" Birdie asked her.

"It's a mess in here. How can I rest in all this clutter?"

"By lying down and closing your eyes, that's how," Birdie said. "If you give my herb tea a chance to work, you'll be asleep in two minutes.

"Let me straighten up first."

"In the morning," Birdie said. "I'll help you straighten up in the morning."

Birdie waited for Albertine to get under the quilt, and she sat down on Clare's bed for exactly two minutes before Albertine fell soundly asleep.

Albertine dreamed that she was in the stands at Wrigley Field. All the players on the field were Colby Malone, and all nine Colbys stopped the game to take off their caps and wave to her. As she waved back, she saw the golden hair on their heads glisten in the sunlight.

A woman's voice in her ear said, "It's not very smart of you to come to the ballpark when you're nine months pregnant. Only a country girl would do something so stupid, but you're not from the country, are you?"

Before she looked at her, Albertine knew that it was Flora Malone scolding her, but this time it was Flora who was trim and beautiful, and it was she who was as fat and ungainly as a cow. Flora's freckled face, greenish eyes, and wavy red hair were surrounded by the white halo of her straw hat, lit from behind by the afternoon sun.

"But you're outa luck, sister," Flora said and shook her head, "'cause I don't know nothin' about delivering babies!"

Albertine felt a long, painful contraction, like a bad menstrual cramp times ten, and it was still hurting when she opened her eyes and saw that she was in the little bedroom with her sister. The radium dial on the Seth Thomas clock said 4:00 a.m. When the contraction eased, Albertine wondered whether she had had others while she was sleeping. Not likely, but her Ma was full of strange stories of women giving birth unexpectedly or refusing to believe that they were in labor. And sometimes in the hospital, women were knocked out entirely with ether when they took their babies by Caesarian section.

In ten minutes, the next contraction started, and from its intensity she knew this was serious labor. Maybe the baby was farther along than her mother thought. Maybe she was really at 40 weeks, not 35. Maybe he was really ready to be born. But ready or not, he was coming in a few hours.

Albertine stayed in bed and timed her contractions on her alarm clock, with its glowing numbers and iridescent hands, including a second hand shaped like an arrow. The next three contractions lasted a minute each and were ten minutes apart. Regular and strong enough to be the real thing. She thought of waking Claribel so she could go get their mother, but what would Ma do? Make her drink more of that chalky tea? Put her back in the bath tub? Burn some incense in the corner and place a clove of garlic under her tongue? Some of Grandmére Elise's old tricks made no sense but seemed to help, and a lot of her remedies were only superstitious rituals intended to make the birthing mother less frightened.

At five o'clock it was still pitch black outside, but Albertine got up to look out the window, anyway, to check on the weather. The inside surface of the glass was covered by a thin layer of ice, so to look through it she had to blow on the frost for a minute until a circle melted away and she could pry up the edges of the ice with her fingernails and create a porthole large enough to look through. Still, she couldn't see much, except for the snow blowing erratically like swarms of white insects in the night. The wind through the alley must make the snow jump like that, it jostles it. Like us, the snowflakes have no choice about where they're going. They're blown around by fate just as we are. All the prayers in the world can't change that, all the rosaries and Masses in all the churches on earth make no difference, no matter what Ma says. It probably makes sense then, Albertine thought, that I haven't wasted too much time in Church.

By seven, when daylight began to show through the little window, the contractions were seven minutes apart and Albertine dreaded what she would have to go through during the day. Her labor with Hank had taken 12 grueling hours and had used up every bit of her energy. She didn't remember it, but her mother told her about how she had used forceps to finally bring Hank out, something midwives never did, but Dr. Bichet was there to direct her and it seemed like the only option left. And poor Hank had a tough beginning, too. When he didn't breathe right away, Ma dunked his head in a bucket of warm water to clear out all the mucus. (Now she had a little rubber bellows to clear the baby's nose so she would not need a bucket for this child, thank God.) And when Hank was born, Albertine was just 20 years old, a kid herself, with a lot more energy and endurance than she had now at 31. The day didn't promise to be much fun, except that at the end of it, she'd have a new baby, the miracle of life.

"Clare!" she called to her sister. "Clare, wake up! Go get Ma. This time, I'm really in labor."

"What time is it?"

"Seven o'clock."

"Gosh, I have to get ready for work."

"Did you hear me? I'm really in labor this time."

"I heard you," Clare yawned. "You really are?"

"I think so!"

"Well, don't get excited. As Ma says, babies are born every day."

"Clare!"

"Well, he's not going to jump out and get in bed with you!"

"Oh, my god, here's another contraction!"

"Okay, I'll go get Ma." Clare slipped her arms into her robe and found her slippers on the braided rug between their beds. "Geez, it's cold!" Clare said as she left the room. "I don't care if Christmas is coming. I hate winter."

The weather didn't seem to matter much to Albertine as she clenched her fists around the edge of the quilt and tried not to think about the pain. Why was she stuck in this drafty room, while Hendrik was down in some fancy hotel in the tropics? He had no idea what she was going through, and he probably didn't even care.

Her mother came into the room just as the contraction subsided. Albertine felt hot, too, but didn't want to let her mother pull back the quilt to examine her.

"When did the contractions start?' Birdie asked as she unwrapped Albertine's fingers from the edge of the bedspread and pulled it back.

"The first one woke me up at four o'clock," Albertine sighed and shivered in the relative cool.

"Why didn't you send for me then?" Birdie asked her.

"There's nothing you can do. Why disturb you?"

"Well, let me help you get to the toilet and then I'll fix you some breakfast and some more herb tea."

"Breakfast? I'm not sure I can eat."

"You'll need your energy, dear," Birdie told her. "At least you got a few hours of sleep. You'll be grateful for that."

She ate the bacon, eggs and toast greedily, then gulped down the tall glass of milk her mother poured for her. By eight o'clock she held a mug of herb tea in both of her hands as her mother called Doc Bichet for the third time during this bout of labor.

Except for Henry, the whole family was up by eight, and to Albertine's ears they made an incredible racket. In his gray Donnelly's uniform, Eugene was barking a Ricky and Roxanne as they made faces at their bowls of oatmeal.

"Eat it!" he scolded them, "it's the only breakfast you get."

"I smell bacon!" Ricky complained. "Why can't I have bacon?"

"Because your aunt ate it all," Elsie joined in. "She's having a baby today. When you have a baby, <u>you</u> can eat bacon."

"But I <u>can't</u> have a baby," Ricky complained.

"Then I guess you'll never get to eat bacon," Elsie laughed.

Albertine felt guilty. If she had known they were the last three slices of bacon, she would have saved them for the kids. Meanwhile, Hank ate his oatmeal quickly and drank his hot chocolate, then hurried to put on his coat, hat, scarf and gloves.

"Where are you going, Sweetheart?" Albertine asked him.

"Are you kidding, Ma?" he smiled at her. "It snowed last night. I can make a quarter by lunchtime just shoveling stoops. Will you be okay without me?"

"I'll be fine, Hank. Be careful, and don't let yourself get too cold."

As he went out, Claribel was buttoning her coat for her walk to the streetcar stop. "Too cold? I'm too cold already," she said, "and I haven't even gone outside."

When things had settled down after breakfast, Birdie tried to make Albertine comfortable in the parlor. If the magnesium tea didn't work this time, the parlor was the best place to go through early labor. Between contractions Albertine tried to distract herself by pinning pieces of fabric together for Elsie as she made her last two dresses that had to be delivered tomorrow, on Christmas Eve. Unfortunately, Albertine didn't do a very neat job, and Elsie had to adjust her work every time.

"Sorry, Elsie," she told her. "I thought I got it right."

"Don't worry," Elsie said. "You've got other things on your mind. Besides, you're saving me time, anyways. And having you here beats working by myself."

By ten o'clock the contractions were five minutes apart and stronger than ever, and Birdie resigned herself to the fact that the herbal remedy wasn't going to work a second time. She called her cousin at the hospital (Fay was on the day shift), and if anything, the lying-in ward was even more crowded than the night before, and they were just as short-handed. Doc Bichet had told Birdie to give Albertine a shot of whiskey, but she didn't like the way alcohol made her mothers sluggish and slow-witted. If Albertine was going to have her baby today, Birdie wanted her to be as sharp as possible. She had to be in control of her own delivery.

At eleven o'clock, Birdie brought Albertine a towel to protect the couch when her water broke, and she went upstairs to wake Henry and to convert their bedroom into a birthing room.

"Henry, I'm sorry to wake you, dear," she said, "but we need this room. It's the only one suitable for a delivery."

"So she's back in labor again?" Henry asked as he sat up, yawned and stretched. "Your magic potion didn't work, after all?"

"I'll thank you not to joke about it, Henry Fontaine," she scolded him. "And hurry up and get a move on! I've got a lot of work to do in here."

"Do I have to make my own coffee?"

"Yes, and make it snappy. I'm going to need every burner on the stove to boil water."

"Don't worry," Henry said. "I won't get in your way."

By one o'clock Birdie had rolled up the bedroom rugs, scrubbed the floor with disinfectant, changed the sheets, set up her birthing chair, pulled out her crib and lined it with fresh linens, set stacks of clean towels on the bedside table, and put blankets over the curtain rods to keep out the draft and warm the room. She had just put her instruments on to boil in a pan on the stove when Albertine's water broke and Doc Bichet rang the front doorbell.

When Elsie opened the door to let him in, the doctor waved to the vacant couch and asked, "Where's the expectant mother?"

The old doctor was less disheveled than usual. His coat had no visible holes except for one torn armpit, his wool cap was new (payment from a patient), and his trousers and jacket were clean, if wrinkled. He had even attempted to shave in the last 24 hours, so instead of a gray stubble, he displayed scabs from half a dozen nasty nicks. The cold afternoon seemed to energize him, or perhaps he was happy that he had been able to sleep all night without attending to Albertine's labor.

"Her water just broke, Doc," Elsie said. "She went to the bathroom to drain."

"Very thoughtful of her, Elsie," the doctor nodded. "And where's you Ma?"

"In the kitchen, I think," Elsie said. "Sterilizing her instruments."

"Well," the doctor said and held up his own worn leather bag, "I hope she's started a pot boiling for mine."

When Doc Bichet stepped into the kitchen, Birdie hurried to him and yanked his bag away from him. "It's about time you got here. Her contractions are three minutes apart, and her water broke. I thought I was going to have to deliver my grandchild on my own."

"It wouldn't be the first time that you didn't wait for me," the doctor grumbled. "Don't be silly, you old fool!" she said and hurried to the stove. "Let's get your tools sterilized and check on Albertine."

They found Albertine standing in the hallway hugging herself in her thick terry cloth robe. "Well, so much for my underpants," she shrugged. "How much longer do I have, Ma? It must be getting close if he's here. Hello, Doctor."

"Let your mother help you upstairs," Doc Bichet said. "She's got the birthing room all ready to make you comfortable."

"Comfortable?"

"Relatively speaking," Doc Bichet shrugged. "I need to take a few minutes to scrub my hands."

Once Albertine arrived in the warm, second-story bedroom, her labor proceeded rapidly. She sat semi-reclining on a stack of pillows on top of the bed, and gave herself up to the contractions which seemed almost constant. Every half hour, Birdie checked her blood pressure, listened to the baby's heart, and gauged Albertine's dilation. In between, she gave Albertine sips of cool water and fed her apple sauce with a spoon. All the while, Doc Bichet sat in the wooden rocking chair with his stethoscope around his neck dozing peacefully but ready to be awakened whenever he was needed.

Albertine sat up straight after her mother declared she was fully dilated. "So is it time to push, then?" she called out. (Still in the rocking chair, Doc Bichet laughed a hearty guffaw. Albertine always amused him.)

"I'll tell you when it's time to push," Birdie told her sternly.

"Well, is it time?"

"Yes, dear," Birdie said. "On the next contraction, it's time."

Albertine closed her eyes and nodded. Finally the time had come, and she felt she had just enough strength to expel the baby before she collapsed in exhaustion.

Birdie moved the birthing chair close to the bed and helped Albertine balance on it so the upright position would help loosen her pelvis and so gravity would help with the delivery.

The baby's head crowned and Doc Bichet got to his feet, but Birdie was able to guide the child into the world, freeing the head, one arm and shoulder, then the others. It was a lovely, tiny boy, white with vernyx, and he took his first breaths and cried without provocation as his whole body blushed red. "It's a boy, dear," Birdie said. "You've got your baby Ronald." The doctor was there with sterile scissors to cut the cord, and Birdie took the baby aside to wash him with a sponge, soap and warm water. She diapered him and wrapped him in a receiving blanket, then presented him to Albertine.

"He's a tiny guy," Birdie said. "Barely four pounds, I'd guess. But he should grow fast."

Albertine held the baby against her breast and spoke gently to him. "There you are, Sweetheart, there you are. You're beautiful, you're so beautiful."

After a few minutes, Doc Bichet took the baby and placed him on a clean towel beneath a lamp and examined him carefully, unwrapping the blanket a little at a time to press his stethoscope against the boy's chest and back. He turned the baby on his stomach and held the boy's head as if he were evaluating an orange at a fruit stand, and then he turned him again and gently lifted his eyelids with his fingertips. He pried open the boy's mouth and looked inside it, and bent over to examine each ear at close range.

Doc Bichet opened the blanket to inspect the umbilical cord, listen to the boy's stomach with the stethoscope and take his pulse on the inside of his thigh. He unpinned the diaper and felt the baby's scrotum with his index finger, and nodded when he found both testicles in place. He picked up the baby and tilted him backwards to watch him arch his spine and tilt his head far to the back. Then the doctor gave the baby back to Birdie, who lay him down in Albertine's arms.

"See if he'll nurse a little bit before the placenta comes," Birdie said.

"It feels so wonderful to hold him, Ma," Albertine said. "I wasn't expecting him to be born this soon, but it's so good to hold him now. He's so tiny!"

The baby took to her breast right away, and Birdie tried to watch, but Doc Bichet pulled her into the hallway where he could speak to her in what passed for privacy in the Fontaine house.

"Everything seems normal enough with the baby, but he's way under weight. You'll have to do everything you can to keep him warm and make sure he nurses. You know he's at risk, Birdie. He's too small and too weak for us to take anything for granted."

"I know what to do," Birdie nodded. "Sit for a while so I can fetch Elsie to help me."

Birdie found Elsie working at her sewing machine, finishing the last dress of the season.

"Elsie!" Birdie began but she was breathless and needed a long moment to compose herself.

"Did I hear a baby crying?" Elsie asked her mother.

"Yes," Birdie nodded, "We have another little boy."

"That's wonderful!" Elsie said happily, but when her mother didn't return her smile, she added, "Is everything all right?"

"Elsie, I need your help," Birdie said.

"Fine, Ma. Give me about twenty minutes to finish this dress, and I'm all yours."

"The sewing can wait, dear," Birdie said. "We need you now."

"Oh, dear," Elsie said, stood up quickly and untied her sewing apron. "Is something wrong?"

"The baby came about a month early and we'll need to work very hard to keep him warm."

"What can I do?" Elsie asked her.

"First, wash your hands with hot water and plenty of soap all the way up to your elbows. And come up to my bedroom to help. Where's your father?"

"Taking a nap in my room."

"And where are the kiddos?" Birdie asked.

"Hank took my two out into the alley, and Lorraine went up to her room with a stack of magazines."

"Well, let's hope they stay busy for a while," Birdie said. "And please come up as soon as you can."

When Birdie came into the bedroom the baby was in the crib and crying weakly, and Doc Bichet was on his knees, stuffing a wad of gauze between Albertine's legs.

"What's wrong, Doc?" she asked. "You didn't pull the cord, did you?"

"Hush," Doc Bichet grumbled. "She delivered the afterbirth and started hemorrhaging."

Birdie checked to make sure the baby was safe in the crib, then went directly to Albertine. Her eyes were closed and she was completely still.

"Albertine!" she called to her. "Wake up now, girl! Stay with us, Sweetheart."

"Why?" she asked without opening her eyes. "It's so luxurious, I can finally get some rest."

"No, dear," Birdie said and touched her cheek. "You have to open your eyes for now. Open them!"

Albertine opened her eyes and gave her mother an irritated frown.

"None of that!' Birdie scolded her. "You have to concentrate."

"Concentrate on what?" Albertine moaned.

"Honey, you're bleeding," Birdie told her. "I can't let you sleep until it stops. Concentrate on making the bleeding stop."

"How will that work, Ma?"

"It works every time. So concentrate."

Meanwhile, Doc Bichet was inserting another wad of gauze, and Birdie turned toward the baby. "Elsie!" she called. "Where is that girl?"

"Here I am," Elsie said as she came through the door and closed it behind her.

"Elsie, your job is to keep the baby warm," Birdie told her. "Do you remember what you did the winter Ricky was born, and he was so small?"

"I held him in a sling under my bathrobe, right next to my skin."

"That's right, you remember. I'll make the sling. You go change into your bathrobe. And wash up again."

"But it's not my baby! Can't Al do it?"

"Your sister is concentrating on stopping her bleeding right now, Elsie. This is something you can do for her child, and I want you to do it right now. We're saving this rocking chair for you."

"I'll be right back," Elsie said and hurried out again.

"Has the bleeding stopped?" Birdie asked Doc Bichet.

"I think so," he said and nodded.

"Thank God," Albertine said. "Now I can sleep."

"Not yet," Birdie corrected her. "Not until I check for myself."

Delicately, Birdie removed the wads of blood-saturated gauze, wiped away the residue, and made sure the bleeding had stopped. Then she replaced the gauze with a clean pad.

"You see, concentration works most of the time," Birdie told her daughter.

"What happens when it doesn't?" Albertine asked.

"Then we have to compress your uterus manually," Birdie said. "Or the patient needs a d and c."

"I'll keep concentrating."

"I think you can rest now," Birdie told her. "I'll keep an eye on you."

Then Birdie went to check on the baby where he lay with eyes wide open. She touched his cheek and it felt cool. So she set to work cutting diapers and pinning them together to make a sling for baby Ronald to sleep in while hanging against his aunt's breast.

In a minute, Elsie came back in her flannel bathrobe with a long nightgown underneath it, unbuttoned to the waist. Birdie fitted the sling around Elsie's neck then pulled her close to the newborn, and unwrapped him so that he was dressed in only his diaper. She placed the baby snugly in the sling, then buttoned Elsie's robe around him.

"Oh dear," Elsie said as she felt the child against her bosom, "he's cold as ice, poor dear. He's freezing."

"Now sit down here," Birdie said, nodding to the rocker. "Sit down here and rock and warm that baby up while Albertine gets some sleep. I'll be back in a minute."

Then Birdie went out into the hallway and crossed the house to the room that Elsie now shared with Gene. She found Henry snoring on top of the double bed, fully clothed and hugging a throw pillow to his chest.

"Henry," she called to him. "Henry."

"What?"

"It's a boy."

"That's nice," he yawned. "Hank has a little brother. Is everything okay?"

"No," she said. "That's why I want you to send a telegram to that blockhead Kinderman down in Florida!"

Chapter Eighteen

The bellhop who handed him the telegram was the size of a boy, but as Hendrik took the yellow envelope from him, he could see that he was actually a very short man with a five o'clock shadow and wrinkles under his eyes. Hendrik thought the guy looked like Zangara, the tiny man who had tried to kill Roosevelt, but they'd sent him to the electric chair. Then Hendrick reached into his pocket and found a quarter to tip him. "Danke," he said and the little man took the coin and hurried away guiltily.

He tore open the envelope and pulled out the telegram, which was typed in smudged capital letters. It was too dark in the ballroom to make it out, so he walked back to the bandstand and held it under the spotlight. It said: YOUR SON BORN 3 PM TODAY. BOTH MOTHER AND BABY IN WEAK CONDITION. PHONE NOW. RETURN HOME SOONEST. HENRY FONTAINE.

Another son. Not bad. But the baby was born prematurely, and that was not good for the child and Albertine. But what could he do about it now? Rush home and comfort his wife, who might be too sick to notice? Be there so Hank would not be afraid? If he left now, there was a chance that Bill could lead the band, but who wants to listen to an hour of trombone solos when they came to hear the saxophone?

Hendrick was staring at the yellow sheet distractedly, not sure what to do, when Pearl pulled it from his fingers, read it, and laughed.

"It's a trick!" she said.

"How could it be a trick?" Hendrik snarled impatiently. "What kind of trick?"

"Albertine is trying to get you home for Christmas. You can't take this seriously. That baby's not due for at least another month."

"The message is from her father."

"She could have signed his name."

"And the baby could be premature. Which is pretty bad, I guess. From what I've heard."

"You've heard old wife's tales," Pearl asserted. "Tales that don't take into account modern medical science."

"Her mom delivers babies for a living. Even Albertine wouldn't lie about having a premature baby."

"Did you hear yourself? Even Albertine. You don't trust her, do you?"

"I'm not one to talk about trust," Hendrik said. "Am I?"

"She cheated on you first," Pearl snapped.

Hendrik took a deep breath, thought of Albertine, and he missed her. Dealing with Albertine was more complicated than handling Pearl, but her problems brought rewards, too. The rumors about Albertine didn't seem so important now, especially if she and the baby were in danger. "You just leave Albertine to me," he said through grit teeth. "She's my wife."

"And what am I?" she asked indignantly. "Tell me, what am I?"

"This is not about you," he insisted.

"Well, it should be about me," she said. "At least I'm faithful to you."

"Come on!" he said and snatched the telegram from her fingers, folded it hastily and slipped it into his coat pocket.

"Listen, Buster, there are a lot of rich men staying at this hotel. Make no mistake: they've noticed me. Every day I get an invitation from at least one millionaire. But like a sap, I've been faithful to you, a saxophone player who doesn't have two dimes to rub together."

"I'm the one who put you in the spotlight."

"Thank you, but my talent did that."

"But I gave you the chance," Hendrik reminded her. "And things have been good for you, haven't they?"

"They were fine until you decided to run after that bitch and her little bastard."

Without thinking, he raised his fist, but he remembered that they were in a public place, and no one would understand why he was so angry.

"The truth hurts, doesn't it, Buster?" she challenged him. "It hurts to know that your slut of a wife just gave birth to Colby Malone's bastard. And you're running back like you're the proud papa. It makes me sick. Quite frankly, it makes me want to puke!"

Hendrik shook his head and wanted to get away from her. She had been waiting for an opportunity to condemn Albertine, and she picked the worst possible moment. He turned away from her and saw Rocko and Billy lighting cigarettes as they headed outside for their break.

"Guys," he called to them, "Wait a second." Hendrik approached them urgently and made a quick look over his shoulder to make sure Pearl wasn't following him.

Sensing his concern, they stopped, held their cigarettes down, and blew their smoke to the side. "What's up?" Rocko asked him.

"I just got a telegram from Henry Fontaine," he said. "Albertine gave birth to a little boy. But neither of them are doing very well. I'm taking the first train North to be with them."

"That's the right thing to do," Rocko nodded. "If there's anything we can do…"

"Cover for me," he said. "Billy, you can play trombone solos on most of our tunes. I've heard you. You can get up front with Pearl."

"I'd be glad to," Billy said. "I was wondering when I'd get the chance!"

Within a few minutes after Elsie took the baby under her robe, he warmed up and began to suckle. "Suck if it makes you feel better," she called softly to the child, "but you're not going to get a drop out of me."

Having such close contact with the newborn relaxed Elsie, and she would have rocked the baby and herself to sleep, except for the minor commotion her mother and Doc Bichet were making as they hovered over Albertine.

"She's burning up, Doc!" Birdie said as she touched her daughter's forehead. "Let me take her temperature. How did she get an infection? I've been so careful."

"You don't know she has an infection," the old doctor grumbled.

"Then how do you explain the fever?"

"Wait for the thermometer, Bird. Let's wait for the facts."

She inserted the thermometer under her daughter's arm and held her wrist to take her pulse.

"Are you sure you didn't yank the cord out?" she accused him.

"Aren't you ashamed to ask me that question?" he pouted and ran his tongue over his teeth. "You don't feed me a mouthful of food all day, and then you accuse me of hurting my favorite girl."

"You have made that mistake in the past," Birdie reminded him. "Too impatient to…" She paused to take out the thermometer.

"What does it say?"

"One hundred two, and you have to add a degree because I used her armpit," Birdie said and shook her head. "If she doesn't have an infection, she caught the flu in the last four hours."

"It could be the result of that bleeding," Bichet said. "Let her rest for a few minutes, and we'll <u>eat</u> something."

"If you're so hungry, go help yourself to some cold chicken from the ice box," Birdie scolded him. "I'm not waiting on you today."

"Cold chicken?" Doc Bichet perked up. "You've been holding out on me."

"Well, go eat your damn chicken! I'll stay up here with the girls and the baby. And wash your hands before you come back."

As soon as the doctor left the room, Albertine rolled over to the side of the bed and threw up a small amount of water and mucus.

"Oh, God," Albertine moaned. "I'm sorry, Ma."

"Don't worry. I rolled up the rugs," Birdie said. "Would you like some water? Some ice chips?"

"A little water," Albertine whispered hoarsely. "To get this taste outa my mouth."

Birdie poured her a glass from the water pitcher on the bedside table, then raised it to Albertine's lips and let her take a small sip.

"How are you feeling?" Birdie asked her.

"Okay," Albertine asked. "How's the baby? Where's the baby?"

"I got him right here," Elsie said and gently touched him through her robe. "You want him back?"

"Naw, you keep him a while longer," Albertine said. "I'm feeling pretty weak right now."

"Don't worry. The baby will be fine," Birdie said. "Let's see about you."

While Doc Bichet and Henry sat in the kitchen together and ate cold chicken, Birdie examined Albertine, found the infection and decided to bring her to the hospital. And if Albertine went, the baby would have to go with her.

"It's nothing to worry about," Birdie said as she wiped Albertine's forehead with a cool cloth, "but for safe keeping, I'll try to get you and little Ronnie into the hospital for a few days."

"Why can't we stay with you?" Albertine asked.

"Because you've got an infection," Birdie told her. "I think the doctors there can handle it better than this old man and I can."

"Ma, I don't want to go anywhere right now," Albertine said. "I don't have the strength."

"I need to call Lucy first, anyway," Birdie said. "And the weather! I forgot about the weather! There was a big snowstorm out there."

"It was still snowing when I changed into my robe," Elsie added as she rocked slowly to comfort the baby. "It didn't seem to be letting up any."

"Have you called Hendrik to say he has a new son?" Albertine asked her mother. "I'm sure he'd come if he knew."

"Your father sent him a telegram," Birdie said. "We don't know if it was delivered. But the message said he should call us, then come home as soon as possible."

"But he hasn't called?"

"Not yet."

"I'm sure he'll come. He has to come. How could he <u>not</u> come?"

"He's far away," Birdie said. "But I'm sure he's already on his way. For all his faults, Hendrik has enough heart to know when his family needs him."

"I'm sorry to spoil your Christmas," Albertine said and began to cry. A deep sadness came over her as she thought of her poor little baby, her own sorry condition, and her separation from her husband on the most important holiday of the year. Hendrik was especially fond of Christmas, too. He would play the Christmas carols on his saxophone as she played her piano, and then break off to sing the verses. He sang them in German, too – Stille Nacht and O Tannenbaum – and he seemed like a little boy trying to please his parents. And even though he didn't want Hank to speak German, he taught him the words to those Christmas songs, and Hendrik seemed delighted when the boy got them right.

"Can I have a turn with the baby?" Albertine asked as her tears subsided. "This infection isn't contagious, is it?"

"No," Birdie said. "If you feel up to it, it will be good for you to sit for a while."

"And Elsie could use a break!" Albertine said. "Wouldn't it be wonderful if you could take turns when you're pregnant? Let someone else carry the baby for a while, so you can have a rest?"

"Well, it's too late for that," Elsie laughed as she stood up from the rocking chair. "And you probably wouldn't find any willing volunteers."

To transfer the baby, Birdie took him out of his sling and wrapped him in a cotton blanket.

"Give your sister the sling," Birdie said to Elsie, "while I change him."

Albertine got out of bed and let Elsie hang the sling of diaper cloth around her neck, then hurried across the room to get a good look at the baby while her mother changed his diaper on top of her dresser. Albertine saw how tiny he was, how thin his arms and legs were, how the end of the cord was already beginning to shrivel, and how perfectly formed were his fingers and toes, his tiny ears, his beautiful little mouth. "Oh my darling," she said and began to tremble with the cold and her fever, until Elsie brought her the heavy terry cloth robe. Albertine steadied herself and was reunited with her baby. It felt different, more real and scarier, too, to hold the baby this way, on the outside. She wanted so much to protect him, but he was so vulnerable now. She felt that he wasn't ready to be on his own. Still, it felt comforting and warm to press him next to her skin, and it was a relief to sit up in the rocker instead of being trapped in the bed. And Albertine could move more freely, too, now that the giant mound was so suddenly gone from her belly.

"Everything's going to be just right," she said softly to her newborn son, and she hoped she was right.

The phone operator in Miami couldn't place Hendrik's long distance call to Chicago. "Nothing's going through, sir," she had told him, "on account of the ice storm in Georgia. Miles of lines are down across the state. They say it could take weeks to restore service." Western Union had the same problem. The wire from Henry had been one of the last messages to make it through.

Hendrik went to the cottage and tossed his other suit into his suitcase along with the clothes from his one bureau drawer, and he left his horn behind. He circled around to the front of the hotel to get a taxi to the station where he would try to catch the midnight train. He didn't even go inside the hotel for fear of seeing Pearl again and having to listen to her insinuations about Albertine. He didn't want to go to jail for beating a woman in public; he needed to get home to his family.

The driver took him along the beach front. The ocean was as beautiful as hammered silver, with a bright moon reflected on its dimpled surface. Silhouettes of palm trees and seaside villas against a violet sky made it seem ridiculous that there would be an ice storm in Georgia, only one state to the north. He knew there were a thousand miles of telephone lines strung on poles all the way up to Chicago. An outage anywhere along the way could interrupt service, and even if there were multiple, redundant wires, a big storm could knock them all out, shutting down all communications.

Though it was a solid, brick building with a spacious terminal hall, the Miami train station was usually a sleepy place (by Chicago standards) with only a few people around. But tonight every bench in the waiting area was full of people and their luggage. Heavy coats were draped over suitcases, in anticipation of the cold weather on the other end of the line.

When Hendrik got to the ticket window and checked the schedule board, every train was marked DELAYED. Miami was the terminus of the line and North was the only direction a train could go from here.

"What a mess!" Hendrik said to the man next to him, a sailor in uniform with a duffel bag that was larger than he was. He had a round face, which in combination with the bag, made Hendrik think of Santa Claus.

"It's one damn mess, all right!" the sailor agreed. "And it's even worse at the bus station! Nobody's gonna make it home for Christmas this year. And there isn't even a problem in Florida. The weather's great here. We might as well stay in Miami and go to the beach on Christmas."

Christmas. Hendrik was glad that Rocko had reminded him to send something to Hank and Albertine, and he hoped the package with the model sailboat and silk scarf got there on time. Although he felt that he would never really be part of the Fontaine family, and the Sunday dinner routine often felt like an unwanted obligation, Christmas day at their house was something that he hated to miss. While he was growing up, the Kindermans had observed Christmas but had never really celebrated it. His father even seemed embarrassed that Hendrik loved Christmas songs and wanted to sing them all the time. And his mother regarded preparing the holiday meal as a huge inconvenience, and not as an expression of love. So it surprised Hendrik when his father wrote to him about their plan to tour Germany in his new Chrysler over the Christmas season. He would show off his success in America at Christmas, when the Germans would be most aware of their own deprivations, which were much worse than the American Depression. Fröhliche Weinachten! I'm rich and you're poor. So there! Well, after all, that's just like Papa to try to make people feel small.

Not sure that he should trust the signs, Hendrik went to the ticket window and spoke to the clerk, who was dressed in a green eyeshade, a leather vest, a bow tie and sleeve garters—like the accountants at the insurance company where Hendrik had worked.

"I want to buy a round trip ticket to Chicago," he told the ticket agent.

"I don't mind selling it to you, pal, but you probably won't get there until New Year's. I've told everyone here that they won't be home for Christmas. The trains aren't running and there's no telling when they will be. So do you still want that ticket?"

"How much for coach class?"

"Thirty-eight fifty."

"Okay. I'll take it. It's the only way out of here."

Hendrik believed that the whole country had an urgency to travel, to be someplace else to share time with someone else. Certainly he felt that way; he was compelled to be on the move. And every obstacle, like this one, would only intensify that desire. So with all that collective will power, all that heightened wander-lust, he was sure the railroad people would clear the tracks, the telephone men would re-string their lines, and the bus drivers would find alternate routes. Ignoring the weather, they would fix things much faster than this cynical clerk believed.

And even if there wasn't a good seat left at the train station waiting room, Hendrik felt he should wait it out there. If he went back to the hotel, he would see Pearl, and if he saw her, and they didn't fight, he might not try to take the train again.

On Christmas Eve morning, Albertine's fever reached 105° and there was still no room at the hospital for her or the baby. Although the snow had stopped falling, it was 20 below zero outside and even colder in the gusty wind. Before he left, Dr. Bichet recommended that they stay at home, and if necessary Elsie and Claribel could take turns keeping the baby warm until Albertine's fever subsided and the winter storm broke. Birdie knew that she could get Albertine through the infection, and they were already feeding the baby condensed milk and egg yolks from sterilized bottles, but she would have preferred a real incubator for the baby and a staff of nurses to watch him for a week or two, until he had put on some weight and his lungs grew stronger. So far he was only taking an ounce of formula at a time, and his color looked jaundiced. His temperature was slightly above normal now, and Birdie hoped he wasn't getting a fever, too.

Even though Albertine and her baby were struggling, Birdie told Henry that the family would have to celebrate Christmas the best they could. After all, Christmas was all about an unexpected baby being born under difficult circumstances. That birth resulted in the salvation of mankind. This one would have a wonderful outcome, too, Birdie believed, so it made this Christmas more special than usual.

On Christmas morning, Henry, Eugene and Larry took their instructions from Birdie, and under supervision from Elsie and Claribel (when they weren't warming the baby) the three inept men prepared the dinner. It was not as elaborate a meal as Birdie would have liked, but there was plenty of good-tasting food.

Albertine wouldn't be able to join them for Christmas dinner. Her fever continued above 104° and shooting pains wracked her head. Whenever she moved, her lower body hurt as if she were being knifed. Instead of sweating, her skin grew hot and dry, her mouth and throat were parched, and every time she swallowed more than a mouthful of water, she vomited it back up in seconds.

In her fever, Albertine forgot about her baby. She dreamed that she and Hendrik lived on the bandstand of a dark, damp basement club, with a bed in the middle of the stage, a bed covered in ragged and stained sheets, a striped pillow without a case, and a moth-eaten blanket. She tried to play the piano, but it was frightfully out of tune, and Hendrik cursed her for playing the wrong notes. He played something deeply sad on his saxophone and asked her to repeat it on the piano, but even though she played the same notes, he cursed her anyway.

Colby Malone appeared wearing a straw hat and a white summer suit, looking like one of the ghosts her mother had described to her. "But, Colby, you're not dead, are you?" she asked the white figure. "I heard you were traded to New York…but tell me please that you're alive and well."

Colby tipped his hat and squinted at her as if she herself was a bright light (and she liked the way his nose scrunched up). Then he stepped back, retreating down a long hallway until he seemed as small as a doll, and he disappeared behind the glowing mist. Now it all seemed ridiculous to her. And humiliating, too. She had been a fool to fall for him. She had thrown her love away.

Then she felt the heat of the stage lights again, and she heard the downbeat from Rocko's bass, and saw the glint off Hendrik's hair and his saxophone. Jake rattled the cymbals with his brushes, which was her cue to lay down the chords beneath Hendrik's lovesick solo. His music sounded painful and incredibly sweet to her, and she was sure that Hendrik played it especially for her. As she stroked the keyboard, she was happy to spot a silk gardenia on top of the piano. Thank God, Pearl was gone for good.

How could she ever doubt him? How could she ever think that Hendrik had fallen out of love with her? When men and women get together, things can happen, but it doesn't mean they have a change of heart. They can be carried away by the moment, the romantic idea that the other person is obsessed with you, by the lure of drink and pleasure, but it can be just an interlude, a short visit to another place that has no connection to the real life that you're committed to, to your family, your husband, your wife, your child. So even if Pearl was able to lure Hendrik away from her for a few weeks, he wouldn't forget Albertine. In fact, now that he's read the telegram, he'll be here in a few hours, to be by my side, and he'll take care of the baby and me. He may be German, and he may sound a little harsh, but Hendrik is kind like my father. Deep down he has a soft heart, a protective heart, a heart that would rather stop beating than betray me.

Albertine found herself sitting in the second pew in a dark church lit only by candles. She held a newborn infant, Hank, she thought. She knew it had to be Notre Dame Church, the French church, but it seemed like a cathedral looming high above her, a dark cavern with elaborate stonework and stained glass windows like patches of multi-colored sky soaking through the heavy granite clouds. The indistinct statues of the Virgin and St. Joseph quivered in the flickering yellow candle light. A priest in white vestments stood behind a marble baptismal font, chanting in Latin. The organ played *Bye-Bye Blackbird*, and Albertine turned around to see her piano teacher Madame Corbet at the keyboard in the choir loft. But Madame never let me play any fun songs for her! When Albertine looked back to the altar, her mother and sisters, and a crowd of nuns from the parish school had all gathered behind the priest. They all stared at her as if she had done something wrong. "It's time to baptize that child!" they called to her.

Of course, she realized, he must be baptized. If anything happens to him, he'll have to be baptized to get into heaven. She stood up and held the baby out to the priest. When he raised his arms, his vestments glowed brightly, and he stared into her face, judging her. Afraid, she pulled the baby back and held him tightly to her breast.

Now she sat at her PBX machine, taking calls for Swanson's Tea and Coffee. The voices on her headset sounded like musical instruments. A trumpet spoke to her. A clarinet complained. A trombone asked for a big order. A chattery banjo left a message from her brother. She connected each wire, transferring each call to the right department, until the saxophone vibrated in her ear, then articulated the words: "No matter what your cares and woe. I'm not coming back to Chi-ca-go! Bye, Bye Birdie!" But it couldn't be Hendrik's saxophone! "How may I direct your call?" she asked. "What party, sir?"

Albertine felt a cold shiver and heard the window creak open, and then she saw Hank climbing in between the curtains. Snow clung to his coat and hat, and he balanced a small bucket which glowed red. He was carrying a pail of burning coal!

"I brought a fire to warm you up, Ma," he said and set the pail on the table next to her bed. The heat raged on her as if she had opened the iron door to a furnace. Her hair nearly melted and her eyes burned.

"I'm warm enough, son," she said. "Why don't you put those down by the window and come back to talk to me?"

He obeyed her without question and set the bucket on the window sill, where the falling snowflakes hissed and sputtered on the coals like angry insects.

"So, have I got a little brother?" he asked.

Albertine nodded.

"And where is he? Can I see him?"

"Where is he?" she cried in alarm. "Where is he? I don't know where he is! Your grandmother took him the same way she took you!"

"I'd rather live with just you and Pa," Hank said. "Can't the four of us just be together?"

"That's my dream," Albertine told him. "But where's the baby? Where's little Ronnie?"

Chapter Nineteen

Albertine woke up with a start, and without thinking she jumped out of bed, but her legs gave way beneath her. She would have fallen to the floor if her father had not been there to catch her.

"Steady, Al," Henry said. "Do you need to use the bathroom?"

"No. I want my baby. Where is he?"

"Your mother and sister took him to the hospital. Your cousin Fay finally had an incubator for him."

"Why didn't they tell me?" Albertine asked. "He's <u>my</u> baby!"

"Honey, you've been delirious for two days. You slept through Christmas while your sisters fed the baby and kept him warm. I'm glad you finally woke up."

"That's not possible!" she cried. "I've only been asleep for a few minutes!"

"Well, I've been sitting here for the past six hours, dear. Let me help you use the toilet and get back in bed."

"They took my baby to the hospital without even telling me? Why did you let them do that, Pa? Why did you let them?"

"They tried to tell you, honey, but you were beside yourself with fever. So they called me in here to watch you. Elsie and your Ma are still at the hospital, and it's nearly time for me to go to work."

"You won't leave me alone, will you, Pa?"

"Claribel will be here soon."

"Oh, Pa! I want my baby!"

"Come on, dear, let me get you settled. Are you thirsty?"

Henry got her to take some cool water and some warm chicken broth, and he saw that her fever had broken at least temporarily. Claribel came home from her job at the store and waited with her father until Albertine drifted off into a restless sleep.

"I think she'll be better now," Henry told Claribel and kissed Clare's forehead before he left for the night shift at

Donnelly's. Clare sat in the rocking chair, knitting some booties for the baby, but she grew bored with it, saw that Albertine would be fine without her, then went downstairs to have dinner and listen to the radio.

By seven o'clock, Clare wondered where her mother and Elsie could be. By eight she was anxious, and by nine o'clock Claribel's nerves made her sick to her stomach. It was clear to her that something had gone terribly wrong. She prayed that the baby would be all right. It would be too cruel if something had happened to the baby.

A little before ten, Elsie came in the front door, clearly upset. When she took off her hat, her hair was wild, her nose and cheeks were wind-burned and red, and her eyes were bloodshot from crying.

Claribel jumped up from the couch, switched off the radio and ran to her sister. "What is it, Elsie?" she asked. "What's wrong?"

Elsie unwrapped her scarf, pulled off her gloves, threw her coat on a chair and collapsed on the sofa. "Pneumonia. The baby has pneumonia."

"What do you mean?" Clare asked her. "How could he have pneumonia? We held him close, right next to our bodies for two days and nights. He was hardly exposed to the air for more than a few seconds. There must be some mistake."

"He had a fever," Elsie reminded her. "That's why Ma kept saying we needed to bring him to the hospital. And she could tell his breathing wasn't clear, just by listening with her stethoscope."

"Did you keep him warm in the taxi?" Clare demanded. "Did you let him get cold?"

"I kept him in the sling under my dress and sweater until Fay opened the incubator for him. We can't blame ourselves, Ma says. He was premature. Even Doc Bichet said his lungs were weak. We shouldn't blame ourselves…but Clare, I do! I do blame myself. What did we do wrong? How did we let that baby get sick?"

"Did our germs infect him?" Clare wondered. "I had a bath every time before I took my turn warming him. I used strong soap, too. I washed my hands until they were raw. It was clumsy with him at first, when the sling didn't hang just right…But that couldn't have hurt him, could it?"

"No, that's not what caused it. Maybe he got infected by Doc Bichet," Elsie said. "That's why Albertine got sick. Ma thinks he was too impatient and did something stupid to make the afterbirth come faster. Maybe he did something just as stupid when he examined the baby. Maybe he kept him out in the air too long. Maybe there was dirt under his fingernails. And he has a cough, doesn't he? He never wears a mask. But Ma says it's not his fault, either. Anything can happen to preemies."

"She always takes up for that dirty old drunk," Clare complained.

"And look what happened!" Elsie said. "The baby's got pneumonia!"

"That poor little baby!" Clare cried. "Wasn't it a great feeling to hold him Elsie? Is there anything like it?"

"Oh Clare, I've had two children of my own, but I have to say that neither of mine were as tiny and precious as that little boy. I felt he had melted into my heart. It made me feel so peaceful, so calm. A lot nicer than being pregnant, I can tell you that!"

"Yes, it was sweet to rock that baby," Claribel confessed. "And when I felt him try to nurse from me, I wept like a baby myself. But they were sweet tears. I was sad for him, but I was happy to be helping him, too."

"I know how you feel, Clare. I didn't cry but I wanted to. I really did. And I want to now, because I have to tell Albertine how sick her baby is."

"Do you really have to tell her now? I think she's asleep, Elsie. Can't you wait until morning?"

"Oh, Clare," Elsie said and tears streaked down her cheeks. "He may not make it through the night."

The two sisters hugged each other and cried for a few minutes, then they climbed the stairs together to talk to Albertine. When they entered the bedroom, Elsie and Clare thought their sister had disappeared, but then they noticed her small shape curled up beneath the blankets in the center of the bed.

"She's sleeping," Elsie whispered.

"Let's come back later," Clare said quietly.

"I'm not asleep," Albertine called from under the blankets. "Where's my baby?"

"Come out from there, Albertine, so we can see you," Elsie told her. "You'll smother yourself."

"I said: where's my baby?" Albertine called again through the covers.

"He's at the hospital," Elsie said softly and sat on the corner of the bed. "Ma and I brought him there and put him in an incubator."

Albertine rose up and flung the blankets off of her as if she were surfacing from under water. She took a deep, cold breath before she called to her sister. "Why didn't you tell me, Elsie? I woke up and he was gone. You nearly frightened me to death. My poor little son. My poor little Ronnie. I thought he had died, Elsie. Isn't that crazy? I dreamed that Hank and I couldn't find him. And then I woke up and he was gone...You might have told me. I'm not so sick that I don't want to know where my baby is!"

"Ma told you, Albertine, but you were too feverish to understand her. Cousin Fay called to say that she had a free incubator. If we could get him to the hospital within the hour, she would hold it for him. He wasn't doing too well," Elsie said. "We thought it might be his last chance."

"Last chance?" Albertine cried. "What do you mean 'last chance'?"

"He's very sick, dear," Elsie said. "He has pneumonia."

"How could he have pneumonia?" Albertine cried angrily. "He's only three days old!"

"His lungs are weak, Al," Elsie said, "because he was born so early."

"But he'll be okay, won't he?" Albertine asked. "Now that he's in the hospital."

"Well," Elsie replied carefully, "his chances are better there, but he's not out of danger. The doctor says he's still very, very sick."

Albertine lay back on the bed and clenched her fists. "God help him," she moaned, then sat up again. "Has anyone heard from Hendrik? Why isn't he here?"

"We haven't heard from him, Al," Elsie said. "Not one word."

"Do I deserve to be so alone?" Albertine moaned. To Clare she seemed small and weak, nearly colorless without makeup, not old-looking so much as extremely tired. "Alright, I've made some mistakes. I haven't always behaved myself, but nobody's perfect. Hendrik does whatever he wants. Why am I being punished?"

"You're not being punished!" Elsie scolded her.

But everything Albertine thought and felt made her believe that she was suffering for a reason. The core of her body ached with every movement, even when she changed positions in bed. Her breasts were swollen and sore. Her head ached, her eyes burned, and her mouth was dry and contaminated with a bitter metallic taste. Her hair was sweaty and clung to her head like a tight, dirty hat. And her baby was sick, taken away to the hospital so she couldn't do anything to help him. She had barely seen the little boy before her fever started, and now she tried hard to remember what he looked like.

Sure, he was a pink newborn with wisps of dark hair, but could I pick him out from anyone else's baby? How old is he now? How long have I been lying in bed? Three days? Four? Isn't there an all-night train from Miami? It would take Hendrik a day, two at most to get here. But Hendrik is punishing me, too. He never wanted another child. He barely pays attention to Hank. All he's interested in is his saxophone, his band, Florida, and his Negro singer with the long legs, full hips and breasts twice the size of mine. And she's probably been filling his head with all kinds of lies about me, about things she didn't know anything about, like that stupid little boxer friend of Claribel's, spreading rumors that couldn't be true, but which Hendrik believed anyway. Rumors that could ruin my life, wreck my marriage, and leave poor Hank and little Ronnie without a father. Did they know the terrible consequences their lies could have on me and my children? And why do my children have to suffer, especially my baby, my poor sick newborn? It could take weeks for him to recover, especially in the dead of winter.

But some would say, Elsie among them, that I brought all this on myself by carrying on at the Top Hat with ball players and mobsters and boxers, falling in love with Colby Malone, and then doing everything I could to make sure Hendrik got me pregnant. A new baby was supposed to make us forget how we had hurt each other. But I should have known that nobody forgets being betrayed. Nobody likes to be tricked into an obligation, either, even when the trap is baited with great sex every night for a month. The glow fades, doesn't it? And being married means you have to give up your freedom and work hard to get along with the one person who knows how to hurt you the most. Not much hope for love, is there? Not if we can't trust each other.

Then she thought of her baby again, a tiny pink boy squinting in the light of an incubator, his little fists clenched as he labored to breathe as fluid built up in his lungs. Why did he have to start his life struggling to take every breath, and why couldn't she be with him?

She felt pressure and pain, and knew it was time to use the toilet, but wasn't sure she had the strength to make it to the bathroom. She looked across the room and saw Clare sitting in the rocker next to the floor lamp. Her eyes were closed, but she didn't seem sound asleep.

"Clare," she called to her, and her voice was both hoarse and strained. "Help me get to the bathroom."

"Okay, sure," Clare said and stepped to the side of the bed as Albertine thrust her feet out from under the blankets.

"Wait," Clare said, "let's get your robe and slippers. Don't want you to catch a chill."

Albertine strained to make every step as they walked across the room and took the few steps down the hallway to the bathroom. Her legs were incredibly heavy, and her whole lower body seemed to be torn by sharp hooks of pain. Once she made it inside the narrow bathroom, Clare helped her take off her robe and then tried to leave her, but Albertine was afraid she'd fall without her. "Don't go," she whispered. "Please stay."

Clare stood over her as Albertine sat on the toilet, dizzy and weak, hardly able to sit upright, shivering from the coldness of the porcelain and the tile. Without Clare's help, she would have been lying on the bathmat, but Clare held her up, made sure she relieved herself, changed her pad, and helped her wash and dry her hands. Albertine felt helpless, and she leaned on her sister on the way back to the bedroom.

Albertine was already climbing (very gingerly) back into bed when she noticed her mother sitting stoop-shouldered in the rocking chair.

"Ma?" Albertine asked, to make sure she wasn't dreaming. "Is that you?"

Birdie had lost her hat, and her hair was windblown and wild. Her brown cloth coat lay in a mound beside the rocker where she had dropped it carelessly, a minute ago.

"I'm very sorry dear," Birdie said in a flat and weary voice. "We did all we could."

"That's okay, Ma," Albertine said and tried to comfort her with the sweetest voice she could make. "I feel a lot better now. How's the baby?"

"That's what I'm trying to tell you," Birdie said softly, and Albertine saw that her mother's face was white and her eyes were full of tears. "We lost him, dear," she moaned. "We lost him."

"What do you mean 'lost him'? You lost him on the way back from the hospital?"

"Oh no, dear, that's not what I mean," Birdie told her and shook her head, and Claribel began crying. "The poor baby died an hour ago."

Albertine leaped from the bed, rushed toward her mother, and knelt before her, gripping Birdie's legs and staring up at her with surprise, anger and disbelief.

"What are you saying?" she demanded. "He can't be dead! He can't be. You took him to the hospital to keep him alive!"

"We did all we could, but the pneumonia had progressed too far, too quickly!" Birdie said and stroked Albertine's shoulder as she lay her head on Birdie's lap and trembled feverishly.

"What about the incubator, Ma?" she said and sobbed bitterly. "You said Lucy and Fay would save him with their incubator."

"I thought they would, dear. But the child was too weak to fight off the pneumonia. He was born too soon. If only he could have waited even one more week."

"My baby!" Albertine cried out and squeezed her mother's legs. "How could you let him die, Ma? You're the one with the goddamn healing hands! You're the midwife who never loses a baby! But you've lost mine! You've lost your own grandson!"

"Oh dear, my heart is broken, too," Birdie said and wept with her daughter. "I would rather die myself than have to tell you this dreadful news. But it fell to me. Oh God, it fell to me…If it's any comfort to you, he was baptized, dear. There was a priest at the hospital. A Jesuit."

"Thank you," Albertine moaned as she remembered her dream of the baptismal font in the dark, cavernous church. "Did he suffer, Ma? Was he in pain?"

"I don't think so, dear," Birdie told her. "He was very quiet. Very still."

"Very quiet," Albertine repeated. "Very still. And then he just stopped breathing?"

Birdie didn't answer her. Instead she stroked Albertine's damp hair and held her head in her lap for a few minutes. Then she said, "Come, dear. Let me help you get back in bed, I'll fix you something to eat and drink."

Albertine didn't eat much because she couldn't stop crying. She wept for four straight hours and couldn't be comforted, even by her father when he came home from work and spoke to her in his deepest, most comforting voice. Birdie stayed with her, though the sound of Albertine's grief was like a knife in her heart. Things had turned out so badly, despite all the care Birdie had given her and the baby. It was too painful to imagine, yet it was real.

Some time before dawn, Albertine finally succumbed to sleep, and Mére Elise appeared to Birdie as she pulled the quilt up to keep her daughter warm. Mére Elise was all in white, and she held a white bundle in her arms, the newly born, newly expired infant. She sat down in the rocking chair and gazed into the baby's face before looking back to Birdie.

"Mére, why…?"

"Hush," Elise whispered. "He belongs with me now."

Chapter Twenty

At noon the next day, Hendrik Kinderman arrived at the Fontaine's house with a four-day growth of beard, a torn overcoat, and trousers that were splattered with mud up to his knees.

When Elsie answered the door, she thought he was a hobo looking for a handout. "Yes?" she asked and gripped the scissors in her apron pocket.

"Elsie, it's me, Hendrik. I came as fast as I could. How are Albertine and the baby? Are they here?" He sounded exhausted and very worried. There were dark circles under his eyes. Then Elsie noticed the pink remnant of his lost thumb.

"Oh, Hendrik, it is you," Elsie said. "Come in out of the cold. We wondered why you didn't come home sooner. You look like you've crawled through hell."

"That's what it felt like. Damn! I have crawled through hell to get here."

"Come in, Hendrik, let me pour you a hot cup of coffee."

"Coffee can wait," Hendrik said. "I want to see Albertine."

"Sure, but come in first. My folks are in the kitchen. Why don't you talk to them for a minute first? They have some news that you need to hear."

"What news? Is Albertine all right?" Hendrik asked as he set his suitcase on the rug and unbuttoned his overcoat.

"She's getting better," Elsie said, "but first come in the kitchen and talk to Ma and Pa."

He walked unsteadily across the house to the kitchen. As he came into the room, both Henry and Birdie stood up from their lunch at the table.

"Hendrik," Birdie asked sternly, determined to give him a piece of her mind, "where have you been?"

"Hello, son," Henry said. "So you got my telegram."

"I did," Hendrik nodded. "And I've been trying to get here for five days."

"Sit down here," Birdie said. Now that she had taken a good look at him, she understood that he had suffered to come back to Chicago to be with his family. "Have some coffee. I'll make you a sandwich."

"Let me see Albertine first. Where is she?" Hendrik demanded and tears came into his eyes as he concluded that she had died while he was struggling to return.

"She's upstairs," Henry told him. "Please take off your coat and sit for a second. We need to talk to you."

"Why? What's wrong?" he sighed and draped his coat over the back of a chair and reluctantly sat down. Birdie placed a mug of coffee in front of him, sat in the next chair and put her arm over his shoulder.

"What is it?" Hendrik asked again. "What's wrong?"

"After the baby was born," Birdie explained, "Albertine got an infection, and she was very sick, but she's on the mend now. She'll be up on her feet in a few days."

"That's good," Hendrik said, lifted the cup in both hands and drank hurriedly, without flinching from the heat. "And the baby? How is the baby?"

"You know, Hendrik, he was born a month prematurely," Birdie said. "He was very weak."

"What are you telling me?" he asked, somehow knowing the answer to her question. "Very weak?"

"His little lungs weren't fully developed. He got pneumonia, and even though we brought him to the hospital, the poor thing didn't pull through."

"You're telling me the baby died?"

Unable to speak any more, Birdie wept quietly as she kept her hand on his shoulder. On reflex he turned to embrace her and began crying, too, from exhaustion as much from grief.

"It looks like you had some trouble getting here, Hendrik," Henry said.

Hendrik broke away from Birdie and drank another sip of coffee before he answered. "The ice storm in Georgia knocked out the phone lines and telegraph, and it shut down the railroad, too. I waited at the station in Miami for the first night, but saw that it was no use. So I cashed in my ticket and hitched a ride on a truck to Biloxi and then got a lift with some sailors to New Orleans. I waited another 18 hours there for the train to Chicago. It was so crowded I had to stand up most of the way. A lot of guys had the same plan as me, to get back to their families."

"So you tried to come home as soon as you got the telegram?" Henry asked.

"That same night. The twenty-third. I even skipped the last show. How could I not come?" Hendrik replied desperately.

"We weren't sure," said Elsie, who had been listening from the doorway. "It took you so long to get here, and we didn't hear a word from you. Albertine felt abandoned."

"Oh, Christ, she must feel terrible," Hendrik said. "To lose the baby!" He held his right hand over his eyes, and his in-laws saw the bright pink scar where his thumb had been. It seemed to be throbbing with pain.

"And you've come all this way to find out that he's gone," Birdie said and hugged him again. "I'm so sorry, Hendrik. We did all we could."

"I'm sure you did," Hendrik said, returned her embrace and leaned heavily on her. He thought for a second that she felt more deeply about the baby's death than he did. She was mourning the child and probably felt guilty that he died while under her care. And Hendrik also felt guilty for not being with Albertine for his son's birth. And in the weariness of his exhaustion, he felt ashamed. It had not been right for him to be away. Albertine had every reason to be angry with him. But when he told her about the terrible journey he'd made to come back to her, maybe she would forgive him.

Hendrik didn't wait for the sandwich. As soon as he finished his coffee, he was on his feet. "Where is she?" he asked.

"In our bedroom," Henry told him.

"I'll come with you," Birdie said.

"No. This is between us two."

If she had been awake when he came in the front door, Albertine would have heard him, she would have known he was in the house, and she would have been ready to challenge him. But the bedroom was dark and she appeared to be asleep. It took him a few seconds to turn on the lamp and sit on the edge of the bed beside her. He waited a minute before she opened her eyes and said, "Am I dreaming again, or is that really you?"

"It's me."

"Hello, Hendrik," Albertine said flatly, without raising her head off the pillow or even trying to touch his hand. "I'd given up hope of ever seeing you again."

"I would have been here sooner, but the ice storm knocked the railroad out of service."

"Is that so?" Her voice was cold and remote.

"I hitched a ride on a truck to New Orleans," he told her.

"Did you?"

"Then I stood up all night on the train to Chicago, so I could be with you."

"Well, you're too late, Heinie." She had never used that awful nickname before, because she knew he hated it.

"I got here as soon as I could. They handed me the telegram in the middle of a show and I left right away. And I didn't stop until I got here. I didn't…"

"Did you hear me?" she cut him off. "It's too goddamn late. Our baby's dead, and where were you? In Florida with that black whore."

"I left as soon as I read the telegram," he argued wearily and his head ached. "It wasn't easy, but I did my best to come home."

"Your best?" she asked bitterly.

"What else could I have done?" he pleaded with her. "The trains stopped running. The phone lines were down."

"You never should have left Chicago," she accused him and her eyes were wild and furious. "If you had stayed, our baby would be alive today. He'd be nursing at my breast right now."

"Are you crazy?" he barked, stunned that she blamed him for the baby's death. "There is no connection. If I'm here, or if I'm there, it wouldn't have changed anything."

"That's where you're wrong, Hendrik. That's where you're so wrong!" She spoke feverishly, unwilling to consider anything he said. "Do you know what forces babies to be born prematurely?"

"Some kind of defect, I suppose."

"Don't you dare say my baby had a defect! He was born prematurely because you abandoned me. Because we had to give up our apartment, and Hank and I had to move into this crowded house with eight other people. And all the while, I knew what you were doing down there in Florida, with complete disregard for my feelings, common decency, or what everyone was thinking about your disgusting escapade!"

"You have no room to talk, Albertine, and I don't need to remind you."

"But I think you do, Hendrik! Remind me of how I have no damn room to talk!"

"Come on, Albertine. I'm sorry I said that. You got under my skin."

"Don't sweep this under the rug, Heinie. Let's get this all out in the open. Remind me why I'm such a slut."

"I didn't call you that."

"Remind me."

"Don't make me."

"Damn you, Heinie. Remind me. Just speak your mind for a change before I puke."

"All right, if you insist, Albertine, I'll tell you about decency and why everyone we know thinks you don't know what the word means."

"Now you're getting somewhere. Now we'll finally get to hear what your filthy mind really thinks about me."

"It doesn't take a filthy mind to understand how you behaved with those small time gangsters, how you drove off to Cicero with them, and came home with your dress torn off your shoulders."

"Where did you hear that lie?"

"And you'd have to be blind not to know that you were playing for drinks in that basement lounge of the Top Hat until you got so drunk that you made a fool of yourself trying to dance with that boxer, the kid who's just 21 years old."

"There's nothing wrong with dancing, Hendrik. If you'd learned how, you would know that."

"I watch people dance every night, dear. I know what it's leading up to. And it's no handshake. It's no little kiss on the cheek."

"So you think I screwed that skinny little boxer! Hah! How else have I ruined my reputation?"

"You know the worst of it," Hendrik said quietly. "Let's just say I forgive you. Let's say it's history, so we can make a new beginning."

"A new beginning? That baby is dead, Hendrik. Will he get a new beginning? No, sir. Tomorrow they're going to bury him in my grandmother's grave. If you've got something on your mind about me, you tell me now. Or this talk about a new beginning is one big joke, Heinie. One big hilarious joke. Remind me. What's the worst thing they say about me?"

"That's enough," he said. "We have played this game long enough."

"Okay, Heinie, if you're afraid to say it, I'll finish it for you. They say that I was Colby Malone's girlfriend, his mistress, that we drank champagne together and had a lot of laughs at the Top Hat, and that I made love to him whenever I could in the big four-poster bed at his swanky Lincoln Park apartment, and that my own son saw us together at the ballpark, but I pretended not to recognize him to avoid making a scene. And worst of all, worst of all they say my baby, my poor lost baby boy was really his son not yours, Heinie. They say he was Colby's bastard. Can you believe it? Can you believe the worst thing they say about me?"

"I don't want to," Hendrik said and looked down at his shoes, which were stained with mud and salt. "But is it true?"

"Is what true?"

"Were you his mistress?"

"Yes," Albertine said. "I'm sorry, Hendrik. I was. Are you having an affair with Pearl?"

"I'm not proud of it, Al. I know now it was a mistake."

"Now that I'm giving you holy hell about it!"

"I knew it was a mistake before I left her," Hendrik whispered. "And is the rest true. Was it his baby?"

"No, of course not," she whispered.

"Are you sure?"

"Of course, I'm sure."

"Tell me the truth. Are you absolutely sure he was my son?"

"Oh, Hendrik, I can't be absolutely sure. The timing is all mixed up. He was born so soon. I don't think he was Colby's child, but…"

"But you can't be sure."

Albertine shook her head.

Hendrik took a deep breath, rubbed his eyes, and ran his hands through his hair. "I can live with that," he said. "I can accept it and move on."

"But I can't, Hendrik. When the baby died, I knew it was over between us. We'll never be able to trust each other again."

"And what about Hank?"

"Since when have you been interested in Hank?"

"He's my son. He's our son."

"You make it sound like we're a family. But we're not any more. Our family is dead, Heinie. We're no good for each other. Go back to your saxophone gig in Florida. Go back to your vicious black whore, and we'll spare ourselves all this pain."

"Pearl is none of those things," he sighed, "but I don't love her, Albertine. I love you."

"I don't believe you. If you loved me, if you really wanted to be with me, you wouldn't have gone to Florida when I needed you here. You wouldn't have abandoned me, and you wouldn't have let our baby die."

"Will you be quiet?" Hendrik insisted. "I didn't let him die. I was trying to earn a living. I didn't know he would be born so soon. I'm sorry. I can make it up to you. Let me try."

She shook her head and trembled with fever as she said, "Come to the funeral tomorrow. See what you've done. And after that…after that I don't care what you do, but I never want to see you again."

This was too much for him to bear, and he didn't have the strength to keep fighting her today. He stood up shakily and hobbled to the door. When he opened it, Birdie and Elsie were standing in the hall.

"She's gone crazy," he told them and drifted to the staircase. "There's no talking to her when she's like that."

It was too cold to open Mére Elise's grave, and the burial ground was covered with a foot of ice and snow, so the service at the cemetery was held in a drafty concrete chapel where the tiny white coffin was placed on a narrow pedestal and it seemed to be levitating at the center of the circle of mourners.

Because of Albertine's weak condition, the family did not request a requiem Mass and decided to have only a brief graveside service. The priest in his purple vestments chanted in Latin, sprinkled the coffin with holy water, blessed it with incense, and then said a few words in English.

Albertine stood, leaning against her mother, breathing steam into the cold, vaulted room. She felt the unreality of the moment, the cruelty of it, the devastation of losing a child so young. Her tears were exhausted by this time, though her body still quaked with painful sobs that pulled at her wounds, and tugged at her rib cage and her soft, tender breasts.

Although this was the smallest casket available, it was at least twice as long as the baby, and Albertine worried that his body would slide around inside it as they lowered the coffin into the ground, and he could lay bunched up at one end of it, folded over, twisted in the white baptismal gown they laid him in. That could not be a comfortable way to rest through eternity, and the image of her child clumped in a ball for all time haunted her. A funeral is supposed to help you say good bye, so you can move on with your life, her mother had told her. Move on with what life? She wondered. With whom. Her mother squeezed her, as if she had read her thoughts, but it was stupid for Albertine to always fall back on her parents. She was 31 years old with a son to raise, and a husband who loved someone else. In a few weeks she could start looking for a job, and soon she could find a place for her and Hank to be on their own.

Her father stood to her left, shuffling his feet in the cold, his eyes tearing up as he thought of how unfair it was for an infant to die, while so many guilty people were walking the earth. Chicago was full of them, of course. There was no logic to it, but the weak and the young couldn't always make it.

Elsie and Eugene stood with their children, who each held a rosary. Elsie offered to sing something, the Our Father she suggested, but Albertine didn't think she could bear it. A few words from the priest, a short blessing was all she wanted, so she told her sister no, and as could have been predicted, Elsie took it the wrong way and had cried bitterly, thinking that Albertine blamed her for the child's death, since she had been the last one to hold him in the sling under her gown, the last one who tried to sustain him with her warmth. But it had been useless, worse than useless, because he had died, anyway, in spite of all their efforts, all their combined love for the tiny boy.

Claribel shared these feelings, but had not expressed them. If this is what comes from love, she wondered, who needs it? Why should I want to attract men if all it gets me is pain, loss, shame and grief? She knew that very few babies died like this, and that if she ever got married, her babies would live and be healthy, but Clare wasn't sure she wanted to take the chance of ending up a broken woman like her sister because she loved a man and wanted a baby.

Lorraine stood next to Larry and daydreamed about the lunch the ladies from the French church were fixing for them to eat when they got back to the house. She knew there would be meat balls and finger sandwiches and chocolate cake, and no one would stop her from eating all that she wanted.

Larry looked past the small white coffin at Albertine, and he was impressed most of all by her beauty. She wore a black hat with a veil (that didn't hide her pale cheeks) and a long pointed feather, dyed black. She held her hands together against her black cloth coat, more to brace herself than to pray. She stood with quiet dignity, in deep mourning, as if she were a young widow and not the mother of a baby who had only lived a few days. Yes, she was deeply hurt, but she seemed resolved to carry on, and unlike every other drab member of the family who wore their worn out clothes as if they were the Depression itself, she looked fresh, well groomed, determined and almost glamorous to him. He always thought that Albertine was the most interesting person in their family – because of her talent, her beauty, her impulsive nature – but today Larry thought he saw something new. His sister was finally aware that her actions had consequences. She was an adult now, and no one needed to protect her any more.

Larry realized that Hendrik wasn't standing beside her, and neither was Hank. They stood closest to the door, as if they were anxious to leave. Larry noticed that Hendrik was looking at Albertine, too, but with a perplexed squint and not admiration. Hendrik was clean shaven and his blonde hair was stiff and shiny. Though Elsie had sewn up the rips in his overcoat, he still looked down and out and discouraged. Maybe he was hurt, too, that Albertine wanted him to go back to Florida.

Hank spent the whole service looking up at his father, whispering questions to him.

"Do you think Ma will be all right?" Hank asked.

After a few seconds, Hendrik put his hand on his son's shoulder and replied, "You know your mother, Hank. She's a very strong woman. Look at her. She hurts today, but she'll be fine tomorrow. Don't worry about her."

"I only saw the baby two times," Hank told him. "Geez, he was small. I wondered how long he would last."

"He was too weak to make it," Hendrik whispered. "Even your Grandma Birdie couldn't save him."

"Both of my aunts took turns keeping him warm. Not Lorraine, though. Her bosom isn't big enough yet."

"Wait a few years," Hendrik smiled and shook his head. "She'll have a nice bosom like Elsie's."

"You mean she'll get fat, too?"

"That might happen."

"Don't joke, Dad. We're at a funeral."

"Okay. I won't joke."

As the priest droned on about baby Ronald's eternal life, Hank asked, "Hey dad? Do you really have to go to Florida tomorrow?"

Hendrik nodded. "We need the money," he said. "And I left my horn down there. What am I without my saxophone?

"You could always buy a new one."

"Not this year. I'll make do with the old one."

Hank wanted to ask his father whether he could go to Florida with him, or at least visit some time. He had never seen the ocean, and it would be great to go to the beach with his Dad and taste salt water for the first time. But Hank was afraid that his father would say 'no' in a way that meant he really didn't want him to visit, and that would spoil the whole day, even more than this funeral for his baby brother.

When the service was over, Hendrik and Hank were the first ones outside, and Hendrik led his son to a patch of the snowy parking lot away from the others, beneath a bare, black oak tree. Then Hendrik held a pocket watch, with a leather fob wrapped around it, in his palm a few inches from Hank's face. "I want you to have this," he said.

"A watch?" Hank asked, but corrected his stupidity immediately. "Nice watch!"

"It was my grandfather's. He gave it to me in Hamburg when I was a few years older than you, the day I climbed on the boat to come to America. Take it."

"Thanks," Hank said and took the watch, which was smaller and lighter than it had seemed at first. It was scuffed and the design was worn off the casing in places, but there were no cracks in the crystal, and when he held it against his ear, it was ticking. "It still works."

"That's right. It was made in Switzerland, where all the good watches are from."

"How often should I wind it?"

"Once a day when you wake up every morning. Take care of it, and you can pass it on to your son, in time."

"I will, Pa. I promise."

"Come on, now. Let's ride back to the house with your mother."

Hank turned to the rest of the family and saw his mother opening her arms for him to come to her. He slipped the watch into his pocket and ran toward her and then collided with her embrace as she squeezed his face against the rough wool and flat buttons of her overcoat. Something broke loose inside him and he began to cry, for the first time since the baby died, and his mother rocked him gently saying, "There, there, that's right, get it out of your system. I didn't think you could hold it in forever."

The sight of Albertine holding Hank this way made Hendrik feel alone, excluded from his family because his wife did not believe that he loved her. This was bad enough for him, being sent back to Florida after losing his son and maybe his wife, but he could fend for himself. He would survive. But things would be worse for Albertine and Hank. She would be both poor and miserable if she had to depend on her parents for everything. It would be a disaster for her, and he felt discouraged and angry that he could do so little to help her. She won't let me! He clenched his teeth, looked up into the leaden sky and felt the cold wind on his neck.

Then Hendrik felt a firm hand on his shoulder, and he heard Henry's deep, raspy voice speaking softly next to his ear.

"It's a sad day," Henry said to him. "I'm sorry for your loss."

"It's your loss, too."

"That's right. It's not right when a baby dies. Makes you feel the world is out of kilter. That nothing makes sense."

"It doesn't make sense," Hendrik shook his head. "Not to me."

"I wanted to thank you, Hendrik," Henry told him.

"For what?"

"For coming back to Chicago as soon as you got my telegram. I know what kind of odyssey you went through to get here."

"You're the only one who understands."

"Sorry that Albertine took it the wrong way. She'll come around."

"I'm not so sure, Henry," Hendrik shrugged but couldn't bring himself to say that he didn't think she would ever change her mind. Instead he said, "Could you please watch out for them while I'm gone?"

Henry patted his back and nodded. "You know I will…Let's catch up before they all drive off without us."

"And do me one more favor, will you, Henry?"

"What's that?"

"Send me another telegram when it's safe to come home."

ABOUT THE AUTHOR

Ron Bitto was born in Chicago, educated on the East Coast, and now lives and works in Houston. He began writing this novel after listening to stories that his grandmother Albertine recorded a few years before she died. On the tapes, she was an unreliable and digressive narrator, but even in her eighties, she commanded attention with the attitude that characterizes her namesake in this novel.

Perfect Pitch is Ron Bitto's fourth novel. He also edited his mother's journals, *Travels with Mary*.

www.ingramcontent.com/pod-product-compliance
Lightning Source LLC
Chambersburg PA
CBHW062109170626
46813CB00002B/379

9780615722573